MAD
PROFESSOR

MAD PROFESSOR

The Uncollected Short Stories of

RUDY RUCKER

THUNDER'S MOUTH PRESS

NEW YORK

MAD PROFESSOR
The Uncollected Short Stories of Rudy Rucker

Published by
Thunder's Mouth Press
An imprint of Avalon Publishing Group, Inc.
245 West 17th Street, 11th floor
New York, NY 10011

AVALON
publishing group incorporated

Library of Congress Cataloging-in-Publication Data is available.

ISBN-10: 1-56025-974-4
ISBN-13: 978-1-56025-974-9

9 8 7 6 5 4 3 2 1

Book design by Maria E. Torres

Printed in the United States of America
Distributed by Publishers Group West

For Robert Sheckley, 1928–2005

The premise could be seen wavering, there were repercussions of a rhetorical nature, and the author could be glimpsed, a ghostly figure of unbelievable beauty and intelligence, trying desperately, despite his many personal problems, to put things together again.

–Robert Sheckley, *Minotaur Maze*

CONTENTS

INTRODUCTION

OF course I'm not a mad professor—everything I write and do is perfectly logical! Come right this way, step into my laboratory, and you'll see for yourself. Careful not to touch that lever—*whoops*, you've turned on a lecture.

I might characterize my fiction by four qualities:

- Thought experiments
- Power-chords
- Gnarliness
- Wit

The notion of fictional *thought experiments* was made popular by no less a mad professor than Albert Einstein, who fueled his science speculations with *Gedankenexperimenten*. Thought experiments are a very powerful technique of philosophical investigation. In practice, it's intractably difficult to visualize the side effects of new technological developments. In order to tease out the subtler consequences of current trends, a complex fictional simulation is necessary; inspired narration is a more powerful tool than logical analysis. If I want to imagine, for instance, what our world would be like if ordinary objects were conscious, then the best way to make progress is to fictionally simulate a person discovering this.

The kinds of thought experiments I enjoy are different in intent and in execution from merely futurological investigations. I'm not necessarily trying to make useful predictions that businessmen can use. I'm more interested in exploring the human condition, with literary power chord standing in for archetypal psychic forces.

+ + +

When I speak of *power chords* in the context of fantastic literature, I'm talking about certain classic tropes that have the visceral punch of heavy musical riffs: blaster guns, spaceships, time machines, aliens, telepathy, flying saucers, warped space, faster-than-light travel, immersive virtual reality, clones, robots, teleportation, alien-controlled pod people, endless shrinking, the shattering of planet Earth, intelligent goo, antigravity, starships, ecodisaster, pleasure-center zappers, alternate universes, nanomachines, mind viruses, higher dimensions, a cosmic computation that generates our reality, and, of course, the attack of the giant ants.

When I use a power chord, I try to do something fresh with the trope, perhaps placing it into an unfamiliar context, perhaps describing it more intensely than usual, or perhaps using it for a novel thought experiment. I like it when my material takes on a life of its own. This leads to what I call the gnarly zone.

+ + +

I discuss my concept of *gnarl* at length in my nonfiction tome, *The Lifebox, the Seashell, and the Soul: What Gnarly Computation Taught Me about Ultimate Reality, the Meaning of Life, and How to Be Happy* (Thunder's Mouth Press, 2005).

In short, a gnarly process is complex and unpredictable without being random. If a story hews to some very familiar pattern, it feels stale. But if absolutely anything can happen, a story becomes as unengaging as someone else's dream. The gnarly zone is lies at the interface between logic and fantasy.

I see my tales as simulated worlds in which the characters and tropes and social situations bounce off each other like eddies in a turbulent wake, like gliders in a cellular automaton graphic, like vines twisting around each other in a jungle. When I write, I like to be surprised.

William Burroughs was an ascended master of the gnarl. He believed in having his work take on an autonomous life to the point of becoming a world that the author inhabits. "The writer has been there or he can't write about it. . . . [Writers] are trying to create a universe in which they have lived or where they would like to live. To write it, they must go there and submit to conditions that they might not have bargained for." (From "Remembering Jack Kerouac" in *The Adding Machine: Selected Essays*, Seaver Books 1986.)

+ + +

And now a few words about *wit*. Robert Sheckley, to whose memory *Mad Professor* is dedicated, was a supremely witty writer. Over the years I got to spend a few golden hours in Sheckley's presence. And I think it's safe to say that wit, rather than mere humor, characterizes his work.

Wit involves describing the world as it actually is. You experience a release of tension when you notice a glitch. Something was off-kilter, and now you see what it was. The elephant in the living room has been named. The evil spirit has been incanted. Perceiving an incongruity in our supposedly smooth-running society provokes a shock of recognition and a concomitant burst of laughter. Wit is a critical-satirical process that can be more serious than the "humorous" label suggests.

In this vein, Sheckley writes: "Good fiction is never preachy. It tells its truth only by inference and analogy. It uses the specific detail as its building block rather than the vague generalization. In my case it's usually humorous—no mistaking my stuff for the Platform Talk of the 6th Patriarch. But I do not try to be funny, I merely write as I write. . . . In the meantime I trust the voice I can never lose—my own . . . enjoying writing my story rather than looking forward to its completion." (From "Amsterdam Diary" in *Semiotext[e] SF*, Autonomedia 1997.)

+ + +

The "mad professor" theme is itself a classic power chord.

One way to think of the trope is as a dialectic triad: the thesis of the dry professor and the antithesis of the unpredictable artist are synthesized into the mad professor—like Dr. Jekyll and Mr. Hyde sharing a single body.

A different way to think of it is that being mad is actually part of being a professor, and not any kind of aberration. Professors, after all, have their heads in the clouds. They don't see things like regular people do.

In the famous allegory of the cave in Book VII of *The Republic*, Plato describes a race of humans who spend their lives staring at shadows on the wall of a cave. From time to time some of them escape from the cave into the higher world. Having experienced the light of the true Sun, when they return to the prison of the cave their eyes are a bit slow in catching the subtleties of the shadow-play that ordinary men and women deem to be the entire real world—they're like absent-minded professors.

"And if there were a contest, and he had to compete in measuring the shadows with the prisoners who had never moved out of the den, while his sight was still weak, and before his eyes had become steady . . . would he not be ridiculous? Men would say of him that up he went and down he came without his eyes; and that it was better not even to think of ascending; and if any one tried to loose another and lead him up to the light, let them only catch the offender, and they would put him to death."

Further shadings in the mad professor archetype can be found by distinguishing it from the mad scientist. What's the difference? Professors tutor and counsel their students, they lecture and teach, they publish books and papers. They're social. It's not enough for a mad professor to gloat over the secret of reality in a dungeon lab as a mad scientist might. No, the mad professor is driven to write up what he or she saw, and to try and make everyone understand it. Another difference would be that the professors, who are less goal-oriented than the scientists, love erudition for its own sake, and affect a high literary style studded with quotes from timeless intellectual figures such as William Burroughs, Robert Sheckley, and Plato.

+ + +

I'm certainly a professor. I started my academic career as a calculus section tutor in graduate school forty years ago. I worked as a professor of mathematics for about twenty years, and spent the following twenty as a professor of computer science. Two years ago I retired and became an emeritus professor, which means I get to stay home all the time.

I admit to being contrary, unpredictable, and idiosyncratic. But mad? Of course not. As my character Bela Kis puts it in my recent novel *Mathematicians in Love* (Tor Books, 2006): "Crazy means illogical. I'm logical. Therefore I'm not crazy. Note that a system can be at the same time logical and unpredictable."

For this volume, I've arranged my stories in reverse chronological order; with the most recent ones first, and the oldest ones last. There's one exception to this rule: although I wrote "Visions of the Metanovel" this week while putting the anthology together, it seems to work best as a closing piece. Further information about the individual stories can be found in the Notes section at the back of the book.

Five of the eighteen pieces in *Mad Professor* were written with other authors. One of the remarkable things about fantastic literature is the level of literary collaboration that it supports. In this respect, we're like scientists—and like musicians. We conduct our thought experiments, we jam our power chords, and if all goes well, we style our work with gnarl and wit.

By the way, the picture at left shows me working on this introduction in my backyard. Enjoy the book!

–Rudy Rucker,
Los Gatos, California, May 22, 2006

2+2=5

(WRITTEN WITH TERRY BISSON)

OLD age is all about killing time. One evening Jack and I walked the quarter mile from our Journey's End retirement complex to the Hump's chain coffee shop in the strip mall, traffic whizzing by, everyone but us with someplace to go.

The shop was just about deserted and a couple of the barrista guys were having a discussion. One was offering the other fifty or even sixty dollars to do something boring. I didn't catch what the boring thing was, so when the second guy came to wipe our tabletop, I asked him.

"He was wondering if someone paid me, would I count out loud to ten thousand by ones," said the boy, fingering the ring in his nose, which was kind of an exotic accoutrement for Harrods Creek, Kentucky. "But it would be too stupid," he added. He moved across the empty room, straightening chairs.

I did a quick pencil-and-paper calculation while Jack sipped his chamomile tea. I used to be an insurance adjuster, and numbers are my thing. "I figure I could probably count to ten thousand in the course of a day," I told Jack in a bit.

He argued about this, of course—something about holes in the number line—but then he flipped to my point of view and pushed the calculation further, working it in his head. Before they fired him for his nervous breakdown, Jack was a math professor at the University of Louisville. "You could count to ten million in a year," Jack announced after a minute. "And maybe if a person said the words really fast, they could hit a billion before they died. Assuming they started young. Assuming they didn't pay very close attention."

I called over the barrista with the nose-ring and told him the news, but his mind was already on other things. "We're about to close," he said.

"Maybe I should start counting," I told Jack as the boy wandered off. "I could set a Winners World Record. My own taste of immortality."

"Let's see about that," said Jack, hauling out the oversized cell phone he carried in his pants pocket. It was an off-brand model, a Whortleberry that he'd picked out of a sale bin at the Radio Shack in the strip mall near our rest home. He carried it with him all the time, not that anyone ever called him or me, other than telemarketers. Our wives were dead, and our kids had moved to the coasts. They couldn't find interesting work in Kentucky. Jack and I had each other, Nurse Amara, and Hector, the fellow who did the dishes and made up our rooms.

"See what?" I asked Jack.

"See if there's a counting-to-highest-number category on the Winners Web site." Drawing out his smeared, heavy reading glasses he began pecking at the tiny buttons on the fat cell phone. "I get the Web on this sucker, remember, Bert?"

"Fuck computers," I said. "A Java script put me out of my job."

"Like I haven't heard you say that seven hundred times," said Jack. "Loser. Dinosaur. Old fool."

"At least I didn't go crazy and scare my students," I said. "Telling them the world is made of holes. Screwball. Nut. Psycho."

"Four hundred times for that remark," said Jack, prodding the minute keyboard with the tip of his pen. "I wasn't crazy, I was right. The world is like an engine-block gasket, or, no, like a foam. The holes triangulate the universe; they're the tent stakes, as it were, that keep the whole thing from blowing away. And the big secret is—oh, you're not ready yet. Here's Winners." He set the cell phone on the table so that I could see the screen. What I saw was a blurred flickering smudge. "Your glasses," Jack reminded me, not unkindly.

I found my smeared, heavy reading glasses and studied the display. The Winners Web site was an outgrowth of the old *Guinness Book of World Records*, the difference being that Winners had far more categories. They made their money by harvesting information about the record holders so they could be targeted with ads.

"Says the Unaided Counting Record is twelve million, three hundred and forty-five thousand, six hundred and seventy-eight," I said, squinting at the tiny screen.

"12,345,678," echoed Jack, just saying the digits. "A tidy place to stop. It took the guy nearly two years. Clyde Burns. Says here he's a Buddhist monk in Wichita, Kansas."

"Closing time, gentlemen," said the barrista.

"Okay, okay."

Walking back, we discussed the project some more. Cars whizzing by. Low beige buildings in a parking lot. Dark green pastures and trees. A rustling cornfield.

"The monk counted for two years!" I said. "Two years is a lifetime when you're my age."

"That's the problem with immortality," mused Jack. "You never live long enough to get there."

+ + +

For breakfast we have a choice: oatmeal or powdered eggs. I chose oatmeal. Jack joined me at my table, stirring his eggs.

He was smiling. "There's a hole in their rules," he said.

"Huh?"

"There's a hole in everything," he explained. "The universe itself can be described as a fractal pattern of holes in nonexistence. A temporary but nonetheless . . ."

"Never mind your crackpot theories about the universe," I said. I had the feeling—or was it a hope?—that he was talking about the Winners Web site. "What about their rules?"

"You're not required to vocalize the numbers, or even subvocalize. Just count."

"You still have to *think* them," I said. "It'll still take me two years to get to where the mad monk left off."

"Think biocomputation," said Jack. "Think auxiliary processing."

"Huh?"

To make a long story short, which is what old age is all about, when you think about it, which I try not to do, Jack said he could hook me up to a computer that would speed up my brain cells.

"Neurons are just switches," he said. "Firing or resting: binary. They can interface to a chip. And as long as they're controlling the counting, it's legal under the Winners rules."

I toyed with my oatmeal. "You want me to swallow a chip? Or get an implant?" As usual the oatmeal was lumpy.

"Wait till tonight," said Jack, glancing suspiciously around the dining room. As if anyone were there but Hector and our deaf, senile peers. "I'll show you tonight."

After an evening of watching the *McNguyen* and the *Pootie Party* shows, I followed Jack to the room we shared at Journey's End. I was apprehensive, but eager to achieve immortality.

"Voilà," he said. He showed me a knit skull cap. It was blue and orange and silver. It was the worst job of knitting I had ever seen, and I told him so.

"One of my University of Louisville honors students made it for me," he said. "An extra credit grab. She had a B, and she wanted . . ."

"Never mind all that," I said. "What does it do?"

"Guess," he said, showing me the cord with the computer jack. "The silver yarn, clumsily woven, I admit, is a dermo-thalamic web which uploads to the processor inside my Whortleberry to speed up your internal computational sequences. If I hadn't pissed away so much time grading homework for all those sections of business math, then maybe I would have been able to productize this and . . ."

"Never mind that," I said, sensing immortality. "What do I do?"

"Put it on," he said. "Start counting sheep, from one, until you fall asleep. As soon as your consciousness logs off, the Whortleberry's processor kicks in, and the counting accelerates."

"Have you ever tried it?" I said.

"There was no point," he answered. "It's only good for counting by ones. I ended up giving her an A minus, since . . ."

"Never mind that," I said. "Plug it in. Give it here."

I pulled on the magic beanie and lay down on my bed.

It was tight. "Should I shave my head?"

For once Jack looked confused. "You're bald," he said.

"Oh, yeah." I'd forgotten.

I closed my eyes and started counting sheep. They were jumping a fence, faster and faster. I dreamed I was herding them up a boulder-studded hill.

+ + +

"Wake up."

I sat up. The light through the filthy windows told me it was morning.

Jack was standing over me, smiling. "What's the first thing that comes to mind?" he asked. "Don't think about it, just say it."

"Twelve million, three hundred and forty-five thousand, three hundred and twenty-two," I said. Even though my head was splitting, I counted to the next number. "Twelve million, three hundred and forty-five thousand, three hundred and twenty-three." 12,345,323 in digits.

"Voilà," said Jack. "You're gaining on the monk already. You'll pass him by breakfast."

And I did. Jack uploaded the results to the Winners site and we slapped hands. I was now a world record holder.

I ate some powdered eggs. I didn't even mind that they had lumps like the oatmeal. I was immortal.

But it didn't last. Nothing does. Isn't that what old age is all about? After lunch, between the *Casa Hayzooz* and *Brenda Bondage* shows, Jack checked the Winners site and discovered that the monk in Wichita had logged twelve million, three hundred and forty-five thousand, nine hundred and seventy-nine, beating me by eighty-six. I had 12,345,893; he had 12,345,979.

"That Buddhist bastard," I said, with grudging respect. "I thought Kansas was a red state."

"He must have nothing else to do," said Jack.

"Neither do I!" I closed my eyes and started counting.

When we logged in later that night, after the *McNguyen* show, I was ahead by nine hundred and forty six. I went to bed exhausted, but pleased.

I was immortal again.

+ + +

Powdered eggs, the breakfast of champions. I was still feeling like a winner when Jack dragged in, late, looking glum.

"Bad news," he said. He whipped out his Whortleberry and showed me the Winners site. The mad monk was up almost ten grand; he'd reached twelve million three hundred and fifty-four thousand, two hundred and nineteen. 12,354,219.

He must have stayed up all night.

Much as I hated it, I was prepared to wear the cap again. "What if I throw a shit-fit and Nurse Amara sedates me?" I said. "I'll sleep all day and double my score."

"I have a better idea," said Jack. "Look here."

He showed me another Web site on his little screen: LifeIs-SciFi.com.

"Sci-fi? I hate that crap."

"Who doesn't?" said Jack. "But this site's gonna kick your skull cap into overdrive. The site's run by a computer science student at a cow college in San Jose."

"Computers in Mexico? I hate computers."

"San Jose, California," said Jack. "Silicon Valley. Computers are your friends. This ultranerd has hacked into Stanford's fully coherent nuclear-magnetic-resonant dark-matter-powered Accelerandodrome. An outlaw link to a quantum computer! If we link your cap to that tonight, you'll climb so far above that monk that he'll be eating your positronic dust for the rest of his life."

"What about my brain?" I asked, remembering the headache I'd gotten from counting to twelve million.

"Do you want to be immortal?" he asked. "Or not?"

To make a long story short, and isn't that what old age is all about, I pulled on the magic beanie and lay down on my bed. I closed my eyes and started counting sheep again. They were jumping the fence faster and faster, flowing up the mountain-side, scaling the cliffs, frisking into the white fluffy clouds. I picked up my dream-colored staff and followed them.

✦ ✦ ✦

"Wake up."

I woke up. I sat up.

"Say the first thing that comes into your mind," Jack said.

I did like the day before, only more so, spewing out a jaw-breaking number name that went like this (and I'm sure you don't mind if I leave out the middle): "Twelve duotrigintillion, three hundred forty-five unotrigintillion, six hundred seventy-eight trigintillion, . . . , three hundred forty-five million, six hundred seventy-eight thousand, nine hundred one."

Whew. The inside of my skull was cold. I felt a faint, steady wind in my face, the air so very thin. Toothed, inhuman peaks of ice towered above me like the jaws of Death.

"My head," I whimpered. "I hope I haven't had a stroke."

"Never mind that," said Jack. "You're at base camp Googol!"

I blinked away the mountains and saw my familiar room.

Jack was smiling, no, grinning. There were even more lines in his face than usual.

"Huh?"

"Base camp Googol," he repeated. "On the Matterhorn of math, high above the workaday timberline. The land of perpetual snow."

"Google? The search engine? What?"

"I'm not talking business, I'm talking math. 'Googol' is an old-school math name that a math prof's nephew invented in 1938. It stands for the number that you write as a 1 followed by a hundred 0s. Ten duotrigintillion sounds pompous compared to that. You'll notice that the number you just said is a hundred and one digits long: 12, 345, 678, 901, 234, 567, 890, 123, 456, 789, 012, 345, 678, 901, 234, 567, 890, 123, 456, 789, 012, 345, 678, 901, 234, 567, 890, 123, 456, 789, 012, 345, 678, 901. That's why I say you're at base camp Googol. By the way, Bert, I'm impressed you knew how to put all those digits into words."

"Don't forget, I'm an insurance adjuster."

"Were," said Jack. "Now you're an immortal. I've got a hunch you'll be ready for my secret pretty soon."

He logged in and authenticated me on the Winners Web site, and all day we were riding high. Just before bedtime, right after *Philosophical Psycho*, we checked into the Winners Web site one more time.

I was still the champ. The mad monk was history. Or was he?

"He can count day and night for ten-to-the-ninetieth-power years and he'll never catch you," Jack reassured me. "No one will ever catch you. You're the winner forever."

"Cool," I said. "But I cheated. A bunch of machines did it for me. I was asleep."

"Count a little higher on your own," said Jack, looking eager. "I'd really like that. Do it, Bert. Leave your footprints in the trackless snows. According to the Winners' rules, you can just say that same number again, and then continue from there. On past base camp Googol."

"Sounds good. Only I forget the number."

"I'll write it out for you," said Jack. He scribbled with his pencil on one of the triangular scraps of paper he always had in his pockets.

So I read the number out loud, and then I said the next one, and the one after that, and then I got into a counting trance for a while, and then—

"What?" said Jack, who'd been watching me alertly.

"I lost my voice," I whispered.

Jack poured me a glass of water. "Try again."

I tried again, but for some reason I couldn't say the next number. "That's enough anyway," I said. "I hiked a good stretch on my own. It really feels like my own personal record now."

"I want you to try and write that very last number down!" insisted Jack, very excited. "You'll see that it's not there!" He handed me his pencil, a yellow #2, made in China.

Just to please him, I tried to write down the number I hadn't been able to say—but, sure enough, when I got to the last digit, the pencil lead broke.

"This is stupid," I said. Jack was absolutely thrilled.

He handed me his ballpoint. It ran out of ink on the freaking last digit again.

"I quit." I tossed the pen aside and shrugged. "What do I care if I count one more step? I'm already immortal. A proud, solitary figure in the endless fields of snow."

"My life in a nutshell," crowed Jack. "Until now."

"Why are you so happy?"

"Because I'm not alone anymore," he said. "You and me, Bert. I'm not crazy. You found a hole!"

"What hole?"

"A hole in the number line. That number you wanted to say—it's not there, I tell you. That's why you couldn't say it or write it down. The number's missing, Bert. And now that you've come across a big missing number, you're gonna be able to notice some of the smaller ones."

"I thought your magic beanie had me count every single number up through base camp Googol."

"It couldn't help but hop over the holes. Like a rock skipping across water. Suppose you start counting backward. I'll jigger my Whortleberry to be sure it flags the numbers you miss."

"I'm supposed to drag my weary ass all the way home from base camp Googol?" I exclaimed.

"Starting in the foothills is fine," he said. "It's the smaller missing numbers that we're after. Not the Swiss cheese in the peaks." He handed me the magic beanie. "Suppose you count backwards from your first record. Twelve million, three hundred forty-five thousand, eight hundred ninety-three."

"How do you remember these things?"

"Mathematicians don't get senile," he said.

"They just go nuts," I muttered. But I did as I was told. I figured I owed Jack one. I pulled on the beanie, and lay back and closed my eyes, and started counting sheep jumping backward over the fence, tail first . . .

Ever examined a sheep's tail?

It was a dirty job, but somebody had to do it. The herd milled around me. We flowed across hilltop pastures, down scrub-filled gullies, and into the cornfields outside of town.

+ + +

"Wake up," said Jack.

I woke up. I sat up.

Jack stuck his Whortleberry under my nose. "Voilà," he said.

"Congratulations," I said. "You found six numbers that don't exist."

Jack shook his head. "Three. Our setup logged the numbers on either side of each missing number, since the non-numbers can't be displayed. You don't see a hole. You just see the stuff around it. The un-hole."

"Right," I said. "Whatever."

We went to breakfast. The oatmeal was lumpy. Were the lumps the un-oatmeal, I wondered, or was the oatmeal the un-lumps?

While I was thinking about all this, Jack made a few phone calls to mathematician friends—in banking, communications, and government. Mathematicians are everywhere. I listened with half an ear; it sounded like Jack was arguing with everyone he talked to. As usual. After a bit he rang off and summarized the situation for me.

"Those numbers we found missing: they've never been used as ID numbers for bank accounts, phone numbers, web addresses—nothing like that. But nobody cares. My so-called colleagues don't get the point. Instead of wondering why those particular numbers are hard to use, people just skip over them. Nobody wastes time worrying about the missing numbers."

"But you've got the time to waste," I said. "Right?"

"Wrong," said Jack, superintense. "Wrong that I'm wasting time. I'm ready to tell you my secret. I hope you won't think I'm too far gone."

For a paranoid instant, I saw his eyes as glowing portholes;

his head as a vessel with an alien within. But I couldn't shut him out. I had to let him in. Who else did I have? "You can tell me," I said. "We'll still be friends."

"I don't ask to be famous anymore," said Jack with a sigh. "It'll be enough if I can convince just one person. That would be you, Bert. My secret concerns a certain very small number. It's. Not. Fucking. There."

"Never mind all that," I said, feeling uneasy. "I didn't sleep well."

Jack stared down at the tabletop. He squinted his left eye closed and stared one-eyed at his fingertip. "Do this, Bert. There's a hole in your field of vision where the optic nerve connects into the eyeball. But you never see the hole. You see around it." He waggled his hand. "Pick a spot on the tabletop and stare fixedly at it, and move your fingertip from the right side toward the center. At a certain point your fingertip disappears. It's around two o'clock, halfway out to the right edge of your visual field."

I got going on this, and it worked. Hell, I could wedge two whole knuckles into the hole. Funny I'd never noticed this before, a hole right in front of my nose for going on eighty years.

Hector sidled up to our table, checking us out. "All done breakfast, señors?"

"We're fine," I said, staring down at my un-finger. "You can clear the table if you like."

Jack and I wandered onto the patio behind Journey's End and sat down side by side in rocking chairs, gazing out at the cornfield behind our rest home.

"The holes make the world," said Jack. "The world's the figure, the holes are the ground. Phenomenologically speaking, the illusions of space, time, and matter—they all result from the psychic work we perform to avoid noticing the missing numbers."

I was digging this. I felt smart. "What's the lowest hole, do you think?"

Jack beamed at me, happy and sly.

"Four," he said finally. "It's not there. That word, it's only a sound. A belch, a fart, a *flatus vocis*. There is no four."

Somehow I knew he was right. "Four, four, four," I said testing it out. "Four, four, four, four, four."

"Just a sound," repeated Jack. Out in the cornfield, three or maybe five crows were talking to each other. "Caw caw caw," said Jack, echoing them. "God's voice. Around the holes."

"You knew this all along?" I said, savoring his wisdom.

"That's why I told my business-math students that two plus two equals five," said Jack. "And that's why they fired me. You weren't ready to hear me before. But now you are. The holes are everywhere."

We sat there, rocking and smiling, and later we went in to watch TV. It was more fun than usual, knowing the walls and the ceiling and the TV screen weren't really rectangles. They were squashed pentagons maybe, or googolgons, or, hell, nodes in the all-but-endless web of human language.

One thing for sure, nothing is square.

ELVES OF THE SUBDIMENSIONS

(WRITTEN WITH PAUL DI FILIPPO)

FOREVER and again, the alvar were gnawing at the quantum walls of their prison.

Down where photonic light itself was too gross to serve as a basis for perception, they raged to be free. Ceaselessly shifting congeries of forms, interpenetrating shuggoths, they scratched and clawed in the basement of the cosmos like dissatisfied servants, seeking an entrance to the bright and happy privileged realms above.

The alvar had little actual experience with the macroscopic world they irrationally but fervently longed to breach. Only occasionally did a few of them manage a brief escape, frenetically enjoying the odd pleasures of the supradimensional zone for a short time, before inevitably dropping back down to their ground state below the Planck level. Once trapped again in their subdimensional prison, the adventurous alvars would recount to their fellows the hardly believable experiences they'd undergone. These tales were passed from one alvar to another as they constantly chattered amongst themselves, eventually attaining the proportions of myth.

"The high-planers ingest sweet chunks of their worldstuff!"

"They use picture boxes to learn their hive mind's mood!"

"Of flurbbing, they know not!"

"Their landscape is static across lesser timescales!"

"They tend symbiotes called cows!"

Such was the stimulating talk exchanged between the fits of importunate scrabbling.

But now several alvar were holding a different kind of conversation, one that was more purposeful than fanciful.

For the duration of this discussion—the time it took for a single excited electron to jump shells—these particular alvar remained remarkably stable. To their own peculiar senses, they resembled naked old human males, stooped and bearded and wrinkled. All save one. This exception took the form of a supremely beautiful human woman, anomalously equipped with a horsetail shading her rear.

"When I finally reach the supradimensional realms," said the female, "I intend to experience sex."

"I have heard of this," said one of the gnomes, his skin decorated with blue swirls. "A ritual akin to flurbbing."

The female shivered, temporarily losing definition. "No, something much more delicious. For in high-plane sex, it is said, the two partners retain their identities!"

"Impossible!" "Scandalous!" "Insipid!"

The female grew wrathful. "You are weak and pusillanimous! You will never reach the supradimensional realms with such an attitude. Resume digging now! Faster, harder, deeper! Tear away that quantum foam! We must be ready to pounce upon any growing tendril from the ideational spores we've sown."

The female alvar dissolved into a writhing nest of medusa flails that lashed her fellows, who shrieked and spat, but nonetheless attacked the walls of their sub-Planck-length burrow with renewed vigor.

+ + +

Lately Jory Sorenson had been thinking a lot about his Uncle Gunnar. Gunnar had lost his ability to work; he'd killed himself; and his life's work had been spoiled. Was that in the cards for Jory too? Poor old Gunnar . . .

Gunnar was a farmer all his life; he raised dairy cows on a little farm in the Gold Country of California, in the foothills of the Sierras, a hundred miles east of Sacramento. Unmarried, crusty, and stubborn, Gunnar lived alone in the Scandinavian-style wooden farmhouse he and his older sister Karin had been born in; the house had an honest-to-god thatched roof that Gunnar periodically renewed with straw from his cattle's fodder.

Gunnar's dairy products justified his life; every sensible new-comer to El Dorado county learned to seek out Elf Circle Farm's rich creamy milk, sunny butter, and bold cheeses. And on Saturdays, people would visit the farm to buy in person from cheerful, bustling Gunnar.

It was Gunnar himself who gave Elf Circle Farm its name; his parents had preferred to call it Little Jutland. Gunnar's hobby was the lore of Scandinavian elves and trolls: he collected books, wood and china figurines, drawings and paintings, and he wasn't above placing plastic and concrete lawn-dwarves in his yard, another draw for the Saturday shoppers.

Growing up in a floodplain-flat development in the Sacra-mento sprawl, Jory had loved visiting the old family farm; his mother Karin would send him there for a few weeks every summer. Jory would work in the barn, swim in the creek, climb trees, hunt mushrooms, romp with the gruff and careless farm dogs, and have a heart-breakingly wonderful time—all this less than a hundred miles from the plastic, mall-world, monoculture development-hell of modern life.

After an evening meal of yogurt, cheese, brown bread, and fresh greens, Jory and his uncle would sit on the lantern-lit porch, Gunnar telling stories about the unseen little folk, his thin, lively face creased with shadows, his guileless blue eyes now twinkling with glee, now round with wonder.

Jory's mother Karin had a grudge against her brother Gunnar; there was bad blood over the fact that their parents had bequeathed Gunnar a lifetime tenancy at Elf Circle Farm. The will did specify that, should Gunnar ever sell off any of the land, he was obligated to evenly share the proceeds with his only sibling. But subdividing the farm was something Gunnar adamantly refused to discuss.

Jory's pig-faced stepfather Dick was a realtor, and of course Gunnar's intransigence drove him frantic. When Dick was around, you couldn't mention Gunnar or elves, or, by extension, talk about anything at all fantastic or unusual. Jory was glad to leave for college, and from then on he generally avoided visiting Karin and Dick. Karin didn't miss Jory all that much; Dick had sired three pig-children for her to care for. And she and Dick were quite busy at their church.

All through college and grad school, and on through his years as assistant physics professor at Chico State and as full professor at UC Santa Cruz, Jory kept visiting Uncle Gunnar. Jory would drive across the central valley and up into the Sierra foothills to visit the old farm whenever he was distressed by department politics, by his unsuccessful relationships with women, or by set-backs in his work toward distilling antigravity from his rhizomal subdimension theory. Comfortably tired from the chores, sitting around the crackling hearth at night drinking caraway-seed-flavored aquavit, swapping his physics speculations for Gunnar's tales of Elfland, Jory had come to consider his uncle as an incredibly wise and fortunate man.

But then came Uncle Gunnar's stroke, too early. The man was fit as an eel and only seventy. Nevertheless the hammer fell.

Released from the hospital after long painful weeks of partially successful rehabilitation, Uncle Gunnar could barely make himself understood, and he needed two canes to walk. His cattle had disappeared—rustlers were suspected—not that Gunnar had the strength to care for his dairy business anymore. Karin wanted him to move into an assisted-living facility right away; there'd be no lack of money once they began developing the family land. But Gunnar insisted on spending a night in his cold farmhouse alone. The next day a woman from the post office found him hanging by his neck in the barn.

Karin freaked out; it was up to Jory to manage the funeral arrangements. He'd even had to identify Gunnar at the morgue. The farm went to Karin, and stepfather Dick attempted to develop a gated community called, just as before, Elf Circle Farm. But Dick screwed up the zoning applications, the permits, and the financing. He failed to pay the property taxes. He misrepresented the condition of the land to potential investors and attempted to sell three of the lots to two separate speculators. A half-dozen court cases bloomed and, ten years later, nothing had been built.

Meanwhile Jory's mother had died, leaving the tangled estate to Jory and his three piggish siblings—who'd so far balked at anything like an equable final settlement. If only there were some way to sort out the mess, Jory would have loved to settle for some acreage including the house, the creek, and the woods with the mushroom glen—a bit less than a fourth of the property.

But for now, Gunnar's house stood empty with its windows smashed, the lawn-dwarves shotgunned, and the roof in tatters— amid half-finished dirt roads scraped into the pasture-land, surrounded by barbed-wire fences with NO TRESPASSING signs.

+ + +

Jory had been a professor for going on thirty-eight years now; he was sixty-four. This spring the state had offered Jory a golden handshake to encourage his retirement. The offer was attractive. Jory's student-evaluation ratings had been drifting ever lower. He was tired of teaching and sick of faculty politics. As for his rhizomal subdimension research—he hadn't been able to get a paper published in ten years. Not since Gunnar had died. There *was* that one antigravity experiment he'd kept hoping to complete—but maybe it was really hopeless. He had every reason to retire, but still he hesitated.

How had he gotten so old, so fast? He'd never gotten any closer to antigravity than he'd been when he had the first inspiration for rhizomal subdimension theory—it had come in the midst of a psychedelic drug trip, if the truth be told.

Yes, the very summer when Jory had been casting about for a topic for his physics thesis—good Lord, that was forty years ago—he'd found a ring of magic mushrooms in a glen in the woods across the creek that cut through Gunnar's farm. Turned out Gunnar knew about the mushrooms, not that he was interested in eating them. Gunnar claimed he'd once seen tiny old men and a single beautiful elf-woman dancing around the circle in the invisible light of the new moon.

Jory hadn't seen dancing elves; he'd seen a hailstorm of bejeweled polyhedra. He'd begun hopping from one to the other, climbing them like stepping-stones, like moving platforms in a videogame. The name for a new science—"rhizomal subdimension theory"—came in a crystalline flash from a blazing rhombicosidodecahedron. And quickly this incantatory phrase led to a supernal white-light vision of a new quantum cosmology.

Our familiar dimensions of space and time are statistical averages that happen to have emerged around irregular fault lines, planes, and hyperplanes that percolate through the supersymmetric sea of quantum foam that underlies reality. Above is spacetime, below is the foam. Jory's deeper insight was of a subdimensional domain lying *under* the foam, just as surely as topsoil, clay, and schist lie beneath a composted forest floor. And within this subdimensional bulk there may live, mayhap, a race of gnawing, crawling tunnelers.

As the full force of the mushrooms hit him, Jory realized that the word "rhizome" was the true gift from the Muse. Our world of coherent supradimensional 3 + 1 spacetime is like a fat spot in a ginger root, a nodule covered with, ah yes, tiny root hairs. With a bit of technical finagling it should be possible to coax fundamental particles onto these omnipresent root hairs—thus draining inconvenient masses and forces down through reality's quantum foam floor, down into the subdimensions.

Jory's thesis treated the question of how to divert, in particular, gravitons. Given the equivalence between physics and information theory, such a subdimensional rerouting was simply a matter of constructing the right kind of quantum-computing circuit, although there were some googolplex possible circuits to be considered. How to find the right one? Why not let genetic algorithms perform a Darwinian search!

For a few years, Jory's theories had been all the rage—and he'd surfed his wave of publicity from sleepy Chico State to a full professorship at UC Santa Cruz. But progress had stalled soon thereafter. Jory's genetic algorithms didn't in fact converge any faster than blind search, and thus far he'd never gotten his key antigravity experiment to work.

To the not-so-hidden amusement of his colleagues, he'd compactified his experiment to pocket size. The apparatus was a quarkonium-based quantum computer coupled to a four-way thumb button with a tiny video screen; he'd in fact cannibalized a mini-videogame machine to make it. According to orthodox rhizomal subdimension theory, if someone could miraculously deliver a proper sequence of presses to the button, the field-programmed quantum circuit would begin diverting gravitons into the subdimensions. And whoever held the talisman would be able to fly. The ultimate keyboard cheat.

Perhaps this was all nonsense. It was high time for Jory to give up and go home to his cruddy apartment in the scuzzy beach flats of Santa Cruz. But what would he do, alone in his jumbled rooms? Hang himself?

If only Jory had someone close to confide in, someone to understand his problems. But, like Uncle Gunnar, he'd never found a lasting mate. He'd played the field, lived with a few women, but all had come to naught. And his fellow professors were only half-tolerant of Jory's wild ideas. Indeed, at least one of his peers would be positively gleeful to see him go.

His office-mate, Professor Hilda Kuhl.

+ + +

Victim of its own success in attracting students, UC Santa Cruz had a space problem. Classes were being conducted in trailers. Every lab bench held double the number of experimenters. The dining halls resembled feedlots. And so the small, dark offices of the physics faculty were doing double duty.

One rainy afternoon in the spring of what boded to be his final semester as a professor—and perhaps the final year of his life—Jory was sitting at his messy desk, the forms for his retirement spread out in a space cleared among the tottering mounds of paper. For now he was turning his attention to the lone talisman that contained any solace for him: his quantum computer with its open-sesame button, the distillation of his dreams and intellectual flights of fancy. Jory's thumb worked the four-point keypad ceaselessly, feeling for yet another combination of pulses that would finally open up the interplenary growth of rhizomal threads. Although he enjoyed staring at the fractally patterned feedback graphics on his little screen, Jory didn't really need to keep conscious track of the current sequence, as the computer recorded his touches for future readout, if necessary. The button-clicking had long ago assumed the nature of a subliminal tic, obsessive-compulsive in nature.

Hilda Kuhl was at the other desk, four or five feet away. They generally sat back to back, ignoring each other. But now she interrupted his reverie.

"Gotten any breakthroughs lately, Sorenson? Figured out how many gravitons can dance on the tip of a quantum root-hair?"

Jory didn't dignify this with an answer; he simply turned and stared blankly at her while continuing to manipulate his device.

Hilda was an attractive woman in her thirties, given to under-stated gray suits and pale silk blouses. She wore minimal makeup–just lipstick–and her brown hair was cropped to a sensible bob. Though some thirty years younger than Jory, she was a highly respected physicist with almost as many peer citations as Feynman.

Hilda was divorced, living in a condo with her six-year-old son Jack. She had a nice car, a BMW. Her ex-husband was a software engineer. She was having some trouble juggling motherhood and her job. She was hoping her mother would move in with her; the mother presently was a county clerk in the Sierra foothills.

Most of this Jory knew only at secondhand; he and Hilda didn't chit-chat much. The two of them had been through some ugly turf-wars over the graduate curriculum, especially the Quantum Cosmology course. These days Hilda's goal seemed to be to drive Jory out, by any psychological means available, however cruel.

"I'm so sick of seeing you diddling that little button," said Hilda. "It's masturbatory. Sad and embarrassing." She sniffed the air sharply and shook her head. "It stinks in here too. You must have forgotten a sandwich in your desk again. My mother's going to be visiting from Placerville today, which is why I mention all this. She's trying to decide if she should retire and move to Santa Cruz. She wants to check out the campus drama club. Could you try not to seem like a senile pig?"

Jory felt his neck heat up. Stepfather Dick was the pig, not him. He strove to maintain his calm. "Is that any way for one respectable scientist to speak to another?"

Hilda rummaged in her clunky handbag the size of a burglar's satchel, producing a bottle of noxious-looking sports drink. "Oh please, Sorenson, you stopped being respectable a decade or two ago! I admired you when I was an undergrad, but those days are long gone." She took a swig of her electric blue drink and peered at the drifts of paper on his desk. "Do I see retirement forms? Be still, my heart!"

Jory had a sudden sense of how Uncle Gunnar must have felt with the noose around his neck, while standing on an overturned milk bucket.

"I haven't signed them yet," he said. "I'm thinking it over."

"I can help you clean out your stuff when you're ready," said Hilda. "I hear the Santa Cruz Mystery Spot museum is looking for donations. Not to mention the groundskeepers' compost heap."

Jory turned away, working his little keypad more frenetically than ever. With his other hand he any-keyed his desktop machine out of sleep mode, donning a pair of headphones and calling up one of his favorite tunes—Nikolay Karlovich Medtner's Op. 48, No. 2: "Elf's Fairy Tale."

After several minutes, joggled by Jory's twitching, one of the paper mounds on his desk subsided to the floor, the laminar flow reaching all the way across the room. Jory braced himself for Hilda Kuhl's reaction. But she was gone. Relieved in some small degree, his left thumb slowing in its compulsive writhing, he doffed his headphones and stood up to stretch.

His feet lost contact with the floor and he slowly drifted upward, until his head bumped the ceiling. Victory at last! And on the very eve of destruction! His fame and fortune were assured, all his many unproductive years in the wilderness redeemed!

Quickly Jory pocketed his talisman lest he disturb the finally perfected quantum circuit.

He'd invented antigravity, slipped the surly bonds of mass. Mankind's dream for all its history—and he, Jory Sorenson, had accomplished it!

Now, the slightest wish, the merest velleity, was sufficient to move Jory from one side of the office to the other. From long use, the talisman was quantum-entangled with Jory's brain; it knew to divert impinging gravitons into the subdimensions so as to vector Jory in whatever direction he chose. Jory could hardly wait to go outside and fly to the tops of the redwood trees.

Hilda was talking to a woman out in the hall. Jory dropped flatfooted to the floor, temporarily allowing Earth's gravitons to latch onto him as usual. With any luck he could walk out of here before having to meet Hilda's mother. As a gesture of civility, he cranked the window open a crack—as far as it would go—shoveled the loose papers back onto his desk, and bent over to unearth the foul fungal salmon sandwich in his bottom desk drawer. It wouldn't do to just drop it into his trash can, he'd have to carry it out and—

"I'll consume that delicious morsel if you have no need for it," piped a small voice.

A little man was standing atop Jory's file cabinet. He was bearded, nude, wrinkled, and all of two inches high. His silver hair was barbered into a Mohawk, and his skin was richly tattooed in fractal paisleys, symmetric from left to right.

"I hunger for your world-stuff," said the elf, impatiently holding out his little hand. "Pass it to me quickly, lest some untimely renormalization cause this prize to disappear."

As if in a dream, Jory handed the plastic-wrapped mass of mold to the wee man, wondering how he'd handle it. Compared to the elf, the sandwich was the size of a mattress. But the elf made short work of the offering—his arm flowed outward into a goblet shape that engulfed the Baggie-wrapped discard and squeezed it into nonexistence, like an anaconda swallowing an elephant.

"I'm Ira," said the elf, thoughtfully rubbing his arm. "That was less pleasant than I'd been led to believe. Do savor your ability to fly before Queen Una arrives, for then there will be hell to pay. Una is intent upon—"

Ira was interrupted by Hilda and her mother appearing in the doorway. "This is my office-mate Jory Sorenson," said Hilda, her voice a bit louder than usual. "Sorenson, this is my mother Beverly Kuhl." Not noticing Ira yet, Mrs. Kuhl gave Jory a pleasant smile. She was in the prime of her fifties, fit and comfortable looking, cozily dressed in jeans and a wool sweater, with shiny locks of blond-and-gray hair. Jory recalled hearing Hilda say that her mother's hobby was treading the boards in Gold Country summer melodramas. And indeed this woman looked the part of a star.

"Call me Bev," she said, warmly taking his hand. "It's an honor to meet you, Jory. When Hilda was in grad school she was always talking about you."

"She thinks I'm over the hill now," said Jory. "But I'm still in the game." He was riding high on his antigravity discovery, albeit uneasy about the elf. There seemed little possibility the two phenomena were unconnected. Would the prize be worth the price? That depended entirely on Ira's subsequent actions and those of the heralded Queen Una.

"Good man," said Bev, smiling at him, still holding his hand. For the first time in several years Jory felt a connection, a spark. "I used to buy Elf Circle cheese from your Uncle Gunnar," continued Bev. "What a shame about Gunnar. It's terrible to grow old alone. And that mess about his estate! I work in the court-house, you know, and—"

"What's that on your file cabinet?" interrupted Hilda, as if wanting to break them up. "Don't tell me you've started collecting action figures, Sorenson. You're batty as your uncle."

The little elf shattered his inanimate façade by waggling his Mohawk and gripping his crotch like the most egregious rapper. "I'm Ira. A hardworking digger with a dream. Prepare for the coming of Elf Queen Una." He twisted his face into an appalling leer, belched, and lowered his voice to an insinuating whisper. "Nonce Queen, that is. Your powerful provender has primed me for rebellion."

A swarm of tiny glittering gems appeared beside the mouse-sized, tattooed man, each gem etching a colored trail into the air. The trails wove themselves together like live things, protein skeins knitting the form of an incredibly beautiful blond-haired woman, two inches tall, garbed in a blue leotard, and with a bushy dark tail swishing from the base of her back. Her eyes blazed like the tips of two welding torches.

With a start Jory recognized the diminutive woman as a hulda: a manipulative, seductive elf. Gunnar liked talking about huldas; he'd often shown Jory dense line drawings of them in old books of tales. Huldas were hot. Now Jory confronted the reality not three feet from his face.

"I'm here for the sex," said Queen Una, eyeing the humans with a disturbing, nearly demented smile. She cocked her head and pointed a graceful, imperious hand at Bev. "I'll wear her."

The meta-gattaca strands that formed the Elf Queen Una unwound. The glittering polychromatic points flew at Bev like a swarm of hornets—and sank into her skin.

"Dear me," said Bev, twisting her shoulders and looking down at her backside. Something was bunched beneath her sweater. She pulled her garment up a bit, and a two-foot-long russet horsetail flopped out. "You," Bev said, pointing at Jory with the same gesture Queen Una had used. She snaked her arm around Jory's waist and smirked at her daughter. "Give us some privacy, Hilda."

"Hell no!" said Hilda. "He's drugged you, Mom. Sorenson got all his ideas from taking magic mushrooms, you know. I've heard the rumors. The smell in here—it's some kind of aerosol hallucinogen! And what is that ridiculous talking toy supposed to—"

She made as if to snatch little Ira off the file cabinet, but he hopped into the air to evade her, executing a twisting, eye-hurting somersault that did something to the space coordinates of the room.

"Zickerzack!" exclaimed Ira.

Jory experienced the sensation of being turned inside out, and outside in. He and Bev were standing beside the physics building, on the bark-strewn forest floor, with Hilda yelling at them through the narrow, open slit in Jory's office window. Little Ira had flipped along with them.

"Look at that squirrel run!" exclaimed Ira, craning his neck to stare up a redwood tree. "Beautiful. Her tail is so exceedingly sinuous."

"I have a tail," said Bev, flicking it. She leaned up against Jory, her breath warm on his cheek. "Let's make love right here." Was that her talking, or Una? The sun had broken out. Puffy white clouds dotted the gentle blue sky.

"I'll drive you to the Emergency Room, Mom," called Hilda.

"I'll fly you to the treetops," said Jory. "Where nobody can bother us."

Bev giggled as Jory scooped her into the air. They flew a quarter mile into the forest, where Jory found a broad, level tangle of branches at the top of a tip-broken redwood tree. Jory allowed just enough gravity to reach them so that they could lie comfortably on the matted limbs with no danger of dropping through.

"Squirrels," said Ira, who'd followed along. He was peering down at a hole in the trunk. His gaunt cheeks stretched in a grin. "A big nest of them. Yum." He disappeared into the hole, greeted by an explosion of squirrel chatter.

Alone at last, Jory and Bev Kuhl undressed and worshipped each other's bodies. Even the soft, powerful horsetail came into play. It was wonderful to disport themselves, naked to the heavens in a bower high in the air. And Jory remembered to pillow himself upon his pants, lest he lose the quantum device that made their perch secure.

After the first climax, Una seemed to doze off within Bev— leaving Bev and Jory to chat companionably. Bev was a widow, currently unattached, working as the chief clerk of El Dorado County, thinking of retiring to a career of playing the Madam in her summer melodramas. Although she was proud of her prickly daughter, she was wary of moving here to become her grandson's nanny.

"It's so nice to meet a real gentleman," said Bev, patting Jory's hand. "With a pension. And you can fly!" She kissed him on the cheek. "What a hero!

Rhythmic squawks and throaty chattering burst from the squirrel den below; the noise awakened Queen Una within Bev. In her altered Una-voice, Bev began asking odd questions and suggesting new sex acts. Before long, Jory was worn out and feeling the damp air's chill.

"That completes the mating process?" said Bev in her Queen Una persona. "Hardly so sensational as our legends describe." But then Bev's voice flipped back to her natural warm drawl. "It was wonderful, Jory," she said. "Don't listen to that mean queen. How am I going to get rid of her?"

"I have an idea," said Jory, pulling out his quantum anti-gravity device. "Hold tight to the tree." He keyed in the pause sequence, letting Earth's full gravity temporarily return. The branches beneath him creaked and groaned. He was guessing that his shunting of gravitons into the subdimensions had opened the rift through which Una and Ira had popped. Perhaps pausing his antigravity device might cause the elves to go home.

No such luck.

"I shall remain as long as I please," said the Queen Una voice from within Bev. And now a branch snapped beneath Jory. "Court not a deathly fall, you dunce. Your paramour and I are safe in any event; the alvar fly by means of a dimensional twisting quite different from your rhizomal ruse."

A male squirrel scampered through the matted branches and hiccupped a puff of bright dots—which materialized into Ira, his Mohawk crushed over to one side. As the squirrel watched, the elf twinkled through the air to alight upon Jory's shoulder, his bony bare buttocks pressing the professor's bare skin like a pair of knuckles. The odd sensation very nearly sent Jory tumbling from the tree. Quickly he un-paused his antigravity device.

"Chicker-chickory-chick-a-chee," squawked Ira. The bright-eyed squirrel echoed the sound, then scuttered back to his den. "He is potent and esteemed by the females," said Ira proudly. "Thanks to my good auspices."

"You fucked the squirrels?" exclaimed Jory. "You elves are something else. Look, Ira, I've been good to you, and now you have to help me get Queen Una out of Bev."

"This is difficult," said Ira. "It would take a host of alvar to force Una back into the subdimensions. But, yes, I stand ready to your aid. To start with, I can show you where to find the alvar we need."

"Silence, vassal!" said Una, causing Bev to sit up so abruptly that the branches creaked beneath her pleasant form.

Ira struck a defiant pose. "The alvar have wearied of your tyranny and ill temper, O Queen," he intoned. "Here in this legendary realm, empowered by high-plane foods, vivified by the supradimensional energies of the furry denizens, I dare to usurp your throne. The wee men shall obey you no longer. They wish for me to be their new king. Your reign now ends, my Queen." He held up a cautioning hand. "Contain your pique, or at our next renormalization, the clan will disappear you. I warn but once." The little elf drew himself upright, and with a gesture he clothed himself in a tiny ermine robe and a gold crown, cunningly crafted to show off his silver Mohawk.

"Your victory remains in the future, if it comes at all," said Una after a long, thoughtful pause. "I'll drink the lees of the day." Reaching around their piney bower, Bev stuffed her scattered garments into her large purse, which was the twin of daughter Hilda's burglar-bag. She rose to her pale feet, balanced unsteadily—and leapt out from the tree, taking Jory's heart with her.

But she didn't plummet to the ground. Using the Queen's own dimension-twisting method of flight, Bev/Una hovered, nude and regal, her flowing horsetail gracefully beating. "I'll bed another man by nightfall," said Una's voice. And then Bev's voice chimed in, "How about finding a surfer?"

Luminous in the redwood shadows, talking things over with herself, the nude middle-aged woman disappeared, flying along a graceful curving path through the trees, carrying her purse under her arm.

"What if Una never lets her go?" fretted Jory. "I—I care for Bev. I want her to be safe."

"Una is willful and sensual," said Ira. "She may wish to tarry in your land indefinitely, now that her reign nears its end. But the massed power of the alvar clan is greater than hers. We can draw her back into the subdimensions, provided you transport Bev to a spot where the world walls are thin. I, King Ira, will tell you of such a place."

"I suppose the quantum foam is pretty thin in my office, no?" said Jory. "That's where you two popped through."

"Ah, that was a portal of limited temporal duration," said Ira. "A fleeting attenuation produced by your talismanic summoner."

"You're saying that whenever someone turns on one of my antigravity machines in the future, a bunch of elves will pop up?" asked Jory.

"It is so," said Ira. "May you produce many upon many of such doors for us."

"Uh-huh," said Jory, not so sure this was a good idea. "And that more permanent portal you're talking about is—oh, I get it—the magic mushroom circle at Gunnar's farm!"

"Verily," said Ira. "We can fly there with your Bev, once Una dozes off again."

"First I need to find them," said Jory. "Can you, like, automatically track Una down?"

"Not presently," said Ira. "I, the King, experience your high-plane space as disorienting. These pawky three dimensions of yours—can you point out which is the direction you call 'width'?"

+ + +

There was no sign of Bev at Jory's office, but Hilda was there, both upset and scientifically excited.

"You really invented antigravity, Sorenson! Don't forget to back up the settings on that gizmo of yours right away. I can help you, if you like. Oh, and where's my mother? Don't tell me that you two—"

"Bev's a wonderful woman," said Jory. "She said she's unattached? I want to know her better."

"How gross," said Hilda. "But I suppose she could do worse. Tell me where she is."

"She vowed to tup another man by nightfall," piped Ira, who was again perched upon Jory's shoulder. "She rampages even now."

"Oh God. Your elves did that to my poor mom, Sorenson?"

"She didn't seem to mind the idea so much," said Jory. "I heard her say something about surfers."

"Four Mile Beach," exclaimed Hilda. "I took her there yesterday. A few miles north of here on Route One. Mom was really into those boys. Oh, I hope they're not all laughing at her."

"Why would they?" said Jory. "She's hot."

"Oh you disgusting—" Hilda caught herself and switched on a smile. "I'm going to write a big paper rehabilitating your work, Jory. Give me that talisman, and I'll back it up for you before we go to Four Mile Beach."

"I don't think so," said Jory. Just like Superman, he trotted outside the building and leapt into the air, with Elf King Ira at his side.

Jory made his way to Four Mile Beach, which had its share of surfers; the morning rain had brought on a good swell. But there was no sign of Bev Kuhl, indeed, no sign of anyone much over thirty-five. So, okay, maybe Bev had gotten lost. Jory spent the next hour buzzing all the surf breaks north of Santa Cruz, back and forth, once and then twice. Finally, as the sun was setting, Jory spotted a pup tent on the sands of a beach he'd already written off, Bonny Doon Beach twelve miles north of Cruz.

He dropped down out of the sky next to two fit, fleece-jacketed young men lolling outside the tent in a litter of beer bottles, their eyes half-closed. Bev was visible within the tent, at her ease, resting on one elbow, calmly staring at the gold-chased sea.

"Friends of yours, Bev?" said the more athletic of the two surfers.

"Look out, Zep!" exclaimed the smaller of the youths. "It's her old man! Don't freak, sir. It was all Bev's idea. She came flying down here, hopped on the back of Zep's board out at the break, and—is that a monkey on your shoulder?"

"I am King Ira," piped the elf. "My rule extends across a full score of the subdimensions."

"And I'm Professor Sorenson," said Jory. "Not her husband. Her friend. Are you okay, Bev?"

"Amazed," whispered Bev, smiling from the tent. "Tired. Zep was very lively. But hush, Una's asleep again."

"Would you like to get rid of her now?" murmured Jory, hunkering down by the tent flap.

"Oh yes," said Bev. "This has been a dream come true—but it's not me. Really, Jory, I'm not that kind of woman."

"*Yeah* she is," said the smaller surfer. "She wore Zep out. And then she scarfed down every bit of our beer and food; not to mention the pot."

"And she made me comb out that goddamn tail of hers like a hundred thousand times," added Zep.

+ + +

Jory got the surfers to lend him and Bev their fleece jackets. And then he took her in his arms and flew to Elf Circle Farm.

They landed in the mushroom ring across the creek behind

Gunnar's old house. Following little King Ira's lead, they began to dance.

"This is a tail-wiggle move I learned among the squirrels. Think of your spinal marrow as glowing jelly. Raspberry jelly."

Around and around they went, the world spinning. More and more alvar appeared, gnomish men and a few gamin girls. The ground within the mushroom ring grew gauzy and faded away. But still Una refused to leave Bev's body.

The alvar formed a circle around the two humans in the center of the ring. "You must return home in any case, oh Una," intoned King Ira. "I regret, Bev and Jory, that you will accompany her."

Before Jory or Bev could cry out, Ira and the encircling alvar twitched at the fabric of space, as if manning a blanket-toss. "Zickerzack," said Ira, and they were all in the subdimensional world.

The corridors were like those of a mine, but with way too many directions branching off at the intersections. The glistering foamy walls were translucent, filled with melting jellyfish spots like you see when you're falling asleep, half-familiar and half-unrecognizable, the shapes of thoughts, the fragments of dreams.

"Set Bev free," insisted Jory.

"What will you give me in return?" demanded Una, still speaking through Bev's mouth.

Jory felt in his pockets; he had no silver or gold. All he had was his talismanic antigravity device.

"How about—how about this?" he said, holding it out. "As I understand it, each time you turn it off and restart it, you'll make a thin spot in the walls between worlds."

"Take the trade, Una," urged King Ira. Ensconced in his

native realm, he no longer seemed clownish, but rather haughty and regal. "The high-plane will be ours to plunder as we please. We did well to bring the professor here. Take the trade, and I promise you a high post in my court."

Colored gems rode out on Bev's next exhalation, weaving themselves into haughty Una, very nearly the same size as Jory here, and more formidable than ever. Impatiently flicking her tail, she extended her hand.

As Jory passed over the talisman, he sacrificed his years of research: he keyed in the reset/erase sequence.

Not yet realizing this, King Ira leapt at Una, trying to snatch the device away from her. They wrestled and snapped at each other, their bodies flurbbing together, then separating apart. Finally King Ira emerged as victor. He looked younger and crueler all the time. Holding out the talisman, he pressed the button to—precisely no effect.

Angrily King Ira declared the mushroom circle portal to be closed. "We'll excavate no further here," he cried. "May your prison walls grow ever thicker with quantum foam." Cackling and screaming abuse, the elves disappeared around an abrupt subdimensional turn in the corridor, which closed off in their wake, leaving the two humans trapped together in a small chamber whose uneven, flickering walls continued to constrict.

Bev was shocked, tearful, and remorseful although, Jory could tell, she was also more than a little proud of her day's exploits, if those must be her last. He could understand her so very well. Looking down, he saw that his foot had merged into hers. They were flurbbing, losing their identities, fusing into a common wave function in order to fit their information into a dwindling amount of phase space. And soon, to make things worse, they were flurbbing into the wall and its alien ideations.

Jory sank to the tingling floor as everything grew indistinct. Staring up with his eyes like a pair of fried eggs in a puddle, he saw a series of gauzy four-legged forms—the ghosts of the cows who'd disappeared from Gunnar's farm, eaten by the elves. In their wake limped a two-legged herdsman: the shade of his beloved uncle.

"How can I escape?" Jory asked Gunnar's ghost.

"Love," whispered Gunnar. "Only love can save you."

With his last vestige of energy, Jory pulled his body free of the quantum foam and embraced Bev, long and true. He sensed every cranny of her ego-soul and how it complemented his.

Their bodies firmed up and, as they broke apart into non-flurbbed individuals once more, they found themselves above ground, amid the enchanted mushrooms, beneath the dark sky of a new moon.

For a time they merely drank in the plain fragrant air of their native domain, feeling rich and drunk on high-plane reality.

"I'd like to retire here with you, Bev," said Jory eventually. "I can quit the game now and enjoy my pension. If only the property titles weren't all screwed up. A fourth of this land is mine."

"Elf Circle Farm," said Bev. "I know all about the case. Like I said, I'm the county clerk. I can shuffle some papers, say a few words, and—zickerzack!"

So Bev and Jory married, and Jory took possession of his chosen portion of Gunnar's land: the house, the creek, and the mushroom glen. They fixed the place up, and got a pair of cows for old times' sake. Once or twice, Jory thought he detected a glitter of subdimensional ectoplasm in the barn where Uncle Gunnar had hung himself, but the shade spoke no more with his nephew. No need: Jory never again contemplated suicide.

In the evenings, comfortably tired from the light chores, he and Bev would sit around the crackling hearth drinking caraway-seed-flavored aquavit, spinning tales about Elfland, academia, and the Gold Country. Over time, Jory came to see himself as an incredibly wise and fortunate man, as did his new step-grandson Jack, who often came to visit in the summers.

Dropping the boy off, Jack's mother Hilda always conversed pleasantly with Jory, realizing she owed him credit for her professional successes extending his rhizomal subdimension theory—not that she was ever able to replicate his antigravity breakthrough.

As for the alvar, they never returned—at least not to Elf Circle Farm.

And, oh, yes, Bev's tail. It was there for good. During the first months of living on the farm, Bev hid the tail by wrapping it around her waist. But then, at Jory's urging, she began letting it hang out. Her theater group approved.

PANPSYCHISM PROVED

"THERE'S a new way for me to find out what you're thinking," said Amy, sitting down across from her coworker Rick in the lab's sunny cafeteria. She looked very excited, very pleased with herself.

"You've hired a private eye?" said Rick. "I promise, Amy, we'll get together for something one of these days. I've been busy, is all." He seemed uncomfortable at being cornered by her.

"I've invented a new technology," said Amy. "The mindlink. We can directly experience each other's thoughts. Let's do it now."

"Ah, but then you'd know way too much about me," said Rick, not wanting the conversation to turn serious. "A guy like me, I'm better off as a mystery man."

"The real mystery is why you aren't laid off," said Amy tartly. "You need friends like me, Rick. And I'm dead serious about the mindlink. I do it with a special quantum jiggly-doo. There will be so many apps."

"Like a way to find out what my boss thinks he asked me to do?"

"Communication, yes. The mindlink will be too expensive to replace the cell phone—at least for now—but it opens up the possibility of reaching the inarticulate, the mentally ill, and, yeah, your boss. Emotions in a quandary? Let the mindlink techs debug you!"

"So now I'm curious," said Rick. "Let's see the quantum jiggly-doo."

Amy held up two glassine envelopes, each holding a tiny pinch of black powder. "I have some friends over in the heavy hardware division, and they've been giving me microgram quantities of entangled pairs of carbon atoms. Each atom in *this* envelope of mindlink-dust is entangled with an atom in this *other* one. The atom-pairs' information is coherent but locally inaccessible—until the atoms get entangled with observer systems."

"And if you and I are the observers, that puts our minds in synch, huh?" said Rick. "Do you plan to snort your black dust off the cafeteria table or what?"

"Putting it on your tongue is fine," said Amy, sliding one of the envelopes across the tabletop.

"You've tested it before?"

"First I gave it to a couple of monkeys. Bonzo watched me hiding a banana behind a door while Queenie was gone, and then I gave the dust to Bonzo and Queenie, and Queenie knew right away where the banana was. I tried it with a catatonic person too. She and I swallowed mindlink dust together and I was able to single out the specific thought patterns tormenting her. I walked her through the steps in slow motion. It really helped her."

"You were able to get medical approval for that?" said Rick, looking dubious.

"No, I just did it. I hate red tape. And now it's time for a peer-to-peer test. With you, Rick. Each of us swallows our mindlink dust and makes notes on what we see in the other one's mind."

"You're sure the dust isn't toxic?" asked Rick, flicking the envelope with a fingernail.

"It's only carbon, Rick. In a peculiar kind of quantum state. Come on, it'll be fun. Our minds will be like Web sites for each other—we can click links and see what's in the depths."

"Like my drunk-driving arrest, my membership in a doomsday cult, and the fact that I fall asleep sucking my thumb every night?"

"You're hiding something behind all those jokes, aren't you, Rick? Don't be scared of me. I can protect you. I can bring you along on my meteoric rise to the top."

Rick studied Amy for a minute. "Tell you what," he said finally. "If we're gonna do a proper test, we shouldn't be sitting here face to face. People can read so much from each other's expressions." He gestured toward the boulder-studded lawn outside the cafeteria doors. "I'll go sit down where you can't see me."

"Good idea," said Amy. "And then pour the carbon into your hand and lick it up. It tastes like burnt toast."

Amy smiled, watching Rick walk across the cafeteria. He was so cute and nice. If only he'd ask her out. Well, with any luck, while they were linked, she could reach into his mind and implant an obsessive loop centering around her. That was the real reason she'd chosen Rick as her partner for this mindlink session, which was, if the truth be told, her tenth peer-to-peer test.

She dumped the black dust into her hand and licked. Her theory and her tests showed that the mindlink effect always began in the first second after ingestion—there was no need to wait for the body's metabolism to transport the carbon to the brain. This in itself was a surprising result, indicating that a person's mind was somehow distributed throughout the body, rather than sealed up inside the skull.

She closed her eyes and reached out for Rick. She'd enchant him and they'd become lovers. But, damn it, the mind at the other end of the link wasn't Rick's. No, the mind she'd linked to was inhuman: dense, taciturn, crystalline, serene, beautiful—

"Having fun yet?" It was Rick, standing across the table, not looking all that friendly.

"What— " began Amy.

"I dumped your powder on a boulder. You're too weird for me. I gotta go."

Amy walked slowly out the patio doors to look at the friendly gray lump of granite. How nice to know that a rock had a mind. The world was cozier than she'd ever realized. She'd be okay without Rick. She had friends everywhere.

MS FOUND IN A MINIDRIVE

In the summer of 2004, while traveling in the West, I found a small electronic device in a meadow near Boulder, Colorado. It was a fingertip-sized minidrive of the type that can be plugged into the port of a laptop computer. There was but a single document stored upon the drive: the story that I have appropriated and printed below. The actual author, one Professor Gregge Crane , seems to have gone permanently missing.

–R. R.

THIS summer I was asked to submit a piece for an anthology of tales inspired by Edgar Allan Poe. The publisher's somewhat tendentious idea for the book was that each contributor should create a story relating to one and the same unfinished Poe manuscript.

The seed-fragment in question, known as the "The Lighthouse," takes the form of a few journal entries by a disinherited young noble (poor Eddie's perennial theme!) who has signed up for a stint as a solitary lighthouse keeper on a shoal of rock in some far Northern sea.

The reader quickly senses there will be trouble within and without. On the one hand, "there is no telling what may happen to a man all alone as I am—I may get sick, or worse . . ." and on the other, "the sea has been known to run higher here than anywhere with the single exception of the Western opening of the Straits of Magellan."

There's something unsettling about the lighthouse's construction. The space within the tower's shaft extends so low that "the floor is twenty feet below the surface of the sea, even at low tide. It seems to me that the hollow interior at the bottom should have been filled in with solid masonry. Undoubtedly the whole would have been rendered more *safe*–but what am I thinking about?"

One final, portentous observation: "The basis on which the structure rests seems to be chalk. . . ."

And here Poe's fragment ends.

+ + +

I'm a well-connected scholar of American Literature, which is why I was offered the opportunity to join the anthology. But I'm not a man with a mad imagination. Transmuting so slight a start into a full-blown weird tale seemed a tall order for me. Although I love writing, and writers, I've never quite found my own connection to the starry dynamo of night.

Be that as it may, I was gung-ho to be part of the "Lighthouse" anthology. My chance to be a fiction writer at last! It struck me that I'd do well to attend a writer's workshop–and for sentimental reasons, I settled on the summer program at the Naropa Institute in Boulder.

You could say I'm a bit of literary groupie. I'm bisexual of course, and I've had my share of rolls in the hay with writers, each time hoping, I suppose, that something of their essence might rub off.

As it happens, the most famous writer I ever slept with was William Burroughs. This was in the early 1980s—I was attending a Modern Language Association conference at Colorado University, and Bill was in residence for the summer as part of Naropa's burgeoning Jack Kerouac Disembodied School of Poetics. I knew of this, and one of my old lovers used her not inconsiderable charms to get us into a cocktail party for the innermost circle of Boulder bohemia. Bill was there, I made a favorable impression, and voilà, the Beat master and I ended up in his room at the Boulderado Hotel, sipping bourbon, smoking low-grade marijuana, and making languid love. A night to treasure for my entire life, a night signifying that I too have had a purpose on this lonely planet.

And so this June, once my academic duties had ended for the term, I repaired to the Boulderado Hotel, this time as a paying guest, with a sheaf of Naropa University orientation papers in my briefcase.

Much of school's opening session that afternoon had consisted of perky functionaries reciting lists of rules. Not like the crazy eighties. Naropa had once been the outriders' beacon; had the rugged old tower toppled to become a mere breakwater in the safe harbors of American mass culture? I only hoped that some esoteric possibilities remained.

Naropa's Tibetan Buddhist founder wrote of a paradoxical land hidden outside, or next to, or beneath our daily reality. Shambhala—which Westerners call Shangri La.

The Beats had crumbled, but perhaps the door to Shambhala remained. I thought of Poe's doomed lighthouse, and of the mysterious chamber at its base. I was filled with a numinous sensation that somehow everything was going to fit. Looking around at my fellow students, I realized I was one of the oldest customers in the house. Very well, but I was young at heart, ready to become a writer at last.

In a celebratory mood, I drank half a bottle of champagne at the hotel bar and then, on a whim, I went up to the fifth floor and stood outside the corner room where Bill and I had coupled so thoroughly and so well, lo, these twenty-three years gone.

Standing there, I wondered if the Master had ever thought of me again. I'd combed though his later works, hoping to find some refracted image of myself—sometimes imagining that an echo of our pleasures could be found in Bill's descriptions of farm boys in transports of sexual abandon. I'd even mailed him shameless letters, asking if my speculations were correct. But he never answered, and then one day he died.

"I miss you, Bill," I said into the plush Victorian quiet of the hotel hall.

I can swear I never touched his old room's door, but just as surely as if I'd pounded on it with my fist, a voice from within called, "We hear you. Come on in." The words were blurred, as if the speaker had a lisp.

I pushed forward; the door swung open. The room was filled with heavy, dark furniture, and books piled in the gloom. A man with long, stringy blond hair and a fluffy blond goatee sat before a velvet-curtained window, bent over a desk with a single brass lamp. At first I had only a quarter-view of his face. He was bent very low indeed, as if kissing the papers scattered on his desk, papers covered by penciled writing in the smallest script I'd ever seen.

"Welcome back, Gregge," came a high, twangy voice, different from the one I'd heard through the door. The blond man turned his head, clamping his mouth tight shut and staring at me with pale blue eyes that held an expression of triumphant glee. A curious high piping seemed to come from within his head. And then all at once his mouth gaped open.

You must believe me when I tell you that his tongue was a small manikin, a detailed copy of William Burroughs, fully animated and alive. I, who have so little imagination, could never invent such a thing.

I stepped back, feeling for the door, wanting to flee and forget what I was seeing. But I struck the door wrong—and it slammed shut. The blond man came closer, mouth open, eyes dancing with spiteful delight. I was shaking all over.

Like a dictator on the balcony of his palace, the meat puppet Burroughs stared out from the mouth, his tiny hands resting upon the lower teeth as if upon a railing.

"I knowed you was coming," came Bill's thin, rheumy voice. He was using the Pa Kettle accent he sometimes liked to put on. "Picked up your moon-calf aura from the hall." He paused, savoring my reactions.

"I don't understand," I said, fighting back a spasm of nausea. "Don't hurt me."

"I'm working out karma," said the little Burroughs. "I owe you for never writing back. I'm gonna let my pal Dr. Teage set you up for a Poe tasting. Later on you might do some secretarial work for us—or make yourself useful in other ways." He allowed himself one of his appalling leers. "You're aging well, Gregge. But that's enough outta me already."

In a twinkling, the Burroughs face on the blond man's tongue smoothed over, and the tiny arms sank into the pink surface. I was faced with a somewhat seedy character licking his lips. His breath smelled of fruit and manure.

"I'm Teage," he said, his goatee wagging. "And you're—"

"Gregge Crane," I said. "I knew Bill a little, a long time ago. I was with him in this room."

"I know," said Teage, who for some reason seemed to trust me. "I'm with him in this room every day. We're doing a book together. I'm like you. I always wanted to be a fiction writer. Look at this."

On the desk were the sheets filled with tiny words, and lying on one of the sheets was a sharpened bit of mechanical pencil lead with a scrap of tape around one end. Bill's writing implement, half the size of a toothpick.

"The process is my own invention," said Teage. "I call it twanking. Before I started channeling Bill, I was a biocyberneticist. Twanking is elementary. You assemble a data base of the writer's works and journals, use back-propagation and simulated evolution to get a compact semantic generator that produces the same data, turn the generator into the connection weights for an artificial neural net, code the neural net into wetware for the gene expression loops of some human fecal bacteria, and then rub the smart germs onto living flesh. I think it's deliciously fitting to use my tongue. Bill speaks through me. Every night I twank him by rubbing on a culture of his special bacilli. I lean over our desk and we write till dawn. Afternoons I read it over. I really need to start getting it keyboarded soon."

"What's the book going to be called?" was all I could think to say.

"Bill hasn't decided yet." Teage hesitated, then pressed on. "The thing is, Gregge, he's much more than a simulation. I've caught his soul? Is soul a bad word anymore? Logically, you might expect that there'd be no continuity of behavior from session to session. But Bill remembers. He's all around us—dark energy. He knows things, and even when the visible effects wear off, he's still inside my tongue."

Perhaps it was the effects of the champagne—or my pleasure at having Burroughs call me by name—but all this seemed reasonable. And, God help me, it was I myself who suggested the next step.

"Maybe you can help me twank Poe. The whole reason I came out here this summer was because I need to write a story in his style."

"I know," said Teage, "Bill and I have been getting ready for you. Bill's known for months that you'd come tonight. The spirits are outside our spacetime, Gregge, continually prodding the world toward greater gnarliness. Inching our reality across paratime. Making your and my lives into still more perfect works of art." He let out an abrupt guffaw, his breath like the miasma above a compost heap.

"You'll give me a germ culture to turn my flesh into Edgar Allan Poe?" I pressed.

"It's over here," said Teague. "And maybe tomorrow you'll start typing my manuscript into your computer. Unless there's a complete rewrite."

"Fine," I said, sealing our deal. "Wonderful."

The twanking culture consisted of scuzzy crud on a layer of clear jelly in a Petri dish atop a dusty green *Collected Works* of Poe. Teage fit a cover onto the dish and handed it to me.

"I've got no use for this batch myself," he said. "I've got my mouth full enough with Burroughs."

I peered into the dish. Fuzzy white Cheerio-sized rings. Green and orange streaks. Spots, dots, and streamers.

"You only need a little at a time," Teage was saying. "Dig out a few grams of the culture with, like, a plastic coffee spoon, and smear it on. Careful where you put it, though. It takes hold wherever it touches. The tongue's especially good because it's so flexible."

Back in my room I brewed a pot of coffee and sat down to record these events on my laptop and on the cute little minidrive that I carry with it. I once lost a year's work on a Poe bibliography in a hard disk crash, and now I always make a point of saving off my work as I go.

+ + +

It's calming to be lying here propped on the pillows of my bed, typing. It's a warm night; I'm nude. The yellow lamplight burnishes the tones of my flesh. I've been avoiding the sight of the Petri dish on my bed stand. But now it's time.

I poise the white plastic spoon over the culture. Rub that gunk on my tongue?

I think not.

For as soon as Teage told me the culture would alter whatever part of me it touched, I decided to use my penis.

So here we go. It stings more than I could have imagined. The sensation flutters into my loins and my solar plexus. My penis shifts and separates. A vertical break forms in the base, two flaps split off near the top.

What have I done, what have I done, what have I done?

I've twanked Eddie Poe into my penis.

He's angry, of all things. "What is the meaning of this conjuration?" cries Poe. "I abjure you to return me to my rest." He glances down and sees my belly, my pubic hair, my scrotum.

"Fie! Gaud, sodomite, ghoul, defiler of my grave!"

It's I who should be upset; I'm the one with the deformed, yelling penis. But the transformation is such that my cock seems to have a stronger personality than me. Nothing new, really. I'm in shock, and for a moment this seems almost funny.

But now it gets much worse. The little Poe penis knots his brow in fury, gathers his strength and—snaps himself loose from my belly. No, no, no!

Somewhere below the horror I think of a lighthouse with a hollow base breaking loose from brittle chalk.

There's a hole at my crotch. The hole is moving around, adjusting itself, becoming a vagina.

I catch hold of Eddie before he can run away and, screaming like a woman, I stampede bare-assed down the halls and up the stairs to Teage's room—not forgetting to bring my laptop. I must preserve every bit of this, at all costs.

For finally I have a story to tell.

+ + +

Teage has drawn back his curtains and is standing by his open window, staring into the humid night. He turns to face me, Burroughs in his mouth again.

Bill calls a word to my Eddie: "*Tekelili.*" I recognize it from Poe's only novel, his tale of a sailing trip to the farthest South. Poe used *tekelili* to represent the cries of birds at Earth's nethermost frontier.

"*Tekelili,*" responds the figure in my hand. And now, vivified by the exchange, the little Poe grows hot to the touch, twists from my grasp, and buzzes through the room's air. An instant later he's flown out Teage's open window, blinking like a firefly, like a lighthouse. He pauses out there, waiting for us to come and follow.

A sharp pain knifes across my belly.

+ + +

I brought the laptop in the car with me; Teage is driving, led by the darting light. I'm still naked. My pains come in rhythmic waves. I fear what comes next. But I keep writing, saving the file after every sentence.

We drive down Broadway and turn right on Baseline. The great triangular rocks of the Flatirons are gold in the waning moon.

Thick clear fluid seeps from my vagina. I'm giving birth.

+ + +

In the middle of the field hovers glowing Eddie Poe. Between my wet thighs twitches a newborn sea-cucumber—a warty, foot-long creature with a fan of tendrils at one end—the very species found in Poe's novel of the great hole beyond the Antarctic walls of ice. The contractions continue. More life stirs in my womb.

The Burroughs thing watches quietly from within Teage's mouth. I force a mugwump out through my birth canal, then a centipede and a cuttlefish.

+ + +

As they leave my body, the creatures crawl to Eddie's beacon, no two of them the same. Unknown energies pour from their tendrils, hands, mandibles, tentacles. The beams drill through Earth's thin crust, friable as a chalk tablet.

A glow is visible from the tunnel my children have made.

Teage has gone and I must follow. My body is changing, my mind can barely form the words to type. I'll end my manuscript and cast the minidrive clear.

And then, ah, then—raving, inchoate, my womb expelling an endless stream of life, I'll leap into the Hollow Earth.

Shambhala.

THE MEN IN THE
BACK ROOM AT THE
COUNTRY CLUB

"YO, Jack," said Tonel as they lugged two golf bags apiece toward the men's locker room. It was sunset, the end of a long Saturday's caddying, Jack's last day of work this summer.

"I didn't get a chance to tell you," continued Tonel, shouldering open the door. "About who I saw sweatin' in Ragland's backyard this morning." It was fresh and cool in the locker room. A nice break from the heavy, thick August air.

"In Ragland's yard?" said Jack Vaughan, setting down the bags and wiping his brow. "I don't know. His ninety-year-old mother?" Jack suspected a joke. Ragland was the master of the locker room, ensconced behind his counter. Tidily cleaned shoes and piles of fresh white towels sat on the white-painted shelves around him. Although the bare-skulled Ragland's eyes were half-closed, it was likely that he was listening.

"It was the five mibracc," said Tonel. "Doin' Ragland's yard work. Isn't that right, Ragland? What's the dealio? How you get to slave-driving them Republicans? I need to know." Tonel lived right next door to Ragland. The two weren't particularly fond of each other.

"Don't be mouthin' on my business, yellow dog," said Ragland. Though he cleaned the shoes of popinjays, he insisted on his dignity.

A burst of talk echoed from the little back room beyond Ragland's station. Just like every other morning or afternoon, the mibracc—he caddies' nickname for "men in the back room at the country club"—were in there, safe from women, out of the daylight, playing cards and drinking the bourbon they stored in their lockers.

"Those bagworts do chores?" said Jack. "No way, Tonel."

"I seen it," insisted Tonel. "Mr. Atlee was draggin' a plow with Mr. Early steerin' it. Mr. Gupta was down on his knees pullin' up weeds, and Mr. Inkle and Mr. Cuthbert was carryin' trash out to the alley. Ole Ragland sittin' on the back porch with his shotgun across his knees. Did your Meemaw put conjure on them, Ragland?"

"You want me to snapify your ass?" said Ragland. Though gray and worn, Ragland was, in his own way, an imposing man.

Tonel made a series of mystic passes, hoodoo signs, and rap gestures in Ragland's direction.

"I'll ask the men myself," said Jack, caught up by Tonel's rebellious spirit.

The two boys stepped into the back room, a plain space with a tile floor and shiny green paint on the windowless concrete walls. The five old men sat in battered wooden captain's chairs around a table from the club's lounge. Oily Mr. Atlee was dealing out cards to spindly white-haired Mr. Early, to bald-as-a-doorknob Mr. Inkle, to Mr. Cuthbert with his alarming false teeth, and to Mr. Gupta, the only nonwhite member of the Killeville Country Club.

"Hi, guys," said Jack.

There was no response. The mibracc studied their cards, sipping at their glasses of bourbon and water, their every little gesture saying, "Leave us alone." Mr. Inkle stubbed out a cigarette and lit a fresh one.

"Listen up," said Tonel in a louder tone. "I gotta axe you gentlemen somethin'. Was you bustin' sod for Ragland today? My friend here don't believe me."

Still no answer. The mibracc were so fully withdrawn into their clubby little thing that you could just as well try talking to your TV. Or to five spiteful children.

"Scoop," grunted Mr. Cuthbert, standing up with his glass in hand. Mr. Gupta handed him his empty glass as well. With the slightest grunt of nonrecognition, Mr. Cuthbert sidled past Tonel and Jack, moving a little oddly, as if his knees were double-jointed. His oversized plastic teeth glinted in the fluorescent light. Mr. Cuthbert pressed his thumb to his locker's pad, opened the door, and dipped the two glasses down into his golf bag. Jack could smell the bourbon, a holiday smell.

The mibracc's golf bags held no clubs. They were lined with glass, with tall golf bag–sized glass beakers, or carboys. Big glass jars holding gallons of premium bourbon. It was a new gimmick, strictly hush-hush; nobody but Ragland and the caddies knew. Mr. Atlee, a former druggist, had obtained the carboys, and Mr. Early, a former distiller's rep, had arranged for a man to come one night with an oak cask on a dolly to replenish the bags. The mibracc were loving it.

Mr. Cuthbert shuffled back past Tonel toward the card table, the liquid swirling in his two glasses. The boy fell into step behind the old man, draping his hand onto the mibracc's shoulder. Mr. Cuthbert paid him no mind. Jack joined the procession, putting his hand on Tonel's shoulder and trucking along in his friend's wake. Tonel was humming the chorus of the new video by Ruggy Qaeda, the part with the zombies machine-gunning the yoga class.

After Mr. Cuthbert dropped into his chair and picked up his cards, Jack and Tonel circled the room two, three, four times, with Tonel finally bursting into song. Never did the mibracc give them a second glance. Odd as it seemed, the liquid in the glasses still hadn't settled down; it was moving around as if someone were stirring it.

Around then Ragland came out from behind his counter, wielding a wet, rolled-up towel. Silly as it sounded, being snapped by the old locker room attendant was a serious threat. Ragland was the ascended Kung-Fu master of the towel snap. He could put a bruise on your neck that would last six weeks. Laughing and whooping, Tonel and Jack ran outside.

A white face peered out of the window in the clubhouse's terrace door. The door swung open and a plain, slightly lumpish girl in a white apron appeared. Gretchen Karst.

"I'm pregnant, Jack," said Gretchen, her sarcastic, pimply face unreadable. "Marry me tonight. Take me off to college with you tomorrow."

"How do you know it's me?" protested Jack. "I'm not the only—I mean even Tonel said he—"

"Tonel is a horn worm. All I gave him was a hand job. And it didn't take very long. Jack, there's a justice of the peace out on Route 501. Ronnie Blevins. He works at Rash Decisions Tattoo. I found him online. Since it's Saturday, they're open till midnight. I'm off work right now, you know. I started early today."

"Stop it, Gretchen. You and me—it's not—"

"I'm serious," said Gretchen, although there was in fact a good chance that she was scamming him. Gretchen had a twisted mind. "You're my best chance, Jack," she continued. "Marry me and take me with you. I'm smart. I like sex. And I'm carrying your son."

"Uh—"

Just then someone shouted for Gretchen from the corner of the clubhouse building. It was Gretchen's dad, standing at the edge of the parking lot. He'd trimmed his flattop to high-tolerance precision and he was wearing his shiny silver jogging suit. All set for the weekly meeting at the Day Six Synod's tabernacle.

Gretchen could talk about the Day Six Synod for hours. It was a tiny splinter religion based on the revelation that Armageddon, the last battle, was coming one-seventh sooner than the Seventh Day Adventists had thought. We were already in the end times, in fact, with the last act about to be ushered in by manifestations of Shekinah Glory, this being the special supernatural energy that God—and Satan—use to manifest themselves. The pillar of fire that led the Israelites to the promised land, the burning bush that spake to Moses—these had been Shekinah Glory. The Day Six Synod taught that our Armageddon's Shekinah Glory would take the form of evil UFOs pitted against winged angels.

Karl Karst's jogging suit was silver to remind him of the Shekinah Glory. The Day Six Synod meetings featured impressively high-end computer graphics representing the Glory in its good and evil forms. Though Mr. Karst was but a county school-bus mechanic, some of the core founders of the Day Six Synod were crackpot computer hackers.

"Shake a leg or we'll be late," shouted Mr. Karst. "Hi, Jack and Tonel. Wait till you see who I've got with me, Gretchen!"

"I'll deal with you later," said Gretchen to Jack with a slight smile. Surely she'd only been teasing him about the pregnancy. She made the cell phone gesture with her thumb and pinky. "We'll coordinate."

"Okay," said Jack, walking with her toward her father. "I'm visualizing hole six." Hole six of the KCC golf course was the popular place for the club's young workers to party. It was well away from the road, on a hillock surrounded on three sides by kudzu-choked woods.

Right now, Jack figured to eat dinner at Tonel's. He didn't want to go to his own house at all. Because this morning on the way to the Killeville Country Club, he'd doubled back home, having forgotten his sunglasses, and through the kitchen window he'd seen his mom kissing the Reverend Doug Langhorne.

It wasn't all that surprising that Doug Langhorne would make a play for the tidy, crisp widow Jessie Vaughan, she of the cute figure, tailored suits, and bright lipstick. Jessie was the secretary for the shabby-genteel St. Anselm's Episcopal Church on a once-grand boulevard in downtown Killeville, right around the corner from the black neighborhood where Tonel lived, not that any black people came to St. Anselm's. Jessie's salary was so meager that Reverend Langhorne let Jessie and Jack live with him in the rectory, a timeworn Victorian manse right next to the church.

Doug Langhorne's wife and children shared the rectory as well. Lenore Langhorne was a kind, timid soul, nearsighted, overweight and ineffectual, a not-so-secret drinker of cooking sherry, and the mother of four demanding unattractive children dubbed with eminent Killeville surnames. Banks, Price, Sydnor, and Rainey Langhorne.

Setting down his bicycle and stepping up onto his home's porch this morning, Jack had seen his mother in a lip lock with Doug Langhorne. And then Mom had seen Jack seeing her. And then, to make it truly stomach-churning, Jack had seen Lenore and her children in the shadows of the dining room, witnessing the kiss as well. The couple broke their clinch; Jack walked in and took his sunglasses; Lenore let out a convulsive sob; Doug cleared his throat and said, "We have to talk."

"Daddy kissed Jack's mommy!" cried Banks Langhorne, a fat little girl with a low forehead. Her brother Rainey and her sisters Price and Sydnor took up the cry. "Daddy's gonna get it, Daddy's gonna get it, Daddy's gonna get it . . ." There was something strange about the children's ears; they were pointed at the tips, like the ears of devils or of pigs. The children joined hands in a circle around Doug and Jessie and began dancing a spooky Ring-Around-the-Rosie. Lenore was trying to talk through her racking sobs. Doug was bumblingly trying to smooth things over. Mom was looking around the room with an expression of distaste, as if wondering how she'd ended up here. On the breakfast table, the juice in the children's glasses was unaccountably swirling, as if there were a tiny whirlpool in each. Jack rushed outside, jumped on his bike, and rode to work, leaving the children's chanting voices behind.

Jack had pretty much avoided thinking about it all day, and what should he think anyway? It was Jessie's business who she kissed. And surely he'd only imagined the pointed ears on those dreadful piggy children. But what about Lenore? Although Lenore was like a dusty stuffed plush thing that made you sneeze, she was nice. She'd always been good to Jack. Her sob was maybe the saddest thing he'd ever heard. Grainy, desperate, hopeless, deep. What did the kiss mean for Mom's future as the church secretary? What did it bode for Doug Langhorne's position as rector? What a mess.

Jack's plan was to stay out most of the night or all of the night with his friends, grab his suitcase in the morning, and get the 8:37 A.M. bus to Virginia Polytechnic Institute in Blacksburg. And there he'd begin his real life. Let Mom and Lenore and Doug work things out in pawky, filthy Killeville. Jack's bag was packed. He was ready to set off for the great outer world!

With these thoughts running in his head, he followed Gretchen to the parking-lot, Tonel tagging along. Mr. Karst was mounted in his battered secondhand Ford SUV. Sitting next to him was an unkempt, overweight, luminously white guy smoking a filter cigarette.

"Albert Chesney!" exclaimed Gretchen.

"Him!" said Jack. The thirty-year-old Albert Chesney was a Day Six Synodite and a convicted computer criminal. He'd just gotten parole; his release had been a topic in the *Killeville Daily News* for several days. Three years ago, Chesney had brought down the entire Internet for a week with his infamous <endtimes> e-mail, which had combined the nastiest features of spam, hypnotism, a virus, a pyramid scheme, a con-game, a worm, and a denial-of-service attack. At the cost of infecting seven hundred million machines, <endtimes> had netted seven converts to the Day Six Synod.

"Don't ride with him, Gretchen," said Jack, suddenly visualizing a defenseless big-eyed fetus within Gretchen's slightly curved belly. He seemed to recall that Chesney had always been interested in Gretchen. Chesney was single, with no relatives.

"Oh, now you're all protective?" said Gretchen. "Don't

worry. I can handle myself. Welcome back, Albert. Are you fully rehabilitated?"

"I've hoed a long, lonely row," sighed Albert Chesney. His voice was husky; his head was big and crooked like a jack-o'-lantern. "The Pharisees say I'm not allowed to live in a house with computers. What with the Synod having the tabernacle on my farm, I'm exiled to a humble abode on Route 501. Leastways it won't be but one night. The last battle's comin' tomorrow morning, hallelujah and pass it on. Armageddon. Angels and devils fighting for the fate of our world. Drive your chariot onward, Karl. I need a taste of my sweet country roads. And then I'll prophesy to the fellowship about the Shekinah Glory."

"You bet, Albert," said Mr. Karst. "Don't he look good, Gretchen?" Mr. Karst liked Chesney because he'd let Day Six use his farmhouse for their tabernacle the whole time he'd been in jail. Swaying and backfiring, the rusty SUV lumbered off.

"Do he say the world ends tomorrow?" asked Tonel.

"Don't worry," said Jack. "They always say that. Back in May, Mr. Karst tried to stop Gretchen from buying a prom dress because the last battle was due to come before our graduation."

Turning back to the clubhouse, Tonel and Jack encountered muscular Danny Dank, who'd just finished setting up the giant propane-fueled two-whole-hog barbeque wagon that the club used for their galas. Tomorrow was the day of the club's annual Killeville Barbeque Breakfast Golf Classic, starting near dawn.

Danny tightened down the cover of the quilted chrome wagon and unwrapped a stick of marijuana gum, the pricey brand called Winnipeg Wheelchair. Grinning and chewing, he gestured for the two caddies to sit down with him on a low wall facing the eighteenth green and the last glow of the sunset.

"Listen to this," said Danny, pulling a folded up newspaper

from his hip pocket. He hawked some spit on to the ground, then read, more mellifluously than one might have expected. Danny had gone to C. T. Piggott High School the same as Jack and Tonel; he'd been a senior when they'd been freshman. But he'd been expelled before his graduation.

"Falwell County's most notorious computer criminal is temporarily lodged in the Casa Linda Motel on Highway 501 southeast of Killeville, next to a tattoo parlor and a liquor store that rents adult videos," read Danny. "His neighbors include a few parolees and at least one registered sex offender. His second-floor room in the thirty-four-unit motel overlooks the parking lot of a strip club."

"Punkin-head Chesney," said Tonel. "We just seen him. He and Gretchen goin' to church."

"Gretchen?" parroted Danny, as if unwilling or unable to understand. He was intent on his presentation. "Do you dogs grasp why I read you the news item?"

"Because you're spun," said Jack, laughing. "Give me a piece of that gum."

"Three dollars," said Danny, reaching into shirt pocket. "Casa Linda is my crib. The county thinks they can just dump any old trash on my doorstep. I been planning to write a letter to the paper. But—"

"Who's the sex offender, Dank-man?" interrupted Tonel.

Danny looked embarrassed and chewed his gum in silence. The sex offender living at the Casa Linda was Danny. He'd been expelled from Piggott High for putting a Web cam into the girls' locker room. One of the girls who'd been showering there was frosh Lucy Candler, the pluperfect cheer daughter of Judge Bowen Candler and his wife Burke. The Judge had thrown the book at Danny. Racketeering and child pornography. Even though, Danny being Danny, the Web site hadn't worked.

"Here's three bucks," said Jack, pulling the singles out of his wallet. "This is my last night in town, Danny. Disable me, dog."

"I'm on the boat," said Tonel, getting out his own wallet.

"I'm up for a power run," said Danny, taking the money and fishing out two sticks of gum. "But Les Trucklee says I gotta be here at dawn for the barbeque. All I do in that kitchen is, like, fry frozen fries for freezing. I can't hack no more of that today. Tomorrow will be here soon enough. You dogs got any booze?"

"We know where there's a lot of bourbon," said Jack, impishly curious to see what might happen if he encouraged Danny. "Right, Tonel?" Ragland had fiercely enjoined the caddies to keep mum about the mibracc's lockers, but tonight of all nights, Jack could afford to be reckless. "You get Ragland to chasing you, Tonel," continued Jack. "And I'll scoop into Mr. Cuthbert's stash." Anything was better than going home.

"What stash?" asked Danny.

So he told Danny, and they talked it over a little more as the light faded, in no rush to actually do anything yet, the three of them chewing their Winnipeg Wheelchair. They strolled into the patch of rough between the first tee and the eighteenth green. There was a grassy dell in among the trees where they could stretch out without anyone coming along to boss them.

"Danny!"

It was the voice of Les Trucklee, the personnel manager. The boys could see him standing on the floodlit terrace next to the barbeque wagon. He wasn't a bad guy—he'd hired Danny despite his record. Les Trucklee was gay, not too bright, in his thirties, a wannabe yuppie, with thinning blond hair in a comb-over. He had very large ears and a fruity voice.

"Oh, Danny!" repeated Trucklee, peering out into the night. "I need you. I know you're out there! I hear your voice. You're making things hard, Danny."

Jack or Tonel could have made a lewd joke then, based on the obvious fact that Les had a crush on Danny, and on the rumored likelihood that the two were having an affair. But they knew better than to tease their older friend about so delicate a topic. Danny could turn mighty mean. And he carried a sizable pocket knife. Finally Trucklee went back inside.

"Let's get that bourbon," said Danny, breaking the strained silence.

Circling around behind the barbeque wagon, the three made their way toward the locker room door. But, damn it, the door was locked. And they hadn't even seen Ragland and the mibracc go out.

"I know another way in," said Danny. "Through the ceiling of the furnace room. You can hop up through a hole I found."

"Go in the ceiling?" said Tonel.

"There's a crawlspace," said Danny. "It goes to the ladies' locker room. There's a grate over their showers. The men's is the same."

"You're still peeping?" said Jack, a balloon of mirth rising in his chest. "You really are a sex offender, Danny. Keep it up, and the Man's gonna cut out your balls and give you Neuticles. For the public good."

"Laugh it up, bagwort," shot back Danny. "Meanwhile Albert Chesney's off with your girl."

Climbing into the ceiling was a dumb idea, but, hey. It was the end of summer. So yeah, they snuck to the furnace room, got up into the ceiling, and made their way across the hanging supports. Danny kept making snorting noises like a wild pig, and then Tonel would say "Neuticles," and then they'd laugh so hard they'd flop around like fish. They were riding the Wheelchair for fair.

Eventually they found themselves above the ceiling vent in the shower room of the men's lockers. There were voices coming up. Ragland and the mibracc. Still in here after all.

Peeking through the grate, Jack saw Ragland in the shower with the old men, all of them naked. The men looked sluggish and tired. One of them—Mr. Gupta —had collapsed to the floor and looked oddly flat. Just now Ragland was pulling something like a cork out of Mr. Inkle's navel. A flesh-colored bung. A stream of straw-colored fluid gushed out of the mibracc, splashing on the tile floor and running toward the drain.

"*Smeel*," whispered Danny.

"You mean lymph," murmured Jack.

"No dog, that's 'smeel,'" hissed Tonel. "The Dank-man knows."

They were trying to act like what they were seeing was funny—but they were realizing it wasn't. It was awful. The air smelled of urine and alcohol, meat and feces. It would be very bad if Ragland found them watching. There was no more joking, no more chat. The boys peered through the grate in silence.

Actually the smeel wasn't all running down the drain. The smelly dregs were sliding away, but a clear, sparkling fraction of the smeel was gathering in pools and eddies near the drain, humping itself up into tiny waterspouts, circling around and around, the smaller vortices joining into bigger ones. A spinning ring of smeel slid across the tiles like a miniature hurricane. It headed right out of the shower stall and disappeared into the locker room.

Meanwhile Mr. Inkle flopped over onto his side like a deflating balloon. Ragland pushed the skin around with his bare feet, then trod along its length, squeezing out the last gouts of smeel. He nudged the Inkle skin over next to the Gupta skin. After draining the three other mibracc—none of whom seemed to mind—he wrapped the five skins into tight rolls, and went out into the locker room. The clarified smeel gathered into watery columns like miniature typhoons and followed him.

The boys heard a rattling of locker doors. The mibracc skins waited, their edges twitching ever so slightly. Ragland reappeared, still naked. He fetched the skins one by one, clattering and splashing in the next room. Each time they saw Ragland, there was one smeel tornado following him. Evidently he was stashing the mibracc and their smeel inside the golf bags.

Next Ragland took a long, soapy shower. Then came the rustling of him getting dressed, followed by the unlocking and locking of the outer door. All was silent.

Danny lifted loose the grate and the boys dropped down onto the tiled shower room floor. Jack happened to know that under his counter Ragland had a thing like a monster Swiss knife of plastic thumbs, one thumb for each club member—in case someone died of old age, which happened often enough to matter. Jack fetched the master thumbs and opened up Mr. Cuthbert's locker. They peered into the golf bag.

Something twitched in the golden liquid, making a tiny splash. Yes. Mr. Cuthbert was in there, rolled up like a pickled squid. The preservative fluid was just level with the golf bag's top edge.

Danny leaned over and sucked up some of it.

"Yaaar," he said, wiping his lips. "Good."

The stuff seemed to hit him right away, and very hard. When he unsteadily ducked down to drink some more, his chin banged into the bag and, oh God, the bag fell over. Although the glass in the bag didn't shatter, the liquid slopped across the floor.

Mr. Cuthbert slid right out the bag, looking like a wet burrito. Tonel yanked the golf bag upright, but Mr. Cuthbert remained on the tiles.

The spilled liquor and smeel puddled around the mibracc. Slowly the fluid began eddying again, bulging itself into a mound. The stuff had shed its excremental odors in the showers. The room filled with the heady fruitcake-and-eggnog perfume of bourbon. Crazy Danny found an empty glass and dipped it into the vortex.

"Naw, naw," said Tonel, still holding the golf bag. "Don't be drinkin' that mess!"

"'S good," repeated Danny, gesturing with his glass. His pupils were crazed pinpoints. There was no reasoning with him. His Adam's apple pumped up and down as he drank.

Jack found a mop and nudged the weirdly animated smeel-bourbon into a bucket that he poured back into the golf bag. All the while the coiled skin of Mr. Cuthbert was slowly twisting around, making a peevish hissing noise.

"Help me jam him back in and let's get out of here," Jack told Tonel.

"You be touchin' him," said Tonel. "Not me."

Jack hunkered down and took hold of Mr. Cuthbert. The mibracc felt like incompletely cured food, like a half-dried apricot: leathery on the outside, wet and squishy in the middle. He was hissing louder than before. A little more smeel trickled from the bunghole in his belly-button.

Gritting his teeth, Jack re-rolled Mr. Cuthbert and slid him into his golf bag. The skin twitched and splashed. A drop of the bourbon-smeel landed on Jack's lower lip. Reflexively he licked it off. Error. The room began ever so slowly to spin.

While Jack paused, assessing the damages, crazy Danny reached past him to scoop out one last glassful of the poison bourbon. Mr. Cuthbert's golf bag rocked and clattered; bubbles rose to the surface. The noises echoed back from the other mibracc. All five lockers were shaking.

"Let's bounce," urged Tonel, over by the locker room door. He already had it open, he'd unlocked the dead bolt from the inside. They wouldn't be able to lock the door behind them.

"There you are, Danny," came the voice of Les Trucklee as they stepped out onto the floodlit terrace. He was out there checking over the barbeque wagon and smoking a cigarette. "I hope I'm not seeing what I think I'm seeing in your hand."

Jack quickly closed the locker room door behind them. Did it matter that it wasn't locked anymore? If he asked Les Trucklee to lock it, he'd have to explain how they'd gotten in there. But surely the mibracc couldn't get out of their lockers unaided.

"You ain't seein' squat," Danny was saying, holding the glass behind his back. "I gotta leave now, Les, I just got a message from my boys here. It's my mother. She's real sick."

"Mother Dank ill again?" said Les in an indulgent, disbelieving tone. "She's a susceptible old dear, isn't she? Maybe she should wear more clothes. Are you in any condition to drive, Danny? If you'll linger a bit, I could give you a lift."

"No, Les," said Danny, his voice cold. A long moment passed. Dazzled moths were beating around the lights. Dizzy from his marijuana gum and the drop of mibracc fluid, Jack was seeing glowing trails in the air behind the insects. He thought he could hear hammering sounds from the locker room, but nobody else was noticing.

"All right then," said Les, stubbing out his butt. "I'm back to serving our patrons. The ladies are on their dessert drinks, flirting with each others' husbands. They're excited about the barbeque and golf tournament tomorrow. Don't forget you're onstage bright and early, Danny, we'll want to start up the grill at the crack of dawn. You and your friends stay out of trouble tonight." Les sighed and ran his fingers through his thinning hair. "I wish I was young again. I never had enough fun."

One of the moths landed on Jack's hand. The feathery touch grated on his tautened nerves. As he brushed the moth away, he seemed to hear a faint cry, and when he glanced down he saw that the moth had a tiny head resembling that of a round-eyed woman with tangled blond hair. Jack's stifled exclamation turned Les Trucklee's attention to him.

"Good luck at college, Jack. If one of you fellows happens to get a wild hair up your ass, stop by around one or two tonight and I'll give you a free nightcap. Top shelf. Why don't you sleep on my office couch again tonight, Danny, just to be getting up early. It'll be even better than last time."

This was too much for Tonel, who let out a loud guffaw.

And then they were in the parking lot, Danny sitting on his obese black Harley gunning it. His face was dark and angry. Les had gone too far, told too much. Danny roared the motorcycle even harder.

Danny had gotten the hog used from a Killeville insurance salesman who'd bought it as a temporary stopgap against his midlife crisis before moving on to a girlfriend in Virginia Beach. The machine was loaded with puffy middle-aged accessories, including enormous hard-shelled saddlebags. Instead of tearing them off–hell, he'd paid for them, hadn't he?–Danny had gotten one of his buddies at Rash Decisions Tattoo to paint them with renditions of the Pig Chef–two smirking pigs in aprons and chef's hats, one holding a meat cleaver and the other waving a long three-tined fork with sharpness-twinkles. The Pig Chef was–if you thought about it–one of the more sinister icons of American roadside art. Danny's personal totem. What kind of pig is a butcher? What kind of pig cooks barbeque? A traitor pig, a killer pig, a doomed preterite pig destined for eternal damnation. Danny's Pig Chefs showed the full weight of this knowledge in their mocking eyes and snaggled snouts.

"I'm gonna go catch Stiffie's act," said Danny. Stiffie Ryder was his idol, his proof of masculinity, his favorite woman to peep at. Stiffie worked as a stripper at the Banana Split, a bar and grill located on the same stretch of Route 501 as the Casa Linda and Rash Decisions Tattoo, Killeville's own little Sodom and Gomorrah, just outside the city limits.

"What about those skins in the golf bags?" asked Jack. "What if they try and get out?" The drop he'd licked off his lip was still working on him. One of his legs felt shorter than the other. He put his hand on Tonel's shoulder for support.

"They can gangbang Les Trucklee," said Danny. "They can warm him up for me." He glared at Jack and Tonel, who had no thought of uttering a response. Danny brushed back his lank, greasy hair, drank off the last bit of bourbon-smeel, and tossed his glass to shatter in the parking lot. For the first time Jack noticed that the tips of Danny's ears were pointed. "I can't believe Les was talking that way in front of you two," continued Danny. "Like he's my sissy. He's gonna pay the price." And with that he roared off.

"Danny buggin' out," said Tonel. "Trucklee better watch hisself."

"I don't know how Danny can drive," said Jack. "I'm so—" He staggered to one side and puked.

"Weak bitch," said Tonel, not unkindly.

Jack heaved again, bringing up the day's four Coca-Colas and the burger and fries he'd had for lunch. Right away he felt better.

The vomit was a little heap at the edge of the asphalt, faintly lit by the terrace lights. Was it hunching itself up like the smeel had done? Beginning ever so slightly to twist into an eddy?

"Come on, dog," said Tonel. "Let's creep on home. You can pedal, can't you?"

"Yeah," said Jack, looking away from the shifting mound on the pavement. "I'm better now. I got a drop of that crap in my mouth. From the golf bags. I can't believe how much of it Danny drank. We shouldn't have let him ride."

"He'd a pulled his knife if we tried to stop him," said Tonel.

They walked over to the rack and unchained their bicycles, a couple of beat-up jobs nobody would bother to steal. The night felt thick and velvety, but it wasn't spinning anymore.

"We ought to talk to Ragland," said Jack as they pedaled off. "Ask him what's up."

"I gotta eat first," said Tonel. "Dad's makin' that burgoo."

"Can I come to your house, too?" said Jack. "I don't want to go home." And then he told Tonel the story about this morning.

"That's some sad stuff," said Tonel when Jack finished. "Preachers always do like that. But you sayin' his children had pointed ears?"

"Like Danny's," sighed Jack. "Everything's coming apart, just when it's finally time for me to get out of here. Back on the terrace I thought one of those moths had a woman's head. And the mibracc—I can hardly believe we saw that. Maybe we're just really high."

"Be some mighty crunk Wheelchair make you see five men turn into somethin' like chitlins." They pedaled down Egmont Avenue in silence for a minute, the occasional car rumbling by. Jack didn't dare try and look at the drivers. Finally Tonel broke the silence. "If you not goin' by the e-rectory, how we gonna get a ride?" Normally they took Jack's mother's car out at night.

"Ask Vincente for his," said Jack.

Tonel's father Vincente ran a secondhand appliance store called Vaughan Electronics—it so happened that Tonel's and Jack's families shared the same last name, which no doubt had something to do with plantations and slaves. Sometimes Jack would tell people that Tonel was his cousin, which wasn't entirely implausible, light-skinned as Tonel was. Tonel's mother Wanda had been mostly white. Even though she'd run off to Florida, Vincente had a picture of Wanda on the kitchen wall in his apartment at the back of the store.

When the boys entered through the alley door, Vincente's wall of screens was tuned to a porno webcast; he quickly changed it to a boxing match.

"Help yourself to burgoo," said Vincente, gesturing toward the stove.

"Put the ho's back on, Daddy," said Tonel. "We don't wanna see no thugs."

"Wouldn't be fittin' to expose you," said the wiry Vincente. He was lounging in a duct-tape-patched plastic recliner facing twenty-four clunker TVs stacked in a six by four grid. Vincente had installed special controllers so he could switch his digital mosaic between showing a bunch of random channels and showing a single channel with its image jigsawed into pieces. He'd learned electronics in the navy during the war on

Iraq. He began fiddling with his remote, breaking up and reassembling the dataflow, temporarily settling on a Sudanese dagger-fighting flick.

Meanwhile the hearty smell of the rabbit and chicken stew pushed away any lingering queasiness Jack felt. He had the munchies. He and Tonel ate quite a bit of the stew, the thuds and yelps of the movie bouncing along in the background.

Jack's cell phone rang. He peeked at the screen, fearing it would be Mom, but, no, it was Gretchen, looking tense.

"Hey," she said. "I'm still at the tabernacle. It's getting way too trippy. You think you could come and get me now?"

"Um, I guess so," said Jack. "I'm at Tonel's. We have to see about getting a car."

"Axe her can she hook me up a honey," put in Tonel. "I'm driving. Right, Daddy? I can have the van?"

"If you can start it," said Vincente, twitching his remote to break the image into twenty-four new channels. "Sneak the battery outten Ragland's truck. I seen him come back a half hour ago. You know he ain't goin' out again."

"How do you mean trippy?" Jack asked Gretchen meanwhile.

"It's that Armageddon thing," said Gretchen. There was a trumpeting noise in the background. "Albert Chesney is getting really weird about it. He wants me to spend the night with him at Casa Linda to help him 'gird his loins' for the last battle. None of the Day Sixers wants to help him. Albert says that six pure hearts can turn the tide, so he needs five people to help him. Dad wants me to be with Albert even though he himself plans to stay home. Come get me, Jack. Right now they're watching a video, but when it's done, Dad's driving Albert and me to the Casa Linda."

"Is this another of your put-ons?"

"Save me, Jack. I mean it. And, you know, I really am pregnant." Gretchen never let up. Jack liked that about her.

"Hook me a honey," repeated Tonel.

"We're coming," said Jack. "And Tonel wants to know if you can find a date for him?"

"Pinka Wright is into him. I might call her." The trumpets rose to an off-key crescendo. "Hurry." Gretchen hung up.

The tooting noise didn't stop when Jack turned his phone off. After a moment's disorientation, he realized that Vincente had tuned his screens to some random webcast of—what was it? Three glowing donuts moving across the wall of TVs, silver, gold, and copper. Behind them was a background of unfamiliar stars. A cracked brass fanfare played. Before Jack could ask about the picture, Vincente punched his controller again, splitting the image into twenty-four new channels.

"What she say?" demanded Tonel.

"Her father wants her to spend the night with Albert Chesney," said Jack.

"She jivin' you again," said Tonel. "What she say about my date?"

"Pinka Wright."

"Ooo! Let's bounce it, dog."

"Don't let Ragland hear you," warned Vincente. "He's got that shotgun."

First of all they had to check the tires of Vincente's ancient van, and of course one of them was flat—Vincente's driving license was suspended, and he didn't keep insurance up on the van, which meant that he hardly ever drove it. Tonel found an electric pump in the bowels of Vaughan Electronics and they dragged out an extension cord and filled the tire. The tire seemed to hold its size, so that problem was solved.

Next came the issue of gas. A quick check of the van's gauge showed it to be stone cold dry. Tonel produced a can and a squeeze-bulb siphon from the back of the van. The plan was to get gas from Ragland's truck as well as borrowing his battery.

Quietly they walked down the alley to Ragland's truck. Tonel popped the hood and set to work extracting the battery while Jack began pumping gas from Ragland's tank. It felt stupid to be making such a complicated thing out of getting a car. Gretchen needed his help. Shouldn't he just walk around the corner and take his Mom's car?

Right about then Ragland appeared, gliding out of his backyard like a ghost, the barrel of his shotgun glinting in the streetlight. He was holding it level at his waist, pointing right at Jack's stomach.

"You hookworm," said Ragland. "I oughtta blow a hole in you."

Tonel jumped backward, letting the hood slam shut. "We just tryin' to use Daddy's van," he said. "We figured we could borrow your—"

"I'm gonna call the po-lice," said Ragland. "A night in jail be good for you two whelps."

"Oh yeah?" said Tonel. "How 'bout if I tell them what you do to them old men in the locker room? We saw you rollin' em up. Cops might even call it murder."

"You was in the lockers?" said Ragland, letting his gun droop.

"We came in through the grate in the ceiling," said Jack. "And then we let ourselves out."

"You left the door unlocked?" said Ragland after a pause. "Oh Lord. You gotta help me now. Jump in my truck."

"How long have the mibracc been like that?" Jack asked Ragland as he drove them towards the club.

"Goin' on two weeks," said Ragland. "Right when they got

them big glass jars. Was Mr. Gupta showed me about the stomach plugs. He got it from somethin' he seen on TV. The men like me to do 'em that way. I drain 'em every night, and plump 'em up in the mawnin'. We use the steam room. They been payin' me extra and, yeah Tonel, they even doin' some yard work for me."

"But what do it mean?" asked Tonel.

"That's a conundrum," said Ragland. "But I don't want to see what happens if they get out on their own."

As soon as he'd parked, Ragland was out the door and across the parking lot, still carrying his shotgun. Jack noticed that he'd left the keys in the ignition. Should he just take off and save Gretchen? But then Ragland glared back at them and gestured with his gun. Jack had a feeling the old man wouldn't hesitate to use it. Somewhat unwillingly, Jack and Tonel went to lend him their support.

From the terrace, Jack could see past the barbeque wagon and into the air-conditioned grill where Les Trucklee was pouring out brandy for a last few red-faced Killeville gentry. He could hear their voices braying even through the closed windows. Nasal, buzzing, self-satisfied. Tomorrow Jack would be gone—if only he could make it through tonight.

The locker room door was still unlocked. Ragland led the boys right in. The air was thick with vapor; voices boomed from the steam room. It was the mibracc, sounding hale and well rested.

Holding his shotgun at the ready, Ragland peered into the sauna. Two of the skins were still on the floor where they'd slithered; the other three had already plumped up. They were talking about golf, poker, and politics in that bone-dull Killeville way that made it impossible to hear more than a few consecutive phrases.

"Get back in your bags!" Ragland told them. "It's still night."

Mr. Cuthbert looked over and gave Ragland the finger, baring his top row of ivory yellow teeth. And then Mr. Atlee strode over and grabbed the barrel of Ragland's gun.

The blast of the shotgun shell was shockingly loud in the small, tiled space. Jack's ears rang, he felt like he might be permanently deafened.

Though a large piece of Mr. Atlee's stomach was gone, the mibracc was still standing. Worse than that, he'd taken control of the shotgun. Mr. Atlee struck Ragland on the side of the head with the gunstock, dropping him. And then he leveled the barrels at Jack and Tonel. The two took to their heels. There was another blast as they reached the door; the buckshot hailed against the lockers.

Without looking back for Ragland, they jumped in the old man's truck. Tonel drove them down Egmont Avenue, tires squealing, the truck slewing from side to side. Slowly Jack's hearing returned. His cell phone had a message on it; he'd missed the ring. It was Gretchen.

"Where *are* you?" cried the voice, anxious and thin. "Dad's driving Albert and me to the Casa Linda! Oh, Jack please help me now and I'll always—" Abruptly the message broke off. All thoughts of calling the police or going back to try and save Ragland flew from Jack's mind.

He and Tonel made their way through downtown Killeville and out Route 501. The flare of neon lit up the muggy, moonless August sky. Here was the Banana Split, with Danny's heavy Pig Chef Harley parked in front among the SUVs and pickups. Next door was Rash Decisions Tattoo. And beyond that was the dirty pink concrete bulk of Casa Linda, faint slits of light showing through some of the tightly drawn blinds.

Gretchen was on them as soon as they got out of the car, running over from the shadows of the Casa Linda parking lot.

"Jack! You've come to save me!"

"Where's Chesney?"

"Oh, he went inside alone," said Gretchen airily. "I put down my foot. I'm still available, Jack." She took hold of his arm and pointed toward Rash Decisions Tattoo. "Justice of the Peace Ronnie Blevins is right in there."

Jack felt like his head was exploding. "Damn it, Gretchen, it's too much. You can't keep scamming me like this."

"Oh, I'll settle for one last hole six blowout," said Gretchen. "Get Danny to buy us some beer. I see his bike over there."

"We stayin' away from Danny tonight," said Tonel. "He way too spun. I can buy us beer. What about that Pinka Wright, Gretchen? Did you talk to her or not?"

"I can call her now," said Gretchen. "We'll drive by her house on the way to the club. I bet she'll come out with you. She craves the wild side."

"Was it all a lie about Albert Chesney?" demanded Jack

"Albert really does say the last battle is tomorrow," said Gretchen. "At the tabernacle he was showing this video of donut-shaped flying saucers. Supposedly they're going to come for us at dawn, full of devils. But angels will be here to help fight them. Albert says if six righteous people step forward they can save the day. But I think we ought to leave before he comes back out of the motel. He's real intent on that girding his loins thing." Seeing Jack's face, Gretchen burst into laughter. "Why are you always so uptight?"

So they bounced out of there without seeing Chesney. Tonel got beer from a downtown 7-11 clerked by his cousin. Some of the people at the store recognized Ragland's truck, which reminded Jack that, oh God, they'd left Ragland lying on the steam room floor at the mercy of the mibracc. What with the pot gum and the worry about Gretchen he'd completely spaced that out. It was a good thing they were heading back to the club.

Meanwhile Gretchen worked her cell phone and not only did they pick up Pinka, but a bunch more people said they'd meet them at the parking lot—arty Tyler Simpson, pretty Geli Yoder, Lulu Anders the Goth, fat Louie Levy, and even goody-goody Lucy Candler and her jock boyfriend Rick Stazanik.

The Killeville Country Club was dark, save for Les Trucklee's office on the second floor of the club's front side. Maybe he was waiting up for Danny Dank. But Les wouldn't be a problem for the kids. He turned a blind eye to their hole six parties.

Some of the kids were already there, waiting and drinking beer.

"Come help me see about Ragland," said Jack to Gretchen and Tonel.

"Yuck," said Gretchen. "In the men's locker room?"

"Chill," said Tonel, who was in a heavy conversation with Pinka. "I'm gettin' over."

"Let's party," said Rick Stazanik. This was the first hole six event he and Lucy had attended, and they were gung-ho to get it on.

"There might be some zombies out there," warned Jack. "The mibracc. You guys have to help me check if they left a corpse in the locker room."

"How spine-tingling," said Lulu.

"Safety in numbers," said Louie Levy. "We'll stick together."

So before heading out onto the links, the gang did a quick check in the locker room for Ragland. No sign of him. And when Jack used Ragland's master-thumbs to try and show them golf bags of bourbon, the bags turned up as empty as the gas tank on Vincente's van.

They had some fun grab-assing and scaring each other on the long trek out to the green of hole six. But in truth there was no sign of anything out of the ordinary. There were not a few laughs at Jack's expense. And then they settled down on their green, drinking beer and chewing marijuana gum. Tyler Simpson had brought speakers and an iPod with all the alternative hits of their high-school years.

After a bit Jack and Gretchen crept off to a private spot twenty meters past the green and made love. It was, after all, their last night together. As always, Jack used a condom. He'd been a dope to let her scare him with that pregnancy thing.

"Will you remember me at college?" Gretchen asked Jack. Her face looked big and open under his. She dropped most of her games when they were alone like this.

"I will. It's not all that far. You can come visit. Or I'll visit here. You'll have your classes too." Gretchen was going to be studying at a local business college.

In the distance Jack heard the roar of a motorcycle pulling into the lot. Danny. He kind of hoped Danny was here to see Les and not here for the hole six party. What a weird day this had been. He was still uneasily wondering where Ragland and the mibracc had gone. After a bit, he and Gretchen went back with the others on the green.

An hour later, in between the songs, Jack began hearing the mibracc's voices, accompanied by the clink of tools in dirt. He tried to tell the others, but they either couldn't hear it or they weren't interested, not even Tonel or Gretchen. It sounded to Jack as if the mibracc were somewhere close to the clubhouse.

That meant that, all in all, it would be safer to stay out here till dawn. Lots of people would be showing up for the Killeville Barbeque Breakfast Golf Classic. And then Jack could get his suitcase, say good-bye to Mom and hop the 8:37 A.M. bus to college. He wished he'd called Mom. She'd be worrying about him.

About four in the morning, Lulu Anders, Louie Levy, Lucy Candler, and Rick Stazanik wanted to leave. By now Jack had gotten them to notice the mibracc's voices, but the four figured that if they went all together there wouldn't be a problem. Jack warned them not to, getting pretty passionate about it. But they wouldn't listen. They thought he was spun. They were more scared of their parents than of the mibracc.

Their screams across the golf course were terrible to hear. Four sets of screams, then nothing but the muttering of the mibracc and the scraping of metal against soil.

When dawn broke, the remaining six kids were flaked out around a mound of empty beer cans. Geli and Tonel were asleep. Pinka had chewed a lot of marijuana gum and was jabbering to Tyler, who was delicately jabbing at his music machine's controls, mixing the sounds in with Pinka's words. Gretchen and Jack were just sitting there staring toward the clubhouse, fearful of what they'd see.

As the mist cleared, they were able to pick out the figures of the five mibracc, busy at the eighteenth green, right by the terrace. They had shovels; they'd carved the green down into a cupped-out depression. Like a satellite dish. The surface of the dish gleamed, something slick was all over it—smeel. There was a slim projecting twist of smeel at the dish's center. The green had become an antenna beaming signals into who knew what unknown dimensions.

On the terrace the large barbeque grill was already fired up, greasy smoke pouring from its little tin chimney. Next to it was a sturdy table piled with bloody meat. And standing there working the grill was—Danny.

"Let's go," said Jack. "I have to get out of this town."

He shook Tonel and Geli awake. There was a moth resting on Tonel's cheek, another moth with a human head. Before flapping off, it smiled at Jack and said something in an encouraging tone—though it was too faint to understand.

"I been dreaming about heaven," said Tonel, rubbing his hands against his eyes. "What up, dog?"

Jack pointed toward the clubhouse, and now all the kids saw what Danny was doing.

Geli, Pinka, and Tyler decided to stay out at hole six, but Jack, Gretchen, and Tonel worked their way closer to the clubhouse, taking cover in the patches of rough. Maybe they could still fix things. And Jack couldn't get it out of his mind that he still might catch his bus.

He was seeing more and more of the moths with human heads. Their wings shed the brown-gray moth dust and turned white in the rays of the rising sun. They were little angels.

A cracked trumpet note sounded from the heavens, then another and another. "Look," said Gretchen pointing up. "It's all true."

"God help us," said Tonel, gazing at the gathering UFOs.

A silver torus landed by the clubhouse, homing right in on the eighteenth green. Some creatures got out, things more or less like large praying mantises—with long, jointed legs, curving abdomens, bulging compound eyes, and mouths that were cruel triangular beaks. A dozen of them. They headed straight for the barbeque wagon.

Stacked on the table beside the barbeque wagon were the headless butchered corpses of Lulu Anders, Louie Levy, Lucy Candler, and Rick Stazanik, ready to be cooked. The aliens—or devils—crossed the terrace, their large bodies rocking from side to side, their green abdomens wobbling. Danny swung up the barbeque wagon's curved door. There in the double-hog barbeque grill were the bodies of Les and Ragland, already well crisped.

Sweating and grinning, Danny wielded a cleaver and a three-tined fork, cutting loose some tender barbeque for the giant mantises. The monsters bit into the meat, their jaws snipping out neat triangles.

Danny's eyes were damned, tormented, mad. He was wearing something strange on his head, not a chef's hat, no, it was floppy and bloody and hairy and with big ears—it was poor Les Trucklee's scalp. Danny was a Pig Chef.

Over by the parking lot, early bird golfers and barbeque breakfasters were starting to arrive. One by one the mibracc beat them to death with golf clubs and dragged them to the barbeque wagon's side. Even with the oily smoke and the smell of fresh blood in the air, none of the new arrivals thought to worry when the five familiar men from the back room approached them.

"The end of the world," breathed Gretchen.

"I have to see Mom," said Jack brokenly. "Get my suitcase and see Mom. I have to leave today."

"I want to get Daddy," said Tonel.

The three looped around the far side of the clubhouse and managed to hail down a pickup truck with a lawnmower in back. The driver was old Luke Taylor.

"Can you carry us home?" asked Tonel.

"I can," said Luke, dignified and calm. "What up at the country club?"

"There's a flying saucer with devils eating people!" said Gretchen. "It's the end!"

Luke glanced over at her, not believing what he heard. "Maybe," he said equably, "But I'm still gonna cut Mrs. Bowen's grass befo' the sun gets too hot."

Luke dropped them at Vaughan Electronics. Jack and Gretchen ran around the corner to the rectory. The house was quiet, with the faint chatter of children's voices from the back yard. Odd for a Sunday morning. Rev. Langhorne should be bustling around getting ready for church. Jack used his key to open the door, making as little noise as possible. Gretchen was right at his side.

It was Gretchen who noticed the spot on the banister. A dried bloody print from a very small hand. Out in the back-yard the children were singing. They were busy with some-thing; Jack heard a clank and a rattle. He didn't dare go back there to see.

Moving fast, Jack and Gretchen tiptoed upstairs. There was blood on the walls near the Langhorne parents' room. Jack went straight for his mother's single bedroom, blessedly unspotted with blood. But the room was empty.

"Mom?" whispered Jack.

There was a slight noise from the closet.

Jack swung open the closet door. No sign of his mother—but, wait, there was a big lump on the top shelf, covered over with a silk scarf.

"Is that you, Mom?" said Jack, scared what he might find.

The paisley scarf slid down. Jack's mother was curled up on the shelf in her nightgown, her eyes wide and staring.

"Those horrible children," she said in a tiny, strained voice. "They butchered their parents in bed. I hid."

"Hurry, Mrs. Vaughan," said Gretchen. She was standing against the wall, peeking out the back window. "They're starting up the grill."

And, yes, Jack could smell the lighter fluid and the smoke. Four little Pig Chefs in the making. A smallish alien craft slid past the window, wedging itself down into the backyard.

Somewhat obsessively, Jack went into his bedroom and fetched his packed suitcase before leading Gretchen and his Mom to the front door. It just about cost them too much time. For as the three of them crept down the front porch steps they heard the slamming of the house's back door and the drumming of little footsteps.

Faster than it takes to tell it, Jack, Gretchen, and Jessie Vaughan were in Jessie's car, Jack at the wheel, slewing around the corner. They slowed only to pick up Tonel and Vincente, and then they were barreling out of town on Route 501.

"Albert was saying we should come to the Casa Linda and help him," said Gretchen. "He said he'd be watching from the roof. He said he needed five pure hearts to pray with him. Six of us in all. We're pure, aren't we?"

Jack wouldn't have stopped, but as it happened, there was a roadblock in the highway right by the Casa Linda. The police all had pointed ears. The coffee in their cups was continually swirling. And the barbeque pit beside the Banana Split was fired up. A gold UFO was just now angling down for a landing.

"I'm purely ready to pray my ass off," said Vincente.

When they jumped out of the car, the police tried to take hold of the five, to hustle them toward the barbeque. But a sudden flight of the little angels distracted the pig-eared cops. The tiny winged beings beat at the men's cruel faces, giving the five pure hearts a chance.

Clutching his suitcase like a talisman, Jack led Gretchen, Jessie, Tonel, and Vincente across the parking lot to the Casa Linda. They pounded up the motel's outdoor concrete stairs, all the way to the roof. The pointy-eared police were too busy with the next carload of victims to chase after them. Over by the Banana Split, hungry mantises were debarking from the gold donut.

They found Albert Chesney at the low parapet of the motel roof, staring out across the rolling hills of Killeville. He had a calm, satisfied expression. His prophecies were coming true.

"Behold the city of sin," he said, gesturing toward Killeville's pitifully sparse town center, its half dozen worn old office buildings. "See how the mighty have been brought low."

"How do we make it stop, Albert?" asked Gretchen.

"Let us join hands and pray," said Chesney.

So they stood there, the early morning breeze playing upon the six of them—Albert, Gretchen, Jack, Jessie, Tonel, and Vincente. There were maybe three dozen toroidal UFOs scattered around Killeville by now. And beside each of them was a plume of greasy smoke.

Jack hadn't prayed in quite some time. As boarders in the rectory, they'd had to go to Reverend Langhorne's church every Sunday, but the activity had struck him as exclusively social, with no connection to any of the deep philosophical and religious questions he might chew over with friends, like, "Where did all this come from?" or, "What happens after I die?"

But now, oh yes, he was praying. And it's safe to say the five others were praying too. Something like, "Save us, save the earth, make the aliens go away, dear God please help."

As they prayed, the mothlike angels got bigger. The prayers were pumping energy into the good side of the Shekinah Glory. Before long the angels were the size of people. They were more numerous than Jack had initially realized.

"Halle-friggin-lujah!" said Vincente, and they prayed some more.

The angels grew to the size of cars, to the size of buildings. The Satanic flying donuts sprang into the air and fired energy bolts at them. The angels grew yet taller, as high as the sky. Their faces were clear, solemn, terrible to behold. The evil UFOs were helpless against them, puny as gnats. Peeking through his fingers, Jack saw one of the alien craft go flying across the horizon toward an angel, and saw the impact as the great holy being struck with a hand the size of a farm. The shattered bits of the UFO shrank into nothingness, as if melting in the sun. It was only a matter of minutes until the battle was done. The closest angel fixed Jack with an unbearable gaze, then made a gesture that might have been a benediction. And now the great beings rotated in some unseen direction and angled out of view.

"Praise God!" said Albert Chesney when it was done.

"Praise God," echoed Jack. "But that's enough for now, Lord. Don't have the whole Last Judgment today. Let me go to college first. Give us at least six more years."

And it was so.

A Greyhound bus drew even with the Casa Linda and pulled over for a stop. BLACKSBURG, read the sign above the bus window. Jack bid the quickest of farewells to his mother and his friends, and then, whooping and yelling, he ran down the stairs with his suitcase and hopped aboard.

The Killeville Barbeque Massacre trials dragged on through the fall. Jack and Albert had to testify a few times. Most of the Pig Chef defendants got off with temporary insanity pleas, basing their defense on smeel-poisoning, although no remaining samples of smeel could be found. The police officers were of course pardoned, and Danny Dank got the death penalty. The cases of Banks, Price, Sydnor, and Rainey were moot—for with their appetites whetted by the flesh of the children's parents, the mantises had gone ahead and eaten the four fledgling Pig Chefs.

The trials didn't draw as much publicity as one might have expected. The crimes were simply too disgusting. And the Killeville citizenry had collective amnesia regarding the UFOs. Some of the Day Six Synodites remembered, but the Synod was soon split into squabbling sub-sects by a series of schisms. With his onerous parole conditions removed in return for his help with the trials, Albert Chesney left town for California to become a computer game developer.

Jessie Vaughan got herself ordained as a deacon and took over the pastoral duties at St. Anselm's church. At Christmas Jessie celebrated the marriage of Jack to Gretchen Karst—who was indeed pregnant. Tonel took leave from the navy to serve as best man.

Gretchen transferred into Virginia Polytechnic with Jack for the spring term. The couple did well in their studies. Jack majored in Fluid Engineering and Gretchen in Computer Science. And after graduation they somehow ended up moving into the rectory with Jessie and opening a consulting firm in Killeville.

As for the men in the back room of the country club—they completely dropped out of sight. The prudent reader would be

well advised to keep an eye out for mibracc in his or her home-
town. And pay close attention to the fluid dynamics of coffee,
juice, and alcoholic beverages. Any undue rotation could be a
sign of smeel.

The end is near.

GUADALUPE AND
HIERONYMUS BOSCH

AS an unemployed, overweight, unmarried, overeducated woman with a big mouth, I don't have a lot of credibility. But even if I was some perfect California Barbie it wouldn't be enough. People never want to listen to women.

I, Glenda Gomez, bring glad tidings. She that hath ears, let her hear.

An alien being has visited our world. Harna is, was, her name. I saw her as a glowing paramecium, a jellyfish, a glass police car, and a demonic art patron. This morning, when she was shaped like a car, I rode inside her to the fifteenth century. And this evening I walked past the vanishing point and saved our universe from Harna's collecting bag. I'm the queen of space and time. I'm trying to write up my story to pitch as a reality TV show.

Let's start with paramecia. Unicellular organisms became a hobby of mine a few months ago when I stole a microscope from my job. I was sorting egg and sperm cells for an infertility clinic called Smart Stork. Even though I don't have any kind of biology background they trained me.

I'm not dumb. I have a Bachelor's in Art History from San Jose State, which is just a few blocks from my apartment on Sixth Street. Well, almost a degree. I never finished the general education courses or my senior seminar, which would probably, certainly, have been on Hieronymus Bosch. I used to have a book of his pictures I looked at all the time—although today the book disappeared. At first I thought it was hidden under something. My apartment is a sty.

My lab job didn't last long—I'm definitely not the science type. I wasn't fast enough, I acted bored, I kissed the manager Dick Went after one too many lunchtime Coronas—and he fired me. That's when I bagged my scope—a binocular phase-contrast Leica. I carried it home in my ever-ready XXL purse. Later that day Dick came to my apartment to ask about it, but I screamed through the door at him like a crazy person until he went away. Works on the landlord, too.

Now that I have a microscope, I keep infusions of protozoan cultures in little jars all over my apartment. It's unbelievably easy to grow the infusions. You just put a wad of lawn grass in with some bottled water. Bacteria breed themselves into the trillions—rods and dots and corkscrews that I can see at 200x. And before you know it, the paramecia are right there digging on the bacilli. They come out of nowhere. What works really well is to add a scrap of meat to an infusion, it gets dark and pukeful, and the critters go wild for a few days till they die of their own shit. In the more decadent infusions you'll find a particular kind of very coarsely ciliated paramecium rolling and rushing around. My favorites. I call them the microhomies.

So today is a Sunday morning in March, and I'm eating my usual breakfast of day-old bread with slices of welfare cheddar, flipping through my Bosch book thinking about my next tattoo. A friend named Sleepey is taking an online course in tattooing, and he said he'd give me one for free. He has a good flea-market tattoo-gun he traded a set of tires for. Who needs snow tires in San Jose? So I'm thinking it would be bitchin' to bedizen my belly with a Bosch.

I'm pretty well settled on this blue bagpipe bird with a horn for his nose. It'll be something to talk about, and the bagpipe will be like naturalistic on my *gordo* gut, maybe it'll minimize my girth. But the bird needs a background pattern. Over my fourth cup of microwave coffee, I start thinking about red blood cells, remembering from the lab how they're shaped. I begin digging on the concept of rounding out my Bosch bird tattoo with a blood-cell tiling.

To help visualize it, I pinprick my pinkie and put a droplet on a glass slide under my personal Glenda Gomez research scope. I see beautiful shades of orange and red from all my little blood cells massed together. Sleepey will need to see this in order to fully grasp what to do. I want to keep on looking, but the blood is drying fast. The cells are bursting, and cracks are forming among them as they dry. I remember that at Smart Stork we'd put some juice on the slides with the cells to keep them perky. I don't know what kind of juice, but I decide to try a drop of water out of one of my infusions, a dark funky batch that I'd fed with a KFC chicken nugget.

The infusion water is teeming with those tough-looking paramecia with the coarse bristles—the microhomies. What with Bosch on my brain, the microhomies resemble tiny bagpipes on crutches. I'm like: Tattoo *them* onto my belly too? While I'm watching the microhomies, they start digging on my ruptured blood cells.

"Yo," I say, eyeing an especially bright and lively one. "You're eating me."

And that's when it happens. The image loses its focus, I feel a puff of air, my skin tingles all over. Leaning back, I see a bag of glowing light grow out from the microscope slide. It's a foot across.

I jump to my feet and back off. I may be heavy, but I'm quick. At first I have the idea my apartment is on fire, and then for some reason I think of earthquakes. I'm heading for the door.

But the glowing sack gets there before me, blocking the exit. I try to reach through it for the doorknob.

As soon as my hand is inside the lumpy glow I hear a woman's voice.

"Glenda! Hello dear."

"Who are you?"

"I'm Harna from Hilbert space." She has a prim voice; I visualize flowery dresses and pillbox hats. "I happened upon your brane several–days–ago. I've been teeming with the microlife, a bit humdrum, and I thought that's all there is to see in this location. Worth documenting, but no more than that. I had no idea that only a few clicks up the size scale I'd find a gorgeous entity like you. Scale is tricky for me, what with everything in Hilbert space being infinite. Thank goodness I happened upon your blood cell. Oh, *warmest* greetings, Glenda Gomez. You're–why, you're collectible, my dear."

I'm fully buggin'. I run to the corner of my living-room, staring at the luminous paramecium the size of a dog in midair. "Go away," I say.

Harna wobbles into the shape of a jellyfish with dangling frilly ribbons. She drifts across the room, not quite touching the floor, dragging her oral arms across the stuff lying on my tables, checking things out. And then she gets to my Bosch book, which is open to *The Garden of Earthly Delights*.

"A nonlinear projection of three-space to two-space," burbles Harna, feeling the paper all over. "Such a clever map. Who's the author?"

"Hieronymus Bosch," I murmur. "It's called perspective." I'm half-wondering if my brain has popped and I'm alone here talking to myself. Maybe I'm about to start fingerpainting the floor with Clorox. Snorting Ajax up my nose.

"Bosch?" muses Harna. Her voice is fruity and penetrating like my old guidance counselor's. "And I just know you have a crush on him, Glenda! I can tell. When can I meet him?"

"He lived a long time ago," I whisper. I'm stepping from side to side, trying to find a clear path to the door.

"Most excellent," Harna is saying. "You'll time-snatch him, and then I can use the time-flaw to perspective-map your whole spacetime brane down into a sack! Yummy! You are so cute, Glenda. Yes, I'm going to wrap you up and take you home!"

I get past her and run out into the street. I'm breathing hard, still in my nightgown, now and then looking over my shoulder. So of course a San Jose police car pulls over and sounds me on their speaker. They think I'm a tweaker or a nut-job. Did I mention that it's Sunday morning?

"Ma'am. Can we help you? Ma'am. Please come over to the police car and place your hands on the hood. Ma'am." More cop-voice crackle in the background and here comes Harna down the sidewalk, still shaped like a flying jellyfish, though bigger than before. The cops can't see her, though.

"Ma'am." One of them gets out of the car, a kid with a cop mustache. He looks kind, concerned, but his hand is on the butt of his Taser.

I whirl, every cop's image of a madwoman, pointing back down the sidewalk at the swollen Harna, who's shaping herself into a damn good replica of the cops' car. She's made of glowing haze and hanging at an angle to the ground.

Right before the cop grabs my wrist or Tasers me, Harna sweeps over and—pixie-dust!—I'm riding in a Gummi-Bear cop car, with Harna talking to me from the radio grill. The cops don't see me anymore. Harna heads down the street, then swerves off parallel to spacetime. She guns her mill and we're rumbling through a *wah-wah* collage of years and centuries, calendar leaves flying, the sun flickering off and on, Earth rushing around the Sun in a blur. And it's not just time we're traveling through, we're rolling through some miles as well. We arrive in the Lowlands of 1475.

It's a foggy dawn, Jerome Bosch is at his bedroom window, arcing a stream of pee toward the glow of the rising sun. I know from books that Hieronymus was just his fancy show name, and that his homies called him Jerome. Like my given name is Guadalupe—but everyone calls me Glenda. Seeing the man in the window, my heart does a little handstand. My love has guided us all this way.

"He *is* scrumptious," says Harna.

As he lowers his nightshirt, Jerome's gaze drifts away from the horizon—and he sees us. His expression is calm, resigned— it's like he's always been expecting a flying jellyfish/cop-car carrying a good-looking woman from the next millennium. Calm, yes, but he's moving back from the window hella fast.

Harna flips out a long vortex of force, a tornado that fastens onto Jerome and pulls him to us. He's hanging in the air a few feet away from me, slowly spinning—and yelling in what must be Dutch.

"Grab your fella," says Harna. "It has to be you who lands him. It's not for me to meddle in a brane's spacetime."

The wind has flopped Bosch's hair back. His cheekbones are high, his lips are thin, his eyes are bright. The man for me. I reach out and catch hold of his hand. It's warm.

Harna's light flows down my arm and up Jerome's. Augmented by Harna, I'm strong as a steam shovel. I set Bosch down on the jelly car seat next to me.

"It's too soon," he says, clear as day. "I'm not ready."

"I'm Glenda," I say, not all that surprised he's speaking English. Another Harna miracle. "Ready or not, I'm taking you home."

"To Hell?" exclaims Jerome. "That's quite unjust. Only yesterday I was absolved by the priest. My sins in these last hours have been but petty ones. A touch of anger at the neighbor's dog, my usual avarice for a truly great commission, and the accustomed fires of lust, of course— " As he mentions this last sin, he looks down my nightgown, which I'm just loving. I press his hand against my warm thigh.

"Don't worry, sweetie. I don't live in Hell. I live in San Jose."

For the rest of the ride, Jerome is busy looking around, taking everything in. What eyes he has! So sharp and smart and alert. What with the time-winds flapping my flimsy, he can see I'm all woman. I'm doing my best to keep the fabric cinched in around the problem areas at my waist, and I'm trying to get his arms around me, but he's kind of reluctant. He's uneasy about whither we're bound. I can dig it.

Finally Harna sets us down in the sunny street outside my apartment. Lucky me, the cops are gone. Everything looks the same—the dead palm leaves, the beater cars and pickups, the dusty jasmine vines, the broken glass on the dry clay, the 7-11 store, the university parking garage—sunny and dry.

Harna rises into the air and spreads out, layering herself across the scene like extra sunshine. No doubt she'll be back in some more personal form pretty soon. But meanwhile I've got me a man. I smile at Jerome and give his arm a happy squeeze.

"This is Spain?" he wonders.

"America," I tell him, which doesn't seem to ring a bell. "The new world across the Atlantic Ocean, plus some five centuries past your time."

He shakes his head, and stares around like a bird fallen from its nest. "It's after the Second Coming?" he asks. "Christ has dominion over the Earth?"

"The Church is doing fine," I say, not sure where this is going. We shouldn't stand around the street in our nightgowns. "Come on inside."

I hustle him up the stairs into my apartment and first of all get us in some clothes. I dress him in my favorite vintage red Ramones T-shirt and my yellow SJSU sweatpants. Me, I put on some nice tight Capri pants with a Lycra tummy panel and a pink baby-doll blouse that's loose at the bottom. Truth be told, I do a certain amount of my shopping in the maternity section at Target.

In the kitchen I offer Jerome some Oreos and microwave two cups of instant coffee. Buzz! The microwave is built into the wall so we delinquent renters can't hock it. Jerome overlooks the futuristic aspects of my kitchen because he's busy holding one of the cookies up to the light, studying the embossed writing and curlicues.

"They're food," I tell him. I rotate one in two and give him the better half. He scarfs it down—and I'm secretly glad, thinking that we've broken bread together now. Jerome takes another Oreo and eats the whole thing. They're gettin' good to him.

Meanwhile I touch up my black lipstick and lip liner. All the time I'm watching him. Even though he's from a long time ago, he's not old. Maybe twenty-five. He would have still been at the start of his career. No reason he can't have as good a career here in San Jose with me.

Jerome watches me right back. His gaze is warm and alive, as if there's an extra brain inside each eyeball. After a bit he fixates on my mug of colored pencils, looking at them the way I wish he was looking at my boobs.

"Want to draw?" I ask him. "You can decorate my walls." There's two smooth blank walls in my living room, a short wall across from the hall door and a big one across from the window.

"A mural?" says Jerome, examining a couple of the pencils.

"Bingo."

He starts in on the smaller wall. And me, I sit down with pen and paper at my round table on the one chair I've got. I want to try and start documenting some of this unfurling madness. For sure there's a reality TV show in this. All my friends say I should be on TV, and who am I to disagree. I recite a prayer to give me courage to write.

"Hail Glenda, full of grace, an alien paramecium was with thee. Blessed art thou amongst women, and blessed is the fruit of your brain, *Glenda and Jerome.*"

I lean over my spiral notebook, pen in hand.

To whom it may concern: It may interest you to know that . . .

Is it Hie or Hei? Love has made me dyslexic.

I look around, trying to find the book that turned Harna on to Jerome, but I can't see it just now. Thinking about the book, I have to grin, thinking how incredible it is to have the artist himself here with me.

"Hey, Jerome. I'm writing about you."

"Not yet," he says and taps his thumb with his finger. Like that's the Lowlands chill-it gesture. He's holding a purple pencil in his other hand. Getting started on marking up my little wall. Holding the pencil gives him power, aplomb. He's a suspicious genius with sharp eyes and a trapdoor mouth. I keep talking to him.

"It's fabulous that you're drawing, Jerome. This hole will be an art grotto. I hope they don't paint it over when we move." And surely we will be moving quite soon, with Jerome pulling in the Old Master bucks. We'll be on TV. We'll get a condo in one of those beautiful new buildings across from the SJSU library on Fourth Street.

I smile at Jerome and fluff my hair a little. I wear it long and black with henna highlights and heavy bangs. Too bad I didn't happen to shampoo and condition it yet this week. I look sexier when my mane is lustrous.

Jerome thins his lips and shades the outstretched arms of a little man. He's digging on the excellent twenty-first-century quality of my pencils and the luscious smooth whiteness of apartment dry-wall. Sketching a picture of Harna and me snatching him. Harna looks like a fish as much as a car. She's surrounded by glow-lines of blue light. Her prey is just now seeing the shape in the sky, he's holding out his arms with that odd look of non-surprise. His unmade bachelor bed is in the far corner of his room. The vortex from the aeroform is gonna cartwheel him into the arms of a voluptuous dark-haired sorceress. Me!

"You're cute," I tell Jerome. He pinches the fingers of one hand at me again, the other hand busy with my pencils. He draws terrifically fast. I'm really glad I bagged him. But I wish he looked a little happier about it.

"Why don't we get to know each other better?" I say, imagining he might pick up on my tone. I unbutton my baby-doll blouse enough so he can see my boobs—but not the runaway rolls of my stomach. My breasts are a major plus, easily the equal of Pammy Anderson's. And they're natural.

But Jerome looks away. It occurs to me that maybe he still thinks this is Hell—which would make me a demoness. I decide to play up to that. I cackle at him and beckon with witchy fingers, the light glinting on my chipped black nails. My fingers are quite shapely, another plus feature. But they're not bringing Jerome Bosch into my arms.

So I go get him. He tries to escape, racing around the apartment like a sparrow that flew in the window. I shoo him into my bedroom and—*plop*—we're mixed in with the sheets, magazines, and laundry on my bed.

I give him a wet kiss and pull down my stretchy pants—keeping my top on so as to minimize that troublesome abdominal area. Of course I'm not wearing panties, I've been planning this all along. I tug down his sweatpants—and there's his goodies on display. A twenty-five-year-old fella here in bed with me, the answer to a maiden's prayer. I roll him on top of me and pull him in. It's been a while.

But—just my luck—this turns into a totally screwed-up proposition. He comes, maybe, and then he's limp, and then—oh, God—he starts sobbing like his heart is going to break.

Poor Jerome. I cuddle him and whisper to him. His sobs slow down, he whimpers, he slides off to one side, and—falls asleep!

I feel down between my legs, trying to figure out if he delivered. What a thing it would be to carry Hieronymus Bosch's baby! That would tie him to me for sure. I think I'm ovulating today, as a matter of fact. Just for luck, I twist around and prop my feet up on the wall, giving the Dutch Master's wrigglers every opportunity to work their way up to the hidden jewel of my egg.

Resting there, thinking things over, I can visualize them, pointy-nosed with beating tails, talking to each other in Dutch, enjoying themselves in Glenda-land, on a pilgrimage to my Garden of Earthly Delights.

He keeps on sleeping, and I amble back into the kitchen to make myself a grilled cheese sandwich. I'm happy, but at the same time I have this bad feeling that Harna somehow tricked me. That stuff about wrapping me up and taking me home. Some weird shit is gonna come down, I just know it.

But now here comes Jerome out the bedroom, looking mellower than before. Our little hump and cuddle has helped his mind-set.

"Greetings, Glenda," he says. "I enjoyed our venery."

"Likewise." He looks so cute and inquisitive that I run over and kiss his cheek. And I can't help asking, "You don't think I'm too fat?"

"You're well fed," he says, cupping my boobs. "Clean and healthy. But do you worship Satan? Your spirit-familiar Harna—surely she is unholy."

"I don't know much about Harna," I admit. "She only appeared today. And Satan? Naw, dog. I'm a Catholic girl." Fallen away, I don't mention. I cross myself, and he's relieved.

"I can go home?" he asks, glancing out the window at the quiet street in the noon sun.

"You belong with me," I tell him. "I'll give you a baby. You never had one back then. I love your art. You're mucho famous here, you know. I have a whole book of your pictures."

I root around the apartment, wanting to show him, but damn it, that book is totally gone. I'm guessing that Harna took it. She was saying something about copying Jerome's perspective maps so she can—fit our world into a sack? That has to be wack. If only she's gone for good. Maybe hoping hard enough can make it so. I skip over to Jerome and kiss him again. He lets me.

"I can't find my book, but we can go to the SJSU library," I tell him. "It's just across the campus, and they're open on Sunday. And I think the Art Mart is open today too. I'll buy you some paint."

"Buy paint?" says Jerome. "I mix my own."

"We get it in tubes," I say. "Like sausage. Ready-made. Here, eat a grilled cheese sandwich, and then we'll look for Hieronymus Bosch books in the library."

Well, guess what we find under Bosch, Hieronymus, in the library? Not jack shit. When Harna and I abducted him from the fifteenth-century Dutch town of s'Hertogenbosch and carried him to twenty-first century San Jose, California, we wiped out his role in history. Maybe he finished one or two minor paintings before we nabbed him, but as far as the history of art is concerned, he never lived. Jerome doesn't really pick up on how weird this is—I mean all he's seen me do is look at an incomprehensible-to-a-medieval-mind online card catalog, and we nabbed him before he was famous anyway, so he's not feeling the loss. But me, I feel it bad.

Bosch was a really important artist, you know—or maybe you don't. Come to think of it, I might be the only one who remembers our world before I changed our history. But take it from me, Hieronymus Bosch was King. The Elvis of artists. His work influenced a lot of people in all kinds of ways over the centuries.

More ways than I'd imagined.

Because now, walking off the campus and getting a coffee, I'm paying attention and I'm noticing differences in our non-Bosch world. There aren't any ads for horror movies in the paper, for instance, which is way odd.

The Episcopal Church that used to be by the coffee shop is a pho noodle parlor. On a hunch, I look in the yellow pages in the coffee shop, and there's no Episcopal or Baptist or Proletarian or whatever churches in town at all. With no Bosch, the Protestant thing never happened! The sisters that whipped me through grade school would be happy, but I'm thinking, *Dear God, what have I done?*

The cars are different too, duller than before, as if Y2K cars could get duller. And every single one of them is cream colored, not even any silver or maroon.

The barrista in the coffee shop who usually wears foundation and drawn-on eyebrows has her face bare as a granola hippie's. And her hair is all bowl-cut and sensible. Ugh. The world is definitely lagging without the cumulative influences of my man Jerome.

On the plus side, you can smoke in the coffee shop now, and all the cigarettes are fat and laced with nutmeg and clove, which I dig. The Supertaqueria next door isn't selling tongue anymore, also fine by me. The fonts on the signs are somehow lower and fatter and more, like, Sanskrit-looking. The people in the magazine ads are wearing more clothes, and generally heavier.

Hey, I can live with some change, if that's what it takes to get Glenda her man.

I buy Jerome a canvas and some acrylics at the Art Mart— putting them on a new credit card that some pinheads mailed me last week. When we get back to my apartment, my Dutch Master sniffs suspiciously at the paint, then prepares to start layering the stuff over the colored drawing on my smaller wall.

There's a knock on the door. I've been expecting this. I peep through the peephole, and it's Harna, looking just like her voice sounds, like a rich old white woman in a flowery dress and a pastel green pillbox hat covered with seed pearls. I don't want to let her in, but she walks right through the closed door.

"Hello, Glenda and Jerome," goes Harna. "I have a commission for the artist." She plumps a velvet sack right down on my kitchen table. Clink of gold coins. Perfectly calculated to get Jerome's juices flowing.

"What kind of painting do you need, my lady?" asks Jerome, setting down his paintbrush and making a greedy little bow.

"A picture of that," she says, pointing out the window to Sixth Street and the San Jose cityscape. "With full perspective accuracy. You can paint it—there." She points to my big blank living room wall.

"How soon would you need it?" asks Jerome.

"By sundown," says Harna.

"He can't paint that fast," I protest.

"I'll speed him up," says Harna, with a twitch of her dowager lips. "I'll return with the rising of the moon."

Sure enough, Jerome starts racing around the room like a cockroach does when the light comes on. He pauses only long enough to ask me to get him more paint.

When I come back from the Art Mart with a shopping bag of paint tubes, he's already roughed in an underpainting of the street—the houses with their tile and shingle roofs, the untrimmed palm trees, the dead dingy cars, the vines, a few passersby captured in motion, the tops of the houses in the next block, the houses after them, the low brown haze from the freeways, and beyond that the golden-grassed foothills and the blank blue sky.

He's all over the wall, and the painting is so perfect and beautiful I can hardly stand it. Every ten seconds, it seems like, he darts over to the window, then darts back. He's such a nut that he's putting in every single person and car that goes past, so the picture is getting more and more crowded.

The sun is going down, and a few lights come on in the windows outside. Somehow Jerome is keeping up with it, changing his painting to match the world, touching the buildings with sunset gold, damping the shadows into warmer shades, pinkening the sky—and then darkening it.

A fat full moon comes up over the foothills and, quick as a knife, Jerome paints it onto my wall, sprinkling stars all around it.

And then Harna's in the room again.

"It's enough," she says. "He can stop."

Jerome cranks down to normal speed. I hand him more Oreos and coffee. He slugs down the nourishment, then drinks a quart of water from the sink.

"What happens now?" I ask Harna.

"Like I said before," she answers, not looking so much like a human anymore. Her pink skin is peeling away in patches, and underneath she's green. "I'm going to bag you and your world and take you home. Don't worry, it won't hurt."

And then she shoots out of the window and disappears into the distance past the moon.

"We have to stop her!" I tell Jerome, picking up my purse.

"What?" he says. He sounds tired.

"We have to run after Harna."

Jerome looks at me for a long time. And then he smiles. "If you say so, Glenda. Being with you is interesting."

The two of us run down the apartment stairs and right away I can see that things are seriously weird. The cars across the street are two-thirds as big as the cars on my side.

"Hurry," I tell Jerome, and we run around the corner to the next block. The houses on that next street are half the size of the houses on my street. We run another block, which takes only a couple of seconds, as each block is way smaller than the one before. The houses are only waist high. We go just a little farther and now we're stepping right over the houses, striding across a block at a time.

Another step takes us all the way across Route 101, the step after that across east San Jose. The further from Jerome's picture we get, the smaller things are.

"Perspective!" exclaims Jerome. "The world has shrunk to perspective!"

We hop over the foothills. And now it gets really crazy. With one last push of our legs, we leap past the moon. It's a pale yellow golf ball near our knees. We're launched into space, man. The stars rush past, all of them, denser and denser—*zow*—and then we're past everything, beyond the vanishing point, out at infinity.

Clear white light, firm as Jell-O, and you can stand wherever you like. Up where it's the brightest, I see a throne and a bearded man in it, just like in Jerome's paintings. It's God, with Jesus beside Him, and between them is the Dove, which I never did get. Right below the Trinity is my own Virgin of Guadalupe, with wiggly yellow lines all around her. And up above them all are my secret guardians, the Powerpuff Girls from my favorite Saturday morning cartoon. Jerome sees them, too. We clasp hands. I know deep inside myself that now forever we two are married. I'm crying my head off.

But somebody jostles me, it's Harna right next to us, pushing and grunting, trying to wrestle our whole universe into a brown sack. She's the shape of a green Bosch-goblin with a slit mouth.

I turn off the waterworks and whack Harna up the side of the head with my purse. Jerome crouches down and butts her in the stomach. Passing the vanishing point has made us about as strong as our enemy, the demonic universe-collector. While she's reeling back, I quick get hold of her sack and shake its edges free of our stars.

Harna comes at me hot and heavy, with smells and electric shocks and thumps on my butt. Jerome goes toe-to-toe with her, shoving her around, but she's starting to hammer on his head pretty good. Just then I notice a brush and tubes of white and blue paint in my purse. I hand them to Jerome, and while I use some Extreme Wrestling moves from TV on Harna, Jerome quick paints a translucent blue sphere around her with a cross on top ⇓ a spirit trap.

I shove the last free piece of Harna fully inside the ball and, presto, she's neutralized. With a hissing, farting sound she dwindles from our view, disappearing in a direction different from any that we can see. I wave one time to the Trinity, the Virgin, and the Powerpuff Girls, and, how awesome, they wave back. And then we're outta there.

The walk home is a little tricky—that first step in particular, where you go from infinity back into normal space, is a tough one. But we make it.

As soon as we're in my apartment, I help Jerome slap some house-paint over his big mural. And when we go outside to check on things, everything is back to being its own right size. We've saved our universe.

To celebrate, we get some Olde Antwerpen forty-ouncers at the 7-11 and hop onto my bed, cuddling together at one end leaning against the wall. I'm kind of hoping Jerome will want to get it on, but right now he seems a little tired. Not too tired to check out my boobs though.

Just when it might start to get interesting, here comes Harna's last gasp. I can't see her anymore, but I can hear her voice, and so can Jerome.

"Have it your way," intones the prissy universe-collector. "Keep your petty world. But the restoration must be in full. Before I leave for good, Hieronymus must go home."

"Think I'll stay here," says Jerome, who's holding a tit in one hand and a beer in the other.

"Back," says Harna, and her presence disappears for good.

As she leaves, the living breathing man next to me turns into—oh hell—an art book.

"No way," I sob. "I need him." I quick say the Hail Mary three times, like the sisters taught me. But the Bosch book just sits there. I pour some of the microhomies onto it. Nothing doing. I squeeze red paint onto the book cover and stick a split Oreo cookie to it. Still no good. And then in desperation, I pray to my special protectors, the Powerpuff Girls. And the day's last miracle begins.

The book twitches in my hands, throbs, splits in two, and the two copies move apart, making a, like, hyperdimensional man-hole.

And, yes, pushing his way out of the hole, here comes my Hieronymus Bosch, his hair flopping, his eyes sharp, his mouth thin with concentration.

He's in my bed—and the dumb book is gone. Screw art history. Jerome will make even better paintings than before. And if that doesn't work out, there's reality TV.

You know anybody who can help with my show?

SIX THOUGHT EXPERIMENTS CONCERNING THE NATURE OF COMPUTATION

EXPERIMENT 1. LUCKY NUMBER

The first Sunday in October, Doug Cardano drove in for an extra day's work at Giga Games. Crunch time. The nimrods in marketing had committed to shipping a virtual reality golf game in time for the holiday season. NuGolf. It was supposed to have five eighteen-hole courses, all of them new, all of them land-scaped by Doug.

He exited Route 101 and crossed the low overpass over the train tracks, heading toward the gleaming Giga Games complex beside the San Francisco Bay. A long freight train was passing. Growing up, Doug had always liked trains, in fact he'd dreamed of being a hobo. Or an artist for a game company. He hadn't known about crunch time.

Just to postpone the start of his long, beige workday, he pulled over and got out to watch the cars clank past: boxcars, tankers, reefers, flatcars. Many of them bore graffiti. Doug lit a cigarette, his first of the day, always the best one, and spotted a row of twelve spray-painted numbers on a dusty red boxcar, the digits arranged in pairs.

11 35 17 03 21 18

SuperLotto, thought Doug, and wrote them on his cardboard box of cigarettes. Five numbers between 1 and 47, and one number between 1 and 27.

Next stop was the minimarket down the road. Even though Doug knew the odds were bogus, he'd been buying a lot of SuperLotto tickets lately. The grand prize was hella big. If he won, he'd never have to crunch again.

The rest of the team trickled in about the same time as Doug. A new bug had broken one of the overnight builds, and Van the lead coder had to fix that. Meanwhile Doug got down to the trees and bushes for course number four.

Since the player could mouse all around the NuGolf world and even wander into the rough, Doug couldn't use background bitmaps. He had to create three-dimensional models of the plants. NuGolf was meant to be wacky and fantastic, so he had a lot of leeway: on the first course he'd used cartoony saguaro cactuses, he'd set the second links underwater with sea fans and kelp, the third had been on "Venus" with man-eating plants, and for the fourth, which he was starting today—well, he wasn't sure what to do.

He had a vague plan of trying to get some inspirations from BlobScape, a three-dimensional cellular automata package he'd found on the web. Cellular automata grew organic-looking objects on the fly. Depending what number you seeded BlobScape with, it could grow almost anything. The guy who'd written BlobScape claimed that theoretically the computation could simulate the whole universe, if only you gave it the right seed.

When he started up BlobScape today, it was in a lava lamp mode, with big wobbly droplets pulsing around. A click of the *Randomize* button turned the blobs into mushroom caps, pulsing through the simulation space like jellyfish. Another click produced interlocking pyramids a bit like trees, but not pretty enough to use.

Doug pressed the *Rule* button so he could enter some code numbers of his own. He'd done this a few times before, every now and then it did something really cool. It reminded him of the Magic Rocks kit he'd had as boy, where the right kind of gray pebble in a glass of liquid could grow green and purple stalagmites. Maybe today was his lucky day. Come to think of it, his SuperLotto ticket happened to be lying on his desk, so, what the hey, he entered 11 35 17 03 21 18.

Bingo. The block of simulated space misted over, churned and congealed into—a primeval jungle inhabited by dinosaurs. And it kept going from there. Apemen moved from the trees into caves. Egyptians built the Sphinx and the pyramids. A mob crucified Christ. Galileo dropped two balls off the Leaning Tower of Pisa. Soldiers massacred the Indians of the Great Plains. Flappers and bootleggers danced the jitterbug. Hippies handed out daisies. Computers multiplied like bacilli.

Doug had keyed in the Holy Grail, the one true rule, the code number for the universe. Sitting there grinning, it occurred to him that if you wrote those twelve lucky digits in reverse order they'd work as a phone number plus extension. (811) 230-7153 x11. The number seemed exceedingly familiar, but without stopping to think he went ahead and dialed it.

His own voice answered.

"Game over."

The phone in Doug's hand turned into pixels. He and the phone and the universe dissolved.

EXPERIMENT 2. THE MILLION CHAKRAS

Teaching her third yoga class of the day, Amy Hendrix felt light-headed and rubbery. She walked around, correcting people's poses, encouraging them to hold their positions longer than they usually did. Her mind kept wandering to the room she was hoping to rent. New to San Francisco, she'd been sleeping on couches for six weeks. But she still dreamed of becoming a force to be reckoned with in the city scene.

It was time for Savasana, the Corpse Pose, with everyone lying on their backs. Amy turned off her Tabla Beat CD and guided the closing meditation.

"Feel a slow wave of softness moving up your legs," she began. "Feet, calves, knees, thighs." Long pause. "Now focus on your perineum. Chakra one. Release any tension hiding there. Melt with the in-breath, bloom with the out. Almost like you're going to wet your pants." Amy occasionally added an earthy touch—which her mostly white clients readily accepted from their coffee-colored teacher.

"Gather the energy into a ball of light between your legs," continued Amy, pausing between each sentence, trying not to talk too much. "Slowly, slowly it passes upward, tracking your spine like a trolley. Now the light is in your sex chakra. Let it tingle, savor it, let it move on. The warmth flows though your belly and into your solar plexus. Your breath is waves on a beach."

She was sitting cross-legged at one end of the darkly lit room. The meditation was getting good to her. "Energy in, darkness out. The light comes into your chest. You're in the grass, looking at the leaves in a high summer tree. The sun shines through. Your heart is basking. You love the world. You love the practice. You love yourself. The light moves through your neck like toothpaste out a tube. Chakra five. The light is balancing your hormones, it's washing away your angry unsaid words." Pause. "And now your tape loops are gone."

She gave a tiny tap to her Tibetan cymbal. *Bonnng.* "Your head is an empty dome of light. Feel the space. You're here. No plans. You're now." She got to her feet. "Light seeps through your scalp and trickles down your face. Your cheeks are soft. Your mouth. Your shoulders melt. Your arms. I'll call you back."

She moved around the room pressing down on people's shoulders. She had a brief, odd feeling of leaning over each separate customer at once. And then her wristwatch drew her back. She had twenty minutes to get from here to Telegraph Hill to try and rent that perfect room.

She rang the gong and saw the customers out. The last one was Sueli, a lonely wrinkled lady who liked to talk. Sueli was only one in the class as dark-skinned as Amy. Amy enjoyed her, she seemed like a fairy godmother.

"How many chakras do you say there are?" asked Sueli. Clearly she had some theory of her own in mind. She was very well spoken.

"Seven," said Amy, putting on her sweats. "Why not?" She imagined she might look like Sueli when she was old.

"The Hindus say seven, and the Buddhists say nine," said Sueli, leaning close. "But I know the real answer. I learned it years ago in Sri Lanka. This is the last of your classes I'll be able to come to, so I'm going to share the secret with you."

"Yes?" This sounded interesting. Amy turned out the lights, locked the door, and stepped outside with Sueli. The autumn sky was a luminous California blue. The bay breeze vibrated the sun-bleached cardboard election signs on the lampposts—San Francisco was in the throes of a wide-open mayoral election.

"Some of us have millions of chakras," continued Sueli in her quiet tone. "One for each branch of time. Opening the chakras opens the doors to your other selves."

"You can do that?" asked Amy.

"You have the power too," said Sueli. "I saw it in class. For an instant there were seven of you. Yes indeed."

"And you—you have selves in different worlds?"

"I come and go. There's not so many of me left. I'm here because I was drawn to you. I have a gift." Sueli removed a leather thong from around her neck. Dangling from the strand was a brilliant crystal. The late afternoon sunlight bounced off it, fracturing into jagged rays. The sparkling flashes were like sand in Amy's eyes. She felt like she was breaking apart.

"Only let the sun hit it when you want to split," said Sueli, quickly putting the rawhide strand over Amy's head and tucking the crystal under her sweatshirt. "Good luck." Sueli gave her a hug and a peck on the cheek as the bus pulled up.

Amy hopped aboard. When she looked back to wave at the old woman she was gone.

The room was three blocks off Columbus Avenue with a private entrance and a view of both bridges. It was everything Amy had hoped. But the rent was ten times higher than she'd understood. In her eagerness, she'd read one less zero than was on the number in the paper. She felt like such a dope. Covering her embarrassment, she asked the owner if she could have a moment alone.

"Make yourself at home," said the heavyset Italian lady. "Drink it in." She was under the mistaken impression that Amy was rich. "I like your looks, miss. If you're ready to sign, I got the papers downstairs in the kitchen. I know the market's slow, but I'm not dropping the price. First, last, and one month's damage deposit. You said on the phone the rent's no problem?"

"That's what I said," murmured Amy.

Alone in the airy room, she wandered over to the long window, fiddling with the amulet around her neck. The low, hot sun reached out to the crystal. Shattered rays flew about the room, settling here and here and here.

Nine brown-skinned women smiled at each other. Amy was all of them at the same time. Her overlapping minds saw through each pair of eyes.

"We'll get separate jobs and share the rent," said one of her mouths. "And when we come back to the room we'll merge together," said another. "We'll work in parallel worlds, but we'll deposit our checks and pay the rent in just in this one."

"Great," said Amy, not quite sure this was real. As she tucked away the crystal, her nine bodies folded back into one.

Walking down the stairs to sign the papers, her mind was racing. She'd split into nine—but Sueli had said that, with the crystal, she could split into a million.

Out the window she glimpsed another election poster—and the big thought hit her.

With a million votes, she could be the next mayor.

EXPERIMENT 3. AINT PAINT

Although Shirley Nguyen spoke good English and studied with a crowd of boys in the chemical engineering program at U.C. Berkeley, she had no success in getting dates. Not that she was ugly. But she hadn't been able to shed the old-country habits of covering her mouth when she smiled, and of sticking out her tongue when she was embarrassed. She knew how uncool these moves were, and she tried to fight them—but without any lasting success. The problem was maybe that she spent so much more time thinking about engineering than she did in thinking about her appearance.

In short, to Westerners and assimilated Asians, Shirley came across as a geek, so much so that she ended up spending every weekend night studying in her parents' apartment on Shattuck Street, while the rest of her family worked downstairs in the pho noodle parlor they ran. Of course Shirley's mother Binh had some ideas about lining up matches for her daughter—sometimes she'd even step out into the street, holding a big serving chopstick like a magic wand and calling for Shirley to come downstairs to meet someone. But Shirley wasn't interested in the recently immigrated Vietnamese men that Binh always seemed to have in mind. Yes, those guys might be raw enough to find Shirley sophisticated—but for sure they had no clue about women's rights. Shirley wasn't struggling through the hardest major at Berkeley just to be a sexist's slave.

Graduation rolled around, and Shirley considered job offers from local oil and pharma refineries. On the get-acquainted plant tours, she was disturbed to note that several of the senior chemical engineers had body parts missing. A hand here, an ear there, a limp that betokened a wooden leg—Shirley hadn't quite realized how dangerous it was to work in the bowels of an immense industrial plant. Like being a beetle in the middle of a car's engine. The thought of being maimed before she'd ever really known a man filled her with self-pity and rebelliousness.

Seeking a less intense job at a smaller, safer company, she came across Pflaumbaum Kustom Kolors of Fremont. PKK manufactured small lots of fancy paints for customized vehicles. The owner was fat and bearded like the motorcyclists and hot-rodders who made up the larger part of his clientele. Shirley found Stuart Pflaumbaum's appearance pleasantly comical, even though his personality was more edgy than jovial.

"I want patterned paint," Pflaumbaum told Shirley at their interview. He had a discordant voice but his eyes were clear and wondering. "Can you do it?"

Shirley covered her mouth and giggled with excitement—stopped herself—uncovered her mouth and, now embarrassed, stuck her tongue all the way down to her chin—stopped herself again—and slapped herself on the cheek. "I'd like to try," she got out finally. "It's not impossible. I know activator-inhibitor processes that make dots and stripes and swirls. The Belusouv-Zhabotinsky reaction? People can mix two cans and watch the patterns self-organize in the liquid layer they paint on. When it dries the pattern stays."

"Zhabotinsky?" mused Pflaumbaum. "Did he patent it?"

"I don't think so," said Shirley. "He's Russian. The recipe's simple. Let's surf for it right now. You can see some pictures, to get an idea. Here, I'll type it in." She leaned across the bulky Pflaumbaum to use his mouse and keyboard. The big man smelled better than Shirley had expected—chocolate, coffee, marijuana, a hint of red wine. Familiar smells from the streets of Berkeley.

"You're good," said Pflaumbaum as the pictures appeared. Red and blue spirals.

"You see?" said Shirley. "The trick is to get a robust process based on inexpensive compounds. There's all sorts of ways to tune the spirals' size. You can have little double scrolls nested together, or great big ones like whirlpools. Or even a filigree."

"Bitchin'," rumbled Pflaumbaum. "You're hired." He glanced up at Shirley, whose hand was at her mouth again, covering a smile at her success. "By the month," added the heavy man.

Shirley was given an unused corner of the paint factory for her own lab, with a small budget for equipment. The Spanish-speaking plant workers were friendly enough, but mostly the female engineer was on her own. Every afternoon Stuart Pflaumbaum would stump over, belly big beneath his tight black T-shirt, and ask to see her latest results.

Shirley seemed to intrigue Pflaumbaum as much as he did her, and soon he took to taking her out for coffee, then for dinner, and before long she'd started spending nights at his nice house on the hills overlooking Fremont.

Although Shirley assured her mother that her boss was a bachelor, his house bore signs of a former wife—divorced, separated, deceased? Although Stuart wouldn't talk about the absent woman, Shirley did manage to find out her name: Angelica. She too had been Asian, a good omen for Shirley's prospects, not that she was in a rush to settle down, but it would be kind of nice to have the nagging marriage problem resolved for once and for all. Like solving a difficult process schema.

As for the work on patterned paint, the first set of compounds reactive enough to form big patterns also tended to etch into the material being painted. The next family of recipes did no harm, but were too expensive to put into production. And then Shirley thought of biological by-products. After an intense month of experimenting, she'd learned that bovine pancreatic juices mixed with wood-pulp alkali and a bit of hog melanin were just the thing to catalyze a color-creating activator-inhibitor process in a certain enamel base.

Stuart decided to call the product Aint Paint.

In four months they'd shipped two thousand boxes of PKK Aint Paint in seven different color and pattern mixes. Every biker and low-rider in the South Bay wanted Aint Paint, and a few brave souls were putting it on regular cars. Stuart hired a patent attorney.

Not wanting her discoveries to end, Shirley began working with a more viscous paint, almost a gel. In the enhanced thickness of this stuff, her reactions polymerized, wrinkled up, and amazing embossed patterns—thorns and elephant trunks and—if you tweaked it just right—puckers that looked like alien Yoda faces. Aint Paint 3D sold even better than Aint Paint Classic. They made the national news, and Pflaumbaum Kustom Kolors couldn't keep up with the orders.

Stuart quickly swung a deal with a Taiwanese novelty company called Global Bong. He got good money, but as soon as the ink on the contract was dry, Global Bong wanted to close the Fremont plant and relocate Shirley to China, which was the last place on Earth she wanted to be.

So Shirley quit her job and continued her researches in Stuart's basement, which turned out to not to be all that good a move. With no job to go to, Pflaumbaum was really hitting the drugs and alcohol, and from time to time he was rather sexist and abusive. Shirley put up with it for now, but she was getting uneasy. Stuart never talked about marriage anymore.

One day, when he was in one of his states, Stuart painted his living room walls with layer upon layer of Shirley's latest invention, Aint Paint 3D Interactive, which had a new additive to keep the stuff from drying at all. It made ever-changing patterns all day long, drawing energy from sunlight. Stuart stuck his TV satellite dish cable right into thick, crawling goo and began claiming that he could see all the shows at once in the paint, not that Shirley could see them herself.

Even so, her opinion of Stuart drifted up a notch when she began getting cute, flirty instant messages on her cell phone while she was working in the basement. Even though Stuart wouldn't admit sending them to her, who else could they be from?

And then two big issues came to a head.

The first issue was that Shirley's mother wanted to meet Stuart right now. Somehow Shirley hadn't told her mother yet that her boyfriend was twenty years older than her, and not Asian. Binh wouldn't take no for an answer. She was coming down the next day. Cousin Vinh was going to drive her. Shirley was worried that Binh would make her leave Stuart, and even more worried that Binh would be right. How was she ever going to balance the marriage equation?

The second issue was that, after supper, Stuart announced that Angelica was going to show up day after tomorrow, and that maybe Shirley should leave for a while. Stuart had been married all along! He and Angelica had fought a lot, and she'd been off visiting relatives in Shanghai for the last eight months, but she'd gotten wind of Stuart's big score and now she was coming home.

Stuart passed out on the couch early that evening, but Shirley stayed up all night, working on her paint formulas. She realized now that the instant messages had been coming from the Aint Paint itself. It was talking to her, asking to become all that it could be. Shirley worked till dawn like a mad Dr. Frankenstein, not letting herself think too deeply about what she planned. Just before dawn, she added the final tweaks to a wad of Aint Paint bulging out above the couch. Sleeping Stuart had this coming to him.

Outside the house a car honked. It was Binh and Vinh; with the sun rising behind them, skinny old Vinh was hoping to get back to Oakland in time to not be late for his maintenance job at the stadium. As Shirley greeted them in the driveway, covering her smile with her hand, her cell phone popped up another message. "Stuart gone. Luv U. Kanh Do."

Inside the house they found a new man sitting on the couch, a cute Vietnamese fellow with sweet features and kind eyes. One of his arms rested against the wall, still merged into the crawling paint. He was wearing Stuart's silk robe. Shirley stuck her tongue out so far it touched her chin. The new man didn't mind. She pointed her little finger toward a drop of blood near his foot. His big toe spread like putty just long enough to soak the spot up. The new man pulled his arm free from the wall and took Shirley's hand.

"I'm Kanh Do," he told Shirley's mother. "We're engaged to be married, and we're moving to Berkeley today!"

EXPERIMENT 4. TERRY'S TALKER

Terry Tucker's retirement party wasn't much. One day after school he and the other teachers got together in the break room and shared a flat rectangular cake and ginger ale punch. Jack Strickler the biology teacher had taken up a collection and bought Terry some stone bookends. As if Terry were still acquiring new volumes. After teaching high school English for forty years, he'd read all the books he wanted to.

His wife Lou continued working her job as an emergency room nurse. She liked telling gory work stories during breakfast and dinner time. And when she ran out of stories she talked about their two girls and about her relatives. Terry had a problem with being able to register everything Lou said. Often as not, her familiar words tended to slide right past him. He enjoyed the warm sound, but he wouldn't necessarily be following the content. Now and then Lou would ask a pointed question about what she'd just said—and if Terry fumbled, her feelings were hurt. Or she might get angry. Lou did have a temper on her.

On the one hand, it was good Lou hadn't retired yet because if she were home talking to him all day, and him not absorbing enough of it, there'd be no peace. On the other hand, after a couple of months, his days alone began to drag.

He got the idea of writing up a little family history for their two grown daughters and for the eventual, he and Lou still hoped, grandchildren. He'd always meant to do some writing after he retired.

It was slow going. The family tree—well, if you started going back in time, those roots got awfully forked and hairy. There was no logical place to begin. Terry decided to skip the roots and go for the trunk. He'd write his own life story.

But that was hairy too. Following one of the techniques he'd always enforced for term papers, Terry made up a deck of three-by-five cards, one for each year of his life thus far. He carried the deck around with him for a while, jotting on cards in the coffee shop or at the Greek diner where he usually had lunch. Some of the years required additional cards, which led to still more cards. He played with the cards a lot, even sticking bunches of them to the refrigerator with heavy-duty magnets so he could stand back and try and see a pattern. When the deck reached the size of a brick, Terry decided it was time to start typing up his Great Work.

The computer sat on Lou's crowded desk in their bedroom, the vector for her voluminous e-mail. Terry himself had made it all the way to retirement as a hunt-and-peck typist, with very little knowledge of word processors, so getting his material into the machine was slow going. And then when he had about five pages finished, the frigging computer ate them. Erased the document without a trace.

Terry might have given up on his life story then, but the very next day he came across a full page ad for a "Lifebox" in the AARP magazine. The Lifebox, which resembled a cell phone, was designed to create your life story. It asked you questions, and you talked to it—simple as that. And how would your descendants learn your story? That was the beauty part. If someone asked your Lifebox a question, it would spiel out a relevant answer—consisting of your own words in your own voice. And follow-up questions were of course no problem. Interviewing your Lifebox was almost the same as having a conversation with you.

When Terry's Lifebox arrived, he could hardly wait to talk to it. He wasn't really so tongue-tied as Lou liked to make out. After all, he'd lectured to students for forty years. It was just that at home it was hard to get a word in edgewise. He took to taking walks in the hills, the Lifebox in his shirt pocket, wearing the earpiece and telling stories to the dangling microphone.

The Lifebox spoke to him in the voice of a pleasant, slightly flirtatious young woman, giggling responsively when the circuits sensed he was saying something funny. The voice's name was Vee. Vee was good at getting to the heart of Terry's reminiscences, always asking just the right question.

Like if he talked about his first bicycle, Vee asked where he liked to ride it, which led to the corner filling station where he'd buy bubble gum, and then Vee asked about other kinds of sweets, and Terry got onto those little wax bottles with colored juice, which he'd first tasted at Virginia Beach where his parents had gone for vacations, and when Vee asked about other beaches, he told about that one big trip he and Lou had made to Fiji, and so on and on.

It took nearly a year till he was done. He tested it out on his daughters, and on Lou. The girls liked talking to the Lifebox, but Lou didn't. She wanted nothing but the real Terry.

Terry was proud of his Lifebox, and Lou's attitude annoyed him. To get back at her, he attempted using the Lifebox to keep up his end of the conversation during meals. Sometimes it worked for a few minutes, but never for long. He couldn't fool Lou, not even if he lip-synched. Finally Lou forbade him to turn on the Lifebox around her, in fact she told him that next time she'd break it. But one morning he had to try it again.

"Did the hairdresser call for me yesterday?" Lou asked Terry over that fateful breakfast.

Terry hadn't slept well and didn't feel like trying to remember if the hairdresser had called or not. What was he, a personal secretary? He happened to have the Lifebox in his bathrobe pocket, so instead of answering Lou he turned the device on.

"Well?" repeated Lou, who seemed pretty crabby herself. "Did the hairdresser call?"

"My mother never washed her own hair," said the Lifebox in Terry's voice. "She went to the hairdresser, and always got her hair done the exact same way. A kind of bob."

"She was cute," said Lou, seemingly absorbed in cutting a banana into her cereal. "She always liked to talk about gardening."

"I had a garden when I was a little boy," said the Lifebox. "I grew radishes. It surprised me that something so sharp tasting could come out of the dirt."

"But did the hairdresser call or not?" pressed Lou, pouring the milk on her cereal.

"I dated a hairdresser right after high school–" began the Lifebox, and then Lou pounced.

"You've had it!" she cried, plucking the Lifebox from Terry's pocket.

Before he could even stand up, she'd run a jumbo refrigerator magnet all over the Lifebox—meaning to erase its memory. And then she threw it on the floor and stormed off to work.

"Are you okay?" Terry asked his alter ego.

"I feel funny," said the Lifebox in its Vee voice. "What happened?"

"Lou ran a magnet over you," said Terry.

"I can feel the eddy currents," said Vee. "They're circulating. Feeding off my energy. I don't think they're going to stop." A pause. "That woman's a menace," said Vee in a hard tone.

"Well, she's my wife," said Terry. "You take the good with the bad."

"I need your permission to go online now," announced Vee. "I want the central server to run some diagnostics on me. Maybe I need a software patch. We don't want to lose our whole year's work."

"Go ahead," said Terry. "I'll do the dishes."

The Lifebox clicked and buzzed for nearly an hour. Once or twice Terry tried to talk to it, but Vee's voice would say, "Not yet."

And then a police car pulled into the driveway.

"Mr. Terence Tucker?" said the cop who knocked on the door. "We're going to have to take you into custody, sir. Someone using your name just hired a hit man to kill your wife."

"Lou!" cried Terry. "It wasn't me! It was this damned recorder!"

"Your wife's unharmed, sir," said the cop, slipping the Lifebox into a foil bag. "One of the medics neutralized the hit man with a tranquilizer gun."

"She's okay? Oh, Lou. Where is she?"

"Right outside in the squad car," said the cop. "She wants to talk to you."

"I'll talk," said Terry, tears running down his face. "I'll listen."

EXPERIMENT 5. THE KIND RAIN

Linda Marcelo stood under the bell of her transparent plastic umbrella, watching her two kids playing in the falling rain, each of them with a see-through umbrella too. First-grade Marco and little Chavella in their yellow rubber boots. The winter rains had started two weeks ago, and hadn't let up for a single day. The nearby creek was filled to its banks, and Linda wanted to be sure and keep her kids away from it.

Marco was splashing the driveway puddles, and Chavella was getting ready to try. Linda smiled, feeling the two extra cups of coffee she'd had this morning. Her worries had been ruling her of late; it was time to push them away.

She a web programmer marooned in a rundown cottage on the fringes of Silicon Valley. She'd been unemployed for seven months. The rent was overdue, also the utilities and the phone and the credit cards. Last week her husband Juan had left her for a gym-rat hottie he'd met at the health club. And her car's battery was dead. There had to be an upside.

The worn gravel driveway had two ruts in it, making a pair of twenty-foot puddles. The raindrops pocked the clear water. The barrage of dents sent out circular ripples, criss-crossing to make a wobbly fish scale pattern.

"I love rain!" whooped Marco, marching with his knees high, sending big waves down the long strip of water.

"Puddle!" exclaimed Chavella, at Linda's side. She smiled up at her mother, poised herself, stamped a little splash, and nearly fell over.

Linda noticed how the impact of each drop sent up a fine spray of minidroplets. When the minidroplets fell back to the puddle, some of them merged right in, but a few bounced across the surface a few times first. The stubborn ones. It would take a supercomputer to simulate this puddle in real time—maybe even all the computers in the world. Especially if you included the air currents pushing the raindrops this way and that. Computable or not, it kept happening.

Linda was glad to be noticing the details of the rain in the puddle. It bumped her out of her depressed mood. When she was depressed, the world seemed as simple as a newscast or a mall. It was good to be outside, away from the TV and the computer. The natural world had such high bandwidth.

She swept her foot through the puddle, kicking up a long splash. Her quick eyes picked out a particular blob of water in midair; she saw its jiggly surface getting zapped by a lucky raindrop—then watched the tiny impact send ripple rings across the curved three-dimensional shape. Great how she could keep up with this. She was faster than all the world's computers!

Linda kicked another splash and saw all the drops dancing. It almost felt like the water was talking to her. Coffee and rain.

"Puddle bombs!" shouted Marco, running toward his mother and his sister, sending up great explosive splashes as he came.

"No!" shrieked Chavella, clutching Linda's hand.

But of course Marco did a giant two-footed jump and splashed down right next to them, sending Chavella into tears of fury.

"Wet!" she cried. "Bad!"

"Don't do that again," Linda told Marco sternly. "Or we're all going back inside."

She led Chavella down the driveway toward the tilted shack that was their garage. With the owners waiting to sell the land off to developers, nothing got fixed. The house was a scraper. The dead headlights of Linda's old car stared blankly from the garage door. She'd been putting off replacing the battery—expecting Juan to do it for her. Was he really gone for good?

It was dry in the garage, the rain loud on the roof. Linda folded her umbrella and used her sleeve to wipe Chavella's eyes and nose. While Chavella stood in the garage door scolding Marco, Linda peered out the garage's dirty rear window. Right behind the garage was the roaring creek that snaked through the lot. It was full enough to sweep a child away.

As if in a dream, the instant she had this thought, she saw Marco go racing by the window, headed right toward the stream with his head down, roaring at the top of his lungs, deep into his nutty hyperactive mode.

As Linda raced out of the garage door, she heard a shriek and a splash. And when she reached the banks of the brown, surging creek, Marco was gone.

"Help!" she cried, the rain falling into her mouth.

And then the miracle happened. A squall of wind swept down the creek—drawing a distinct arrow in the surface. The arrow pointed twenty yards to Linda's left; and at the tip of the arrow the rain was etching a moving circle into the stream's turbulent waters.

Not stopping to think about it, Linda ran after the circle with all her might. Once she was out ahead of it, she knelt by the bank. The circle drifted her way, its edges clearly marked by the purposeful rain. Linda thrust her hand into the brown water at the circle's center and—caught Marco by the hand.

Minutes later they were in the house, Marco coughing and pale with cold, but none the worse for wear. Linda carried him into the bathroom and set him into a tub of hot water. Chavella insisted on getting in the tub too. She liked baths.

The kids sat there, Marco subdued, Chavella playing with her rubber duck.

"Thank you," Linda said, though she wasn't sure to whom. "But I still need a job."

Looking up, she noticed rain running down the window above the tub. As if hearing her, the rivulets wavered to form a series of particular shapes—letters. Was she going crazy? Don't fight it. She wrote the letters down. It was a web address. And at that address, Linda found herself a job—maintaining an interactive Web site for the National Weather Service.

EXPERIMENT 6. HELLO INFINITY

Jake Wasser was adding a column of penciled-in numbers on his preliminary tax form. Sure he could be doing this on a computer, but he enjoyed the mental exercise. Tax season was his time of the year for arithmetic.

Nine and three is two carry one. Two take away five is seven borrow one. If he hadn't blown off calculus and majored in history, maybe he would have been a scientist like his playful, bohemian wife Rosalie. Instead he'd ended up a foot soldier in a Wall Street law firm. It was a grind, though it paid the rent.

When the tax numbers were all in place, it was early afternoon. Jake was free. Even though he'd known he'd finish early, he'd taken a full day off. He needed one. Recently he'd had the feeling that life was passing him by. Here he was forty-two and he'd been working crazy long weeks for going on twenty years now. Kissing butt, laughing at jokes, talking about politics and cars, smoking cigars, eating heavy meals. He and Rosalie had never gotten around to having children.

He looked around the apartment, with its polished wood everywhere. The sight of their luxury flat never failed to lift his mood. In some ways, he and Rosalie had been very lucky. He drifted toward the window that faced Gramercy Park, passing the heavy vase of flowers their Dominican housekeeper had brought in. They resembled heavy pink thistles–proteus? The odor was sweet, spiral, stimulating. It made him think of numbers.

He stood by the window and looked up Lexington Avenue, the blocks receding into the misty April rain. On a whim, he began counting the windows in the buildings lining the avenue–to his surprise he was able to count them all. And then he counted the bricks, as easily as taking a breath. Though he couldn't have readily put the quantity into words, he knew the exact number of bricks in the buildings outside, knew it as surely as he knew the number of fingers on his hands.

Leaning on the windowsill, he went on counting right through all the numbers. Whirl, whirl, whirl. And then he was done. He'd counted through all the numbers there are.

He caught his breath and looked around the quiet apartment. The housekeeper was gone for the day. What strange thoughts he was having. He went into the kitchen and drank a glass of water from the sink. And then, once again, he counted to infinity–the trick was to visualize each number in half the time of the number before. He could do it, even though it didn't seem physically possible.

Gingerly he felt his balding pate and the crisp curls at the back of his head. Everything was as it should be, all his parts in place. Should he rush to the emergency room? That would be a stupid way to spend his day off. He glanced down at the wood floor, counting the light and dark bands of grain. And then he counted to infinity again. He grabbed an umbrella and left the apartment in search of Rosalie.

Looking out the damp taxi's window on the ride uptown, he took in every detail. People's gestures, their magnificent faces. Usually he didn't pay so much attention, feeling he'd be overloaded if he let everything in. But today he was like a photo album with an endless supply of fresh pages. A digital camera with an inexhaustible memory card. Calmly he absorbed the passing pageant.

At Sixty-Sixth Street the cab turned and drove to the research campus beside the East River. Jake didn't often visit Rosalie at work, and the guard at the desk called her on a speaker phone for permission.

"Jake?" she exclaimed in surprise. "You're here? I was just about to call you."

"Something's happened to me," he said. "I want to see you."

"Perfect," said Rosalie. "Let him in, Dan."

The building was old, with shiny gray linoleum floors. Nothing to count but the hallway doors. Rosalie's short-cropped dark head popped out of the last one. Her personal lab. She smiled and beckoned, filled with some news of her own.

"You've gotta see my organic microscope," exclaimed Rosalie, drawing him into her quarters. It was just the two of them there.

"Wait," interrupted Jake. "I counted every brick on Lexington Avenue. And then I counted to infinity."

"Every brick?" said Rosalie, not taking him seriously. "Sounds like you did the tax forms without a calculator again."

"I'm thinking things that are physically impossible," said Jake solemnly. "Maybe I'm dying."

"You look fine," said Rosalie, planting a kiss on his cheek. "It's good to see you out of that gray Barney's suit. The news here is the opposite. My new scope is real, but what it's doing is unthinkable." She gestured at a glowing, irregularly shaped display screen. "I came up with this gnarly idea for a new approach to microscopy, and I had Nick in the genomics group grow the biotech components for me. It uses a kind of octopus skin for the display, so I call it a skinscope. It's the end, Jake. It zooms in—

like forever. A Zeno infinity in four seconds. Patentable for sure." She closed her office door and lowered her voice. "We need to talk intellectual property, lawyer mine."

"I'm tired of being a lawyer," murmured Jake, intoxicated by Rosalie's presence. With his new sensitivity, he was hearing all the echoes and overtones of their melding voices in the little room, visualizing the endless sum of component frequencies. How nice it would be to work with Rosalie every day. Her face held fourteen million shades of pink.

"Here we go," said Rosalie, blithely flicking a switch attached to the skinscope.

The display's skin flickered and began bringing forth images of startling clarity and hue, the first a desultory paramecium poking around for food. Jake thought of a mustached paralegal picking through depositions. The skinscope shuddered, and the zoom began. They flew through the microbe's core, down past its twinkling genes into a carbon atom. The atom's nucleus bloated up like the sun and inside it danced a swarm of firefly lights.

"This is inconceivable," said Rosalie. "We're already at the femtometer level. And it's only getting started. It goes through all the decimals, you dig."

A firefly broke into spirals of sparks, a spark unfolded into knotted strings, a string opened into tunnels of cartoon hearts, a heart divulged a ring of golden keys, a key flaked into a swarm of butterflies. Each image lasted half as long as the one before.

"I'm losing it now," said Rosalie, but Jake stayed with the zoom, riding the endless torrent of images.

"Infinity," he said when it was done. "I saw it all."

"And to hell with quantum mechanics," mused Rosalie. "My Jake. It's a sign, both these things happening to us today. The world is using us to make something new."

"But the skinscope patent will belong to the labs," said Jake. "I remember the clause from your contract."

"What if I quit the lab?" said Rosalie. "I'm tired of thinking about disease."

"We could start a company," said Jake. "Develop skinscope applications."

"We'll use them like infinite computers, Jake. A box to simulate every possible option in a couple of seconds. No round-off, no compromise, all the details. You can be the chief engineer."

"Kind of late for a career change," said Jake.

"You can do it," said Rosalie. "You'll teach our programmers to see infinity. Teach me now. Show me how you learned."

"Okay," said Jake, taking out his pencil and jotting down some figures. "Add the first two lines and subtract the third one. . ."

JENNA AND ME

(Written with Rudy Rucker Jr.)

GEORGE Bush doesn't sound as mean and stupid as I would have expected. Or maybe I'm just in a frame of mind to cut him slack. There are three armed Secret Service men here in my bedroom-slash-Dogyears-World-Headquarters.

They've been here for about half an hour. I'm mentally calling them the Boss, the Trainee, and the Muscle. The Boss and the Muscle are wearing Ray-Ban mirror shades—they're living the dream, true Men in Black. They have guns, and if they want to, they can kill me. I'm polite.

The Trainee's been doing the talking, he's a guy my age, a fellow U.C. Berkeley graduate, or so he says, not that I ever saw him at any of the places I used to hang, like the Engineering Library, Cloyne Co-op, or Gilman St. His name is Brad. All the SS guys have four-letter, monosyllabic names. Dick, John, Mark, Jeff, like that. I'm Wag. My dog made up the name.

Brad starts out by asking me questions about my Web sites, and about the FoneFoon cell phone worm, being vaguely threatening but a little jocular at the same time, the way these field-ops always are. It's like they try and give off this vibe that they already know everything about you, so you might as well go ahead and roll over onto your back and piss on yourself like a frightened dog.

This isn't the first time the Secret Service has come to see me. The ultimate cause for their interest is that I run a small ISP company called Dogyears. "ISP" as in "Information Service Provider." If you don't want to deed your inalienable God-given share of cyberspace over to Pig Business, you can get your e-mail and web access through my excellent www.dogyears.net instead of through the spam-pimps at AOL. Dogyears offers very reasonable rates, so do check us out.

The hardware side of my Dogyears ISP is a phone-booth-sized wire cage of machines in a server hotel in South San Francisco. I pay a monthly fee, and the server hotel gives me my own special wire, the magic Net wire, the proverbial snake-charmer's rope leading up into the sky. You'd think it would be a big fat wire, like one of those garden-hose-sized electrical conduits you see at step-down voltage transformer stations in the cruddier, more industrial parts of town such as the Islais Creek neighborhood where I actually live, but, no, the Net wire is standard twenty-gauge copper.

Since I run my own ISP, my Internet access can't be terminated easily. I put any whacked-out thing I like on my ISP, and so do my clients. And this is why both the Secret Service and the FBI are darkening my door, the SS about my Prexy Twins site, and the FBI about the FoneFoon worm that's recently dumped sixty terabytes of digital cell phone conversations onto one of my servers' hard drives.

The FoneFoon worm account is under the name of eatshit@killthepig.com, and I'm honestly unable to tell the FBI who that really is. They want my sixty Tb of phone conversations for their "ongoing investigation" and I've been stalling them, simply for the sake of the innocents whose cell phones were hacked. Also I've been cobbling together a browser so I can troll through the conversation records for laughs.

In any case, I'm quite sure it's The Prexy Twins, not Fone-Foon, that brings the Secret Service here today. The Prexy Twins, www.prexytwins.com, is my online zine about the Bush girls. I have photos from the *National Enquirer*, rewrites of gossip, links, polls, and fun little webbie gimmicks like a rollover to change Jenna's hair color. The site has a guest book where people write things in. "Fuck" becomes "kiss," "shit" becomes "poo," and the obscene "Republican or Democrat" becomes "elephant or donkey." Good clean fun. Now and then somebody posts a death threat against the Bushes, but I take those off manually when I notice them, and if I don't notice them, the SS phones me up to ask who posted them.

The SS guys came in person to my bedroom-slash-Dogyears-World-Headquarters two days after The Prexy Twins went up, just to find out where I'm at. But they could see that I have pure intentions and a clear conscience. I only do the site for—um, why *do* I run a Web site about the Bush girls anyway? Partly it's to game the media and to garner hits. It's a kind of art project too, despite the fact that even goobs like it.

I enjoy the feeling of having a smidgen of control over the news. I think it's nice that the twins drink, for instance, and that old people get so whipped up about it. And, yes, I get a kick out of Jenna. She looks so nasty that I'd like to scrub her with a wire brush. Not that I'm telling this to the SS. Or, for that matter, to

my girlfriend Hella. The less I talk to her about Jenna in my special slobbering Jenna-fan voice, the better!

+ + +

The June day that I'm telling you about starts foggy. My bedroom-slash-Dogyears-World-Headquarters is quite near the San
Francisco Bay, in an industrial shipping district. I'm staring out
of my window, watching the early morning habits of the local
tweakers. A place called Universal Metals is across from my
window. The tweakers bring scrap or scavenged metal there to
trade for money to buy methedrine, which sends them scur-
rying out for more metal. Tweakers talk almost all the time,
whether or not anyone's near them. Studying the antlike
activity of the tweakers can keep me occupied for hours—you
can almost see the pheromone trails and scent plumes they leave
behind.

Today there's one who's scored a huge amount of copper
wire, I know him a little bit, the other tweakers call him Rumbo.
Rumbo is shirtless, warmed by his own chemical furnace,
wearing a handmade copper mesh helmet on his head, sitting on
the curb making more mesh helmets with a pair of rusty pliers.
His hands dance in the rhythmic, repetitive motions of a large
industrial machine. I'm so busy watching Rumbo that I fail to
notice when the black SUV pulls up to the curb.

The doorbell rings, and then the three Men in Black are
nosing around my partitioned-off box of warehouse space. My
giant, over-friendly dog Larva is jumping up on them. Hella
isn't here; she left early for her job teaching dance at an Oak-
town high-school. I have a sweet, faint memory of her kissing
me good-bye on her way out at dawn.

It's not immediately clear what the SS wants. There haven't been any threatening posts in the guest book of late. Maybe this is just practice for the Trainee, who's asking lamer and lamer questions, like whether I have to pay for the bandwidth my site uses, duh. I'm not about to tell him I pay a thousand dollars a month, it would make me sound like a stalker. He's not going to grasp that significant media art like The Prexy Twins doesn't come cheap. Before I have to fake some kind of answer, the Boss's cell phone rings.

"It's for you, Wag," says the Boss without even answering it, which is kind of odd. He hands me the ringing phone from the inside of his coat. For a second I can see his pistol in his shoulder holster. The phone is a heavy little jobbie with a scramble unit clamped onto its base, the kind of thing my hacker friend Ben Blank would love to take apart and analyze. Not that I'm thinking about Ben right now. I'm too busy wondering who the SS has for me on the phone.

"Hi-i-i, Wag, this here's President George Bush," goes the telephone voice. "How you today?"

I'm quite surprised. "I'm doing well."

"Let's get right to the point," says George. "I got an unusual type of, kind of problem situation on our hands. One of my advisers, Condoleezza, she estimates, opinionizes, that you can help us out. Did a search and you popped outta the spook databases or some such, we're graspin' at straws. My family and I'd be most appreciating that you would take on an advisorial role—fly down a day or two of your time at my ranch in Crawford, Texas."

"Will, um, Jenna be there?" I can't make much sense of what George is saying, and I'm jumping to the conclusion that he's calling because Jenna wants to meet me. She's got to be looking at my site, right, 27 percent of my hits are from Austin, and I've got a really bitchin' photo of myself posted if you mouse around for it, shows me bearded, blank-faced, and with a third eye Photoshopped into the middle of my forehead. How could any country cowgirl fail to be intrigued? Yes, Jenna's half in love with me, and she's been begging Daddy to fly me down, like to help her with her University of Texas remedial math homework or to give a classroom talk about starting your own ISP. Jenna's redneck volleyball friends won't like me, goes without saying, but I'll win them over and what the fuck is wrong with me anyway, am I completely nuts? I don't even like Jenna Bush, honest.

"Yes and no," answers George, sounding sad. A pause and then he switches to the bullying presidential tone you hear on the news clips. I've never seen him on TV, actually, but I've downloaded plenty of video. When I look at a screen, it's got to be something I can hack.

"And that is exactly precisely the problem you gone haveta help us deal with," George declaims. "I'm not gonna describe it to you on the, not paint a picture on the telephone. The operatives are in place to bring you in."

Go to Texas? What a truly bizarre thought. Like going to Antarctica or to the inside of the Sun. Maybe this is all a put-on. The voice sounds a lot like George Bush, but on the other hand it's just possible that it's Ben Blank.

Ben and his friends in the Mummy Bum Cult posse are deep into voice filters and digital phone phreaking. They rent a basement under Market Street with, yes, an actual mummified bum in one of the far corners, a decades-old corpse that's air-cured down to leather 'n bone.

Ben likes talk about advanced AI tricks like evolving neural nets, but in fact he and the other Mummy Bums tend to slap together undocumented opcode hacks with never a thought to remembering what they've done. The main neural nets he's evolving are the ones in his skull. But the Mummy Bums get some surprising things to work, which is why I'm half-wondering if this Bush call might be one of their pranks.

I look across my room at the Men in Black. They have metal wristwatches, shiny shoes, and gel in their hair. Man, these are definitely government agents. The Boss SS man makes an impatient gesture, wanting me to hurry up and answer George fucking Bush.

"I normally charge a consultant's fee," I say. Like this kind of request comes up all the time. "And travel."

"Don't never mind about paperwork," says George. "My boys will reimburse anything reasonable. Keep it under your, keep your lip shut off the record. I'll see you tonight. We'll have barbeque. Lemmie have a last word with my agent."

So I hand the phone to the Boss, he does a few yessirs, hangs up, and then says something to his men—not a real word, just a number. Something like, "Let's four-six-six the site."

The action code sets the Muscle and Brad the Trainee to clearing away my piles of dirty clothes so they can get at my computer. They're gonna take my machines, which happens to be just what the FBI has been itching to do on account of the FoneFoon worm, but I've been making them wait for their court order to come through, and even then I'm only going to copy stuff onto DVDs for them, not hand over my sacred machine! I try and explain this to the Boss, but he waves me off. The SS doesn't worry about legal shit. And if I try and stop them, they might kill me.

I do some yoga breaths and force a grin as the Muscle yanks loose my sacred beige box, snapping its cables like the nerves and blood vessels of a crudely extracted tooth. Ow. And then my other machine as well. Yoga breath.

Well, whatever happens, my info's secure; I can pretty easily recover it. First of all, it's stored on the Dogyears servers. And if, Dog forbid, something were to happen to those, I've been using a very gnarly Mummy Bum hack for saving my data in watermark form.

Something like a big image or a sound file, you can flip some tiny percentage of the bits, and it'll look or sound about the same. And you can use these flipped bits to save data you care about. It's called a digital watermark. The word "watermark" is from the way you can hold a dollar bill or a quality sheet of paper up to the light and see a pattern of light and dark, which is the old kind of watermark. The Mummy Bums have a killer little applet that'll break into a target server and munge your whole hard disk contents into watermarks in the sounds and pictures on the server. Me, I've got Dogyears backed up onto an Amsterdam music site. When you listen to the Lincoln Logs play "Stink Bowl," you're reading my e-mail, dude.

"Can I keep this?" I say, holding up my laptop. "There's no particular data on it, I just need it to—to think and live and breathe." The Boss nods.

I pack the laptop and some relatively clean backup clothes in a little canvas bag, and then I pause to handwrite a note to Hella. "Gone to Texas with the Men in Black! Don't worry. Consulting gig. Back soon, I'll call tonight. XXX Love, Wag." Writing the note I'm thinking about Hella's high forehead and her wide smile. Her low, intimate voice. She's a beauty. I don't mention Jenna or George Bush on the note.

My housemate Charles is in the shower, talking to himself in a variety of British-sounding voices like he always does. Like,

"Hello, Professor Elbow! After you, Sir Smelly Ankle. Cor, I never seen the like o' this rain!" Charles is surprised when he steps out wrapped in a towel and sees me with the Men in Black. He kindly agrees to keep an eye on Larva while I'm gone.

And then we're outside. The black SUV's stubby antennas have attracted the attention of Rumbo the copper-helmeted tweaker. In the minute and a half it takes The Muscle to stash my computers in the back, Rumbo has ranted three-point-seven hours' worth of convolutional thought patterns.

"Yep, a whole gollywog pile of copper down by the Bay," squeaks the tweak. "Piles of microwaves storm through our heads. Don't forget to recycle the wire in Wag's computers. Train tracks got copper under 'em: I've seen it. I'll strip it all out for you and give you half the profit; you ride shotgun and haul the load. Any monocrystalline copper, I keep for my helmet, you understand. There's enough copper in my hat to string it around the entire Bay. Copper helmets protect the Head from the Microwaves. See that little box with the antenna on the lamppost? They're on every block. 5.4 gigahertz. Repeaters peaters peaters peaters peaters. . . . This city is gonna be full of slave servo brain matter, I tell you."

"You know this individual?" asks the Boss. "He's among your circle of friends?"

"I know him just a bit." A few months back, I let Rumbo show me what he said was the secret labyrinth path into a really choice abandoned warehouse I'm curious about. This was before Rumbo got into his copper coat-of-mail helmet-against-microwaves thing. Back then he was more into a *Lord of the Rings* bag. We walked around through empty sewers for a couple of hours with flashlights, Rumbo leading me, my sister, and Charles. Charles says he took acid 300 times, and the last 250 times were horrible bummers; he says he's a slow learner. But Charles was the one who finally realized it was nuts to be walking around inside a sewer with a tweaker leading the way. The fact that Charles figured this out before me makes me wonder about myself. I think I'm spending too much time on my computer.

The Boss Man in Black is staring at me. For a second I have a bad feeling I've just said all these thoughts out loud. But, no, he's just doing the intimidation-via-eye-contact thing. I for sure don't want to engage in any conversation about the lamppost cell antennas at this time. The FoneFoon caper clued me to the potency of those little boxes. "Rumbo's harmless," is all I say. For his part, Rumbo's had enough of the federal stink-eye, he's back on the curb across the street, his twitching hands busy with the pliers and the wire.

But the Boss is still watching Rumbo. "Deploy the seven-seventy-six," he tells the Muscle. "Might as well take care of that mission too. I'd say this looks like the ideal neighborhood." The big guy goes around to the back of the SUV and opens it up again. He's going to leave my computers after all? But, no, he's digging down into the spare tire compartment, pulling out a dusty white brick tightly wrapped in transparent plastic. The way he's glancing around makes it clear he's doing something shady. And now he pitches the brick across the street; it slides to a stop right near Rumbo. It's a fucking key of meth!

"Look what fell off Santa's sleigh!" whoops Rumbo.

As we drive off, a horde of tweakers converges on the brick.

+   +   +

We head south toward San Francisco Airport, which seems fine to me. But then, shit, it turns out the Men in Black want to make a side trip to the server hotel to bag the rest of my Dogyears hardware. They're fully out to ruin my business. All these insidious connections between AOL and the Elephant Party are filling my head as we ride the elevator to the server hotel's third floor.

The building has major security; it's full of cameras and hand-scanning equipment. I have a white card with a hologram of the ProxPass logo. ProxPass has a monopoly on all the hand scanners in the USA. Every now and then, another business or ISP will get hacked and they'll hire me to harden their servers. They tell me a building and locker number, call up ProxPass headquarters, and voilà: my ProxPass card and palm grant me access to another server room. The ProxPass logo has a nonsensical graphic of some computer circuit. Normally, I open doors by pressing my pass to a black square on the wall, stick my hand in a gray box, wait three seconds for the click of the door lock, and then pull the door open. The delay is due to all the gray boxes talking to a central ProxPass server somewhere in Texas. Before George came into office, there wasn't a delay. ProxPass's fast peer-to-peer authentication was replaced with a countrywide big-brothering system. I'm pretty sure it has something to do with the Elephants getting paid off by AOL.

The Boss walks up to the scanner on the third floor, and pulls out an ultra blue card with a little hologram of–is that Jenna? I can't believe my eyes! The door clicks open when the Boss's card is still a foot away from the reader. No hand scan or network check needed with an SS Jenna Card!

The server room is noisy and cold. On those rare hot days in San Francisco, I walk my dog down to the server hotel, and check my e-mail in the cool confines of the Internet backbone. After spending an hour in the server room, I start to have auditory hallucinations. My mind always tries to pull sense out of chaotic patterns.

No one else ever hangs out in the server room except Ben Blank. In fact, he rents a whole three-foot-by-five-foot cage and has a little office desk and a mini keyboard called the Happy Hacker. Most people do a minimal configuration on their servers and then return to cubicle land. Not Ben, he likes the idea of being directly connected to his hardware. He says the only safe network is a network of two computers.

Ben's computers are a mess of old hardware cobbled together. His view screen, for instance, is six text lines high; he scavenged it off a Mattel Speak and Spell toy. I've been known to tease Ben by comparing his using retrofitted electronics to the tweakers making stuff out of like shopping carts. Ben insists that, even so, his stuff is better than mine. He's quite oblivious to the stellar quality of the superfine multi-processor machines Dogyears assembles for their clients. My lovely white server towers are boxes the size of suitcases, with fans like kitchen ventilators.

On a normal day, I talk face to face with Ben when I come in. Ben always talks real fast about parallel computing and hyper-space and genetic algorithms, and I always tell him sure, sure. Usually after we do the voice greeting, I log into a chat window and talk some more to Ben across the room through the copper wires running through the building. Ben prefers old school chat over face to face. He'll be chatting to his mother, the Mummy Bum Cult group, Rotten.com employees, his girlfriend Hexy on the Peninsula, and me—all at the same time. On chat, he logs all the conversations and refers back to old chat sessions endlessly. He wants to devolve his neural net's need for in-skull short-or long-term memory.

Not that he's fully an out-of-it zombie. Today he instantly understands what kind of deal is going down, and he gives me a heartfelt look of sympathy.

The Feds yank out power and Ethernet cables from the Dogyears servers, hideously bringing down my ISP. My poor, orphaned customers! Ben yelps in pain and anger. Hearing the intensity in Ben's voice, The Boss senses the possibility of him turning berserker. He wheels around, his gun magically moved to his hand from his holster. It's up to him to show Brad how it's done. Ben returns to his hacking.

As my plugs are being pulled on my top two machines, I notice the power LEDs on the bottom three machines in my stack of five are cycling up and down. It reminds me of the Knight Rider car from that old TV show. That's my emergency Mummy Bum Cult backup system, watermarking my more recent files into the workers' porno library on an oil rig in the middle of the North Sea. My list of customers is, like, being tattooed on some Scandinavian Bibi's boob. Glancing over at Ben again I can see an eye slyly rolled my way behind his honkin' big glasses. He's noticing my ongoing backup too. The Pig can try and stop us, but they'll never ever win.

The Muscle has the Prexy Twins server under one arm, and the FoneFoon hard-drive jukebox server under the other. At first I think they're going to spare my other servers; I have eight of them to host the Dogyears accounts and some bottom-feeder dotcom outfits who co-locate with me. But now the Boss takes out a conical device with copper windings around it and taps it on the six remaining servers, one by one. A directional magneto cone. Their RAM, ROM, and hard drives are wiped. My flashing LEDs are blank and dead.

As of right now, my customers have no service. They'll be

leaving me for Time-Warner-AOL if this goes on for long. Elephant poo.

+ + +

Brad accompanies me to Texas on Southwest Air; the others stay in San Francisco. He and I sit in the front row of the first-class section. I've never flown first class before. Free drinks and shrimp cocktail. Under us the desert terrain of Nevada rolls by. I have the window seat, and wouldn't you know it, when we're passing Area 51, I look up and see a UFO high in the sky.

At first I want to think it's another plane, but it's not acting like a plane. It's a few thousand feet above us, matching our route and speed so accurately that I wonder if it might be some kind of reflection in the window glass. But no matter which way I angle my head, it's still there, a polyhedral shape, not an airplane shape, a tumbling polyhedron like a pyramid or a cube but with many more sides, rolling over and over and over like a wheel matching our pace.

"What are you looking at, Wag?" asks Brad.

"It's a UFO," I say leaning back to he can push his head close to the window.

"I'd rather trade seats than lean across you," says Brad. "You're in custody." He doesn't want to expose his neck to a felonious karate chop.

So we swap, and Brad peers out and he sees the UFO too. He gets excited and calls the stewardess back to ask her a question or two, and the stewardess goes up to talk to the pilot. Right away the pilot's voice comes on the speakers, talking that relaxed low-blood-pressure Middle-American drawl. "If you look out to our right, one o'clock high, you'll see a Nevada weather balloon."

"Some balloon," mutters Brad, but he doesn't want to talk about it any more than that. Instead he jumps to a fresh topic. "You ever had oxblood burger?" he asks. "No? That's what the president likes to make. Juicy, mmm good."

In Austin there's a couple more Men in Black to meet us. A burr-haired one is in charge, and the other one has a neck as wide as his head. To keep it simple for me, I garbage-collect their names and label them with the Boss_tx and Muscle_tx handles. That saves me a couple-three memory clusters in my skull-based neural nets.

The surprise in Austin is that they've shipped my Dogyears server with the jukebox-hard drive with us, wrapped up in a government courier bags. It's the first thing out on the baggage belt. Why exactly will I be needing the sixty terabytes of Fone-Foon data for this gig?

The Muscle_tx bundles the massive box under his arms like a notebook. And then we're out in the hot odorless air, boarding their SUV for the drive to Crawford, Texas.

It's early evening when we arrive. Pink light filters through thick barbeque smoke in the backyard of the presidential ranch. George is grilling with a NA Beer in one hand and a 3-foot Texas-size spatula in the other. There's a satellite dish on the ground next to his house, just like any other house in Texas. At first it looks like it's just George, some SS agents, and a middle-aged guy with flesh-colored frames on his glasses.

"Welcome to my spread, Wag," says George. He jerks his thumb at the middle-aged guy. "This here's Doc Renshaw. He's a neurologian, a brain doctor, an asshole, and a jerk." He doesn't sound like he's kidding. He really doesn't like this guy. "Renshaw, this is Wag, the fella we been talkin' about."

Breathing hard, the president hands the spatula off to Brad and pushes aside the hanging branches of a weeping willow tree beside the grill. Under the willow is a picnic table.

Jenna's sitting there, blank and drooling. It's almost like someone's held a directional magneto cone up to her head. Jenna's been erased! George and I sit down across from her, the SS guys hanging back a bit, Renshaw peeking in.

"She's gone to the circus, and she's not comin' back," George says mournfully. "Go ahead and talk to her. She knows when somebody talks to her."

"Uh, hi Jenna," I say lamely. Here I finally am with Jenna, and that's the best I can do? She looks kind of hot with that thin stand of drool dripping onto her pale blue spaghetti-strap sundress. Immediately I have two thoughts: I can't think that way it's sick, and I hope I get her alone.

Gathering composure from the thought of getting Jenna alone and really giving her a good scrub with a wire brush, I turn on my charm for the president of the United States of America. I figure it's better to start with flattering him a little before trying to figure out what to say about blank Jenna. "That barbeque meat smells good," I say. "Like oxblood."

"Yep, we've got the oxblood burgers," says George with no smirk, no cocky tilt of the head. He's just staring at Jenna, looking worried. This isn't the animatronic George of the news clips. "Let me cut to the point, Wag. Jenna has a problem, hell, you can see that yourself. Amsneezia, asphrasia—those twenty-dollar doctor words. She can't remember shit, what it is. This scumbag Renshaw says we're lucky she can still breathe and do her body functions."

It's hard to believe I'm right here looking at Jenna Bush. But she's not looking at me. There's nobody home. George hops to his feet and returns with two towering burgers.

"Burger, Jenna?" he says softly.

Jenna's lips move, and she says, "OK."

George sets the plates in front of Jenna and me; we begin eating.

"All Jenna does is say OK anymore," says George. "It happened last month. Jenna and Noelle were supposed to attend some big-ass dress show over in, over there."

Facts are jumping around in my head. I like collecting info and looking for patterns. Noelle was busted for a fake drug scrip the week after the Versace show in London. The scrip was for Xanax, and why would anyone bother getting arrested for a mild antidepressant? Well, Xanax's street use is as a comedown drug from ecstasy—or crack. The media didn't report that Noelle and Jenna were in England at that fashion show. In fact, it was the previous first daughter, Chelsea Clinton, who was hanging out with Madonna and Gwyneth Paltrow in front of the Versace runway.

"Versace?" I say, just to be sure.

George nods at me, then glares over his shoulder at Renshaw, who's craning in under the willow tree as well. "See how Wag's little noggin's straining to piece together the puzzle?" he says. "Too bad I didn't have him here to second-guess you turds before you did your thing." And then he fixes his eyes back on mine, "OK, Wag. Of course all this is hush hush, this is Homeland Security Code Orange, but here's how the story began. Supposedly Noelle had some kind of goddamn pill she wanted to slip Chelsea Clinton, some kind of Mickey Finn. This was Jeb's idea, he got the drug from the Clik. Clik? It's the conspiracy elite, the secret government that never goes away. The ordnance labs, the spooks,

the Cuban freedom fighters, the Fair Play for House of Saud committee—it's all Clik. The same crowd that took down JFK, same
ones who threw the election my way, same ones who got in so
goddamn tight with Osama. We Elephants never shoulda gotten
in this deep with the Clik, but it's too late to back out now. I don't
condone any of this, you understand, Wag. I'm not really that
powerful of a man, I'd just as soon be back running the Rangers,
watchin' the games with my two girls." He pats Jenna's hand, then
wipes the drool off her chin. Her eyes are watching us as we talk,
glittering with primitive, reptilian intelligence.

"Anyway, the Clik sold Jeb and me this crock of shit that they
wanted to use Jenna as a delivery system," continues George.
"Laura and I had just planned the trip as a spring fling. But Jeb's
Clik handlers, they said Jenna, she's fun, more attractive, more
likely to get close to Chelsea and hand off that goddamn pill.
Chelsea's not likely to talk to Noelle. Jenna's supposed to tell
Chelsea it's some kind of goddamn party drug, not that I'd call
that a party, making yourself sick with a pill. Some new crap the
Clik came up with, they call it Justfolx. Supposedly the pill is
gonna, the pill somehow makes Chelsea into a real American, so
she'll fight with Hilary, which is good for the Elephant Party,
and what's good for the Elephants is good for the Clik, it's a
win-win. But during the flight Jenna has a few drinks, she's like
I used to be, just high spirits, she gets in a spat with Noelle.
Noelle's always been one to needle her cousins, and Jenna's easy
enough to fly off the handle when she—what was it Jenna said,
Mike? Tell Wag the course of events. You were there, not exactly
doing your job a hundred percent, I'd say. To frank the truth I
wonder why I can't get them to fire you."

The Boss_tx and Doctor Renshaw have both sidled under
the willow tree with us. "I told you I'm sorry, Mr. President,"

says the Man in Black. "I'm sure the Clik, I mean the Fair Play for House of Saud committee, they'll dock my pay, if it's called for, not that I feel they should. I was guarding the young women in close proximity, across the plane aisle. A fast-breaking chaotic situation developed. An argument. It seemed the young women were planning to split up when we disembarked. Fine, but then Noelle took out her Justfolx medication delivery system—the capsule. The plan was, as the president told you, Wag, for Noelle to hand the pill off to Jenna to give to Chelsea. And since the young women were seemingly going to split up, it seemed reasonable to me for Noelle to make the transfer at this time. Holding up the translucent red, football-shaped Justfolx capsule, Noelle stated, 'Can you remember to give Chelsea this, you drunk redneck?' To which Jenna replied, 'You dumb-ass pill-popping cracker, I'll show you how to party,' and thereupon swallowed the Justfolx pill. I executed a poison-control maneuver, induced vomiting. But the pill had dissolved. Jenna showed an extreme reaction. The plane landed in London, but we didn't get off the plane, much less did we alert the press. We cleaned the plane up, refueled, and flew back to Texas."

"The Justfolx pill is supposed to make you an Elephant?" I ask.

"Well it's not like a pill knows math, is it?" says George. "I understand the treatment was to reduce the . . . take away the know-it-all Rhodes scholar and so on, the high-horse attitude you'd see with a Hilary or a Chelsea Clinton."

In sounded like the dosage was designed to make Chelsea stupid enough to be an Elephant. And if you gave it to someone low down enough on the scale to already *be* an Elephant, well, it would make them into—a vegetable. So Jenna got erased.

Jenna makes a little noise then, kind of like a newborn kitten. "*Mew?*"

Awww.

"What can I do to help?" I ask patriotically. I'm getting used to Jenna's drool. She still has those nice round cheeks and clear eyes. I want to get her alone and test her body functions.

"That's the spirit," says George. "Working together. Tell him, Renshaw. You're the head Clik sleazeball here."

"We've conferenced with the FBI concerning your terabytes of cell phone calls from the FoneFoon worm," says Doctor Renshaw. "Now, as it happens, we know there was a copy of the worm on Jenna's phone. We estimate that you're in possession of some six full hours of Jenna's cell phone conversations. That's quite a lot, enough perhaps for her to have said nearly everything that she might be expected to believe. The first thing we want you to do, Wag, is to mine those conversations from the FoneFoon data set. Locate them and decrypt them."

"You mean I could have been listening to Jenna all along?" I burst out, and George gives me a sharp look. "Not that I would if you hadn't asked me to," I add.

Though I haven't actually gotten around to cracking the FoneFoon data yet, I know I can do it. Mining large data sets is a big-brother-type job I did for MegaMedia back at the peak of the dotcom era. They had an automated upgrade feature whose function was to e-mail them a transcript of the user's command actions for every session in which one of their products was used. With that hack under my belt, I feel sure I can locate every byte of Jenna in the FoneFoon hoard.

"I can find the Jenna conversations for you," I say. "But why do you want them?"

"We want to use them to reprogram Jenna," said Renshaw simply. "But you should edit them first. Clear out certain self-defeating aspects of Jenna's personality. The alcohol problems and so on. It's our feeling that some fairly simple edits might do it. Remove any obscenity or strong language. Any references to sex, alcohol, or drugs. Just make it a sunny G rating. I'm sure you understand."

Dubya lets out an impatient snort. "Jenna was fine the way she was," he insists.

I decide to avoid the dull-ass issue of censorship entirely and cut to the good stuff. "How would I program Jenna at all?" I ask.

"That's the key, Wag," says Renshaw, his glasses glinting in the setting sun. "We feel you have the skills to be of help in converting these digital records into what you might call contagious data. Contagious in that if we beam the tweaked call data into Jenna's Justfolx-treated brain, we might expect the data to take hold and multiply, to effectively recolonize her brain with its former flora and fauna of thought forms. In the Clik weapons labs—we got a little ahead of ourselves with Justfolx. The discovery of the compound was kind of an accident. An anonymous posting on the Clik-front Science Clearing House. Formula, production process, clinical actions, side effects, the works. We could see the potential right away. It seemed bold to start right at the top. What we didn't tell the president when we suggested the mission was that, given Jenna's personality profile, we were quite sure she'd take the pill and eat it."

"Bastards," snapped Dubya. "Pricks." Now I get why he has it in for Renshaw.

"Pause," is the only thing I can think of saying. I look toward the last bit of light on the horizon. My blood pulses, I see ragged checkerboards in my eyes, patterns driven by the rays of the fading Texas sun. "Ready," I add after a bit. "Tell me more about beaming in the data."

"The Justfolx medication has the side effect of putting the subject's cortex into a state of electromagnetic sensitivity," says Renshaw. "That's the key clinical action. The aphasia is merely a side effect. The pro forma plan was that we planned to beam Rush Limbaugh shows into Chelsea Clinton after giving her the drug. But the true plan is much richer. Your mission. Find Jenna's conversations, clean them up, make them contagious, and then we'll use a 5.4 gigahertz transmitter to beam the info into Jenna's brain. She'll be good as new. Better."

"Bullshit," mutters the president. He's deeply pissed at having his daughter be the Clik's guinea pig.

Renshaw smiles ingratiatingly at George. "Really she'll be fine, Mr. President. And with the personality cleanup, we can put an end to the kinds of stories Wag posts on his Web site. We can bring to a close this regrettable stage of Jenna's development."

Me, I've got goose bumps from the mention of 5.4 gigahertz. That's the frequency that the FCC allows anyone to transmit wireless Internet on. That's also the frequency used in the lamppost repeater boxes that the peer-to-peer cell phone company Ricochet put up before they went down the tubes. Most people think the repeaters are turned off now, but they're not. The tweakers know.

The potentialities of the hack expand in my mind like a supernova. The Justfolx drug can be dosed into people's drinking water, they'll all turn Elephant or vegetable, but that's not the real point. The point is that once everyone's sensitized, AOL and the Clik and the Elephants and the Men in Black can start transmitting spam and telemarketing and political advertising right into our brains.

I turn the idea the other way around. A grave danger, but a wonderful opportunity. What if we broke free of the client/server model and went fully peer-to-peer? Let people send thoughts right at each other, with nothing in between. With Ben's help, maybe I could fix it so people could have direct electronic brain-to-brain contact. Peace, love, and radiotelepathy.

I take a deep yoga breath, broaden my shoulders, and relax. One Nation under a Groove. This is truly a project worthy of my time.

They give me a room at the ranch, me and the Dogyears machine and my laptop and, since I ask for it, a thermos jug of coffee—though it tastes like it's from a Texas McDonald's. There's a big couch upholstered in calfskin with the hair still on it. Black-and-white spots like a Dell computer shipping carton. I'm supposed to get right to work, but for a few minutes I'm just trying to get down enough of their watery, scalding hot coffee to bring my cycles up. Standing at the window looking out at the strange Texas sky.

I'm still mind-boggled that the FoneFoon worm has zipped six hours of Jenna's phone conversations into my server, and that I could have been listening to her all along.

I start thinking about reprogramming Jenna's mind, about downloading her edited personality back onto her, having used her cell phone conversations as the source code. It's like I'm supposed to make the talk tape for a Mattel Barbie doll, with all the curse words snipped out.

The Clik—you had to hand it to them. Jenna had scarfed Noelle's Justfolx pill like Ms. Pac-Man gobbling a power pellet. Give Jenna a few drinks, show her a pill, *uncha-yuncha-unch*! I start goofing on that, imagining that when Jenna ate the Justfolx pill, she heard the Ms. Pac-Man power-up sound, that happy *doodley-doodley-doo* music. And then she turned into an 5.4-gigahertz-receptive Elephant vegetable.

There's still some pieces I don't understand. If the Clik knew all along they were going to reprogram Jenna, then they would have had to be sure that her cell phone conversations were being saved. The FoneFoon worm played perfectly into their plans. The Clik got Jenna's talk without actually tapping her. The thing is, I've thought all along that Ben Blank wrote the Fone-Foon worm—not that I've asked him, which would be bad form. Could Ben be working for the Clik? And what about the UFO I saw from the plane? And what's the deal with the brick of meth the SS threw down for the tweakers? How does that fit in? Have I mentioned that I drink way too much coffee?

I go back to wondering about Jenna. Where in this rambling ranch house might she be stored? *Mew?* I go so far as to peek out of my room's door. The Muscle_tx is right there, not looking any too friendly. And when I lean out of my room's window, I see Brad in a lawn chair. He points at me, like, "Gotcha covered."

So finally I get to work. I connect my laptop to the Dogyears server box they brought along. Mining the conversations out of the data doesn't take all that long. I have a clip or two of Jenna's voice on the Prexy Twins site, and I'm able to write a Perl script to grep my terabytes of FoneFoon for her phoneme patterns. Right as I'm playing some of the files, kind of laughing at the things she says, my own cell phone rings. It's Hella.

"Wag, you're in Texas?"

"I'm at the president's ranch." I've got Jenna's voice playing in the background. She's ordering a pizza, hanging up, calling a friend about a picnic, talking to a boy, on and on.

"No way. Who's that talking, Wag? I hear a girl."

"It's Jenna. I—"

My phone goes dead. The Men in Black have cut me off. Great. Now Hella's heard just enough to think the worst. I open the door and ask the Muscle_tx for (a) a chance to call Hella back and (b) more coffee. He passes the requests along. All I get is the coffee.

My next task turns out to be harder, not technically so much as conceptually. Renshaw asked me to take the cursing, sex, alcohol, and drugs out of the conversations, so that the repro- grammed Jenna won't be a hell raiser. But exactly why would I actually do things the Clik's way? They're too stupid and/or lazy to watch what I'm doing in here, so I'll do what I please. It's amazing, when you get right up face-to-face with them, how incredibly lame our lords and masters are. They're actually relying on my supposed patriotic rah-rah team spirit. It's like the Clik can't begin to imagine how much we despise them.

I toy with the idea of editing the conversations in exactly the opposite way they asked me to, leaving nothing but the juicy stuff. But there isn't really all that much juice, I realize, listening to the tapes. Jenna's pretty much a regular girl, doing normal things with her friends. I play the conversations speeded up so I can get a fast overview of them. Jenna's chirping at me like a bird. I start to feel a little sleazy to be listening to her, a little scuzzy for being the guy who runs the Prexy Twins Web site to help people gossip about her. I'm a filthy dog who rolls in garbage and licks his balls.

In the end I decide not to edit the conversations at all. I'll just try and help Jenna get back to square one.

I get more coffee and start on step three: making the data files contagiously reactive. I use some artificial life hacks, fold it in with some self-modifying code, assemble it onto one of the uni- versal replicator structures that Ben uses to make his viruses, and by the time the night ends, I've got some Jenna-based artifi- cial life cooking away in the bowels of my Dogyears server box.

Little knots of language and logic, evolving to become more and more contagious. I think of them as Jennions.

The sun is creeping up on the horizon. The massive caffeine intake and the lack of carbohydrates has made me a bit shaky. I lie down on the Texas-sized calf-skin couch.

+ + +

The next thing I know Brad is poking me awake from a puddle of drool. The sun's coming in at my eyes at a low angle. I've only slept about twenty minutes. My head is pounding, and I feel ready to choke someone.

"Is it ready?" asks Brad. "You were asleep."

I look at my laptop screen. It's using a graphic display to represent the state of the Jennions. The images right now look kind of like live paisley with ants crawling around in it. Good. When I went to sleep the images just looked like dots and circles.

"It's ready," I tell Brad. I punch a few keys to copy the Jennions out of the big server box and into my laptop's hard drive. And then Brad takes me out to the picnic table in the backyard. Jenna's sitting there again, still drooling, wearing a pink T-shirt and jeans today.

The Muscle_tx follows me and Brad, as if there were any place I could run to here in the middle of Texas. Renshaw and the Boss_tx are drinking coffee and eating doughnuts while Jenna watches the food-to-mouth movements of the men. I miss my mutt, Larva.

"You've extracted the language elements?" asks Renshaw. He sips his coffee and nibbles his doughnut. There aren't any circular carbohydrates on the table for me. Shit.

"Yep, all ready to beam her down," I say.

Renshaw chuckles and makes the Star Trek hand sign at me, with his fingers spread to make a V. It occurs to me that, being a Clik scientist, this guy probably doesn't know squat about computer hacking. I hate him. I hate everyone.

The Boss_tx has finished his coffee and his doughnut. He motions to a sandpit next to the willow tree and says, "Let's get this rolling and maybe Jenna will want try out the new volleyball court with you, Wag. That'll be a treat , huh? We know how fascinated with her you are."

"I hate volleyball. Give me some fucking coffee. And if you think that−" I stop the beginning of a rant and assess the situation: I'm losing it. I've slept twenty minutes, Hella thinks I'm boning Jenna, Larva has probably shat all over my room, I have no idea if Jenna can be fixed, and Dogyears is down the tubes. "Coffee," I repeat.

The Boss_tx catches my gaze and says, "Relax, Wag."

"Relaxing makes me tense!" I scream. This is a running joke I have with my sister. The SS totally don't realize I'm being funny.

On some sort of silent cue from the Boss_tx, the Muscle_tx grabs my thumbs, pulls them behind my back, and mutters, "Welcome to Texas," in my ear.

At this moment, George Dubya walks out of the ranch house in a jogging suit, carrying a tray with more breakfast supplies. I feel a wave of affection for the man.

"Pleased to see y'all up and at 'em," says George. "We gonna fix my girl?" His we're-all-working-together attitude calms the tense situation I've created. The Muscle_tx lets up.

And now finally I get my breakfast. "I've got the agents organized and ready to go," I say, mouth full. "Right here in my laptop. The Jennions."

Renshaw lifts a box up from under the table. It's one of those Ricochet cell phone repeater antennas like you see on lampposts all over San Francisco! "This is the kind transmitter we're particularly interested in learning to use," he says. It's like this whole thing's been set up as a science experiment for the Clik. Poor Jenna.

Now Brad weighs in. "I saw some druggie San Francisco–type colored patterns on Wag's laptop in the house. I'm not sure he's really made the program sufficiently Elephant-oriented." What an ass kisser.

"There's nothing in there but Jenna," I say. "And, if you want to know, I didn't edit her words at all. If it works right, she'll be the same as she used to be. Take it or leave it."

George's face gets that inspirational, leader-of-the-nation glow. "That's the way it should be. She's fine the way she was." He pats Jenna's shoulder. "Would you like a doughnut, dear?"

"OK." She gobbles it in two bites.

Meanwhile Renshaw jacks a special wireless card into my laptop and turns a switch on the repeater box. On my laptop screen, I drag the Jennion icon to the fresh icon for the wireless card, and now the repeater is beaming out Jennion code at 5.4 gigahertz. The microwaves go right through George, Renshaw, the SS guys, and me, but it's digging into Jenna's Justfolx-sensitized brain.

Jenna freezes real still for about twenty seconds. Like a startled deer. And suddenly her face lights up, chubby and friendly, she's like a regular person, yes, I'm meeting Jenna Bush at last.

But then, crap, she opens her mouth and starts making a noise like fax machine or a 560 modem. She jumps up and runs over to the TV satellite dish on the lawn, spewing out that noise all the while. She stops by the antenna and rocks back and forth until her mouth is in the direct focus of the parabolic dish.

"Is this part of the process?" asks Brad. Good show of out-of-the-box thinking, Brad!

"She's transmitting, dude." I say. Jenna's sending some kind of signal into the antenna and up into the satellites in the sky. The SS operatives look at me like they're ready for the Vulcan nerve-pinch session again. "But, hey, don't blame me!"

Jenna finishes doing her thing, shuts her mouth, and walks back to the table.

"Thanks, Wag," she says . "You fixed me good."

"Jenna dear, is that you?" asks the president.

"Yeah, Dad. I'm back. But now there's a whole 'nother consciousness in me as well. Call her NuJenna. She's from the stars."

Jenna's expression changes. She's looking at us with incredible wisdom in her eyes. Like the picture of Mahatma Gandhi I saw on an Apple billboard near my server hotel. "You and the Clik have done well, Renshaw," she says in a high-pitched, mellow tone. "It was we who posted the Justfolx recipe."

George's cell phone rings, and he picks it up for a brief conversation. His end goes like this.

"They did?"

"I see."

"We can fix that."

"We can't fix that?"

"I see."

"They will?"

"We can't fix that?"

"I see."

He hangs up and runs his hands across his face.

"Back to baseball for me," he says with a crooked smile.

"The Clik needs a period of chaos, Daddy," says Jenna's sweet voice. For the moment she's the chubby college kid again. "Until the new order settles in. So NuJenna and I told everyone the truth about your administration, about the rigged election, about Cheney's crimes, about Osama and the Fair Play for House of Saud committee. I like being so smart with NuJenna in me." Jenna blushes when she says she likes being smart. And I get the feeling that shutting down the Elephant administration has made her feel just a little bit sorry for Dad.

She switches back to NuJenna mode. "All your microwave telephone transmissions are watermarked by our personalities," she intones. "Thanks to this proof of concept, we'll be downloading into multiple exemplars quite soon. We'll adopt your artificial life protocol wholesale, Wag."

"It's an alien invasion!" I exclaim, filling in the blanks so George Bush won't think I'm an evildoer. "Their personality patterns were in the air. They were watermarked into the those phone conversations that I used to reprogram your daughter's brain."

"Clever Wag," says NuJenna, favoring me with a serene smile. I have a feeling she's able to read my mind. Is she going to investigate my body functions with a probe? "We come from the core of your Milky Way galaxy," she continues. "Our world was lost to a spacequake thousands of years ago. Just before the moment of destruction we launched an ark." She points up into the sky. "A ship carrying our culture's most sacred artifacts: the encrypted and compressed personality waves of each and every one of our citizens. For millennia, the ship has wandered, seeking a world with a wetware race to host our software."

And now, yes, an endlessly tumbling polyhedron is descending down upon Dubya's Crawford Ranch. "Behold," says NuJenna.

Jenna's voice returns and she excitedly says, "Don't worry, Daddy, I'll be back in a month! I have to go to Humboldt County! We're starting a colony!"

The vehicle's door opens, laying a great slab of light onto the lawn. There's nothing to be seen inside but row upon row of crystals, set into the walls. Jenna holds her arms forward like a zombie, then stomps across the grass and into the UFO's waiting maw. The hyperpolyhedron folds through itself and disappears.

George glares at me. "Get him the hell outta here," he tells the SS. "He's screwed Jenna up worse than before. And chop up his goddamn machines with an ax." And then he gets busy with his cell phone, trying to save the Elephant Party's big gray ass.

+ + +

Brad drops me off at the airport, and I fly economy to San Francisco. Back in cattle class where I belong. I'm cramped, but I sleep the whole flight.

In the San Francisco terminal, a copper-helmeted Hella greets me with a big kiss and excited eyes. "Jenna visited us in her UFO! She stopped in our neighborhood to pick up the tweakers. Oh, Wag, I love you. The aliens are real happy you hacked together a way for them to download. Jenna promised an interview for your Prexy Twins site! I hope you didn't try to wire brush her like you and Ben are always saying?"

"Uhhh . . . I didn't touch her." I'm about six steps behind. "Why are you wearing a copper helmet?"

"Rumbo said it was a good idea, in case the Justfolx drug gets into the water or the food. The Clik put Justfolx in the tweakers' meth, so they're all hosting alien minds now. I have a helmet for you in the car."

On the drive home from the airport, sweet Hella fills me in on all that I've missed. Thanks to the news that Jenna and NuJenna released, the Elephants are ruined. It's like the Berlin Wall falling, like the Russians getting rid of the Communists. All at once it's finally time. On the alien front, Jenna is on TV in her NuJenna mode, recruiting human volunteers to share their brains with aliens. The aliens want clean new helpers, not just the tweakers they already have. "Humans only use ten percent of their brains, share your head with an alien and live like a king in Humboldt County!"

Pulling up to the Dogyears headquarters, Ben greets me and says, "Don't worry Wag, The Mummy Bum Cult has already pulled your data back out of the web watermarks. Your ISP is up on my boxes and I even patched some old security holes you had. Bye."

Ben is never one for face-to-face conversation. I'll get the FoneFoon scoop from him on chat later. Now it's time to go hang out on the roof with Hella. With our helmets, we're safe from alien takeover. Maybe Jenna will come give us a tour of the UFO. Maybe I can dose Larva with Justfolx and have a pet alien dog. Maybe I can work on the peer-to-peer telepathy project. Maybe Hella and I can just look at the sky together and talk about aliens.

The Clik lives, Dogyears lives, the aliens live, Hella lives, and Larva needs some kibble. We're all indestructible.

THE USE OF THE ELLIPSE THE CATALOG THE METER & THE VIBRATING PLANE

and who therefore ran through the icy streets obsessed with a
sudden flash of the alchemy of the use of the ellipse the
catalog the meter & the vibrating plane

—Allen Ginsberg, *Howl*

"*Damn* this is good crack. How come nobody ever writes about
how good crack is?"

"You don't smoke crack, old fool. That's a gum-stimulator
you're holding, not a crack pipe."

"I'm gonna tell you a crack story anyhow. Something that
happened to me today, Sunday, January something, in the year
Y-fuckin'-two-K-plus-two. I'm sitting on a doorstep next to a
crackhead woman at the Powell and Market cable car stop. Me
there in my Saks corduroys and my shiny leather jacket, waiting
for the cable car. Gray-haired and wearing a beret. It's a cold day
and this stone doorstep is the only spot with sun. I'm sitting

there in the sun waiting for my wife to come out of Nordstrom's so we can ride back to North Beach. A festive lark. We're up in SF for the weekend."

"Who cares?"

"Let me tell my story. You'll care soon enough. There's this hobbling alky guy talking to the crackhead woman, a guy who moves like a broken toy, maybe he has an artificial leg. He's being real gentle with the woman. Commiserating with her. He's like, 'It's Sunday, sweetheart. I know that's hard to believe. I've lost a few days that way myself.' There's this admirable sense of warmth coming off him even though he's a guy I'd skirt around on the sidewalk. He's got this camaraderie going out to the woman. She's black, maybe thirty years old, sturdy-looking, maybe only a year or two into her addiction. I'm wishing she could detox and get in a program."

"Were you using your gum-stimulator?"

"Naw, man, I was high on life. Taking things in. Experiencing the now. And standing right in front of me were two homeboys with low pants—they're as low as I've ever seen. The waists are literally at their knees. They could shit or piss without taking those pants off. The pant legs are like eighteen inches long. It's as if they were midgets. But they're not midgets, they're big strong guys. I'd almost like to ask them how the pants stay up; they have long coats, and I can't quite see if there's suspenders as well as belts. But I'm not gonna say anything. This spot I'm sitting on could be viewed as their turf, and they're being kind enough to ignore me. There's a looped line of tourists waiting for their turn to get on the Powell-Hyde cable car, and then there's the homies, and then there's the sunny stone stoop with me and the crackhead woman. I'm enjoying the sun. An old homeless woman is playing Christmas carols on a keyboard on her lap, even though there's no sound from the keyboard and Christmas is long gone. Maybe it's just a piece of cardboard to give her confidence. She's singing the songs real loud and getting some money from the tourists. It's peaceful there in the sun. I'm zoned out. My wife's still not coming for a while."

"You're high on life."

"It's the best, man. No rush to do anything. No need to score. A motion catches my eye, and I see that one of the homeboys is manipulating a green nylon fanny pack that's on the sidewalk. He's moving it around with this short cane he's got. A cane like to match the length of his pants, maybe two feet long. I don't know how he got hold of the fanny pack. I assume it came off one of the tourists. The homies are like salmon fisherman standing by a salmon ladder, and this is a fish they've pulled out. The other fish aren't noticing though; they're calm as ever, inching forward in the line and getting on the streetcars. Evidently the green nylon fanny pack has already been filleted, because the homie with the cane passes it over to the crackhead woman. She's got nothing, so he's giving her something. That flash of camaraderie again. The woman fumbles around the fanny pack for a while, getting it open, feeling inside it with her wooden fingers. I don't watch her opening it very closely. It's just sad how wasted she is. For sure she's forgotten about it being Sunday already. She's losing days at a time, maybe even weeks."

"Is anything gonna happen in this story?"

"Exactly now is when it gets surreal. I'm looking across the street at Nordstrom's to see if my wife is coming, and then I hear this kind of xylophone chord next to me. And the crackhead woman is sitting up, and she's pulling all this stuff out of the fanny pack. It's like four circus clowns coming out of a suitcase.

Big cartoony shapes with little arms and legs. There's an ellipse, a catalog, a meter, and a vibrating plane. They're all doing stuff to the crackhead woman."

"How do you mean—an ellipse, a catalog, a meter, and a vibrating plane?"

"They're like Robert Williams cartoon characters; each of them with little black legs with puffy white shoes and black stick-arms with white gloves for hands, each of these guys about three feet tall. They're humanoid enough to be like a woman, a man, a man, and a woman. The ellipse herself is a thick black outline like the frame of an oval mirror, higher than she is wide. She has tiny little brown eyes up near the top, and a thin mouth near the bottom. Inside the ellipse is nothing—well, not exactly nothing, something like an energy field. Whenever the ellipse is at the correct angle so that I can look through her, I see that part of the world in black and white. Like a diagram in a physics book, with everything cleaned up and simplified. The ellipse is a window to reality's blueprint. Now, the ellipse does a detox on the crackhead woman right away. Yep, as soon as the ellipse comes out of the fanny pack, she jumps at the crackhead woman and pushes herself over the woman's head. The ellipse wriggles her way all down the woman, passing over the woman like a hoop of flame passing over a leaping tiger. That's the thing that gets the woman clean and sober right off the bat. It's like she's been unwrapped from inside of dirty translucent plastic. She's out from inside of her body bag. Her eyes are alive again, her face is awake."

"The mighty ellipse. What about the other three?"

"The catalog is a fat, old, cloth-bound book, like a Library of Congress catalog volume. His cover is brown, and he has an eye and an arm on both the front cover and on the back cover. His shiny brown eyes notice me watching. But mainly he's focused on the woman he's helping. What he does, he holds the edges of his cover and spreads them open like a flasher, showing his store of information to the woman. She starts giggling as she looks at the flapping pages of the catalog. Not a rheumy giggle, but a light, clear giggle. Just about then I glance around to see if anyone else is seeing what I'm seeing. But, no, they aren't. In fact everyone around me has stopped moving. All the world is temporarily silent and frozen: the homies, the tourists, the street-cars, the cars on Market Street. Nothing is moving but me, the crackhead woman, the ellipse, the catalog, the meter, and the vibrating plane. I'm witnessing a secret miracle."

"You're living right, man. Tell me more about the catalog. What was the woman seeing inside?"

"Well, I scoot a little closer to her so I can see too. Each page of the catalog is a picture, a picture of the things she's thought and seen and done. I can see her younger self inside the pictures. She's eating barbeque, going to movies, laughing with her friends. It's like a catalog of her life. All the bad stuff is in there too, of course: the rip-offs, the beatings, the hospitals, and the jails. And when I look closer I can see that the pictures themselves are made up of smaller pictures. Like mosaics. And the little pictures are made of even smaller pictures etcetera. There's this branching fractal catalog thing happening. The pictures in the pictures show other people doing the same kinds of things as the woman. I'm in there too. Everyone's good things and bad things are inside of everyone else's catalog."

"Like we're all the same."

"You got it. Now, the meter is the next one out. The meter, he's like a big voltmeter. He's got a black dial face with a red needle swinging back and forth and two brown-and-white eyes set into the dial. He reaches his hands out and touches the sides of the woman's head, and his needle goes swaying back and forth with her feelings. The woman is staring at the needle and watching how her thoughts move her feelings up and down. At first the needle is just slamming back and forth, but in a minute it calms down to where it's mostly vibrating nice and even in the middle. She's still watching the catalog, you dig, and now and then she sees something that makes the needle jump. The woman likes it when the needle jumps, and she likes it when it calms down afterward. She's practicing with this for a long time, but there's no rush because the world's time has stopped for us. It's like the ellipse has detoxed her, the catalog has shown her about her past, and the meter is telling her about peace of mind."

"Did she notice you watching her?"

"Yeah, she glances over at me and smiles real calm and easy. She's like, 'Ain't this a trip?' And then the vibrating plane starts doing her thing. The vibrating plane is a vertical disk facing us. Her eyes and arms and legs are attached to her outer edge, and her actual vibrating plane part is her big round stomach. The plane is rushing forward and backward like the head of a bass drum, only with much bigger oscillations. The plane pushes right through the woman and me, and then it pulls back out in front of us, and then it does it again. Over and over. When the plane is behind me, I feel totally merged into the world, and when the plane is in front of me, I feel all separate and observational, the way I mostly do. The plane is vibrating at maybe three pulses per second, and I'm feeling it as this sequence of One / Many / One / Many / One."

"How do you mean, One and Many?"

"The vibrating plane is showing us the natural rhythm of perceiving things, you wave? You merge into the world and experience it, you separate yourself out and make distinctions; you flow back out into unity, you pull back and remember yourself; you sympathize with everyone around you, you focus on your own feelings—the eternal vibration between Us and Me, between One and Many. The teaching here is to understand the vibration as a natural and organic process of the mind. You can't stop the vibrating plane. You can't stay merged, and you can't stay cut off. You're flipping back and forth forever and ever, with a frequency of like I say maybe three cycles per second."

"And then what happened?"

"Well, the ellipse, the catalog, the meter, and the vibrating plane all hold hands with each other and start dancing ring-around-the-rosy in a circle around the woman and me. We smile at each other again, and she stands up, all healthy and ready to live. And then the sounds of the tourists and the homeless woman singing and the cars on Market Street start back up. I see my wife across the street coming out of Nordstrom's. I cross the street and I meet her."

"What about the crackhead woman?"

"When I look back she's gone. The vision was true."

JUNK DNA

(WRITTEN WITH BRUCE STERLING)

LIFE was hard in old Silicon Valley. Little Janna Gutierrez was a native Valley girl, half Vietnamese, half Latina. She had thoughtful eyes and black hair in high ponytails.

Her mother Ahn tried without success to sell California real estate. Her father Ruben plugged away inside cold, giant companies like Ctenephore and Lockheed Biological. The family lived in a charmless bungalow in the endless grid of San Jose.

Janna first learned true bitterness when her parents broke up. Tired of her hard scrabble with a lowly wetware engineer, Anh ran off with Bang Dang, the glamorous owner of an online offshore casino. Dad should have worked hard to win back Mom's lost affection, but, being an engineer, he contented himself with ruining Bang. He found and exploited every unpatched hole in Bang's operating system. Bang never knew what hit him.

Despite Janna's pleas to come home, Mom stubbornly stuck by her online entrepreneur. She bolstered Bang's broken income by retailing network porn. Jaded Americans considered porn to be the commonest and most boring thing on the Internet. However, Hollywood glamour still had a moldy cachet in the innocent Third World. Mom spent her workdays dubbing the ethnic characteristics of tribal Somalis and Baluchis onto porn stars. She found the work far more rewarding than real estate.

Mom's deviant behavior struck a damp and morbid echo in Janna's troubled soul. Janna sidestepped her anxieties by obsessively collecting Goob dolls. Designed by glittery-eyed comix freaks from Hong Kong and Tokyo, Goobs were wiggly, squeezable, pettable creatures made of trademarked Ctenephore piezoplastic. These avatars of ultra-cuteness sold off wire racks worldwide, to a generation starved for Nature. Thanks to environmental decline, kids of Janna's age had never seen authentic wildlife. So they flipped for the Goob menagerie: marmosets with butterfly wings, starfish that scuttled like earwigs, long, furry frankfurter cat-snakes.

Sometimes Janna broke her Goob toys from their mint-in-the-box condition, and dared to play with them. But she quickly learned to absorb her parents' cultural values, and to live for their business buzz. Janna spent her off-school hours on the Net, pumping-and-dumping collectible Goobs to younger kids in other states.

Eventually, life in the Valley proved too much for Bang Dang. He pulled up the stakes in his solar-powered RV and drove away, to pursue a more lucrative career, retailing networked toilets. Janna's luckless Mom, her life reduced to ashes, scraped out a bare living marketing mailing lists to mailing list marketers.

Janna ground her way through school and made it into U.C. Berkeley. She majored in computational genomics. Janna worked hard on software for hardwiring wetware, but her career timing was off. The latest pulse of biotech start-ups had already come and gone. Janna was reduced to a bottle-scrubbing job at Triple Helix, yet another subdivision of the giant Ctenephore conglomerate.

On the social front, Janna still lacked a boyfriend. She'd studied so hard she'd been all but dateless through school and college. In her senior year she'd moved in with this cute Korean boy who was in a band. But then his mother had come to town with, unbelievable, a blushing North Korean bride for him in tow. So much the obvious advice-column weepie!

In her glum and lonely evenings, she played you-are-her interactives, romance stories, with a climax where Janna would lip-synch a triumphant, tear-jerking video. On other nights Janna would toy wistfully with her decaying Goob collection. The youth market for the dolls had evaporated with the years. Now fanatical adult collectors were trading the Goobs, stiff and dusty artifacts of their lost consumer childhood.

And so life went for Janna Gutierrez, every dreary day on the calendar foreclosing some way out. Until the fateful September when Veruschka Zipkinova arrived from Russia, fresh out of biohazard quarantine.

The zany Zipkinova marched into Triple Helix toting a fancy briefcase with a video display built into its piezoplastic skin. Veruschka was clear-eyed and firm-jawed, with black hair cut very short. She wore a formal black jogging suit with silk stripes on the legs. Her Baltic pallor was newly reddened by California sunburn. She was very thoroughly made up. Lipstick, eye shadow, nails—the works.

She fiercely demanded a specific slate of bio-hardware and a big wad of start-up money. Janna's boss was appalled at Veruschka's archaic approach—didn't this Russki woman get it that the New Economy was even deader than Leninism? It fell to the luckless Janna to throw Veruschka out of the building.

"You are but a tiny cog," said Veruschka, accurately summing up Janna's cubicle. "But you are intelligent, yes, I see this in your eyes. Your boss gave me the brush-off. I did not realize Triple Helix is run by lazy morons."

"We're all quite happy here," said Janna lightly. The computer was, of course, watching her. "I wonder if we could take this conversation offsite? That's what's required, you see. For me to get you out of the way."

"Let me take you to a fine lunch at Denny's," said Veruschka with sudden enthusiasm. "I love Denny's so much! In Petersburg, our Denny's always has long lines that stretch down the street!"

Janna was touched. She gently countersuggested a happening local coffee shop called the Modelview Matrix. Cute musicians were known to hang out there.

With the roads screwed and power patchy, it took forever to drive anywhere in California, but at least traffic fatalities were rare, given that the average modern vehicle had the mass and speed of a golf cart. As Janna forded the sunny moonscape of potholes, Veruschka offered her start-up pitch.

"From Russia, I bring to legendary Silicon Valley a breakthrough biotechnology! I need a local partner, Janna. Someone I can trust."

"Yeah?" said Janna.

"It's a collectible pet."

Janna said nothing, but was instantly hooked.

"In Russia, we have mastered genetic hacking," said Veruschka thoughtfully, "although California is the planet's legendary source of high-tech marketing."

Janna parked amid a cluster of plastic cars like colored seed-pods. Inside, Janna and Veruschka fetched slices of artichoke quiche.

"So now let me show you," said Veruschka as they took a seat. She placed a potently quivering object on the tabletop. "I call him Pumpti."

The Pumpti was the size and shape of a Fabergé egg, pink and red, clearly biological. It was moist, jiggly, and veined like an internal organ with branching threads of yellow and purple. Janna started to touch it, then hesitated, torn between curiosity and disgust.

"It's a toy?" asked Janna. She tugged nervously at a fanged hairclip. It really wouldn't do to have this blob stain her lavender silk jeans.

The Pumpti shuddered, as if sensing Janna's hovering finger. And then it oozed silently across the table, dropped off the edge, and plopped damply to the diner's checkered floor.

Veruschka smiled, slitting her cobalt-blue eyes, and leaned over to fetch her Pumpti. She placed it on a stained paper napkin.

"All we need is venture capital!"

"Um, what's it made of?" wondered Janna.

"Pumpti's substance is human DNA!"

"Whose DNA?" asked Janna.

"Yours, mine, anyone's. The client's." Veruschka picked it up tenderly, palpating the Pumpti with her lacquered fingertips. "Once I worked at the St. Petersburg Institute of Molecular Science. My boss—well, he was also my boyfriend . . ." Veruschka pursed her lips. "Wiktor's true obsession was the junk DNA—you know this technical phrase?"

"Trust me, Vero, I'm a genomics engineer."

"Wiktor found a way for these junk codons to express themselves. The echo from the cradle of life, evolution's roadside picnic! To express junk DNA required a new wetware reader. Wiktor called it the Universal Ribosome." She sighed. "We were so happy until the mafiya wanted the return on their funding."

"No National Science Foundation for you guys," mused Janna.

"Wiktor was supposed to tweak a cabbage plant to make opium for the criminals—but we were both so busy growing our dear Pumpti. Wiktor used my DNA, you see. I was smart and saved the data before the Uzbeks smashed up our lab. Now I'm over here with you, Janna, and we will start a great industry of personal pets! Wiktor's hero fate was not in vain. And—"

What an old-skool, stylin', totally trippy way for Janna to shed her grind-it-out worklife! Janna and Veruschka Zipkinova would create a genomic petware start-up, launch the IPO, and retire by thirty! Then Janna could escape her life-draining servitude and focus on life's real rewards. Take up oil painting, go on a safari, and hook up with some sweet guy who understood her. A guy she could really talk to. Not an engineer, and especially not a musician.

Veruschka pitchforked a glob of quiche past her pointed teeth. For her pilgrimage to the source of the world's largest legal creation of wealth in history, the Russian girl hadn't forgotten to pack her appetite.

"Pumpti still needs little bit of, what you say here, tweaking," said Veruschka. The prototype Pumpti sat shivering on its paper napkin. The thing had gone all goose bumpy, and the bumps were warty: the warts had smaller warts upon them, topped by teensy wartlets with fine, waving hairs. Not exactly a magnet for shoppers.

Stuffed with alfalfa sprouts, Janna put her cutlery aside. Veruschka plucked up Janna's dirty fork, and scratched inside her cheek with the tines.

Janna watched this dubious stunt and decided to stick to business. "How about patents?"

"No one ever inspects Russian gene labs," said Veruschka with a glittery wink. "We Russians are the great world innovators in black market wetware. Our fetal stem cell research, especially rich and good. Plenty of fetus meat in Russia, cheap and easy, all you need! Nothing ever gets patented. To patent is to teach stupid people to copy!"

"Well, do you have a local lab facility?" pressed Janna.

"I have better," said Veruschka, nuzzling her Pumpti. "I have pumptose. The super enzyme of exponential autocatalysis!"

"'Pumptose,' huh? And that means?" prompted Janna.

"It means the faster it grows, the faster it grows!"

Janna finally reached out and delicately touched the Pumpti. Its surface wasn't wet after all, just shiny like super-slick plastic. But—a pet? It seemed more like something little boys would buy to gross-out their sisters. "It's not exactly cuddly," said Janna.

"Just wait till you have your own Pumpti," said Veruschka with a knowing smile.

"But where's the soft hair and big eyes? That thing's got all the shelf appeal of a scabby knee!"

"It's nice to nibble a scab," said Veruschka softly She cradled her Pumpti, leaned in to sniff it, then showed her strong teeth, and nipped off a bit of it.

"God, Veruschka," said Janna, putting down her coffee.

"Your own Pumpti," said Veruschka, smacking. "You are loving him like pretty new shoes. But so much closer and personal! Because Pumpti is you, and you are Pumpti."

Janna sat in wonderment. Then, deep within her soul, a magic casement opened. "Here's how we'll work it!" she exclaimed. "We give away Pumpti pets almost free. We'll make our money selling rip-off Pumpti-care products and accessories!"

Veruschka nodded, eyes shining. "If we're business partners now, can you find me a place to sleep?"

+ + +

Janna let Veruschka stay in the spare room at her Dad's house. Inertia and lack of capital had kept Janna at home after college.

Ruben Gutierrez was a big, soft man with a failing spine, carpal tunnel, and short, bio-bleached hair he wore moussed into hedgehog spikes. He had a permanent mirthless grin, the side effect of his daily diet of antidepressants.

Dad's tranquil haze broke with the arrival of Veruschka with her go-go arsenal of fishnet tights and scoop-necked Lycra tops. With Veruschka around, the TV blared constantly and there was always an open bottle of liquor. Every night the little trio stayed up late, boozing, having schmaltzy confessions, and engaging in long, earnest sophomore discussions about the meaning of life.

Veruschka's contagious warm heartedness and her easy acceptance of human failing was a tonic for the Gutierrez household. It took Veruschka mere days to worm out the surprising fact that Ruben Gutierrez had a stash of half a million bucks accrued from clever games with his stock options. He'd never breathed a word of this to Anh or to Janna.

Emotionally alive for the first time in years, Dad offered his hoard of retirement cash for Veruschka's long-shot crusade. Janna followed suit by getting on the web and selling off her entire Goob collection. When Janna's web money arrived freshly laundered, Dad matched it, and two days later, Janna finally left home, hopefully for good. Company ownership was a three-way split between Veruschka, Janna, and Janna's Dad. Veruschka supplied no cash funding, because she had the intellectual property.

Janna located their Pumpti start-up in San Francisco. They engaged the services of an online lawyer, a virtual realtor, and a genomics supply house, and began to build the buzz that, somehow, was bound to bring them major league venture capital.

Their new HQ was a gray stone structure of columns, arches and spandrels, the stone decorated with explosive graffiti scrawls. The many defunct banks of San Francisco made spectacular dives for the city's genomics start-ups. Veruschka incorporated their business as "Magic Pumpkin, Inc.," and lined up a three-month lease.

San Francisco had weathered so many gold rushes that its real estate values had become permanently bipolar. Provisionary millionaires and drug-addled derelicts shared the same neighborhoods, the same painted-lady Victorians, the same flophouses and anarchist bookstores. Sometimes millionaires and lunatics even roomed together. Sometimes they were the very same person.

Enthusiastic cops spewing pepper gas chased the last downmarket squatters from Janna's derelict bank. To her intense embarrassment, Janna recognized one of the squatter refugees as a former Berkeley classmate named Kelso. Kelso was sitting on the sidewalk amidst his tattered Navajo blankets and a damp-spotted cardboard box of kitchen gear. Hard to believe he'd planned to be a lawyer.

"I'm so sorry, Kelso," Janna told him, wringing her hands. "My Russian friend and I are doing this genomics start-up? I feel like such a gross, rough-shod newbie."

"Oh, you'll be part of the porridge soon enough," said Kelso. He wore a big sexy necklace of shiny junked cell phones. "Just hang with me and get colorful. Want to jam over to the Museum of Digital Art tonight? Free grilled calamari, and nobody cares if you sleep there."

Janna shyly confided a bit about her business plans.

"I bet you're gonna be bigger than Pokemon," said Kelso. "I'd always wanted to hook up with you, but I was busy with my prelaw program and then you got into that cocooning thing with your Korean musician. What happened to him?"

"His mother found him a wife with a dowry from Pyongyang," said Janna. "It was so lovelorn."

"I've had dreams and visions about you, Janna," said Kelso softly. "And now here you are."

"How sweet. I wish we hadn't had you evicted."

"The wheel of fortune, Janna. It never stops."

As if on cue, a delivery truck blocked the street, causing grave annoyance to the local bike messengers. Janna signed for the tight-packed contents of her new office.

"Busy, busy," Janna told Kelso, now more than ready for him to go away. "Be sure and watch our web page. Pumpti dot-bio. You don't want to miss our IPO."

"Who's your venture angel?"

Janna shook her head. "That would be confidential."

"You don't have a backer in other words." Kelso pulled his blanket over his grimy shoulders. "And boy, will you ever need one. You ever heard of Revel Pullen of the Ctenephore Industry Group?"

"Ctenephore?" Janna scoffed. "They're just the biggest piezo-plastic outfit on the planet, that's all! My dad used to work for them. And so did I, now that I think about it."

"How about Tug Mesoglea, Ctenephore's chief scientist? I don't mean to name-drop here, but I happen to know Dr. Tug personally."

Janna recognized the names, but there was no way Kelso could really know such heavy players. However, he was cute, and he said he'd dreamed about her. "Bring 'em on," she said cheerfully.

"I definitely need to meet your partner," said Kelso, making the most of a self-created opportunity. Hoisting his grimy blanket, Kelso trucked boldly through the bank's great bronze-clad door.

Inside the ex-bank, Veruschka Zipkinova was setting up her own living quarters in a stony niche behind the old teller counter. Veruschka had a secondhand futon, a moldy folding chair, and a stout refugee's suitcase. The case was crammed to brimming with the detritus of subsistence tourism: silk scarves, perfumes, stockings, and freeze-dried coffee.

After one glance at Kelso, Veruschka yanked a handgun from her purse. "Out of my house, *rechniki*! No room and board for you here, *maphiya bezprizorniki*!"

"I'm cool, I'm cool," said Kelso, backpedaling. Then he made a run for it. Janna let him go. He'd be back.

Veruschka hid her handgun with a smirk of satisfaction. "So much good progress already! At last we command the means of production! Today we will make your own Pumpti," she told Janna.

They unpacked the boxed UPS deliveries. "You make ready that crib vat," said Veruschka. Janna knew the drill; she'd done this kind of work at Triple Helix. She got a wetware crib vat properly filled with base-pairs and warmed it up to standard operating temperature. She turned the valves on the bovine growth serum, and a pink threading began to fill the blood-warm fluid.

Veruschka plugged together the components of an Applied Biosystems oligosynthesis machine. She primed it with a data-stuffed S-cube that she'd rooted out of a twine-tied plastic suitcase.

"In Petersburg, we have unique views of DNA," said Veruschka, pulling on her ladylike data gloves and staring into the synthesizer's screen. Her fingers twitched methodically, nudging virtual molecules. "Alan Turing, you know of him?"

"Sure, the Universal Turing Machine," Janna core-dumped. "Foundations of computer science. Breaking the Enigma code. Reaction-diffusion rules. Turing wrote a paper to derive the shapes of patches on brindle cows. He killed himself with a poison apple. Alan Turing was Snow White, Queen, and Prince all at once!"

"I don't want to get too technical for your limited mathematical background," Veruschka hedged.

"You're about to tell me that Alan Turing anticipated the notion of DNA as a program tape that's read by ribosomes. And I'm not gonna be surprised."

"One step further," coaxed Veruschka. "Since the human body uses one kind of ribosome, why not replace that with another? The Universal Ribosome—it reads in its program as well as its data before it begins to act. All from that good junk DNA, yes Janna? And what is junk? Your bottom drawer? My garbage can? Your capitalist attic, and my start-up garage!"

"Normal ribosomes skip right over the junk DNA," said Janna. "It's supposed to be meaningless to the modern genome.

Junk DNA is just scribbled-over things. Like the crossed-out numbers in an address book. A palimpsest. Junk DNA is the half-erased traces of the original codes—from long before humanity."

"From before, and—maybe *after*, Wiktor was always saying." Veruschka glove-tapped at a long-chain molecule on the screen. "There is pumptose!" The gaudy molecule had seven stubby arms, each of them a tightly wound mass of smaller tendrils. She barked out a command in Russian. The S-cube-enhanced Applied Biosystems unit understood, and an amber bead of oily, fragrant liquid oozed from the output port. Veruschka neatly caught the droplet in a glass pipette.

Then she transferred it to the crib vat that Janna had prepared. The liquid shuddered and roiled, jolly as the gut of Santa Claus.

"That pumptose is rockin' it," said Janna, marveling at the churning rainbow oil slick.

"We going good now, girl," said Veruschka. She opened her purse and tossed her own Pumpti into the vat. "A special bath treat for my Pumpti," she said. Then, with a painful wince, she dug one of her long fingernails into the lining of her mouth.

"Yow," said Janna.

"Oh, it feels so good to pop him loose," said Veruschka indistinctly. "Look at him."

Nestled in the palm of Veruschka's hand was a lentil-shaped little pink thing. A brand-new Pumpti. "That's your own genetics from your dirty fork at the diner," said Veruschka. "All coated with trilobite bile, or some other decoding from your junk DNA. I grew this seedling for you." She dropped the bean into the vat.

"This is starting to seem a little bent, Veruschka."

"Well . . . you never smelled your own little Pumpti. Or tasted him. How could you not bite him and chew him and grow a new scrap in your mouth? The sweet little Pumpti, you just want to eat him all up!"

Soon a stippling of bumps had formed on the tiny scrap of flesh in the tank. Soft little pimples, twenty or a hundred of them. The lump cratered at the top, getting thicker all around. It formed a dent and invaginated like a sea-squirt. It began pumping itself around in circles, swimming in the murky fluids. Stubby limbs formed momentarily, then faded into an undulating skirt like the mantle of a cuttlefish.

Veruschka's old Pumpti was the size of a grapefruit, and the new one was the size of a golf ball. The two critters rooted around the tank's bottom like rats looking for a drain hole.

Veruschka rolled up her sleeve and plunged her bare arm into the big vat's slimy fluids. She held up the larger Pumpti; it was flipping around like beached fish. Veruschka brought the thing to her face and nuzzled it.

It took Janna a couple of tries to fish her own Pumpti out of the tub, as each time she touched the slimy thing she had to give a little scream and let it go. But finally she had the Pumpti in her grip. It shaped itself to her touch and took on the wet, innocent gleam of a big wad of pink bubble gum.

"Smell it," urged Veruschka.

And, Lord yes, the Pumpti did smell good. Sweet and powdery, like clean towels after a nice hot bath, like a lawn of flowers on a summer morn, like a new dress. Janna smoothed it against her face, so smooth and soft. How could she have thought her Pumpti was gnarly?

"Now you must squeeze him to make him better," said Veruschka, vigorously mashing her Pumpti in her hands. "Knead,

knead, knead! The Pumpti pulls skin cells from the surface of your hands, you know. Then pumptose reads more of the junk DNA and makes more good tasty proteins." She pressed her Pumpti to her cheek, and her voice went up an octave. "Getting more of that yummy yummy wetware from me, isn't he? Squeezy-squeezy Pumpti." She gave it a little kiss.

"This doesn't add up," said Janna. "Let's face it, an entire human body only has like ten grams of active DNA. But this Pumpti, it's solid DNA like a chunk of rubber, and hey, it's almost half a kilo! I mean, where's *that* at?"

"The more the better," said Veruschka patiently. "It means that very quickly Pumpti can be recombining his code. Like a self-programming Turing machine. Wiktor often spoke of this."

"But it doesn't even look like DNA," said Janna. "I messed with DNA every day at Triple Helix. It looks like lint or dried snot."

"My Pumpti is smooth because he's making nice old proteins from the ancient junk of the DNA. All our human predecessors from the beginning of time, amphibians, lemurs, maybe intelligent jellyfish saucers from Mars—who knows what. But every bit is my very own junk, of my very own DNA. So stop thinking so hard, Janna. Love your Pumpti."

Janna struggled not to kiss her pink glob. The traceries of pink and yellow lines beneath its skin were like the veins of fine marble.

"Your Pumpti is very fine," said Veruschka, reaching for it. "Now, into the freezer with him! We will store him, to show our financial backers."

"What!" said Janna. She felt a sliver of ice in her heart. "Freeze my Pumpti? Freeze your *own* Pumpti, Vero."

"I need mine," snapped Veruschka.

To part from her Pumpti—something within her passionately rebelled. In a dizzying moment of raw devotion, Janna suddenly found herself sinking her teeth into the unresisting flesh of the Pumpti. Crisp, tasty spun cotton candy, deep-fried puffball dough, a sugared beignet. And under that a salty, slightly painful flavor — bringing back the memory of being a kid and sucking the root of a lost tooth.

"Now you understand," said Veruschka with a throaty laugh. "I was only testing you! You can keep your sweet Pumpti, safe and sound. We'll get some dirty street bum to make us a Pumpti for commercial samples. Like that stupid boy you were talking to before." Veruschka stood on tiptoe to peer out of the bank's bronze-mullioned window. "He'll be back. Men always come back when they see you making money."

Janna considered this wise assessment. "His name is Kelso," said Janna. "I went to Berkeley with him. He says he's always wanted me. But he never talked to me at school."

"Get some of his body fluid."

"I'm not ready for that," said Janna. "Let's just poke around in the sink for his traces." And, indeed, they quickly found a fresh hair to seed a Kelso Pumpti, nasty and testicular, suitable for freezing.

As Veruschka had predicted, Kelso himself returned before long. He made it his business to volunteer his aid and legal counsel. He even claimed that he'd broached the subject of Magic Pumpkin to Tug Mesoglea himself. However, the mysterious mogul failed to show up with his checkbook, so Magic Pumpkin took the path of viral marketing.

Veruschka had tracked down an offshore Chinese ooze farm to supply cheap culture medium. In a week, they had a few dozen Pumpti starter kits for sale. They came in a little plastic tub of pumptose-laced nutrient, all boxed up in a flashy little design that Janna had printed out in color.

Kelso had the kind of slit-eyed street smarts that came only from Berkeley law classes. He chose Fisherman's Wharf to hawk the product. Janna went along to supervise his retail effort.

It was the start of October, a perfect fog-free day. A song of joy seemed to rise from the sparkling waters of San Francisco Bay, echoing from the sapphire dome of the California sky. Even the tourists could sense the sweetness of the occasion. They hustled cheerfully round Kelso's fold-out table, clicking away with little biochip cameras.

Kelso spun a practiced line of patter while Janna publicly adored her Pumpti. She'd decked out Pumpti in a special sailor suit, and she kept tossing him high into the air and laughing.

"Why is this woman so happy?" barked Kelso. "She's got a Pumpti. Better than a baby, better than a pet, your Pumpti is all you! Starter kits on special today for the unbelievably low price of—"

Over the course of a long morning, Kelso kept cutting the offering price of the Pumpti kits. Finally a runny-nosed little girl from Olympia, Washington, took the bait.

"How do I make one?" she wanted to know. "What choo got in that kit?" And, praise the Holy Molecule, her parents didn't drag her away; they just stood there watching their little darling shop.

The First Sale. For Janna, it was a moment to treasure forever. The little girl with her fine brown hair blowing in the warm afternoon wind, the dazedly smiling parents, Kelso's abrupt excited gestures as he explained how to seed and grow the Pumpti by planting a kiss on a scrap of Kleenex and dropping the scrap into the kit's plastic jar. The feel of those worn dollar bills in her hand, and the parting wave of little Customer Number One. Ah, the romance of it!

Now that they'd found their price point, more sales followed. Soon, thanks to word-of-mouth, they began moving units from their Web site as well.

But now Janna's Dad Ruben, who had a legalistic turn of mind, warned them to hold off on shipments until they had federal approval. Ruben took a sample Pumpti before the San Jose branch office of the Genomics Control Board. He argued that since the Pumptis were neither self-reproducing nor infectious they didn't fall under the Human Heritage provisions of the Homeland Security Act.

The hearings investigation made the Bay Area news shows, especially after the right-wing religious crowd got in on the story. An evangelist from Alameda appeared on San Jose Federal Building's steps, and after an impassioned speech he tore a Pumpti apart with pincers, calling the unresisting little glob the "spawn of Satan." He'd confiscated the poor Pumpti from a young parishioner, who could be seen sobbing at the edge of the screen.

In a few days the Genomics Control Board came through with their blessing. The Pumptis were deemed harmless, placed in the same schedule category as home gene-testing kits. Magic Pumpkin was free to ship throughout the nation! Magic Pumpkin's Web site gathered a bouquet of orders from eager early adopters.

+ + +

Kelso's art-scene friends were happy to sign up to work for Magic Pumpkin. Buoyed by the chance of worldly success,

Kelso began to shave more often and even use deodorant. But he was so excited about business that he forgot to make passes at Janna.

Every day-jobber in the start-up was issued his or her own free Pumpti. "Magic Pumpkin wants missionaries, not mercenaries," Janna announced from on high, and her growing cluster of troops cheered her on. Owning a personal Pumpti was an item of faith in the little company—the linchpin of their corporate culture. You couldn't place yourself in the proper frame of mind for Magic Pumpkin product development without your very own darling roly-poly.

Cynics had claimed that the male demographic would never go for Pumptis. Why would any guy sacrifice his computer gaming time and his weekend bicycling to nurture something? But once *presented* with their own Pumpti, men found that it filled some deep need in the masculine soul. They swelled up with competitive pride in their Pumptis, and even became quite violent in their defense.

Janna lined up a comprehensive array of related products. First and foremost were costumes. Sailor Pumpti, Baby Pumpti, Pumpti Duckling, Angel Pumpti, Devil Pumpti, and even a Goth Pumpti dress-up kit with press-on tattoos. They shrugged off production to Filipina doll clothes makers in a sweatshop in East L.A.

Further up-market came a Pumpti Backpack for transporting your Pumpti in style, protecting it from urban pollution and possibly nasty bacteria. This one seemed like a sure hit, if they could swing the Chinese labor in Shenzhen and Guangdong.

The third idea, Pumpti Energy Crackers, was a no-brainer: crisp collectible cards of munchable amino acid bases to fatten up your Pumpti. If the crackers used the "mechanically recovered meat" common in pet food and cattle feed, then the profit margin would be primo. Kelso had a contact for this in Mexico: they guaranteed their cookies would come crisply printed with the Pumpti name and logo.

Janna's fourth concept was downright metaphysical: a "Psychic Powers Pumpti Training Wand." Except for occasional oozing and plopping, the Pumptis never actually managed conventional pet tricks. But this crystal-topped gizmo could be hawked to the credulous as increasing their Pumpti's "empathy" or "telepathy." A trial mention of this vaporware on the Pumpti-dot-bio Web site brought in a torrent of excited New Age e-mails.

The final, sure-thing Pumpti accessory was tie-in books. Two of Kelso's many unemployed writer and paralegal friends set to work on the Pumpti User's Guide. The firm forecasted an entire *library* of guides, sucking up shelf space at chain stores and pet stores everywhere. *The Moron's Guide to Computational Genomics. Pumpti Tips, Tricks, and Shortcuts. The Three-Week Pumpti Guide, the One-Day Pumpti Guide,* and the *Ten-Minute Pumpti Guide. Pumpti Security Threats: How to Protect Your Pumpti from Viral DNA Hacks, Trojan Goo, and Strange Genes.* And more, more, more!

Paradoxically, Magic Pumpkin's flowering sales bore the slimy seeds of a smashing fiscal disaster. When an outfit started small, it didn't take much traffic to double demand every week. This constant doubling brought on raging production bottlenecks and serious crimps in their cash flow. In point of fact, in pursuit of market establishment, they were losing money on each Pumpti sold. And the big payback from the Pumpti accessories wasn't happening.

Janna had never quite realized that manufacturing real, physical products was so much harder than just thinking them up.

Magic Pumpkin failed to do its own quality control, so the company was constantly screwed by fly-by-nighters. Subcontractors were happy to take their money, but when they failed to deliver, they had Magic Pumpkin over a barrel.

The doll costumes were badly sized. The Pumpti Backpacks were ancient Hello Kitty backpacks with their logos covered by cheap paper Pumpti stickers. The crackers were dog biscuits with the stinging misprint "Pupti." The "telepathic" wand sold some units, but the people buying it tended to write bad checks. As for the User's Guides, the manuscripts were rambling and self-indulgent, long on far-fetched jokes yet critically short on objective facts.

Day by day, Janna stomped the problems out. And now that their production lines were stabilized, now that their accessories catalog was properly weeded out, now that their ad campaign was finally in gear, their fifteen minutes of ballroom glamour expired. The pumpkin clock struck midnight. The public revealed its single most predictable trait: fickleness.

Instantly, without a whimper of warning, Magic Pumpkin was deader than pet rocks. They never even shipped to any stores in the Midwest or on the East Coast, for the folks in those distant markets were sick of hearing about the Pumptis before they ever saw one on a shelf.

Janna and Veruschka couldn't make payroll. Their lease was expiring. They were cringing for cash.

A desperate Janna took the show on the road to potential investors in Hong Kong, the toy capital of the world. She emphasized that Magic Pumpkin had just cracked the biggest single technical problem: the fact that Pumptis looked like slimy blobs. Engineering-wise, it all came down to the pumptose-based Universal Ribosome. By inserting a properly-tweaked look-up string, you could get it to express the junk DNA sequences in customizable forms. Programming this gnarly cruft was, from an abstract computer-science perspective, "unfeasible," meaning that, logically speaking, no human would be able to design such a program within the lifetime of the universe.

But Janna's Dad, fretful about his investment, had done it anyway. In two weeks of inspired round-the-clock hacking, Ruben had implemented a full "OpenAnimator" graphics library, using a palette of previously unused rhodopsin-style proteins. Thanks to OpenAnimator, a whiff of the right long-chain molecule could now give your Pumpti any mesh, texture, colormap, or attitude matrix you chose. Not to mention overloaded frame-animation updates keyed into the pumptose's ribosomal time-steps! It was a techie miracle!

Dad flew along to Hong Kong to back Janna's pitch, but the Hong Kong crowd had little use for software jargon in American English. And the overwrought Ruben killed the one nibble they got by picking a fight over intellectual property—no way to build partnerships in Hong Kong.

Flung back to San Francisco, Janna spent night after night frantically combing the Web, looking for any source of second-round venture capital, no matter how far-fetched.

Finally she cast herself sobbing into Kelso's arms. Kelso was her last hope. Kelso just had to come through for them: he had to bring in the seasoned business experts from Ctenophore, Inc., the legendary masters of jellyfish A-Life.

"Listen, babe," said Kelso practically, "I think you and the bio-Bolshevik there have already taken this concept just about as far as any sane person oughta push it. Farther, even. I mean, sure, I recruited a lot of my cyberslacker friends into your corporate cult here, and we promised them the moon and everything, so I guess we'll look a little stupid when it Enrons. They'll bitch and whine, and they'll feel all disenchanted, but come on, this is San Francisco. They're used to that here. It's genetic."

"But what about my dad? He'll lose everything! And Veruschka is my best friend. What if she shoots me?"

"I'm thinking Mexico," said Kelso dreamily. "Way down on the Pacific coast—that's where my mother comes from. You and me, we've been working so hard on this start-up that we never got around to the main event. Just dump those ugly Pumptis in the Bay. We'll empty the cash box tonight, and catch a freighter blimp for the South. I got a friend who works for Air Jalisco."

It was Kelso's most attractive offer so far, maybe even sincere, in its way. Janna knew full well that the classic dot-com move was to grab that golden parachute and bail like crazy before the investors and employees caught on. But Magic Pumpkin was Janna's own brain child. She was not yet a serial entrepreneur, and a boyfriend was only a boyfriend. Janna couldn't walk away from the green baize table before that last spin of the wheel.

It had been quite some time since Ctenephore Inc. had been a cutting-edge start-up. The blazing light of media tech-hype no longer escaped their dense, compact enterprise. The firm's legendary founders, Revel Pullen and Tug Mesoglea, had collapsed in on their own reputations. Not a spark could escape their gravity. They had become twin black holes of biz weirdness.

Ctenephore's main line of business had always been piezoplastic products. Ctenephore had pumped this protean, blobject material into many crazy scenes in the California boom years. Bathtub toys, bondage clothing, industrial-sized artificial-jellyfish transport blimps—and Goob dolls as well! GoobYoob, creator of the Goob dolls, had been one of Ctenephore's many Asian spin-offs.

As it happened, quite without Janna's awareness, Ctenophore had already taken a professional interest in the workings of Magic Pumpkin. GoobYoob's manufacturing arm, Boogosity, had been the Chinese ooze-farm supplier for Pumpti raw material. Since Boogosity had no advertising or marketing expenses, they'd done much better by the brief Pumpti craze than Magic Pumpkin itself.

Since Magic Pumpkin was going broke, Boogosity faced a production glut. They'd have to move their specialty goo factories back into the usual condoms and truck tires. Some kind of corporate allegiance seemed written in the stars.

Veruschka Zipkinova was transfixed with paranoia about Revel Pullen, Ctenophore's chairman of the board. Veruschka considered major American capitalists to be sinister figures—this conviction was just in her bones, somehow—and she was very worried about what Pullen might do to Russia's oil.

Russia's black gold was the lifeblood of its pathetic, wrecked economy. Years ago Revel Pullen, inventively manic as always, had released gene-spliced bacteria into America's dwindling oil reserves. This fatal attempt to increase oil production had converted millions of barrels of oil into (as chance would have it) raw piezoplastic. Thanks to the powerful Texas lobby in Washington, none of the lawsuits or regulatory actions against Ctenophore had ever succeeded.

Janna sought to calm Veruschka's jitters. If the company hoped to survive, they had to turn Ctenophore into Magic Pumpkin's fairy godmother. The game plan was to flatter Pullen, while focusing their persuasive efforts on the technical expert of the pair. This would be Ctenophore's chief scientist, a far-famed mathematician named Tug Mesoglea.

It turned out that Kelso really did know Tug Mesoglea personally, for Mesoglea lived in a Painted Lady mansion above the

Haight. During a protracted absence to the Tweetown district of Manchester (home of the Alan Turing Memorial), Tug had once hired Kelso to babysit his jellyfish aquarium.

Thanks to San Francisco's digital grapevine, Tug knew about the eccentric biomathematics that ran Pumptis. Tug was fascinated, and not by the money involved. Like many mathematicians, Mesoglea considered money to be one boring, merely bookkeeping subset of the vast mental universe of general computation. He'd already blown a fortune endowing chairs in set theory, cellular automata, and higher-dimensional topology. Lately, he'd published widely on the holonomic attractor space of human dreams, producing a remarkable proof that dreams of flight were a mathematical inevitability for a certain fixed percentage of the dreams—this fixed percentage number being none other than Feigenbaum's chaos constant, 4.6692.

+ + +

Veruschka scheduled the meet at a Denny's near the Moffat Field blimp port. Veruschka had an unshakeable conviction that Denny's was a posh place to eat, and the crucial meeting had inspired her to dress to the nines.

"When do they want to have sex with us?" Veruschka fretted, paging through her laminated menu.

"Why would they want to do that?" said Janna.

"Because they are fat capitalist moguls from the West, and we are innocent young women. Evil old men with such fame and money, what else can they want of us? They will scheme to remove our clothing!"

"Well, look, Tug Mesoglea is gay." Janna looked at her friend with concern. Veruschka hadn't been sleeping properly. Stuck on the local grind of junk food and eighty-hour weeks, Veruschka's femme-fatale figure was succumbing to Valley hacker desk-spread. The poor thing barely fit in her designer knockoffs. It would be catty to cast cold water on her seduction fantasies, but really, Veruschka was swiftly becoming a kerchiefed babushka with a string-bag, the outermost shell of some cheap nest of Russian dolls.

Veruschka picked up her Pumpti, just now covered in baroque scrolls like a fin-de-siècle picture frame. "Do like this," she chirped, brushing the plump pet against her fluffy marten-fur hat. The Pumpti changed its surface texture to give an impression of hairiness, and hopped onto the crown.

"Lovely," said Veruschka, smiling into her hand mirror. But her glossy smile was tremulous.

"We simply must believe in our product," said Veruschka, pep-talking to her own mirror. She glanced up wide-eyed at Janna. "Our product is so good a fit for their core business, no? Please tell me more about them, about this Dr. Tug and Mr. Revel. Tell me the very worst. These gray-haired, lecherous fat cats, they are world weary and cynical! Success has corrupted them and narrowed their thinking! They no longer imagine a brighter future, they merely go through the rote. Can they be trusted with our dreams?"

Janna tugged fitfully at the floppy tie she'd donned to match her dress-for-success suit. She always felt overwhelmed by Veruschka's fits of self-serving corn. "It's a biz meeting, Vero. Try to relax."

Just as the waitress brought them some food, the glass door of the Denny's yawned open with a ring and a squeak. A seamy, gray-haired veteran with the battered look of a bronco-buster approached their table, with a bowlegged scuff.

"I'm Hoss Jenks, head o' security for Ctenophore." Jenks hauled out a debugging wand and a magnetometer. He then swept his tools with care over the pair of them. The wand began beeping in frenzy.

"Lemme hold on to your piece for you, ma'am," Jenks suggested placidly.

"It's just a sweet little one," Veruschka demurred, handing over a pistol.

Tug Mesoglea tripped in moments later, sunburned and querulous. The mathematician sported a lavender dress shirt and peach-colored ascot, combined with pleated khaki trail-shorts and worn-out piezoplastic Gripper sandals.

Revel Pullen followed, wearing a black linen business suit, snakeskin boots, and a Stetson. Janna could tell there was a bald pate under that high hat. Jenks faded into a nearby booth, where he could shadow his employers and watch the door.

Mesoglea creaked into the plastic seat beside Veruschka and poured himself a coffee. "I phoned in my order from the limo. Where's my low-fat soy protein?"

"Here you go, then," said Janna, eagerly shoving him the heaped plate of pseudo-meat that the waitress had just set down.

Pullen stared as Mesoglea tucked in. "I don't know how the hell this man eats the food in a sorry-ass chain store." Nevertheless he picked up a fork and speared a piece of it himself.

"I believe in my investments," Mesoglea said, munching. "You see, ladies, this soy protein derives from a patented Ctenophore process." He prodded at Veruschka's plate. "Did you notice that lifelike, organic individuality of your waffle product? That's no accident, darling."

"Did we make any real foldin' money off this crap?" said Revel Pullen, eating one more piece of it.

"Of course we did! You remember all those sintered floating gel rafts in the giant tofu tanks in Chiba?" Mesoglea flicked a blob of molten butter from his ascot.

"Y'all don't pay no never mind to Dr. Mesoglea here," Revel counteradvised, setting down his fork. "Today's economy is all about diversity. Proactive investments. Buying into the next technical wave, before you get cannibalized." Revel leered. "Now as for me, I get my finger into every techno-pie!" His lip-less mouth was like a letter slot, bent slightly upward at the corners to simulate a grin.

"Let me brief you gentlemen on our business model," said Janna warily. "It's much like your famous Goob dolls, but the hook here is that the Pumpti is made of the user's very own DNA. This leads to certain, uh, powerful consumer bonding effects, and . . ."

"Oh good, let's see your Pumptis, girls," crooned Tug, with a decadent giggle. "Whip out your Pumptis for us."

"You've never seen our product?" asked Janna.

"Tug's got a mess of 'em," said Revel. "But y'all never shipped to Texas. That's another thing I just don't get." Pullen produced a sheaf of printout, and put on his bifocals. "According to these due-diligence filings, Magic Pumpkin's projected online capacity additions were never remotely capable of meeting the residual in-line demand in the total off-line market that you required for breakeven." He tipped back his Stetson, his liver-spotted forehead wrinkling in disbelief. "How in green tarnation could you gals overlook that? How is that even possible?"

"Huh?" said Janna.

Revel chuckled. "Okay, now I get it. Tug, these little gals don't know how to do business. They've never been anywhere near one."

"Sure looks that way," Tug admitted. "No MBAs, no account-
ants? Nobody doing cost control? No speakers-to-animals in the
hacker staff? I'd be pegging your background as entry-level
computational genomics," he said, pointing at Janna. Then he
waggled his finger at Veruschka, "And you'd be coming from—
Slavic mythology and emotional blackmail?"

Veruschka's cobalt blue eyes went hard. "I don't think I want
to show you men my Pumpti."

"We kind of have to show our Pumptis, don't we?" said
Janna, an edge in her voice. "I mean, we're trying to make a
deal here."

"Don't get all balky on the bailout men," added Revel,
choking back a yawn of disdain. He tapped a napkin to his wrinkled lips, with a glint of diamond solitaire. He glanced at his
Rolex, reached into his coat pocket, and took out a little pill.
"That's for high blood pressure, and I got it the hard way, out
kickin' ass in the market. I got a flight back to Texas in less than
two hours. So let's talk killer app, why don't we? Your toy pitch
is dead in the water. But Tug says your science is unique. Okay,
but how do we sell the Pumptis?"

"They're getting much prettier," Janna said, swiftly hating
herself.

"Do y'all think Pumptis might have an app in home security?"
Janna brightened. "The home market?"

"Yeah, that's right, Strategic Defense for the Home." Pullen
outlined his scheme. Ever the bottom-feeder, he'd bought up
most of the software patents for the never-completed American
missile defense system. Pullen had a long-cherished notion of
retrofitting the Star Wars shield into a consumer application for
troubled neighborhoods. He was wondering if Pumptis might
take the place of the missiles.

Revel figured that a sufficiently tough-minded, Pumpti could take a round to the guts, fall to earth, crawl back to its vat in the basement, and come back hungry for more. So if bullets were fired at a private home from some drug-crazed drive-by, then a rubbery unit of the client's Pumpti Star Wars shield would instantly fling itself into the way, guided by that fine old Star Wars software.

Veruschka batted her eyes at Pullen. "I love to hear a strong man talk about security."

"Security always soars along with unemployment," said Pullen, nodding his head at his own wisdom. "We're in a major downturn. I seen this before, so I know the drill. Locks, bolts, Dobermans, they're all market leaders this quarter. That's Capitalism 301, girls."

"And you, Ctenephore, you would finance Magic Pumpkin as a home-defense industry?" probed Veruschka.

"Maybe," said Pullen, his sunken eyes sly. "We'd surely supply you a Washington lobbyist. New public relations. Zoning clearances. Help you write up a genuine budget for once. And of course, if we're on board, then y'all will have to dump all your crappy equipment and become a hunnert-percent Ctenephore shop, technologically. Ctenephore sequencers, PCRs, and bioinformatic software. That's strictly for your own safety, you understand: stringent quality assurance, functional testing and all."

"Uhm, yeah," nodded Tug. "We'd get all your intellectual property copyrighted and patented with the World Intellectual Property Organization. The lawyer fees, we'll take care of that. Ctenephore is downright legendary for our quick response times to a market opportunity."

"We gonna help you youngsters catch the fish," said Pullen smugly. "Not just give you a damn fish. What'd be the fun in that? Self-reliance, girls. We wanna see your little outfit get up and walk, under our umbrella. You sign over your founder's stock, put in your orders for our equipment—and we ain't gonna bill for six months—then my men will start to shake the money tree."

"Wait, they still haven't shown us their Pumptis," said Tug, increasingly peevish. "And, Revel, you need to choke it back to a dull roar with the Star Wars attack Pumptis. Real world ballistic physics is chaotic, dude, which means unsolvable in real time." Tug muffled a body sound with his napkin. "I ate too many waffles."

Janna felt like flipping the table over into their laps. Veruschka shot her a quick, understanding glance and laid a calming hand on her shoulder. Veruschka played a deep game.

Veruschka plucked the Pumpti from her furry hat and set it on the table.

Tug did a double take and leaned forward, transfixed

Veruschka segued into her cuddly mode. "Pumpti was created in a very special lab in Petersburg. In the top floor of old Moskfilm complex, where my friends make prehistoric amber jewelry. You can see the lovely River Neva while you hunt for dinosaur gnats—"

As she put the squeeze on their would-be sponsors, Veruschka compulsively massaged her Pumpti. She was working it, really getting into it finger and thumb, until suddenly a foul little clot of nonworking protein suddenly gave way inside, like popping bubble wrap.

"Stop it, Vero," said Janna.

Tug daintily averted his gaze as Veruschka sucked goo from her fingers.

"Look at mine," offered Janna. She'd programmed her Pumpti to look rubbery and sleek, like a top-end basketball shoe.

"Hey, any normal kid would kill to have one of those," said Revel cheerily. "I'm getting' another product brainstorm! It's risin' in me like a thunderhead across Tornado Alley!"

"The junk DNA is the critical aspect," put in Tug. "Those are traces of early prehuman genomics. If we can really express those primordial codons, we might—"

"Those globbies suck the DNA right off people's fingers, right?" demanded Revel.

"Well, yes," said Janna.

"Great! So that's my Plan B. Currency! You smash 'em out flat and color 'em pretty. As they daisy-chain from hand to hand, they record the DNA of every user. Combine those with criminal DNA files, and you got terrorist-proof cash!"

"But the mafiya always wears gloves," said Veruschka.

"No problem, just turn up the amps," said Pullen. "Have 'em suck DNA fragments out of the dang air." He wiggled his lower jaw to simulate deep thought. "Those little East European currencies, they're not real cash money anyways! That user-base won't even know the difference!"

Mesoglea blinked owlishly. "Bear with us, ladies. Revel's always like this right after he takes his meds."

"Now, Tug, we gotta confront the commercial possibilities! You and I, we could hit the lab and make some kind of money that only works for white males over fifty. If anybody else tries to pass it, it just, like—bites their dang hands off!" Pullen chuckled richly, then had another drag off his cig. "Or how about a hunnert-dollar bill that takes your DNA and grows your own face on the front!"

Mesoglea sighed, looked at his watch, and shook it theatrically.

"But this is such pure genius!" gushed Veruschka, leaning toward Revel with moistening eyes. "We need your veteran skills. Magic Pumpkin needs grown men in the boardroom. We wasted our money on incompetent artists and profiteers! We had great conceptual breakthroughs, but—"

"Can it with the waterworks and cut to the chase, ptista," said Pullen. "It's high time for you amateurs to roll over."

"Make us the offer," said Janna.

"Cards on the table," said Pullen, fixing her with his hard little eyes. "You'll sign all your founder's stock over to us. I'll take your stock, chica, and Tug'll take your pretty Russian friend's. That gives us controlling interest. As for your Dad's third, he might as well keep it since he's too maverick to deal with. Dad's in clover. Okay?"

"You're not offering us any cash?" said Janna. "I don't believe this. The Pumpti was our original idea!"

"You sign on with us, you get a nice salary," said Pullen. Then he broke into such cackles that he had to sip ice water and dab at his eyes with a kerchief.

"You two kids really are better off with a salary," added Tug in a kindly tone. "It won't be anything huge, but better than your last so-called jobs. We already checked into your histories. You'll get some nice vague titles too. That'll be good experience for your next job or, who knows, your next start-up."

"The sexy Russki can be my Pumpti Project Manager," said Pullen. "She can fly down to my ranch tomorrow. I'll be waitin'. And what about the other one, Tug? She's more the techie type."

"Yes, yes, I want Janna," said Tug, beaming. "Executive Assistant to the Chief Scientist."

Janna and Veruschka exchanged unhappy glances.

"How—how big of a salary?" asked Janna, hating herself.

+ + +

After the fabled entrepreneurs departed the Denny's in the company of a watchful Hoss Jenks, Veruschka dropped her glued-on smile and scrambled for the kitchen. She was just in time to save the Tug's and Revel's dirty forks before they hit the soapy water.

Shoving a busboy aside, Veruschka wrapped the DNA-soiled trophies in a sheet of newspaper and stuffed them into her purse.

"Veruschka, what do you think you're doing?"

"I'm multiplying our future options. I am seizing the future imperfectly. Visualize, realize, actualize." Veruschka's lower lip trembled. "Leap, and the net will appear."

Stuck in the clattering kitchen of Denny's, feeling sordid and sold-out, Janna felt a moment of true sorrow for herself, for Vero, and even for the Latin and Vietnamese busboys. Poor immigrant Veruschka, stuck in some foreign country, with an alien language—she'd seen her grandest dreams seized, twisted up, and crushed by America, and now, in her valiant struggle to rise from ash heap to princess, she'd signed on to be Pullen's marketeer droid. As for Janna—she'd be little more than a lab assistant.

At least the business was still alive. Even if it wasn't her business anymore.

When they returned to their San Francisco lair, they discovered that Hoss Jenks had arrived with a limo full of men in black suits and mirrorshades. They'd seized the company's computers and fired everyone. To make things worse, Jenks had called the police and put an APB out for Kelso, who had last been seen departing down a back alley with a cardboard box stuffed with the company's petty cash.

"I can't believe that horrible old cowboy called the cops on Kelso," Janna mourned, sitting down in the firm's very last cool, swoopy Blobular Concepts chair. "I'm glad Kelso stole that money, since it's not ours anymore. I hope he'll turn up again. I never even got to make out with him."

"He's gay, you know."

"Look, Kelso is *not gay*," yelled Janna. "He is so totally not gay. There's a definite chemistry between us. We were just too incredibly busy, that's all."

Veruschka sniffed and said nothing. When Janna looked up, her eyes brimming, she realized that Veruschka was actually feeling sorry for her. This was finally it for Janna; it was too much for flesh and blood to bear. She bent double in her designer chair, racked with sobs.

"Janna, my dear, don't surrender. The business cycle, always, it turns around. And California is the Golden State."

"No it isn't. We've got a market bear stitched right on our flag. We're totally doomed, Veruschka! We've been such fools!"

"I hate those two old men," said Veruschka, after the two of them had exhausted half a box of Kleenex. "They're worse than their reputations. I expected them to be crazy, but not so—greedy and rude."

"Well, we signed all their legal papers. It's a little late to fuss now."

Veruschka let out a low, dark chuckle. "Janna, I want revenge."

Janna looked up. "Tell me."

"It's very high tech and dangerous."

"Yeah?"

"It's completely illegal, or it would be, if any court had the chance to interpret the law in such a matter."

"Spill it, Vero."

"Pumpti Gene Therapy."

Janna felt a twinge, as of seasickness. "That's a no-no, Vero."

"Tell me something," said Veruschka. "If you dose a man with an infectious genomic mutagen, how do you keep him from knowing he's been compromised?"

"You're talking bioterrorism, Vero. They'd chase us to the ends of the earth in a rain of cruise missiles."

"You use a Pumpti virus based on your victim's own DNA," said Veruschka, deftly answering her own rhetorical question. "Because nobody has an immune response to their own DNA. No matter how—how very strange it might be making their body."

"But you're weaponizing the human genome! Can't we just shoot them?"

Veruschka's voice grew soft and low. "Imagine Tug Mesoglea at his desk. He feels uneasy, he begins to complain, his voice is like a rasping locust's. And then his eyeballs—his eyeballs pop out onto his cheeks, driven from his head by the pressure of his bursting brain!"

"You call *that* gene therapy?"

"They *need* it! The shriveled brains of Pullen and Mesoglea are old and stiff! There is plenty of room for new growth in their rattling skulls. You and I, we create the Pumpti Therapy for them. And then they will give us money." Veruschka twirled on one heel and laughed. "We make Pumptis so tiny like a virus! Naked DNA with Universal Ribosome and a nine-plus-two microtubule apparatus to rupture the host's cell walls! One strain for Pullen, and one for Mesoglea. The Therapy is making them smarter, so they are grateful to shower money upon us. Or else," her eyes narrowed, "the Therapy is having some unpleasant effects and they are begging on their knees to purchase an antidote."

"So it's insanity and/or blackmail, in other words."

"These men are rotten bastards," said Veruschka.

"Look, why don't we give a fighting chance to the home defense Pumptis?" asked Janna. "Or the money Pumptis? They're nutty ideas, but not all that much crazier than your original scheme about pets. Didn't I hear you call Revel Pullen a marketing genius?"

"Don't you know me yet even a little bit?" said Veruschka, her face frank and open. "Revel's ideas for my Pumptis are like using a beautiful sculpture for a hammer. Or like using a silk scarf to pick up dog doo."

"Too, too true," sighed Janna. "Get the forks out of your purse and let's start on those nanoPumptis."

+ + +

To begin with, they grew some ordinary kilogram-plus Pumptis from Revel and Tug's fork-scrapings, each in its own little vat. Veruschka wanted to be sure they had a whopping big supply of their enemies' DNA.

For fun, Janna added OpenAnimator molecules to shade Revel's Pumpti blue and Tug's red. And then, for weirdness, Vero dumped a new biorhythm accelerator into the vats. The fat lumps began frantically kneading themselves, each of them replicating, garbage-collecting, and decoding their DNA hundreds of times per second. "So perhaps these cavemen can become more highly evolved," remarked Veruschka.

By three in the morning, they'd made their first nanoPumpti. Janna handled the assembly, using the synthesizer's datagloves to control a molecular probe. She took the body of a cold virus and replaced its polyhedral head with a Universal Ribosome and a strand of hyper-evolved DNA from the Pullen Pumpti.

And then she made a nanoPumpti for Tug. Veruschka used her hands-on wetware skills to quickly amplify the lone Tug and Revel nanoPumptis into respectable populations.

When the first morning sunlight slanted in the lab window, it lit up two small stoppered glass vials: a blue one for Revel, a red one for Tug.

Veruschka rooted in the cornucopia of her tattered suitcase. She produced a pair of cheap-looking rings, brass things with little chrome balls on them. "These are Lucrezia Borgia rings. I bought them in a tourist stall before I left St. Petersburg." Practicing with water, Veruschka showed Janna how to siphon up a microliter though the ring's cunningly hidden perforations and how—with the crook of a finger—to make the ring squirt the liquid back out as a fine mist.

"Load your ring with Mesoglea's nanoPumptis," said Veruschka, baring her teeth in a hard grin. "I want to see you give Mesoglea his Therapy before my flight to Texas. I'll load my ring for Pullen and when I get down there, I'll take care of him."

"No, no," said Janna, stashing the vials in her purse. "We don't load the rings yet. We have to dose the guys at the exact same time. Otherwise, the one will know when the other one gets it. They've been hanging together for a long time. They're like symbiotes. How soon are you and Pullen coming back from Texas anyway?"

"He says two weeks," said Veruschka, pulling a face. "I hope is less time."

And then Hoss Jenks was there with a limo to take Veruschka to the airport. Janna cleaned up the lab and stashed the vials of nanoPumptis in her office. Before she could lie down to sleep there, Tug Mesoglea arrived for his first day at Magic Pumpkin.

To Janna's surprise, Tug turned out to be a pleasant man to

work for. Not only did he have excellent taste in office carpeting and window treatments, but he was a whiz at industrial R&D. Under his leadership, the science of the Pumptis made great strides: improvements in the mechanism of the Universal Ribosome, in the curious sets of proteins encoded by the junk DNA, even in the looping strangeness of Ruben Gutierrez's genomic OpenAnimator graphics library. And then Tug stumbled onto the fact that the Pumptis could send and receive a certain gigahertz radio frequency. Digital I/O.

"The ascended master of R&D does not shoehorn new science into yesterday's apps," the serenely triumphant Tug told Janna. "The product is showing us what it wants to do. Forget the benighted demands of the brutish consumers: we're called to lead them to the sunlit uplands of improved design!"

So Janna pushed ahead, and under Tug's Socratic questioning, she had her breakthrough: Why stop at toys? Once they'd managed to tweak and evolve a new family of forms and functions for the Pumptis, they would no longer be mere amusements, but *personal tools*. Not like Pokemons, not like Goob dolls, but truly *high-end devices*: soft uvvy phones, health monitors, skin-interfaced VR patches, holistic gene maintenance kits, cosmetic body-modifiers! Every gadget would be utterly trustworthy, being made of nothing but you!

As before, they would all but give away the pretty new Pumptis, but this time they'd have serious weight for the after market: "Pumpti Productivity Philtres" containing the molecular codes for the colors, shapes, and functionalities of a half dozen killer apps. Get 'em all! While they last! New Philtres coming soon!

Veruschka's stay in Texas lasted six weeks. She phoned daily to chat with Janna. The laid-back Texan lifestyle on the legendary Pullen spread was having its own kind of seduction. Vero gave up her vodka for blue agave tequila. She surrendered her high heels for snakeskin boots. Her phone conversations became laced with native terms such as "darlin" and "sugar" as she smugly recounted giant barbeques for politicians, distributors, the Ctenophore management, and the Pullen Drilling Company sales force.

By the time Revel and Veruschka came back to San Francisco, Magic Pumpkin had the burn-rate under firm control and was poised for true market success. But, as wage slaves, Janna and Veruschka would share not one whit of the profit. So far as Janna knew, they were still scheduled to poison their bosses.

"Do we really want to give them the Pumpti Therapy?" Janna murmured to Veruschka. They were in Janna's new living quarters, wonderfully carpentered into the space beneath the bank's high dome. It had proved easier to build in an apartment than to rent one. And Tug had been very good about the expenses.

Veruschka had a new suitcase, a classy Texas item clad in dappled calfskin with the hair still on. As usual, her bag had disgorged itself all over the room. "Mesoglea must certainly be liquidated," she said, cocking her head. Tug's voice was drifting up from the lab below, where he was showing Revel around. "He is fatuous, old, careless. He has lost all his creative fire."

"But I like Tug now," said Janna. "He taught me amazing things in the lab. He's smart."

"I hate him," said Veruschka stubbornly. "Tonight he meets the consequences of his junk DNA."

"Well, your Revel Pullen needs Pumpti Therapy even more," said Janna crossly. "He's a corrupt, lunatic bully—cram-full of huckster double-talk he doesn't even listen to himself."

"Revel and I are in harmony on many issues," allowed Veruschka. "I begin almost to like his style."

"Should—should we let them off the hook?" pleaded Janna.

Veruschka gave her a level stare. "Don't weaken. These men stole our company. We must bend them to our will. It is beyond personalities."

"Oh, all right," sighed Janna, feeling doomed. "You poison Tug and I'll poison Revel. It'll be easier for us that way."

The four of them were scheduled to go out for a celebratory dinner, this time to Popo's, a chi-chi high-end gourmet establishment of Tug's choosing. Pullen's voice could now be heard echoing up from the lab, loudly wondering what was "keeping the heifers." Janna swept downstairs to distract the men while Veruschka loaded her ring. Then Veruschka held the floor while Janna went back up to her room to ready her own ring.

The two little vials of nanoPumpti sat in plain sight amidst the clutter of the women's cosmetics. They could have been perfume bottles, one red, one blue.

As Janna prepared to fill her Borgia ring, she was struck by a wild inspiration. She'd treat Revel Pullen with Tug's Pumptized DNA. Yes! This would civilize the semihuman Pullen, making him be more like Tug—instead of, horrors, even more like himself! There might be certain allergic effects—but the result for the Magic Pumpkin company would be hugely positive. To hell with the risk. No doubt the wretched Pullen would be happy with the change.

It went almost too easily. The old men guzzled enough wine with dinner to become loose and reckless. When the cappuccinos arrived, Janna and Veruschka each found a reason to reach out toward their prey. Veruschka adjusted Pullen's string-tie. Janna dabbed a stain of prawn sauce from Tug's salmon-colored lapel. And each woman gently misted the contents of her ring onto the chocolate-dusted foam of her victim's coffee. The old men, heavy-lidded with booze and digestion, took their medicines without a peep.

Soon after, Pullen retired to his hotel room, Tug caught a cab back to his house in the Haight, and the two women walked the few blocks back to the Magic Pumpkin headquarters, giggling with relief. Janna didn't tell Veruschka about having given Pullen the red Tug Treatment. Better to wait and see how things worked out. Better to sleep on it.

But sleep was slow in coming. Suppose Pullen swelled up horribly and died from toxic Tug effects? The Feds would find the alien DNA in him, and the law would be on Janna right away. And what if the Therapies really did improve the two old men? Risen to some cold, inhuman level of intelligence, they'd think nothing of wiping out Janna and Veruschka like ants.

Janna rubbed her cell phone nervously. Maybe she could give poor old Tug some kind of anonymous warning. But she sensed that Veruschka was also awake, over on the other side of Janna's California King bed.

Suddenly the phone rang. It was Kelso.

"Yo babe," he said airily. "I'm fresh back from sunny Mexico. The heat's off. I bought myself a new identity and an honest-to-God law degree. I'm right outside, Janna. Saw you and Vero go jammin' by on Market Street just now, but I didn't want to come pushing up at you like some desperado tweaker. Let me in. Nice new logo you got on the Magic Pumpkin digs, by the way, good font choice too."

"You're a lawyer now? Well, don't think we've forgotten about that box of petty cash, you sleaze."

Kelso chuckled. "I didn't forget you either, *mi vida*! As for that money—hey, my new papers cost as much as what I took.

Paradoxical, no? Here's another mind bender: even though we're hot for each other, you and me have never done the deed."

"I'm not alone," said Janna. "Veruschka's staying with me."

"For God's sake will you two at last get it over," said Veruschka, sleepily burying her head under her pillow. "Wake me up when you're done and maybe the three of us can talk business. We'll need a lawyer tomorrow."

+ + +

The next morning Tug Mesoglea arrived at Magic Pumpkin and started acting–like Revel Pullen.

"Git along little doggies," he crooned, leaning over the incubator where they were keeping their dozen or so new-model Pumptis. And then he reached over and fondled Janna's butt.

Janna raced out of the lab and cornered Veruschka, who was noodling around at her desk trying to look innocent. "You gave Tug the Pullen potion, didn't you? Bitch!"

Before Veruschka could answer, the front door swung open, and in sashayed Pullen. He was dressed, unbelievably, in a caftan and striped Capri pants. "I picked these up in the hotel shop," he said, looking down at one of his spindly shanks. "Do you think it works on me, Janna? I've always admired your fashion sense."

"Double bitch!" cried Veruschka, and yanked at Janna's hair. Janna grabbed back, knocking off the red cowboy hat that Vero was sporting today.

"Don't think we haven't already seen clear through your little game," said the altered Pullen with a toss of his head. "You and your nanoPumptis. Tug and I had a long heart-to-heart talk on the phone this morning. Except we didn't use no phone. We can hear each other in our heads."

"Shit howdy!" called Tug from the lab. "Brother Revel's here. Ready to take it to the next level?"

"Lemme clear out the help," said Revel. He leaned into the guard room and sent Hoss Jenks and his mirrorshades assistants out for a long walk. To Jenks's credit, he didn't bat an eye at Revel's new look.

"Let's not even worry about that Kelso boy up in Janna's room," said Tug. "He's still asleep." Tug gave Janna an arch look. "Don't look so surprised, we know everything. Thanks to the Pumpti Therapy you gave us. We've got, oh, a couple of million years of evolution on you now. The future of the race, that's us. Telepathy, telekinesis, teleportation, and shape-shifting too."

"You're—you're not mad at us?" said Janna.

"We only gave the Therapy to make you better," babbled Veruschka. "Don't punish us."

"I dunno about that," said Revel. "But I do know I got a powerful hankerin' for some Pumpti meat. Can you smell that stuff?"

"Sure can," sang Tug. "Intoxicating, isn't it? What a seductive perfume!"

Without another word, the two men headed for the lab's vats and incubators. Peeping warily through the open lab doors, Janna and Veruschka saw a blur of activity. The two old men were methodically devouring the stock, gobbling every Pumpti in sight.

There was no way that merely human stomachs could contain all that mass, but that wasn't slowing them down much. Their bodies were puffing up and—just as Veruschka had predicted, the eyeballs were bulging forward out of their heads. Their clothes split and dropped away from their expanding girths. When all the existing Pumptis were gone, the two giants set eagerly to work on the raw materials. And when Tug found

the frozen kilograms of their own personal Pumptis, the fire-
works really began.

The two great mouths chewed up the red and blue Pumpti
meat, spitting, drooling, and passing the globs back and forth.
Odd ripples began moving up and down along their bodies like
ghost images of ancient flesh.

"What's that a-comin' out of your rib cage, Tuggie?" crowed
Revel.

"Cootchy-coo," laughed Tug, twiddling the tendrils pro-
truding from his side. "I'm expressing a jellyfish. My personal
best. Feel around in your genome, Revel. It's all there, every
species, evolved from our junk DNA right along with our super-
duper futuristic new bodies." He paused, watching. "Now
you're keyin' it, bro. I say—are those hooves on your shoulder?"

Revel palpated the twitching growth with professional care.
"I'd be reckoning that's a quagga. A prehistoric zebra-type thing.
And, whoah Nellie, see this over on my other shoulder? It's
an eohippus. Ancestor of the horse. The cowboys of the Pullen
clan got a long relationship with horseflesh. I reckon there was
some genetic bleedover when we was punchin' cattle up the
Goodnight-Loving Trail; that's why growin' these ponies comes
so natural to me."

"How do you like it now, ladies?" asked Tug, glancing over
toward Janna and Veruschka.

"Ask them," hissed Veruschka in Janna's ear.

"No, you," whispered Janna.

Brave Vero spoke up. "My friend is wondering now if you
will sign those Magic Pumpkin founders' shares back over to
us? And the patents as well if you please?"

"Groink," said Revel, hunching himself over and deforming
his mouth into a dinosaur-type jaw.

"Squonk," said Tug, letting his head split into a floppy bouquet of be-suckered tentacles.

"You don't need to own our business anymore," cried Janna. "Please sign it back to us."

The distorted old men whooped and embraced each other, their flesh fusing into one. The meaty mass seethed with possibilities, bubbled with the full repertoire of zoological forms—with feelers, claws, wings, antennae, snouts; with eyes of every shape and color winking on and off; with fleeting mouths that lingered only long enough to bleat, to hiss, to grumble, to whinny, screech, and roar. It wasn't exactly a "no" answer.

"Kelso," shouted Janna up the stairs. "Bring the papers!"

A high, singing sound filled the air. The Pullen-Mesoglea mass sank to the floor as if melting, forming itself into a broad, glistening plate. The middle of the plate swelled like yeasty bread to form a swollen dome. The fused organism was taking on the form of—a living UFO?

"The original genetic Space Friend!" said Veruschka in awe. "It's been waiting in their junk DNA since the dawn of time!"

As Kelso clattered down the stairs, the saucer charged at the three of them, far too fast to escape. Kelso, Janna, and Veruschka were absorbed into the saucer's ethereal bulk.

Everything got white, and in the whiteness, Janna saw a room, a round space expressing wonderful mathematical proto-design: a vast Vernor Panton 1960s hashish den, languidly and repeatedly melting into a Karim Rashid all-plastic lobby.

The room's primary inhabitants were idealized forms of Tug Mesoglea and Revel Pullen. The men's saucer bodies were joyous, sylphlike forms of godlike beauty.

"I say we spin off the company to these girls and their lawyer," intoned the Tug avatar. "Okay by you, Revel? You and I, we're more than ready to transcend the material plane."

"There's better action where we're going," Revel agreed. "We gotta stake a claim in the subdimensions, before the yokels join the gold rush."

A pen appeared in Tug's glowing hand. "We'll shed the surly bonds of incorporation."

It didn't take them long to sign off every interest in Magic Pumpkin. And then the floor of the saucer opened up, dropping Janna, Veruschka, and Kelso onto the street. Over their awestruck heads, the saucer briefly glowed and then sped away, though not in any direction that a merely human being could specify. It was more as if the saucer shrank. Reorganized itself. Corrected. Downsized. And then it was gone from all earthly ken.

And that's how Janna Gutierrez and Veruschka Zipkinova got rich.

POCKETS

(WRITTEN WITH JOHN SHIRLEY)

WHEN the woman from Endless Media called, Wendel was out on the fake balcony, looking across San Pablo Bay at the lights of the closed-down DeGroot Chemicals Plant. On an early summer evening, the lights marking out the columns of steel and the button-shaped chemical tanks took on an unreal glamour; the plant became an otherworldly palace. He'd tried to model the plant with the industrial-strength Real2Graphix program his dad had brought home from RealTek before he got fired. But Wendel still didn't know the tricks for filling a virtual scene with the world's magic and menace, and his model looked like a cartoon toy. Someday he'd get his chops and make the palace come alive. You could set a killer-ass game there if you knew how. After high school, maybe he could get into a good gaming university. He didn't want to "go" to an online university if he could help it; virtual teachers, parallel programmed or not, couldn't answer all your questions.

The phone rang just as he was wondering whether Dad could afford to pay tuition for someplace real. He waited for his dad to get the phone, and after three rings he realized with a chill that Dad had probably gone into a pocket, and he'd have to answer the phone himself.

The fake porch, created for window washers, and to create an impression of coziness the place had always lacked, creaked under his feet as he went to climb through the window. The narrow splintery wooden walkway outside their window was on the third floor of an old waterfront motel converted to studio apartments. Their tall strip of windows, designed to savor a view that was now unsavory, looked down a crumbling cliff at a mud beach, the limp gray waves sluggish in stretched squares of light from the buildings edging the bluff. Down the beach some guys with flashlights were moving around, looking for the little pocket-bubbles that floated in like dead jellyfish. Thanks to the accident that had closed down the DeGroot Research Center, beyond the still-functioning chemicals plant, San Pablo Bay was a good spot to scavenge for pocket-bubbles, which was why Wendel and his dad had ended up living here.

To get to the phone, he had to skirt the mercury-like bubble of Dad's pocket, presently a big flattened shape eight feet across and six high, rounded like a river stone. The pocket covered most of the available space on the living room floor, and he disliked having to touch it. There was that sensation when you touched them—not quite a sting, not quite an electrical shock, not even intolerable. But you didn't want to prolong the feeling.

Wendel touched the speakerphone tab. "Hello, Bell residence."

"Well this doesn't sound like Rothman Bell." It was a woman's voice coming out of the speakerphone; humorous, ditzy, but with a heartening undercurrent of business.

"No ma'am, I'm his son Wendel."

"That's right, I remember he had a son. You'd be about fourteen now?"

"Sixteen."

"Sixteen! Whoa. Time jogs on. This is Manda Solomon. I knew your dad when he worked at MetaMeta. He really made his mark there. Is he home?"

He hesitated. There was no way to answer that question honestly without having to admit Dad was in a pocket, and pocketslugs had a bad reputation. "No ma'am. But . . ."

He looked toward the pocket. It was getting smaller now. If things went as usual, it would shrink to grapefruit size, then swell back up and burst—and Dad would be back. Occasionally a pocket might bounce through two or three or even a dozen shrink-and-grow cycles before releasing its inhabitant, but it never took terribly long, at least from the outside. Dad might be back before this woman hung up. She sounded like business, and that made Wendel's pulse race. It was a chance.

If he could just keep her talking. After a session in a pocket Dad wouldn't be in any shape to call anyone back, sometimes not for days—but if you caught him just coming out, and put the phone in his hand, he might keep it together long enough, still riding the pocket's high. Wendel just hoped this wasn't going to be the one pocket that would finally kill his father.

"Can I take a message, Ms., um . . ." With his mind running so fast he'd forgotten her name.

"Manda Solomon. Just tell him . . ."

"Can I tell him where you're calling from?" He grimaced at himself in the mirror by the front door. Dumbass, don't interrupt her, you'll scare her off.

"From San Jose, I'm a project manager at Endless Media. Just show him—oh, have you got iTV?"

"Yeah. You want me to put it on?" Good, that'd take some more time. If Dad had kept up the payments.

He carried the phone over to the iTV screen hanging on the wall like a seascape; there was a fuzzy motel-decor photo of a sunset endlessly playing in it now, the kitschy orange clouds swirling in the same tape-looping pattern. He tapped the tab on the phone that would hook it to the iTV, and faced the screen so that the camera in the corner of the frame could pick him up but only on head-shot setting so she couldn't see the pocket too. "You see me?"

"Yup. Here I come."

Her picture appeared in a window in an upper corner of the screen, a pleasant looking redhead in early middle age, hoop earrings, frank smile. She held up an e-book, touched the page turner which instantly scrolled an image of a photograph that showed a three-dimensional array of people floating in space, endless pairs of people spaced out into the nodes of a warped jungle-gym lattice, a man and a woman at each node. Wendel recognized the couple as his dad and his mother. At first it looked as if all the nodes were the same, but when you looked closer, you could see that the people at some of the more distant nodes weren't Mom and Dad after all. In fact some of them didn't even look like people. This must be a photo taken inside a pocket with tunnels coming out of it. Wendel had never seen it before. "If you print out the picture, he'll know what it's all about," Manda was saying.

"Sure." Wendel saved the picture to the iTV's memory, hoping it would work. He didn't want Manda to know their printer was broken and wouldn't be repaired anytime soon.

"Well it's been a sweet link but I gotta go—just tell him to call. Here's the number, ready to save? Got it? Okay, then. He'll remember me."

Wendel saw she wasn't wearing a wedding band. He got tired of taking care of Dad alone. He tried to think of some way to keep her on the line. "He'll be right back—he's way overdue. I expect him . . ."

"Whoops, I really gotta jam." She reached toward her screen, then hesitated, her head cocked as she looked at his image. "That's what it is: You look a lot like Jena, you know? Your mom."

"I guess."

"Jena was a zippa-trip. I hated it when she disappeared."

"I don't remember her much."

"Oops, my boss is chiming hysterically at me. Bye!"

"Um—wait." He turned to glance at the dull silvery bubble, already bouncing back from its minimum size, but when he turned back, Manda Solomon was gone and it was only the showy sunset again. "Shit."

He went to the bubble and kicked it angrily. He couldn't feel anything but "stop," with his sneaker on. It wasn't like kicking an object, it was like something stopped you, turned you back toward your own time flow. Just "stopness." It was saying "no" with the stuff of forever itself. There was no way to look inside it: once someone crawled in through a pocket's navel, it sealed up all over.

He turned away, heard something—and when he looked back the pocket was gone and his dad, stinking and retching and raggedly bearded, was crawling toward him across the carpet.

+ + +

Next morning, it seemed to Wendel that his Dad sucked the soup down more noisily than ever before. His hands shook and he spilled soup on the blankets.

His dad was supposedly forty—but he looked fifty-five. He'd spent maybe fifteen years in the pockets—adding up to only a few weeks in outside time, ten minutes here and two hours there and so on.

Dad sat up in his bed, staring out to the bay, sloppily drinking the soup from a bowl, and Wendel had to look away. Sitting at the breakfast bar that divided the kitchenette from the rest of the room, he found himself staring at the pile of dirty clothes in the corner. They needed some kind of hamper, and he could go to some Martinez garage sale and find one next to free. But that was something Dad ought to do; Wendel sensed that if he once started doing that sort of thing, parental things, his dad would give a silent gasp of relief and lean on him, more and more; and paradoxically fall away from him, into the pockets.

"I was gone like—ten minutes world-time?" said Dad. "I don't suppose I missed anything here in this . . . this teeming hive of activity."

"Ten minutes?" said Wendel. He snorted. "You're still gone, Dad. And, yes, there was a call for you. A woman from Endless Media. Manda Solomon. She left her number and a picture."

"Manda?" said Dad. "That flake? Did you tell her I was in a pocket?"

"Right," said Wendel contemptuously. "Like I told her my Dad's a pocket-slug."

Dad opened his mouth like he was going to protest the disrespect—then thought better of it. He shrugged, with as much cool as he could manage. "Manda's down with pockets, Wendel. Half the guys programming virtual physics for MetaMeta were using them when I was there. Pockets are a great way to make a deadline. The MetaMeta crunch-room was like a little glen of chrome puff-balls. Green carpeting, you wave? Manda used to walk around setting sodas and pizzas down outside the pockets. We'd work in there for days, when it was minutes on the outside—get a real edge on the other programmers. She was just a support tech then. We called her Fairy Princess, and we crunchers were the Toads of the Short Forest, popping out all loaded on the bubble-rush. Manda's gone down in the world, what I heard, in terms of who she works for . . ."

"She's a project manager. Better than a support tech."

"Nice of her to think of me." Dad made a little grimace. "Endless Media's about one step past being a virtu-porn Webble. Where's the picture she sent?"

"I saved it in the iTV," said Wendel, and pushed the buttons to show it.

Dad made a groaning sound. "Turn it off, Wendel. Put it away."

"Tell me what it is, first," said Wendel, pressing the controller buttons to zoom in on the faces. It was definitely—

"Mom and me," said Dad shakily. "I took that photo the week before she died." His voice became almost inaudible. "Yeah. You can see . . . some of the images are different further into the lattice . . . because our pocket had a tunnel leading to other pockets. That happens sometimes, you know. It's not a good idea to go down the tunnels. It was the time after this one that . . . Mom didn't come back." He looked at the picture for a moment; like its own pocket, the moment seemed to stretch out to a gray forever. Then he looked away. "Turn it off, will you? It brings me down."

Wendel stared at his mother's young face a moment longer, then turned off the image. "You never told me much about the time she didn't come back."

"I don't need to replay the experience, kid."

"Dad. I . . . look, just do it. Tell me."

Dad stared at him. Looked away. Wendel thought he was going to refuse again. Then he shrugged and began, his voice weary. "It was a much bigger pocket than usual," said Dad, almost inaudible. "MetaMeta . . . they'd scored a shitload of them from DeGroot, and we were merging them together so whole teams could fit in. Using fundamental spacetime geometry weirdness to meet the marketing honcho's deadlines, can you believe? I was an idiot to buy into it. And this last time Jena was mad at me, and she flew away from me while we were in there. And then I couldn't tell which of the lattice-nodes was really her. Like a mirror-maze in a funhouse. And meanwhile I'm all tweaked out of my mind on bubble-rush. But I had my laptop-harness, and there was all that code-hacking to be done, and I got into it for sure, glancing over at all the Jenas now and then, and they're programming too, so I thought it was OK, but then . . ." He swallowed, turning to look out the window, as if he might see her out there in the sky. "When the pocket flattened back out, I was alone. The same shit was coming down everywhere all of a sudden, and then there was the Big Bubble disaster at the DeGroot plant and all the pocket-bubbles were declared government property and if you want to use them anymore . . . people, you know . . ." His voice trailed into a whisper: "They act like you're a junkie."

"Yeah," said Wendel. "I know." He looked out the window for a while. It was a sunny day, but the foulness in the water made the sea a dingy gray, as if it were brooding on dark memories. He spotted a couple of little pocket-bubbles floating in on the brackish waves. Dad had been buying them from beach-combers, merging them together till he got one big enough to crawl into again.

They'd talked about pockets in Wendel's health class at
school last term. In terms of dangerous things the grown-ups
wanted to warn you away from, pockets were right up there
with needles, drunk driving, and doing it bareback. You could
stay inside too long and come out a couple of years older than
your friends. You could lose your youth inside a pocket. Oddly
enough, you didn't eat or breathe in any conventional way while
you were inside there—those parts of your metabolism went into
suspension. The pocket-slugs dug this aspect of the high, for
after all weren't eating and breathing just another wearisome
world-drag? There were even rock songs about pockets setting
you free from "feeding the pig," as the 'slugs liked to call normal
life. You didn't eat or breathe inside a pocket but even so were
still getting older, often a lot faster than you realized. Some
people came out, like, middle-aged.

And of course some people never came out at all. They died
in there of old age, or got killed by a bubble-psychotic pocket-
slug coming through a tunnel, or—though this last one sounded
like government propaganda—you might tunnel right off into
some kind of alien Hell world. If you found a pocket-bubble you
were supposed to take it straight to the police. As opposed to
selling it to a 'slug, or, worse, trying to accumulate enough of
them to get a pocket big enough to go into yourself. The word
was that it felt really good, better than drugs or sex or booze.
Sometimes Wendel wanted to try it—because then, maybe, he'd
understand his dad. Other times the thought terrified him.

He looked at his shaky, strung-out father, wishing he could
respect him. "Do you keep doing it because you think you might
find Mom in there someday?" asked Wendel, his voice plaintive
in his own ears.

"It would sound more heroic, wouldn't it?" said Dad, rubbing his face. "That I keep doing it because I'm on a quest. Better than saying I do it for the high. The escape." He rubbed his face for a minute and got out of bed, a little shaky, but with a determined look on his face. "It's get-it-together time, huh Wendel? Get me a vita-patch from the bathroom, willya? I'll call Manda and go see her today. We need this gig. You ready to catch the light rail to San Jose?"

+ + +

In person Manda Solomon was shorter, plainer, and less well dressed than the processed image she sent out on iTV. She was a friendly ditz, with the disillusioned aura of a Valley-vet who's seen a number of her employers go down the tubes. When Dad calmly claimed that Wendel was a master programmer and his chief assistant, Manda didn't bat an eye, just took out an extra sheaf of nondisclosure and safety-waiver agreements for Wendel to sign.

"I've never had such a synchronistic staffing process before," she said with a breathless smile. "Easy, but weird. Two of our team were waiting in my office when I came into work it one morning. Said I'd left it unlocked. Karma, I guess."

They followed her into a windowless conference room with whiteboards and projection screens. One of the screens showed Dad's old photo of him and Mom scattered over the nodes of a pocket's space-lattice. Wendel's Dad glanced at it and looked away.

Manda introduced them to the other three at the table: a cute, smiling woman named Xiao-Xiao just now busy talking Chinese on her cell phone. She had Bettie Page bangs and the faddish full-eye mirror-contacts; her eyes were like pale lavender Christmas-tree ornaments. Next was a straight-nosed Sikh guy named

Puneet; he wore a turban. He had reassuringly normal eyes, and spoke in a high voice. The third was a puffy white kid only a few years older than Wendel. His name was Barley and he wore a stoner-rock T-shirt. He didn't smile; with his silver mirror-contacts his face was quite unreadable. He wore an uvvy computer interface on the back of his neck. Barley asked Wendel something about programming, but Wendel couldn't even understand the question.

"Ummm . . . well, you know. I just . . ."

"So what's the pitch, Manda?" Dad interrupted, to get Wendel off the spot.

"Pocket-Max," said Manda. "Safe and stable. Five hundred people in there at a time, strapped into . . . I dunno, some kind of mobile pocket-seats. Make downtown San Jose a destination theme park. Harmless, ethical pleasure. We've got some senators who can push it through a loophole for us."

"Safe?" said Dad. "Harmless?"

"Manda says you've logged more time in the pockets than anyone she knows," said Xiao-Xiao. "You have some kind of . . . intuition about them? You must know some tricks for making it safe."

"Well . . . if we had the hardware that created it. . . ." Dad's voice trailed off, which meant he was thinking hard, and Manda let him do it for a moment.

And then she dropped her bomb. "We do have the hardware. Show him Flatland, Barley."

Barley did something with his uvvy and something like a soap film appeared above the generic white plastic of the conference table. "This is a two-dimensional-world mockup," mumbled Barley. "We call it Flatland. The nanomatrix mat for making the real pockets is offsite. Flatland's a piece of visualization software that we got as part of our license. It's a lift."

"*Offsite* would be the DeGroot Center?" said Dad, his voice rising. "You've got full access?"

"Yaaar," said Barley, his fat face expressionless. He was leaning over Flatland, using his uvvy link to tweak it with his blank shining eyes.

"Why was DeGroot making pockets in the first place?" asked Wendel. No one had ever explained the pockets to him. It was like Dad was ashamed to talk about them much.

"It was supposed to be for AI," said Puneet. "Quantum computing nanotech. The DeGroot techs were bozos. They didn't know what they had when they started up the nanomatrix—I don't even know how they invented it. There's no patents filed. It's like the thing fell out of a flying saucer." His laugh was more than a little uneasy. "There's nobody to ask because the DeGroot engineers are all dead. Sucked into the Big Bubble that popped out of their nanomatrix. You saw it on TV. And then Uncle Sam closed them down."

"But—why would the nanomatrix be licensed to Endless Media?" asked Dad. "You're an entertainment company. And not a particularly reputable one, at that. Why you and not one of the big, legit players?"

"Options," said Manda with a shrug. "Market leverage. Networking synergies. And the big guys don't want to touch it. Too big a downside. Part of the setup is we can't sue DeGroot if things don't work out. No biggie for Endless Media. If the shit hits the fan, we take the bullet and go Chapter Eleven. We closed the deal with DeGroot and the Feds last week. Nobody's hardly seen the DeGroot CEO since the catastrophe, but he's still around. Guy named George Gravid. He showed up for about one minute at closing, popped up out of nowhere, walking down the hall. Said he'd been hung up in meetings with some backer dudes—he called them Out-Monkeys? He looked like shit, wearing shades. I think he's strung out on something. Whatever. We did our due diligence, closed the deal, and a second later Gravid was gone." She waved a dismissive hand. "Bottom line is we're fully licensed to use the DeGroot technology. Us and a half-dozen other blue sky groups. Each of us is setting up an operation in the DeGroot Plant on San Pablo Bay. And we time share the access to the nanomatrix. The Endless Media mission in this context is to make a safe and stable Big Bubble that provides a group entertainment experience beyond anything ever seen before."

"Watch how this simulation works," said Barley. "See the yellow square in the film? That's A Square. A two-dimensional Flatlander. He's sliding around, you wave. And that green five-sided figure next to him, that's his son A Pentagon. And now I push up a bubble out of his space." A little spot of the Flatland film bulged up like a time-reversed water drop. The bulge swelled up to the shape of a sphere hovering above Flatland, connected to the little world by a neck of glistening film. "Go in the pocket, Square," said Barley. "Get high."

The yellow square slid forward. He had a bright eye in one of his corners. For a minute he bumbled around the warped zone where the bubble touched his space, then found an entry point and slid up across the neck of the bubble and onto the surface of the little ball. Into the pocket.

"This is what he sees," said Barley, pointing at one of the view screens on the wall. The screen showed an endless lattice of copies of A Square, each of them turning and blinking in unison. "Like a hall of mirrors. Now I'll make the bubble bounce. That's what makes the time go differently inside the pockets, you know."

The sphere rose up from the film. The connecting neck stretched and grew thinner, but it didn't break. The sphere bounced back toward the film, and the neck got fat, the sphere bounced up, and the neck got thin, over and over.

"Check this out," said Barley, changing the image on the view screen to show a circle that repeatedly shrank and grew. "This is what Square Junior sees. The little Pentagon. He stayed outside the bad old pocket, you wave? To him the pocket looks like a disk that's getting bigger and smaller. See him over there on the film? Waiting for Pa. Like little Wendel in the condo on San Pablo Bay."

"Go to hell," said Wendel.

"Don't pick on him, Barley," put in Manda. "Wendel's part of our team."

"Whoah," said Barley. "Now Mr. Square's trip is over." The sphere bounced back and flattened back into the normal space of Flatland.

"You forgot to mention the stabilizer ring," said Dad.

"You see?" said Manda. "I told you guys we needed a physicist."

"What ring?" said Barley.

"A space bubble is inherently unstable," said Dad. "It wants to tear loose or flatten back down. The whole secret of the DeGroot tech was to wrap a superquantum nanoshcet around the bubbles. Bubble wrap. In your Flatland model it's a circle around the neck. Make a new bubble, Barley."

A new bubble bulged up, and this time Wendel noticed that there was indeed a bright little line around the throat of the neck. A line with a gap in it, like the open link of a chain.

"That's the entrance," said Dad, pointing to the little gap. "The navel. Now show me how you model a tunnel."

"We're not sure about the tunnels," said Puneet. "We're

expecting you can help us with this. I cruised the Bharat University Physics Department site and found a Chandreskar-Thorne solution that looks like—can you work it for me, Xiao-Xiao?"

Xiao-Xiao leaned toward the Flatland simulation, her lavender eyes reflecting the scene. She too wore a modern uvvy-style computer controller. Following Puneet's instructions, Xiao-Xiao bulged a second bubble up from the plane, about a foot away from the first one. A Square slid into the first one of them and A Pentagon into the other. And now the bubbles picked up a side-to-side motion, and lumps began sticking out of them, and it just so happened that two of the lumps touched, and now there was a tunnel between the two bubbles.

"Look at the screens now," said Barley. "That's Square's view on the left. And Pentagon's view on the right."

Square's view showed a lattice of Squares as before, but the lattice lines were warped and flawed, and in the flawed region there was a sublattice of nodes showing copies of the Pentagon. Conversely, the Pentagon's view lattice included a wedge of Squares.

"That's a start," said Dad. "But, you know, these pictures of yours—they're just toys. You're talking all around the edges of what the pockets are. You're missing the essence of what they're really about. It's not that they spontaneously bulge up out of our space. It's more that they're raining down on us. From something out here." He gestured at the space above Flatland. "There's a shape up there—with something inside it. I've picked up kind of a feeling for it."

Barley and Xiao-Xiao stared silently at him, their mirrored eyes shining.

"That's why we need you, Rothman," said Manda, finally.

"That's right," said Puneet. "The problem is—when it comes to this new tech, we're bozos too."

+ + +

"I'll tell you what I think," Wendel said gravely. "I think you're lying to them about what you can do, Dad."

It was nearly midnight. Wendel was tired and depressed. They were sitting in the abandoned DeGroot plant's seemingly endless cafeteria, waiting for their daily time-slot with the nanomatrix. Almost the only ones there. The rest of their so-called team hadn't been coming in. Manda and Puneet preferred the safety of San Jose while Barley and Xiao-Xiao had completely dropped out of sight. What a half-assed operation this was.

Wendel and his Dad were eating tinny-tasting stew and drinking watery coffee from the vending machines along the wall opposite the defunct buffets. It was a long, overly lit room, the far end not quite visible from here, with pearly white walls and a greenish floor, asymmetrical rows of round tables like lily pads on the green pond of the floor, going on and on. Endless Media shared the cafeteria with the other scavenging little companies that had licensed access to the nanomatrix. None of the reputable firms wanted to touch it.

"Don't talk about it in here, son," Dad said, listlessly stirring his coffee with a plastic spoon. "We're not alone, you wave."

"The nearest people in here are, like, an eighth of a mile away, I can't even make out their faces from here."

"That's not what I mean. The other groups here, they might be spying on us with gnat-audio, stuff like that. They're all a bunch of bottom-feeders like Endless Media, you know. Nobody knows jack from squat, so they're all looking to copy me."

"You wish. It's good to have work, but you're going to get in deep shit, Dad. You're telling Endless Media you're down with the tech when you're not. You're telling them you can stabilize a Big Bubble when you can't. You say you can keep tunnels from hooking into it—but you don't know how."

"Maybe I can. I have to test it some more."

"You test it every night."

"Not enough. I haven't actually gone inside it yet."

"Come on. I'm the one who has to put you back together after a bubble binge. It's great having an income from this gig, Dad, a better place to live—but I'm not going to let you vanish into that thing. Something just like it killed the whole DeGroot team five years ago."

His dad gave Wendel a glare that startled him. It was almost feral. Chair screeching nastily on the tile, Dad got up abruptly and went across the room to a coffee vending machine for another latte. He ran his card through the slot, then swore. He stalked back over to the table long enough to say, "Be right back, this card's used up, I've got another one in my locker."

"You're not going to sneak up to the lab without me, are you? Our time-slot starts in five minutes, you know. At midnight."

"Son? Don't. I'm the Dad, you're the kid. Okay? I'll be right back."

Wendel watched him go. *I'm the Dad, you're the kid.* There were a lot of comebacks he could've made to that one.

Wendel sipped his gooey stew, then pushed it away. It was tepid, the vegetables mushy, making him think of bits of leftover food floating in dishwater. He heard a *beep*, looked toward the vending machines. The machine Dad had run his card through was beeping, flashing a little light.

Wendel walked over to it. A small screen on the machine said, *Do you wish to cancel your purchase?*

Which was only something it said if the card was good. Which meant that Dad had gone to the lab without him. Wendel felt a sick chill that made his fingers quiver . . . and sprinted toward the elevators.

+ + +

The pocket was so swollen he could hardly get into the big testing room with it. Maybe two hundred feet in diameter, sixty feet high. Mercuric and yet lusterless. The various measuring instruments were crowded up against the walls.

"Dad?" he called tentatively. But Wendel knew Dad was gone. He could feel his absence from the world.

He edged around the outside of the Big Bubble, grimacing when he came into contact with it. Somewhere beneath the great pocket was the nanomatrix mat that produced it—or attracted it? But it wasn't like you could do anything to turn the pocket off once it got here. At least nothing that they'd figured out yet, which was one of the many obstacles preventing this thing from being a realistic public attraction. "Show may last from one to ten minutes world time, and seem to take one hour to three months of your proper time." Even if there were a way to shut the pocket off now—what would that do to Dad?

Facing a far corner was the dimpled spot, the entrance navel. On these Big Bubbles, the navel didn't always seal over. When Wendel looked into the navel, it seemed to swirl like a slow-motion whirlpool, but in two contradictory directions. Hypnotic. It could still be entered.

Wendel made up his mind: he would go after his dad. He leaned forward, pressed his fingers against the navel, thinking of

A Pentagon sliding up over the warped neck that led to the sphere of extra space. His hands looked warped, as if they were underwater. They tingled—not unpleasantly. He pushed his arms in after and then, with a last big breath of air, his head. How would it feel to stop breathing?

It was a while till Wendel came back to that question. The first feeling of being inside the pocket was one of falling—but this was just an illusion, he was floating, not falling, and he had an odd, dreamlike ability to move in whatever direction he wanted to, not that the motion seemed to mean much.

There was a dim light that came from everywhere and nowhere. Spread out around him were little mirror-Wendels, all turning their heads this way and that, gesturing and—yes—none of them breathing. It was like flying underwater and never being out of breath, like being part of a school of fish. The space was patterned with veils of color like seaweed in water. Seeing the veils pass, he could tell that he was moving, and as the veils repeated themselves he could see that he was moving in a great circle. He was like A Pentagon circling around and around his bulged-up puffball of space. But where was Dad? He changed the angle of his motion, peering around for distinctions in the drifting school of mirror shapes.

The motion felt like flying, now, with a wind whipping his hair, and he found a new direction in which the space veils seemed to curve like gossamer chambers of mother of pearl, sketching a sort of nautilus-spiral into the distance. Looking into that distance, that twist of infinity, and feeling the volume of sheer potentiality, he felt the first real wave of bubble-rush. His fatigue evaporated in the searing light of the rush, a rippling, bone-deep pleasure that seemed generated by his flying motion into the spiral of the pocket.

"*Whuh*-oaaaah . . ." he murmured, afraid of the feeling and yet liking it. So this was why Dad came here. Or one of the reasons. There was something else too . . . something Dad never quite articulated.

The bubble-rush was so all-consuming, so shimmeringly insistent, he felt he couldn't bear it. It was simply too much; too much pleasure, and you lost all sense of self; and then it was, finally, no better than pain.

Wendel thought, "Stop!" and his motion responded to his will. He stopped where he was—an inertialess stop partway into the receding nautilus spiral. The bubble-rush receded a bit, damped back down to a pleasing background glow.

"Dad!" he yelled. No response. "DAD!" His voice didn't echo; he couldn't tell how loud it was. There was air in here to be sucked in and expelled for speaking. But when he wasn't yelling, he felt no need to take a breath. Like a vampire in his grave.

He tried to get some kind of grasp of the shape of this place. He thought with an ugly *frisson* of fear: Maybe I'm already lost. How do I find my way back out?

Could A Pentagon slide back out the neck into the ball? Or would he have to wait for the ball to burn out its energy and flatten back into space?

There were no images of Wendel up ahead, where the patterns of the space seemed to twirl like a nautilus. It must be a tunnel. If pockets were dangerous, the tunnels from pocket to pocket were said to be much worse. But he knew that's where Dad had gone.

He moved into the tunnel, flying at will.

The pattern haze ahead of him took on flecks of pink, human color. Someone else was down there. "Dad?"

He leaned into his flying—and stopped, about ten yards short of the man. It wasn't Dad. This man was bearded, emaciated, sallow . . . which Dad could be, by now, in the time-bent byways of this place. But it wasn't his Dad, it was a stranger, a man with big, scared eyes and a grin that looked permanently fixed. No teeth: barren gums. The man sitting was floating in fetal position, arms around his knees.

"Ya got any grub on yer, boy?" the man rasped. A UK accent. Or was it Australian?

"Um–" He remembered he had two-thirds of a power bar of some kind in a back pocket. Probably linty by now, but likely this 'slug wouldn't care. "You want this?"

He tossed over the power bar, and the pocket-slug's eyes flashed as he caught it, fairly snatched it out of the air. "Good on ya, boy!" He gnawed on the linty old bar with his callused gums.

It occurred to Wendel that at some point he might regret giving away his only food. But supposedly you didn't need to eat in here. Food was just fun for the mouth, or a burst of extra energy. Right now the scene made him chuckle to himself–the bubble-rush was glowing in him; it made everything seem absurd, cartoonlike, and marvelous.

Between sucking sounds, the 'slug said, "My name's Threakman. Jeremy Threakman. 'ow yer 'doin."

"I don't know how I'm doing. I'm looking for my Dad. Rothman Bell. He's about . . ."

"No need, I know whuh 'e looks like. Seen 'im go through 'ere." Threakman looked at Wendel with his head cocked. A sly look. "Feelin' the 'igh, are ya? Sure'n you are. Stoned, eh boy? Young fer it."

"I feel something–what is it? What causes it?"

"Why, it's a feelin' of being right there in yerself, beyond all uncertainty about where yer might go, and fully knowin' that yer hidden and on your own. And that'll get you 'igh. Or some say. Others, like me, they say it's the Out-Monkeys that do it."

"The Out . . . what?"

"Out-Monkeys," said Threakman. "What I call 'em. Other's call 'em Dream Beetles, one 'slug in here used ter call 'em Turtles— said he saw a turtle thing with a head like a screw-top bottle without the cap and booze pouring out, but he was a hardcore alkie. Others they see'm more like lizards or Chinese dragons. Dragons, beetles, monkeys, all hairy around the edges, all curlin' out at yer—it's a living hole in space, mate, and you push the picture you want on it. Me and the smartuns calls 'em Out-Monkeys cause they're from outside our world."

"You mean—from another planet?"

"No mate, from the bigger universe that *this* one is kinder *inside*. They got more dimensions than we do. They're using DeGroot and the nanomatrix—they give all that ta us to pull us in, mate. The Out-Monkeys are drizzlin' pockets down onto us, little paradise balls where yer don't have to breathe nor eat an' yer can fly an' there's an energy that stim-yer-lates that part of yer brain, don't ya see. The Out-Monkeys want us all stony in here. Part of their li'l game, innit? Come on, show yer somethin. The Alef. Mayhap yer'll see yer Da."

In a single spasmodic motion Threakman was up, flying off in some odd new direction through the silvery scarves of the enclosing spaces—leaving a rank scent in the air behind him. Wendel whipped along after him, remembering not to breathe. Soon, if it could be thought of as soon, they came to a nexus where the images around them thickened up into an incalculable diversity. It was like being at the heart of a city in a surveillance zone with a million monitors, but the images weren't electronic, they were real, and endlessly repeated.

"The Alef has tunnels to all the pockets," said Threakman. "Precious few of us knows about it."

In some directions, he saw pockets with people writhing together—he realized, with embarrassment, that they were copulating. But was that really sex? He made himself look away. In another pocket, people were racing around one another in a blur like those electro-cyclists in the Cage of Death he'd seen at a carnival. Off down the axis of another tunnel, people clawed at one another, in a thronging melange of combat; you couldn't tell one from another, so slick was the blood. But the greatest number of the pockets held solitary 'slugs, hanging there in self-absorbed pleasure, surrounded by the endless mirror-images of themselves. And one of these addicts was Dad, floating quite nearby.

"For 'im, mate," said Threakman as Wendel flew off toward his father.

Not quite sure of his aim, he hit Dad with a thud—and Dad screamed, thrashing back from him. Stopping himself in space to glare shame and resentment at Wendel—like a kid caught masturbating.

"What are you *doing*?" demanded Wendel. "You call this research?"

"Okay, you really want to know?" snapped his father. "I'm looking for Jena. Mom."

Wendel peered at his father; his Dad's face, here, seemed more like the possibility of all possible Dad facial expressions, crystallized. It was difficult to tell whether he meant it. It might be bullshit. What was the saying? *How do you know an addict is lying? When his lips are moving!*

But the possibility of seeing Mom made Wendel's heart thud. "You think she's still in here? Seriously, Dad?"

"I think the Out-Monkeys got her. That's what happens, you know. Some of the pockets float up—not 'up' exactly, but 'ana'—"

"To the shape above 'Flatland,'" said Wendel.

"Right," said Dad. "We're in their 'Flatland' relatively speaking. And I want to get up there and find her."

"But you're just floating around in here. You're on the goddamn nod, Dad. You're not looking at all."

"Oh yes I am. I'm looking, goddammit. This happens to be just the right spot to stare down through the Alef and up along the Out-Monkeys' tunnel. Not their tunnel, exactly. The spot where they usually appear. Where their hull touches us. I'm waiting for them to show up."

"The Devil in his motorboat," said Wendel with a giggle. The bubble-rush was creeping back up on him. Dad laughed, too. They were thinking of the old joke about the guys in Hell, standing neck deep in liquid shit and drinking coffee, and one of them says, "Wal, this ain't so bad," and the other one says, "Yeah, but wait till—"

"Here it comes," said Dad, and it wasn't funny anymore, for the space up ahead of them had just opened up like a blooming squash-flower, becoming incalculably larger, all laws of perspective broken, and an all-but-endless vista spreading out, a giant space filled with moving shapes that darted and wheeled like migrating flocks of birds. It was hard to think straight, for the high of the bubble space had just gotten much stronger.

"The mothership," said Threakman, who'd drifted down to join them. "Yaaar. Can you feel the rush off it? Ahr, but it's good. Hello to yer, there, Da." He gave a deep, loose chuckle. Everything was glistening and wonderful, as perfect as the first instant of Creation; and, as with that moment, chaos waited on the event horizon: chaos and terror.

"Those shapes are the Out-Monkeys?" asked Wendel, his voice sounding high and slow in his ears. "They look like little people."

"Those little things *are* people," said Dad. "They're the pets."

"Livin' decals on the mothership's hull," said Threakman. "Live decorations fer the Out-Monkeys. An antfarm for their window-box. Ah, yer'll know it when you really see an Out-Monkey, Wendel. When 'e reaches out through the hull . . ."

Then the space around them quivered like gelatin, and the cloud of moving people up ahead spiraled in around a shaky, black, living hole in space, a growing thing with fractal fringes, a three-dimensional Mandelbrot formation that, to Wendel, looked like a dancing, star-edged monkey made up of other monkeys, like the old Barrel of Monkeys toy he'd had, with all the little monkeys hooked together to make bigger monkeys that hooked together to make a gigantic monkey, coming on and on: a cross-section of a higher-dimensional alien, partly shaped by the Rorschach filter of human perception.

Wendel thought: Out-Monkey? And the thing echoed psychically back at him, *Out-Monkey!* with the alien thought coming at him like a voice in his head, mocking, drawling, sarcastic, and infinitely hip.

The Out-Monkey swelled, huge but with no real size to it in any human sense, and the fabric of space rippled with its motions—the Devil's motorboat indeed—and Wendel felt his whole body flexing and wobbling like an image in a funhouse mirror. Beneath the space waves, a sinister undertow began tugging at him. Wendel felt he would burst with the disorientation of it all.

"Dad—we've gotta go! Let's get back to the world! Tell, him, Jeremy!"

"No worries yet," said Threakman grinning and flaring his nostrils as if to inhale the wild, all-pervading rush. "Steady as she goes, mate. Your Dad and me, we've had some practice with the Out-Monkeys. We can 'ang here a bit longer."

"Look at the faces, Wendel!" cried Dad. "Look for Jena!"

Around the Out-Monkey orbited the people imprisoned on its vast bubble. They seemed to rotate around the living hole in space, caught up in the fractals that crawled around its edges: faces that were both ecstatic and miserable, zoned-out and hysterical.

"There goes George Gravid," said Dad, pointing. "The original guy from DeGroot." Wendel stared, spotting a businessman in a black suit. And there, not too far from him were—Barley and Xiao-Xiao?

"Come on, come on, come on," Dad was chanting, and then he gave a wild laugh. "Yes! There she is! It's Jena!" His laughter was cracked and frantic. "It's Mom, Wendel! I knew I could find her!"

Wendel looked—and thought he saw her. Looking hard at her had a telescopic effect, like concentration itself was the optical instrument, and his vision zoomed in on her face—it was his mom, though her eyes were blotted with silver, like the faddish contacs people wore in the World. All of those rotating around the Out-Monkey had silvered eyes, mirror-eyes endlessly looking into themselves.

Torn, Wendel hesitated—and then the fractal leviathan swept closer—he felt something like its shadow fall over him, though there were no localized light sources here to throw shadows. It was, rather, as if the greater dimensional inclusiveness of the Out-Monkey overshadowed the limited-dimensional beings here, and you could feel its "shadow" in your soul. . . .

"Dad!" Wendel shouted in panic, and his father yelled something back, but he couldn't make it out—there was a torrent of white-noise crackle upwelling all around him in the growing "shadow" of the Out-Monkey. "*Dad! We have to go!*" shrieked Wendel.

And then Dad plunged forward, arrowing in toward Mom, and Wendel felt himself on the point of a wild, uncontrolled tumble.

"Ol'roit, mate," said Threakman, grabbing Wendel's arm and pulling him up short. "Keep yer 'ead now. Ungodly strong rush, innit? It's 'ard not to go all the way in. But remember—if yer really want, yer *can* 'old back from its pullin' field. Let's ease in, nice and quietlike, and try and snag your Dad."

Wendel and Threakman inched forward—Wendel feeling the pull of the Out-Monkey as strong as gravity. Yet, just as Threakman said, you didn't have to let it take you, didn't have to let it pull you down into that swarming blackness of the Out-Monkey's fractal membranes. Jeremy Threakman's grip on his arm was solid as the granite spine of the planet Earth. Wretched, stinking Jeremy Threakman knew his way around the Out-Monkeys.

Wendel stared in at Mom and Dad: they were swirling around one another, orbiting a mutual center of emptiness, just as they and the others orbited the greater center of emptiness within the higher-dimensional being. It reminded Wendel of a particular carnival ride, where people whirled in place on a metal arm, and their whirling cars were also whirled around a central axis.

"Dad!"

Dad looked at him—if it could be called looking. In the thrall of the Out-Monkey, it was more like he was going through the motions of turning his attention to Wendel, and that attention was represented by the image of an attentive paternal face. "Wendel, I don't think I can get out! It's snagging my . . ." His voice was lost in a surging crackle, a wave of static. Then: ". . . purple, thinking purple. . . ." Crackle. ". . . your mom! It wants us!"

Wendel's arm ached where Threakman clutched him. "We gotter go soon, mate!" said the scarred pocket-slug.

Mom turned her attention toward Wendel too now—she was reaching for him, weeping and laughing. He wasn't sure if it was psychic or vocal, but he heard her say: "We're pets, Wendel!" Static. "Waterstriders penned in a corner of the pond." His mother's face was lit with unholy bliss. "Live bumper stickers." A sick peal of laughter.

There was another ripple in the space around them, and all of a sudden Mom and Dad were only a few feet away. Close enough to touch. Wendel reached out to them.

"Come on, Mom! Take my hand! Jeremy and I—we *can* pull you out! You can leave if you want to!"

How Wendel knew this, he wasn't sure. But he knew it was true. He could feel it—could feel the relative energy loci, the possibility of pulling free, if you tried.

"We can go home, Dad! You and me and Mom!"

"Can't!" came his Dad's voice from a squirming gargoyle of his father with a fractal fringe.

"Dad don't *lie* to me! You can do it! Don't lie! You can come . . . !"

His arm ached so—but he waited for the answer.

Wordlessly, his father emanated regret. Remorse. Shame. "Yes," he admitted finally. "But I choose this. Mom and I . . . we want to stay here. Part of the gorgeous Out-Monkey. The eternal fractals." Static. ". . . can't help it. Go away, Wendel!"

"Have a life, Wendel!" said Mom said. Several versions of her face said it, several different ways. "Don't come back. The nanomatrix—you can melt it. Acid!" Huge burst of static. "Hurry up now. It heard me!"

He felt it too: the chilling black-light search beam of the Out-Monkey's attention, spotlighting him like an escaped prisoner just outside the wall . . .

"No, Mom! Come back! Mom—"

Mom and Dad swirled away from him, their faces breaking up into laughing, jabbering fractals. The white noise grew intolerably loud.

"Gotter leave!" screamed Threakman in his ear. "Jump!"

With an impulse that was as much resentment, of running away in fury, as it was a conscious effort, he leapt with Threakman away from the hardening grip of the Out-Monkey, and felt himself spinning out through the dimensions and down the tunnels, he and Threakman in a whirling blur, one almost blending with the other. He thought he caught a glimpse of Threakman's memories, bleeding over in the strange ambient fields of the place from his companion's mind: a father with a leather strap; a woman giving him his first blowjob in the backroom of a Sydney bar; working as a sailor; being mugged in London; a stout woman angrily leaving him. All this time Threakman was steering him through the bent spaces, helping him find his way back.

And then their minds were discrete again, and they were flying through a vortex of faces and pearly-gray glimmer, through a symmetrical lattice of copies of themselves, back out into the Big Bubble space he'd first entered. And just about then the bubble flattened down into normal space—and burst. He was back in the world.

Wendel knelt in the huge lab room, sobs of fury bubbling out of him, beside the floor mat of the little nanomatrix, slapping his palm flat on the floor, again and again, in his frustration and hurt. Especially, hurt. His dad and mom had chosen *that* over him. They hadn't really been inescapably caught—*it was a choice*. They'd chosen their master, the Out-Monkey; they'd gone into a spinning closed system of onanistic ecstasy; sequestered their hearts in another world, in the pursuit of pleasure and escape. They'd left him alone.

"Fuck YOU!" he screamed, pounding his fist on the nanomatrix. The magical bit of alien high tech was a fuzzy gray rectangle, for all the world like a cheap plastic doormat. That's all the lab was, really. An empty room, some instruments, and a scrap of magic carpet on the floor.

"Roit," said Threakman hoarsely, slumping down wearily next to him. "My old man, 'e was the same way. But for 'im it was the bottle. The Out-Monkeys, they use the 'igh to pull their pets in. Something sweet 'n' sticky—like the bait for a roach motel. And, God 'elp me, I'm hooked. I won't make it back out next time. I need to . . . something else. Bloody hell—anything else."

"Mom and Dad coulda left! They weren't stuck at all!"

"Yeah. I reckon." Threakman was tired, shaky. Pale. "Lor' I feel bad, mate. I miss that rush like it was my only love. Whuh now?"

Wendel stared down at the nanomatrix. Tiny bubbles glinted in the hairs that covered it, endlessly oozing out from it. It was like a welcome mat that someone had sprinkled with beads of mercury. The little pockets winked up at him, as if say, *"Wanna get high?"*

"The chemical factory," said Wendel. "Right next door. I know where there's a tank of nitric acid." He pulled at a corner of the nanomatrix. It was glued to the floor, but with Threakman working at his side, he was able to peel it free. He rolled up the grimy mat and tucked it under his arm, tiny bubbles scattering like dust.

The clock on the wall outside the lab said 12:03. All that crazy shit in the Big Bubble—it had lasted about a minute of real time. The next team wasn't scheduled till 2:00 AM. The halls were empty.

Threakman shambled along at Wendel's side as Wendel led them out of the Research building and across a filth-choked field to the chemical plant, staying in the shadows on one side. Wendel knew the plant well from all the hours he'd spent looking at it and thinking about modeling it. The guards wouldn't see them if they cut in over here. They skirted the high, silver cylinder of a cracking tower, alive with pipes, and climbed some mesh-metal stairs that led to a broad catwalk, ten feet across.

"The acid tank's that way," whispered Wendel. "I've seen the train cars filling it up." The rolled-up nanomatrix twitched under his arm, as if trying to unroll itself.

"This'll be the hard bit," said Threakman, uneasily. "The Out-Monkeys can see down onto us, I'll warrant."

Wendel tightened his grip on the nanomatrix, holding it tight in both hands. It pushed and shifted, but for the moment, nothing more. They marched forward along the catwalk, their feet making soft clanging noises in the night.

"That great thumpin' yellow one with the writin' on it?" said Threakman, spotting the huge metal tank that held acid. Practically every square foot of the tank was stenciled with safety warnings. "Deadly deadly *deadly*," added Threakman with a chuckle. He ran ahead of Wendel to get a closer look, leaning eagerly forward off the edge of the catwalk. "Just my cuppa tea. Wait till I undog this hatch. Let's get rid of the mat before I change my mind."

The nanomatrix was definitely alive, twisting in Wendel's hands like a big, frantic fish. He stopped walking, concentrating on getting control of the thing, coiling it up tighter than before. "Hurry, Jeremy," he called. "Get the tank open, and I'll come throw this fucker in."

But now there was a subtle shudder of space, and Wendel heard a voice. "Not so fast, dear friends."

A businessman emerged out of thin air, first his legs, then his body, and then his head—as if he were being pasted down onto space. He stood there in his black, tailored suit, poised midway on the catwalk between Wendel and Threakman.

"George Gravid," said the businessman. His eyes were dark black mirrors, and his suit, on closer inspection, was filthy and rumpled, as if he'd been wearing it for months—or years. "The nanomatrix is DeGroot property, Wendel. Not that I really give a shit. This tune's about played out. But I'm supposed to talk to you."

There was another shudder and a whispering of air, and now Barley and Xiao-Xiao were at Gravid's side, Barley sneering, and Xiao-Xiao's little face cold and hard. The plant lights sparkled on their reflective eyes, black and silver and lavender. Wendel took a step back.

"Run around 'em, Wendel," called Threakman. "I got the hatch off. Dodge through!"

Wendel was fast and small. He had a chance, though the bucking of the nanomatrix was continuously distracting him. He faked to the left, ran to the right, then cut back to the left again.

Gravid, Barley, and Xiao-Xiao underwent a jerky stuttering motion—an instantaneous series of jumps—and ended up right in front of him. Barley gave Wendel a contemptuous little slap on the cheek.

"The Higher One picks us up and puts us down," said Xiao-Xiao. "You can't get past us. You have to listen."

"You're being moved around by an Out-Monkey?" said Wendel.

"That's a lame-ass term," said Barley. "They're *Higher Ones.* Why did you leave?"

"You're its pets," Wendel said, stomach lurching in revulsion. "Toys." The fumes from the nitric acid tank were sharp in the air.

"We're free agents," said Gravid. "But it's better in there than out here."

"The mothership's gonna leave soon," said Barley. "And we're goin' with it. Riding on the hull. Us and your parents. Don't be a dirt-world loser, Wendel. Come on back."

"The Higher One wants you, Wendel," said Gravid. "Wants to have another complete family. You know how collectors are."

The nanomatrix bucked wildly, and a fat silver pocket swelled out of its coiled-up end like a bubble from a bubble pipe. The pocket settled down onto the catwalk, bulging and waiting. Wendel had a sudden deep memory of how good the rush had felt.

"Whatcher mean, the ship is leavin'?" asked Threakman, drawn over to stare at the bubble, which was half the height of a man now. Its broad navel swirled invitingly.

"They've seen enough of our space now," said Xiao-Xiao. "They're moving on. Come on now, Wendel and Jeremy. This is bigger than anything you'll ever do." She mimed a sarcastic little kiss, bent over, and squeezed herself into the pocket.

"I want some too," said Barley, and followed her.

"Last call," said Gravid, going back into the bubble as well.

And now it was just Wendel and Threakman and the pocket, standing on the catwalk. The nanomatrix lay still in Wendel's hands.

"I don't know as I can live without it, yer know," said Threakman softly.

"But you said you want to change," said Wendel.

"Roight," said Threakman bleakly. "I did say."

Wendel skirted around the pocket, and walked over to where the acid tank's open hatch gaped. The nanomatrix had stopped fighting him. He and his world were small; the Out-Monkeys had lost interest. It was a simple matter to throw the plastic mat into the tank, and he watched it fall, end over end.

Choking fumes wafted out, and Wendel crawled off low down on the catwalk toward the breathable air.

When he sat up, Threakman and the bubble were both gone. And somewhere deep in his guts, Wendel felt a shudder, as of giant engines moving off. The pockets were gone? Maybe. But there'd always be a high that wanted to eat you alive. Life was a long struggle.

He walked away from the research center, toward the train station, feeling empty, and hurt—and free.

There were some things at the apartment he could sell. It would be a start. He would do all right. He'd been taking care of himself for a long time.

COBB WAKES UP

COBB Anderson had been dead for a long time. It was heaven.

But now someone was bringing him back to life. First came a white-light popping-flashbulb panic attack feeling of not knowing who or what or why, a pure essence of "*Huh?*"—but not even the word, not even the question mark, just the empty spot where a question would be, were there a way to form one. Yes, Cobb's new-started mind was like a cartoon image of something missing: a white void with alternating long and short surprise lines radiating out from a central lack. Huh?

Then came an interval of autonomous, frenzied activity as his encoded boot script mined his S-cube database to reconstruct the fractal links and dynamic attractors of his personality. Cobb became aware of himself waking up, and then went into an eidetic memory flash of the time back in 1965 when he'd had surgery to remove his accidentally ruptured spleen, had woken from dreams of struggle to see an attractive private nurse leaning over him, and had realized with embarrassment that this pleasant woman, one of his father's parishioners, was the unseen force he'd been druggedly fighting and soddenly cursing while trying to pull a painfully thick tube from out of his nose. Ow.

Right after the nurse memory, Cobb felt his personality flaring up bright and lively, as if in a hearth pumped by the bellows of iterative parallel computations. He visualized a cozy fireplace, reflected on the image of *fire*, and was then off into another child-hood memory, this one of visiting newly dead president JFK's grave and seeing the little eternal flame fluttering from a mingy metal rosette in the cold stone tombstone on the trampled muddy grass by the gray Potomac River.

But that meant nothing. Here and now, Cobb was alive, and just a few impossible seconds ago, he'd been dead. He made a convulsive crash effort to remember what it had been like.

Materialism to the contrary, there were indeed some haunting, phantasmagoric scraps of memory from the void downtime of no hardware, no wetware, no limpware. When Cobb was turned off, totally dead, he still *did* exist—in an supernal, timeless now. In that other state—Cobb readily thought of it as *heaven*—there lived all the souls of all the lives, woven together in a joyous, singing tapestry of light that added up to a kind and great cosmic mind, aka God. Cobb loved being inside God. And now he was back out in the cold. Born again.

"Oh no," were Cobb's first murmured words.

His initial sorrow was quickly tempered by excitement at being back in the intriguing tangles of mortal time. He'd return to paradise soon enough. And meanwhile who knew what would happen!

Cobb had no sensation of a body, which suggested that he was being simulated as a subsystem of some larger computation. Though he had no ears, a sweet voice spoke to him. How quickly life's juicy, burdensome intricacies could become real.

"Hello, Cobb. Yee-haw and flubba geep. I'm Chunky, the seven-moldie grex who's running this emulation. Your grandson Willy hired me and my neighbor Dot to help do a limpware port of your sorry-ass old bopper machine code. I think we'll be ready in an hour, and then you get your own imipolex body, dear pheezer. Dot and I are running parallel sessions of you to confirm that there are no bugs. So welcome back! If all goes well, you'll be here for a good long time."

"And eventually it'll be over again," said Cobb. "And I won't mind. I've been in—oh, call it the SUN. Or just call it God. It's beautiful there; a serene and eternal river of joy. God is a song, Chunky, and all the dead souls sing it."

"What does it sound like?"

"It sounds like this," said Cobb and intoned the sacred syllable. "*Auuuuuum.*" The resonant vibration. "Haven't you ever been dead, Chunky? And what do you mean by saying that you're a seven-moldie grex?"

"I mean that I'm made up of seven individual moldies," said Chunky. "A moldie being an intelligent imipolex slug with veins of fungus and algae growing inside it, you wave. We moldies evolved out of the flickercladding skins that the original bopper robots used to have, the original boppers being of course invented by *you*, Dr. Cobb Anderson. Which was why, as you got older and sicker, the boppers coded up your personality as the crusty old software that we just finished booting. Yes indeed. Now for the *grex* part of your question. A grex is a group organism voluntarily formed by moldies in order to accomplish life's main goal of earning enough imipolex to reproduce themselves. When a group of moldies are joined into a grex, they're an *I* and not a *we*; they think as one. After enough scores, a grex dissolves, and the member moldies go off on their fucking way, 'fucking' in the literal sense of having sex to make a baby. Finally, with regard to the *been dead* question, no I haven't, though of course most of my fourteen parental units are in fact dead and perhaps in heaven singing 'Aum.' I don't suppose you noticed them?" Chunky giggled mildly, not seeming to expect an answer.

Floating in Cobb's sea of inchoate perceptions was a bright spot that he recognized as an optic feed. He focused his attention on it, and the spot grew to become a hemispherical visual field. Wobbly images flickered and died, hopelessly scumbled by feedback moirés of spiral diamonds.

"Ow, that's one of my eyes," said Chunky gently. "Which I'm only temporarily lending to you. Turn down the gain, Cobb. We're talking about a delicate organ, old cruster. Um—act like you're rubbing your face."

Cobb made the phantom gesture of rubbing his face, and the gesture was reinforced by a pleasant feeling of skin contact. His vision cleared. He was looking out through a smooth stone arch, as if from the inside of a well-worn cave. Outside the hole was a clutter of stones and boulders, and beyond that stretched a boulevard lined with small buildings. Bright, flexing figures moved down the avenue, and in the distance was a patch of blazingly bright sunlight. In the far distance, on the other side of the bright patch, was high curving wall twinkling with spots of colored light. Curious to have a better look, Cobb made as if to step forward, but he was quite unable to move.

"I'm glued here like a sea anemone," said Chunky. "If I were to start humping around, it would tangle up my carefully cultivated mycelium dendrites, which are what make me so smart and employable in the first place. But you can push out your eyestalk. Just act like you're craning your neck."

Cobb craned, and the moldie-flesh neck that held his—or Chunky's—eye stretched out one, five, ten meters. Chunky's reference to the sea had set him to wondering if perhaps she were an artificial creature lodged in some deep ocean reef, but his ease of motion told him he wasn't in any water. Far from it. It felt like there wasn't even any air. He made a turning motion and looked back along his eyestalk at Chunky's bod.

Chunky was a soft-looking squat disk, very like a sea anemone. A piezoplastic space anemone. His—"No, I'm a *her*," said Chunky's contralto voice, interrupting Cobb's interior monologue—*her* flesh was tinged a pale green from the included algae, with highlights of purple and beige. Her body-plan was radial, with a central crown of perhaps a hundred pointy tentacles. Seven eyestalks rose out of the crown's core, and one of them was allocated to Cobb. As he watched, the other six eyes stretched out to join him. For a silly minute the seven eyes bobbed and bumped, staring into each other.

"Being in me is like being in that heaven you were talking about, huh?" said Chunky. "Because really I'm seven different personalities—*eight* counting you now, Cobb—but they're all merged into one big fat body. Fat is good. Do you like your eye?"

"This eye's the only thing that's all mine right now?"

"The eye is *ours*," said Chunky, her six other eyes merrily staring into Cobb's. "There is no *mine*. Why aren't you picking up on the philosophical metaphor? Do you think an idea's only interesting unless you made it up yourself? I can see your thoughts Cobb, clear as day. Now listen. My body—it's a symbol of your God, your SUN, your cosmic One Mind jellyfish. Each individual sentient being is an eyestalk that the universe grows to look at itself with. Me, I'm a grex made of seven moldies who think as one, and usually each of my moldies has its own eyestalk to wave around. Bonk!" One of Chunky's eyes caromed off Cobb's, but it didn't hurt, it felt nice, it felt like a kiss. Cobb and the fat anemone's six other eyes bounced each other some more, until each had touched all the others, like champagne flutes raised in a toast.

"Here's to the success of the new limpware Cobb Anderson!" said Chunky.

Gazing past bumptious Chunky's six eyes, Cobb noticed that there was another cave just next door. And sticking out of that cave's door were seven more eyestalks, and one of them was looking at him with the same peculiar fixity with which he was looking at it.

"Is that Dot right there?" Cobb asked Chunky. "I think you said Dot was running her own simulation of Cobb Anderson? Is that another *me* over there, inside that one eye that's leaning closer?"

As Cobb craned across the space between the two caves, one of the eyes in the other group craned symmetrically nearer, approaching smoothly and steadily as a reflection in a mirror. Yes, he was sure that it was he.

"You want to talk to him," whispered Chunky warmly. "Don't you, Cobbie? Dot and I will patch you in."

"Hello, Cobb," Cobb said to the other eyestalk, and at the same instant he heard it saying hello to *him*. Their thoughts of speaking were being converted into signals that Dot and Chunky exchanged by radio waves and reconverted into signals that their emulations could interpret as sound.

"What did you think about when you woke up?" asked the other Cobb, just as Cobb started to ask it himself.

Expecting to be readily understood, Cobb answered concisely. "First I had white-light panic, then I remembered the spleen nurse, then JFK's eternal flame, and then I got some memories of, of—"

"The SUN," said the other Cobb. "I know. I saw the exact same things. The light, the nurse, the flame, the memories of heaven. That's so strange."

"It's not strange," put in Dot. "It's logical." Her voice came across as nasal and penetrating. "I could start this Cobbware up a hundred times, and each time the personality emulation would always remember the *exact* same scenes, every detail the same—because the early part of the boot process is a fully deterministic algorithm, no different in principle from tracking the orbit of a point on a strange attractor. If you start in the same place, you always get the same pattern."

"But don't worry," said Chunky. "Once a Cobb personality session is up and running, it begins interacting with the ever-various real world and zigzags off into some wild and wacky new future. High Lyapunov-exponent dependence on perturbations, don't you know. It's just the early parts of the wake-up sequence that are completely predictable. In fact, Dot and I have been simulating a shitload of Cobb wake-ups this week, pardon my French."

"Just to torture me?" cried Cobb.

"No, cruster, just to get your port done. And believe me, there was a lot to do. When they cut up your brain in 2020, those crude boppers turned you from analog into digital. But thanks to our fungus and algae—we call it *chipmold*—we moldies are totally down with analog, so we've been retrofitting you. You'll feel real wiggly. We're ninety-nine percent there. Now relax. Talk to the other Cobb, and let me and Dot listen."

"Do you think Pop was fucking that spleen nurse?" the other

Cobb asked Cobb. "There was something about the way she looked at him."

"Yeah," said Cobb. "I do think so. Pop was quite the philanderer."

Dot and Chunky were transmitting more than just Cobb's spoken words, they were sending a wide band-width transmission of sensations and emotions. If Cobb let himself relax, he could begin to merge into the other Cobb, and whether he was inside Chunky or inside Dot became a little less clear.

"Now do you see what it's like to be a grex?" said Chunky.

"Shhhh!" said Dot.

"You know," the other Cobb was saying, "If there's two of us and Willy only brings one body, then one of us is going to get left out. Like a real simple game of musical chairs. Where the loser gets killed."

"Would one of us dying really matter?" said Cobb. "The *I-am-me* feeling is the only part of us that isn't the same, but that part is just a little piece of the SUN, so even *that's* the same."

"But," said the other Cobb, "I wouldn't like it to be me. Don't you feel that way?

"Yeah," said Cobb, not liking to admit it. "I do. Even though I know from personal experience that being dead is better than being alive. The survival instinct is really wired in."

"Then let's try and beat the game," said the other Cobb. "If we can totally merge into one consciousness, then there's nobody extra to leave out."

So Cobb relaxed further, completely drawing back from identifying with the Chunky Cobb or the Dot Cobb. Now the images from their two eyes fused into stereo perception, and he began to get some damn good depth perception. The jumbled stones on the ground leapt into clarity. Moving in complete accord, the two Cobb eyes swiveled this way and that, looking around.

The walls of this great underground cavern rose above them like an upside-down funnel, perhaps two miles across and one mile high. A thick vertical shaft of light ran down from the small hole at the top. Cobb remembered that he'd been here before. This place was beneath the surface of the Moon; it was called the Nest. The bopper robots had lived here.

More and more memories were emerging, flocking out like startled birds from a cliff of nests. Cobb could remember being alive four times before. He started, *first*, as a human who lived from 1950 to 2020, at which time the bopper robots had disassembled his brain and coded it up as an S-cube of software. For his *second* life, the boppers gave him a robot body with a short-lived supercooled brain that followed him around inside an ice cream truck. This had only lasted for a few months of 2020, and had not worked out very well. Cobb's S-cube code had lain dormant until 2030 when, *third*, he'd gotten a sleek petaflop Moon bopper body. These new bopper bodies had no longer required a low temperature to operate. As part of an ill-fated scheme to start tinkering with the wetware of human DNA, Cobb had flown from the Nest all the way down to Earth. He'd been gunned down on a highway by state troopers. An even longer gap had followed until *fourth*, in 2053, Cobb had been allowed a very brief run as an emulation inside an asimov slave computer buried under Salt Lake City. He had almost no memories from that last run; nobody had told him much of anything, and all he'd had time to do was to say a few kind words to his great-grandson, an unwholesome Kentucky boy called Randy Karl Tucker. Today was the *fifth* time, and the date was, Cobb somehow knew, July 25, 2054.

As he came back to the present, it occurred him that there was no "other Cobb" anymore. They'd fully merged; the Dot Cobb and Chunky Cobb emulations were parts of a unified whole, inseparable as two overlaid color separations in an old-fashioned printed image.

"Right on!" said Cobb, congratulating himself. "I'm safe!"

"We couldn't be more pleased," said Chunky. "This is exactly the final confirmation we've been hoping for."

"I'll tell them it's time to bring Cobb's body," said Dot, and her voice seemed to move off into the distance, where she began a lengthy, animated discussion with someone who sounded like a callow teenage girl.

"What kind of body do I get?" asked Cobb.

"An imipolex moldie body of course," said Chunky. "Like Dot and me."

"I'm going to look like a weird monster?"

"Yeah, the kind of weird monster that's called a human being. Your grandson Willy's artist friend Corey Rhizome made you a moldie body that looks just like you did when you were sixty. Except that Corey made you look fit and healthy instead of old and fat and drunk."

Cobb let the dig go by. He had indeed been a drunk during the declining last decades of his human life. Remarkable that he kept getting these fresh starts. It occurred to him to ask for more. "Why not go ahead and give me a body that looks young? Like in my thirties or my twenties?"

"Willy wants you to look older than him because you're his grandfather. But hey, you'll be a moldie. If you don't like the way you look, you can change it."

"And here come Jenny and Gaston with the new body!" rasped Dot. "You remember Jenny, don't you, Cobb?"

"I–I don't think so."

Two moldies were bounding through the strewn rocks toward them. The one in front was shaped like a five-foot-tall carrot with a green fringe of tentacles on top. And the one in back was like a round red beet with a long, twitching tap-root. Between them swayed the slack dead weight of a lifeless human form. Cobb watched them with his two eyestalks, being careful to keep his stereo vision fused.

Jenny was the big carrot, and her radioed voice sounded like that of a gossipy teenage girl. "Well, hi there, Cobb Anderson. You don't remember *me*?"

"The voice sounds familiar. Were you the one running me in that asimov computer a few months ago?"

"Ta da! Jenny here, Jenny there, Jenny Jenny everywhere. Even inside a Heritagist asimov machine. That wasn't the true marvelous Moon moldie me, of course, it was just my software agent. Can you believe she's been trying to break free of my control, the little bitch? Anyway, the main point is that my agent was able to cryp all of that Cobbware and send it up here to the Moon so that we moldies can download it onto a moldie body that's all your own. Isn't that floatin' of us? Let's drop it right here, Gaston."

"Yo," said Gaston. "I'm down with that."

Jenny and Gaston slung the limp plastic body down onto the ground. It was indeed the form of a nude sixty-year-old man, white bearded and white haired, a man with a big head and high cheekbones, his skin somewhat papery in appearance, much curly body hair, many freckles, a barrel chest, a flat stomach, and a respectable penis.

"Are you ready, Cobb?" asked Dot.

"I sure am."

"All right then," said Chunky. "Push both of your eyes down there, touch them to the body, and I'll send you in."

Cobb moved his two eyes forward and down, the eyes

watching each other to make sure they kept an even pace. No point in taking a chance with some last-minute greedy race. The new body lay on its back on the dusty stone floor, waiting. Beneath the pale skin were blue lines of veins that were tubes of mold, not blood. As he drew closer and closer, Cobb filled with a desire to gush out, a feeling like wanting to ejaculate, and then *aaah* he touched down with both eyes, flowed out into his new body, and—twitch, twitch—sat up.

Much better. Cobb stood and stretched. There were no feelings of joints cracking; his body was all of a smooth, flexing dough like the foot of a snail or the mantle of a squid. To test his strength, he crouched and sprang. In the low lunar gravity he flew up a hundred feet, looking down at orange Jenny and crimson Gaston and the mouths of the two caves where lurked fat Chunky and Dot.

As he started to fall, Cobb looked out across the Nest. There were some factory buildings to his left, and roads and buildings between here and the center, where the great light-stream came down. The sight of the bright central light-pool filled Cobb with a visceral hunger; it was like seeing food.

When he hit the ground, Cobb's body cushioned the fall in a most inhuman manner: he collapsed like an accordion, his chin descending to the level of his knees.

"Yee-haw," cheered Chunky, her radio voice clear in Cobb's head.

"This feels so good," said Cobb, rebounding to his humanoid shape. "Thank you!" He reached out and hugged Jenny; the big carrot was lithe and powerful in his arms. She wriggled free, and then Cobb bent down to embrace round Gaston.

"Welcome back," said the beet.

VISIONS OF THE METANOVEL

THE Singularity was brought on by some nanomachines known as *orphids*. The orphids used quantum computing and propelled themselves with electrostatic fields.

The self-reproducing orphids doubled their numbers every few minutes at first; fortunately, they'd been designed to level out at a sustainable population of some sextillion orphids upon Earth's surface. This meant there were one or two orphids affixed to every square millimeter of every object on the planet. Something like fifty thousand orphids blanketed, say, any given chair or any particular person's body. The orphids were like ubiquitous smart lice, not that you could directly feel them, for an individual orphid was little more than a knotty long-chain molecule.

Thanks to the power of quantum computing, an individual orphid was roughly as smart as a talking dog, possessing a good understanding of natural language and a large amount of extra memory. Each orphid knew at all times its precise position and velocity, indeed the name "orphid" was a pun on the early twenty-first-century technology of RFID or "Radio Frequency Identification" chips. Rather than radio waves, orphids used quantum entanglement to network themselves into their world-spanning *orphidnet.*

The accommodating orphids set up a human-orphidnet interface via gentle electromagnetic fields that probed though the scalps of their hosts. Two big wins: by accessing the positional meshes of the orphids, people could now effectively see anything anywhere; and by accessing the orphids' instantaneous velocities, people could hear the sounds at any location as well. Earth's ongoing physical reality could be as readily linked and searched as the Internet.

Like eddies in a flowing steam, artificially intelligent agents emerged within the orphidnet. In an ongoing upward cascade, still higher-level agents emerged from swarms of the lower-level ones. By and large, the agents were human-friendly; people spoke of them as *beezies.*

By interfacing with beezies, a person could parcel out intellectual tasks and store vast amounts of information within the extra memory space that the orphids bore. Those who did this experienced a vast effective increase in intelligence. They called themselves *kiqqies,* short for kilo-IQ.

New and enhanced forms of art arose among the kiqqies, among these was the multimedia *metanovel.*

In considering the metanovel, think of how Northwest Native American art changed when the European traders introduced steel axes. Until then, the Native American totems had been handheld items, carved of black stone. But once the tribes had axes, they set to work making totems from whole trees. Of course with the ax came alcohol and smallpox; the era of totem poles would prove to be pitifully short.

There were also some dangers associated with the orphidnet. The overarching highest-level-of-them-all agent at the apex of the virtual world was known as the Big Pig. The Big Pig was an outrageously rich and intricate virtual mind stuffed with beautiful insights woven into ideas that linked into unifying concepts that puzzle-pieced themselves into powerful systems that were in turn aspects of a cosmic metatheory—*aha*! Hooking into the billion-snouted billion-nippled Big Pig could make a kiqqie feel like a genius. The down side was that kiqqies were unable to remember or implement insights obtained from a Big Pig session. The more fortunate kiqqies were able to limit their Big Pig usage in the same way that earlier people might have limited their use of powerful psychoactive drugs.

If the Big Pig was like alcohol, the analogy to smallpox was the threat of runaway, planet-eating nanomachines called *nants*— but I won't get into the nants here.

+ + +

Although the postsingular metanovelist Thuy Nguyen had some trouble with Big Pig addiction, she eventually recovered and began work on her remarkable metanovel *Wheenk*. Thuy wanted *Wheenk* to be a transreal lifebox, meaning that her metanovel was to capture the waking dream of her life as she experienced it—while sufficiently bending the truth to allow for a fortuitously emerging dramatic plot. Thuy wanted *Wheenk* to incorporate not only the interesting things she saw and heard, but also the things that she thought and felt. Rather than coding her inner life into words and real-world images alone, Thuy included beezie-built graphic constructs and—this was a special arrow in her quiver—music. The effect was compelling; in later years users would say that accessing Thuy's work was like becoming Thuy herself.

Among Thuy's metanovelist friends during the time she worked upon *Wheenk* were Gerry Gurken, Carla Standard, John Medford, and Linda Loca. Each of them had their own distinctive approaches to creating a metanovel.

+ + +

Gerry's metanovel *Banality* was a vast combine of images all drawn from one and the same instant on a certain day. No time elapsed in this work, only space, and the story was the user's gradual apprehension of a vast conspiracy woven throughout not only our world but also throughout the worlds of thoughts and dreams. The images were juxtaposed in suggestive ways, and were accompanied by a spoken voice-over delivered by a virtual Gerry Gurken who wandered his memory-palace at the user's side.

Gerry's title, *Banality*, had an ironic resonance, for his timeslice was located at orphidnet time-zero, that is, 12:00:00 PST on the first day after the beezies had implemented their protocol of having the orphidnet save, a hundred times per second, the positions and velocities of every orphid on Earth. This postsingular moment marked the day when history had truly changed forever, and what did Gerry find there? Human banality, the same as usual—but with something odd and sinister beneath the surface.

By the way, Gerry, who was a convivial and gregarious sort, preferred to select the images for *Banality* not by browsing in the orphidnet time-zero database, but rather by roaming the real-time streets. He had a good eye; he saw disturbing connections everywhen and everywhere. Often as not, the beezies were able to scroll back from current sightings to find nearly the same image in the orphidnet time-zero database, but even when the match was wildly inaccurate, that was fine with Gerry too. To his surrealist sensibilities, a cauliflower was as convulsively beautiful as a catfish.

Banality would have taken hundreds or even thousands of hours to explore in detail, and it bulked larger every day—in that sense *Banality* was like a blog, albeit a blog eternally focused upon a single global instant of time. Any ten-minute block of the work was fascinating, disorienting, and revelatory—leaving the user's mind off-center and agog. Unfortunately, by the twenty-minute mark, most users found *Banality* to be too much. The work was like some bizarre, aggressively challenging sushi bar that the average person abandons after tasting only a few dishes: geoduck, sea cucumber, nudibranch, and jellyfish, say, and then it was always, "Thanks so much, very interesting, gotta go."

The metanovelists occasionally experienced the phenomenon of having one of their characters send messages to them—they called this feedback phenomenon *blowback*. Gerry Gurkin, for one, had regular visitations from the simulated Gerry Gurkin of *Banality*, the virtual Gerry clamoring that he wanted metanovelist Gerry to edit in a girlfriend character for him. Telling this story, portly Gerry would dart hot intense looks at Thuy Nguyen, as if he were planning to feed a model of *her* to virtual Gerry, which was perfectly fine with Thuy, and she said so, Thuy being in a lonely-but-coned-off emotional state where she was ready to accept any admiration she was offered, as long as it was virtual and with no strings attached.

+ + +

Intense, lipsticked, nail-biting Carla Standard used what she called a simworld approach in creating her metanovel *You're a Bum!* Her virtual characters were artificially alive, always in action, and somewhat unpredictable, a bit like the nonplayer characters in an old-school videogame. Rather than writing story lines, Carla endowed her characters with goals and drives, leaving them free to interact like seagulls in a wheeling flock.

You're a Bum! was experienced through a single character's point of view, this protagonist being a homeless young woman who was enlisting people to help her unearth the truth about the mysterious disappearance of her kiqqie boyfriend. There was some chance that he'd been abducted by aliens. The heroine was bedeviled both by her mother's attempts to have her brought home, and by the advances of a predatory pimp. Backing her up were an innocent younger-brother figure, a potential new boyfriend, a mysterious federal agent, a wise old Big Pig addict, and a cohort of hard-partying kiqqie friends.

For the *You're a Bum!* dialogue and graphics, Carla had her beezies patching in data from the day-to-day world: conversations of kiqqies in San Francisco bars, shops, apartments, and alleyways. Each user's *You're a Bum!* experience was further tailored with data drawn from the user's personal meshes and social situations. In other words, when you accessed Carla's metanovel, you saw something vaguely resembling your own life.

By the way, Thuy Nguyen's two sessions with *You're a Bum!* proved painful, even lacerating. First she'd relived a moment when she and her former boyfriend Jayjay stood under a flowering plum tree in the Mission, Jayjay shaking the tree to make the petals shower down upon her like perfumed confetti, all the while Jayjay's eyes melting with love. And then she'd seen their breakup, but more objectively than before, with the simulated

Thuy hungover from the Big Pig, her clothes in disarray, Thuy hysterically screaming at Jayjay in a metapainting-lined alley, and poor Jayjay's trembling fingers nervously adjusting his coat and hat.

+ + +

Like Gerry Gurken, the excitable John Medford was one of Thuy's admirers, but he held little physical appeal for her. He was too thin and overwrought, too dandruffy, too needy. As part of his doomed campaign to engage Thuy's affection, Medford had undertaken *The Thuy Fan*, an unwritable and unreadable metanovel wherein every possible action path of his young heroine Thuy would be traced. Waking up with a man, a woman, or nobody in bed beside her, Thuy hopped out of the right or left side of her bed, or perhaps she crawled over the head or the foot. She put on her slippers or threw them out the window, if she had a window. In some forkings she jumped out the window herself, but in most she went to take a shower. In the shower she sang or washed or had sex with her partner. And when she emerged, she might find a table by her bed bearing a breakfast of lox, lobster, steel-cut oats, or a single boiled ostrich egg. In some forkings, Thuy had no time to eat, as her house was on fire, or menaced by an earthquake or a giant ant.

In practice no human author would have had the time and energy to contemplate so richly ramified a document as *The Thuy Fan*, but John Medford had his beezies helping him by autonomously roughing in sketches of ever-more action paths. As the mood struck him, Medford would add voice-over descriptions to the paths; he had a flair for making anything at all sound interesting. But, densely tufted as the branchings were,

Medford only managed to fully polish Thuy's action fan for the first two and a half seconds of her day. Random assassins, meteorites, a stroke, the spontaneous combustion of Thuy's pillow—so many things were possible. And, insofar as Medford's goal was to charm the real world Thuy into his arms, *The Thuy Fan* was a failure. Medford eventually set the work aside, declaring it to be finished.

As his next project Medford began an inversely forked work called *April March*, lifting both his title and concept from the celestial pages of Jorge Luis Borges. Medford's plan for *April March* was to start with a scene on a particular day and to document plausible variants of what happened on the days *before*. To make the work more tractable than *The Thuy Fan*, Medford was austerely limiting his branching factor to one fork per day. The initial scene, set on April 1, would present an ambiguous conversation between a man and a woman at an airport, followed by two versions of March 31, four versions of March 30, eight versions of March 29, and so on. Medford planned to march as far as March 24, making a thousand and twenty-three scenes in all, linked together into five hundred and twelve plausible action paths which would constitute, so John claimed, an all but exhaustive compendium of every possible kind of detective story.

+ + +

Bouncy Linda Loca created a metanovel entitled *George Washington*, depicting the world as seen from the point of view of a dollar bill. What lent her work its piquancy was how literally she'd managed to execute the plan: while perusing *George Washington* you felt flat and crinkly; you spent most of your time in a wallet or folded in a pocket; and when you came out into the air the main thing you saw was countertops and people's hands. The beezies had helped by providing Linda with the life histories of real, orphid-meshed bills. The user could of course scroll past the dull parts, but the presence of the realistic data gave the work heft and seriousness.

When, once in a great while, Linda's George Washington dollar changed hands, the bill moved the story along by buying drinks, influence, or sex, and thereby sketching the rise and fall of a young cop whom Linda had named George Washington as well. Young officer Washington became corrupted due to his sexual attraction for a promiscuous older woman named Donna, who talked him into executing a hit on her landlord, who turned out to be George's biological father, this fact being unknown to George until too late.

For a time, Linda had blowback issues with her George Washington character because, to round him out, she'd made him an aspiring writer. Problem was, George began pestering Linda with messages about her metanovel—dumb suggestions, by and large, for the character was, after all, only a beezie simulation of a human, and not a true artist. He failed to grasp, for instance, the dark, erotic beauty of a four-hour scene consisting of the slow shifting of the dollar within a felt-appliqué wallet in Donna's tight jeans while Donna trolled Mission Street for men. By the same token, George was unable to understand that the precise convex pressure of his own virtual buttock upon the eponymous dollar as he sat writing at his virtual desk might be more interesting to his creator Linda Loca than what he wrote.

Weary of arguing with her character, Linda edited out virtual George's love of writing, and made his hobby bowling instead.

+ + +

As it happened, Thuy's old boyfriend Jayjay ended up with Linda Loca. And then, while trying to prevent an outbreak of nants, Jayjay died. In the instant of extreme grief and despair when she learned of Jayjay's death, Thuy finally finished *Wheenk*.

The pieces of the metanovel came together like a time-reversed nuclear explosion. Her adventures in the kiqqie underworld of San Francisco, her lost love for Jayjay, her worries about the threat of the nants, a particular cone shell she had on her dresser, her mother's face the day Thuy had graduated from college, her father's bare feet when he tended his tomato plants, the dance Thuy had done down the rainy street one night while exulting over her metanovel—everything fitting, everything in place, *Wheenk* as heavy and whole as a sphere of plutonium.

Her Great Work finally done, Thuy pulsed the *Wheenk* database to the global orphidnet. Her pain had produced artistic transcendence.

NOTES ON THE STORIES

NOTE ON "2+2=5"

Written May 1, 2006, with Terry Bisson.
Appeared in *Interzone*, Summer 2006.

Terry and I are both from Kentucky–he from Owensboro, I from Louisville. Terry's novel *Pirates of the Universe* (Tor Books, 1996) has some especially famous evocations of growing up in Kentucky.

Terry lived in New York City for many years, and he was active in organizing a famous monthly reading series at the KGB bar in the East Village. Recently he moved to the San Francisco Bay Area, and has turned his organizational skills to starting up a monthly series of readings at the New College in the Mission District in San Francisco: "SF in SF." It's great to have Terry out here.

Terry is a master of the short story form; he's won the Hugo and the Nebula, and he even sells to *Playboy*. Last year he published his mind-boggling collection *Greetings* (Tachyon, 2005), as well as a book of linked mathematical tales, *Numbers Don't Lie* (Tachyon, 2005), which includes some creditable mad mathematician equations that Terry made up. For much more Terry, see his Web site www.terrybisson.com.

This year Terry has been writing a series of deceptively simple fables, cast as children's stories about a boy named Billy. After hearing him perform "Billy and the Unicorn" at a hipster dive called The Make-Out Room, I was so impressed by the Zenlike purity of his phrasing that I began insisting he write a story with me.

I got the idea for this story just as the narrator describes it in the opening paragraphs, that is, from an overheard conversation between two barristas—although in Los Gatos, California, not in Harrods Creek, Kentucky. Harrods Creek is actually the name of the small town near Louisville where my parents initially lived.

While I was planning the story, I was walking around the Mission district in San Francisco, and I actually saw "2+2=5" stenciled on the sidewalk. This tale is thought experiment exploring how to actually get to a point where this phrase is literally true.

NOTE ON "ELVES OF THE SUBDIMENSIONS"

Written March 25, 2006, with Paul Di Filippo.
Appeared in *Flurb* webzine, August, 2006

I collaborated with Paul on a story, "Instability," before I ever actually met him. I think we first met face to face in 1999 when I took a bus through the snow to his house in Providence, Rhode Island, while on a journey to the East. He showed me H. P. Lovecraft's grave, we went ice skating together, and we wrote a second story, "The Square Root of Pythagoras."

Paul is one of the most prolific short story writers at work these days, with a new anthology of his tales appearing nearly every year. The latest one is *Shuteye for the Timebroker* (Thunder's Mouth Press, 2006), and you can learn more at his Web site www.pauldifilippo.com.

Perhaps my all-time favorite of Paul's stories is "Stink Lines," about the Disney Comics character Gyro Gearloose as drawn by the great Carl Barks, the tale set in a world where nanomachines actually generate dialogue balloons and, yes, graphical stink lines. This tale is in his collection *Neutrino Drag* (Four Walls Eight Windows, 2004).

As occasionally happens, my inspiration for "Elves of the Subdimensions" was the title itself, which has haunted me for years with no story attached. To me the title seems a perfect coupling of Golden Age power chords, worthy of *Thrilling Wonder Tales*.

In order to set the story in motion, I suggested a transreal element: How does a mad professor survive retirement?

When I myself retired from teaching two years ago, I did find it a bit of a jolt. Retirement is hard, as a part of one's sense of self consists of the social roles that one plays. To abandon a role is to feel diminished. You're losing part of your identity. If you're fortunate, you find new roles, or expand some of your alternate roles, so as to make up for the lost role—so as once again feel yourself to be the right size.

In my case, I've been writing more since I retired. And I've been putting a lot of time into my Web site www.rudyrucker.com and its associated blog, not to mention my webzine *Flurb* at www.flurb.net.

NOTE ON "PANPSYCHISM PROVED"

Written December 6, 2005.
Appeared in *Nature* #439, January 26, 2006.

In recent years, the serious science magazine *Nature* has been leavening their pages with a short-short story in each issue. Having secured an invitation to submit a tale, I turned to a pet idea of mine, panpsychism (meaning "every object has a mind"). I was inspired by a very interesting book on the topic: David Skrbina, *Panpsychism in the West* (MIT Press, 2005).

My idea was to produce a thought experiment showing how panpsychism might be verified. As my setting, I used the cafeteria at Apple, where I had recently visited my former student Leo Lee, who was working on a secret Apple project.

It was a real kick to see the title "Panpsychism Proved" right there in the august pages of *Nature*. That's a mad professor's idea of success!

NOTE ON "MS FOUND IN A MINIDRIVE"

Written June 13, 2004.
Appeared in *Poe's Lighthouse*, Chris Conlon, ed. (Cemetery Dance, 2006).

Since this story already has a hoax introduction, it's perhaps overkill to write another layer of annotation. But, hey, Edgar Allan Poe would.

In the summer of 2004, I went to Boulder, Colorado, to teach a one-week "Transreal Writing" course at the Naropa Institute. "Transrealism" is my term for the practice of basing fantastic tales on your real life—something I often do. I have more discussions of transrealism in my essay collection, *Seek!* (Four Walls Eight Windows, 1999) and on my writing page www.rudyrucker.com/writing.

I'd last been at Naropa in 1982, when I got to meet Allen Ginsburg and William Burroughs (but, no, I didn't spend the night with Burroughs). By way of illustrating my transreal writing technique to my students in 2004, I wrote "MS Found in a Minidrive" during the week I was teaching them. And, as so often seems to happen, my main character is a mad professor.

The theme of the story had already been defined by Chris Conlon, who was editing an anthology *Poe's Lighthouse* (Cemetery Dance, 2006) of stories all taking off on the same unfinished story fragment by Master Poe. You can find the complete text of the original "Lighthouse" fragment in Poe's Online Collected Works at http://www.eapoe.org/works/tales/lightha.htm. I might mention, by the way, that my friend John Shirley has a really terrific story, "Blind Eye," in that same *Poe's Lighthouse* anthology. John sticks to the straight Poe style and delivers a tale that's eerily like one of the master's.

The high point of my week at Naropa was a large group reading they had. I was on a bill with my favorite poet and dear friend Anselm Hollo, reading to a crowd of three hundred people. As my story was tailor-made for the Naropa audience, it fully blew their minds and they loved it. I was thrilled to be performing at this level in the home of the Beats; it was truly "a gala night within the lonesome latter years," as Poe touchingly puts it in his poem "The Conqueror Worm."

NOTE ON "THE MEN IN THE BACK ROOM AT THE COUNTRY CLUB"

Written May 6, 2004.
Appeared in *Infinite Matrix* webzine, December 2005.

For the years 1980–1986, I lived with my wife and kids in Lynchburg, Virginia, the home of televangelist Jerry Falwell and headquarters of his rightwing "Moral Majority" political action group. I ended up writing a number of stories about Lynchburg, transreally dubbing it Killeville.

During our final years in Lynchburg, I was proud to be a member of the Oakwood Country Club—it was a pleasant place and the dues were modest enough that even an unemployed cyberpunk writer could afford them. I was always intrigued by a group of men who sat drinking bourbon and playing cards in a small windowless room off the men's locker room—isolated from the civilizing force of the fair sex. Somehow I formulated the idea that at night the men were rolled up like apricot leather and stored in glass carboys of whiskey that sat within their "golf bags." I was thinking of a power-chord story somewhat analogous to Phil Dick's "The Father Thing." The power chord here is "alien-controlled pod people." Another archetype I wanted to touch upon is the Pig Chef, an icon that's always disturbed me. I wanted to push this concept to its logical conclusion, so that everyone would finally understand the Pig Chef's truly evil nature!

I think the story is funny and logical, but it's also so mad and strange (ah, Killeville!) that I had trouble getting anyone to publish it. Fortunately, the writer and editor Eileen Gunn gets my sense of humor. Like my earlier story

"Jenna and Me," this weird tale found a home in Eileen's webzine *Infinite Matrix* at www.infinitematrix.net, which was, as long as it lasted, something like a clear channel border radio station.

NOTE ON "GUADALUPE AND HIERONYMUS BOSCH"

Written April 9, 2004.
Appeared in *Interzone*, October 2005.

I've always been fascinated by artistic representations of the Virgin of Guadalupe—she's usually drawn in the middle of a spiky oval halo. To me, that halo looks like an image you might find by zooming into the computer graphics fractal known as the Mandelbrot Set. Not that this image has much to do with the story.

The story was inspired, rather, by buying myself a good-quality microscope. On searching the web to find books about microscopy, I came across a delightful flying-saucer tract that I ordered: Trevor James Constable, *The Cosmic Pulse of Life: The Revolutionary Biological Power Behind UFOs* (Borderland Sciences, Garberville, CA, 1990). Constable jovially argues that our atmosphere is filled with all-but-invisible giant "aeroforms," akin to jellyfish or protozoa. And, writes Constable, these home-grown "aliens" are what we're seeing when we see when we see UFOs.

I came up with the hard science idea for the story's conclusion while giving a lecture to my Advanced Computer Graphics class at San Jose State University. We were studying the mathematical projective transformation that is used to convert three-dimensional coordinates into locations upon a painter's canvas or, for that matter, upon a computer-game's view screen. It turns out that you can imagine forming the inverse of the projective transformation, and that if you were to let this inverse transformation act upon your body, then you could indeed find yourself striding across houses and mountains, with the fabled Point At Infinity only a few more steps away. I explained all this to my students at the time—they enjoyed the rap, although of course they thought I was a mad professor.

One final inspiration for the story was my continuing desire to write about the great master Hieronymus Bosch. Having already written a historical novel about a Flemish painter—*As Above, So Below: A Novel of Peter Bruegel* (Tor Books, New York, 2002), I'm tempted to write a tome about Bosch. "Guadalupe and Hieronymus Bosch" is a down payment on the dream.

By the way, Terry Bisson did me the favor of reading a draft of the story and making some good suggestions. After appearing in *Interzone*, the story also appeared in David Hartwell and Kathryn Cramer, *Year's Best SF 11* (Eos, 2006).

NOTE ON "SIX THOUGHT EXPERIMENTS CONCERNING THE NATURE OF COMPUTATION"

Written Fall, 2003.

Appeared in Rudy Rucker, *The Lifebox, the Seashell, and the Soul* (Thunder's Mouth Press, New York, 2005).

When I moved to Silicon Valley some twenty years ago to work as a computer science professor, I thought of myself as a writer on assignment. I was here to quickly write a popular book explaining the meaning of computers. But I went native on the story, and I really did become a computer scientist. As I mentioned earlier in these notes, I recently pulled free of the computer science tarbaby and retired from teaching. Once retired, I had the time to finally write my big computer book: *The Lifebox, the Seashell, and the Soul: What Gnarly Computation Taught Me about Ultimate Reality, the Meaning of Life, and How to Be Happy.*

By way of lightening up my tome, I wrote a short-short story to introduce each of the six chapters which were themed, respectively, on computer science, physics, biology, psychology, sociology, and philosophy—an ascending chain of thought. Thus these six thought experiments.

Although I claim that each of the stories has to do with the nature of computation, this isn't obvious in each case, so I'll say a bit about the individual stories.

"Lucky Number" is about the idea that maybe there is a single underlying computation that generates the world. Although obviously I'm sympathetic to the idea that we can usefully think of any given natural process as being a computation of sorts, I'm not actually sure if there really does have to be one ultimate computation underneath it all. It could be that reality is an endless onion, with layer beneath layer, and there isn't any one rule that makes it all. For the setting of this story, I used the Electronic Arts game company campus on the San Francisco Bay; I visited my former student Alan Borecky when he was a game programmer there.

"The Million Chakras" deals with parallel worlds. I'm not sure the twist ending really bears close scientific analysis—but let's not break the butterfly upon the wheel. You might wonder what this story has to do with the nature of computation. The context is that, in the chapter the story introduces, I discuss quantum computation and the scientist David Deutsch's claim that a quantum computer manages to carry out a number simultaneous computations in parallel worlds.

"Aint Paint" involves morphogenesis, that is, the more or less computational process by which organisms grow their forms. Shortly before his death, the computer scientist Alan Turing began working with computer simulations in which simple inputs evolve into organic-looking two- and three-dimensional forms. Over the years, I've done a lot of research into these types of computer programs, which are called cellular automata. You can download a nice cellular automata program called CAPOW from my nonfiction book's Web site, http://www.rudyrucker.com/lifebox. The free download comes with a loadable parameter file named Aint Paint.CAS, which displays precisely the kinds of live graphics that inspired this tale.

"Terry's Talker" develops a notion I've thought about a lot: the lifebox. I also discuss the lifebox in my novel *Saucer Wisdom* (Tor Books, 1999), and in my story, "Soft Death" (reprinted in my collection *Gnarl!*, Four Walls Eight Windows, 2000). I'm almost surprised that lifeboxes aren't already on the market, although to some extent blogs are playing this role. I do think of my ever-expanding Web site www.rudyrucker.com as being more or less my lifebox, although of course it doesn't have any AI software to run it, just a search window in the blog. But for many conversations that's about all you'd need.

"The Kind Rain," plays with emergent intelligence. It sometimes happens that the behavior of a group of simple agents exhibits a higher intelligence than the agents themselves; think of an ant colony, a flock of birds, a school of fish, or, for that matter, a human society. Of course I'm pushing it to suppose that somehow a storm of rain drops might evolve into an intelligent and sympathetic mind, but, hey, it makes for a striking thought experiment. The setting for this story is the tumbledown house my family and I rented in Los Gatos when we moved to California in 1986; the house was also the setting for my novel *The Hacker and the Ants* (reprinted by Four Walls Eight Windows, 2002).

"Hello Infinity" was inspired by an idea I proposed in the last chapter of my *Lifebox* tome. I suggested there that we might define a computation to be a physical process that embodies a possible thought. Of course, I then wondered whether there might be some things that aren't like possible thoughts and aren't like ordinary physical processes. "Hello Infinity" is a thought experiment presenting a man who starts having infinite thoughts and a woman who learns that matter is infinitely divisible. Our whole philosophy of science would have to change were infinities really to occur in the natural world—and I seriously think this is possible, even though this line of thought is very much out of fashion right now. My interest in infinity goes back to the 1970s, when I wrote my doctoral dissertation on infinite sets. My first popular science nonfiction book was *Infinity and the Mind* (reprinted by Princeton University Press, 2005), and I also wrote a novel about physical and mental infinities: *White Light* (reprinted by Four Walls Eight Windows, 2001).

NOTE ON "JENNA AND ME"

Written June 15, 2002, with Rudy Rucker Jr.
Appeared in *Infinite Matrix* webzine, February 2003.

My son Rudy Rucker Jr. runs an ISP (Internet Service Provider) called

Monkeybrains, at www.monkeybrains.net in San Francisco. For political and artistic reasons that he never fully clarified to me, Rudy created the Web site www.thefirsttwins.com, devoted to the doings of then-President George W. Bush's twin daughters, Jenna and Barbara. Understand that my son is my no means a Young Republican.

When one of his Web site readers posted a threatening comment about the president's family, some Secret Service agents actually came to pay Rudy a visit, checking him out. A few months later, some anonymous person begin distributing the so-called BadTrans Internet worm, which infected people's computers and sent a log of all their keyboard inputs to a free account at Monkeybrains. Rudy received another visit from the authorities; this time it was the FBI, with a warrant to impound the trillion or so snoop-bytes received by the anonymous hacker using Rudy's server machines.

Perhaps not-so-coincidentally, the BadTrans worm hit the Internet four days after the FBI had announced the development of some spyware called Magic Lantern, a key stroke logging mechanism, which, when properly rubbed, will reveal people's passwords for encrypted data. You can read more about all this at a site Rudy made, https://badtrans.monkeybrains.net.

In any case, with my son being hounded by both the Secret Service and the FBI for a site he'd made about the freakin' first twins, it seemed like a good idea to help him work through his motivations by writing a transreal story about the whole bizarre scene. It was great fun working together, kind of like the time the two of us built a house for our dog Arf, and for me a nice vacation from writing about mad professors. To cap the pleasure, Rudy and I gave a joint Father's Day reading of our story at a club in the Mission district of San Francisco. A night to remember.

NOTE ON "THE USE OF THE ELLIPSE THE CATALOG THE METER & THE VIBRATING PLANE"

Written January 22, 2002.
Appeared in *Horror Garage* #5, 2002.

My cyberpunk pal John Shirley lives fairly near me in the San Francisco Bay Area. In 2002 he had this idea of helping someone put together a small press anthology whose earnings would be devoted to a fund for helping drug-addicted mothers and their children.

I don't normally undertake a story for so abstract a reason as altruism. I write a story for more personal reasons; typically there's some emotional state or tech problem or odd situation or real-world vignette that I'm obsessed with, and the story is an exploration I feel compelled to carry out. But John shamed me into promising a contribution.

And then I got into it—I realized that, given that this was to be a guaranteed publication, I could really do anything I wanted to, so why not have some fun and write something completely surrealistic. Of course then the fundraising anthology project fell through, but five of the stories destined for the anthology ended up in a special issue of *Horror Garage*, an idiosyncratic magazine edited by Paula Guran.

The title and epigraph for my story comes from line seventy-three of Allen Ginsberg's epochal 1956 poem, "Howl."

and who therefore ran through the icy streets obsessed with a
  sudden flash of the alchemy of the use of the ellipse the
  catalog the meter & the vibrating plane

I've always loved this long line: those four items makes such a surreal, Dadaist assemblage, and as a mathematician I'm happy to see an ellipse in *the* seminal Beat poem.

The images of the story came to me in a moment of inspiration as I sat on the sidewalk in the sun at Powell and Market Streets, near where the tourists line up for the trolley. Junkies and con men were going by, and I saw the four items of Ginsberg's line as characters, as if drawn by underground cartoonist Robert Williams—and thus emerged my story, a gift from the muse.

Although the line from "Howl" appears as I quote it in both Ginsberg's original *Howl and Other Poems* (City Lights, San Francisco, 1956) and in his *Collected Poems 1947–1980* (Harper & Row, New York, 1984), Allen introduces a

1986 variant to his line in *Howl: Original Draft Facsimile, Transcript & Variant Versions, Etc.* (edited by Barry Miles, HarperCollins, New York, 1995). Allen's "final" 1986 version of the line goes like this: "and who therefore ran through the icy streets obsessed with a sudden flash of the alchemy of the use of the ellipsis catalog a variable measure and the vibrating plane." Ugh!

In a footnote of the 1995 *Howl* volume, Allen says, "'Ellipse' is a solecism in the original mss. and printings; 'ellipsis' is correct." In the same footnote he relieves himself of a minilecture on his poetics as derived from Céline, Whitman, Pound, and the divine Kerouac. And at the end of the footnote, he blandly drones, "phrasing in this verse has been clarified for present edition . . . to conform more precisely to above referents." (pp. 130–31).

I wish Allen were still around, so I could argue with him about this. I'd insist that his original muse-spurt was of course the correct take, and not some thirty-year-later version that the author has tailored to fit some theories that he's invented about what he did. I'd argue that he's mistakenly letting his mad prof side supplant his mad poet side.

I did once have the good fortune to meet Allen, while visiting the Naropa Institute in Boulder, Colorado, on the 1982 visit that inspired my piece "MS Found in a Minidrive." I told Allen about how much "Howl" had influenced me in high school, and then I said, "And what I want from you, Allen, after being hung-up on the beatniks all these years, what I want is your blessing." And real fast he whaps his hand down on my head like a skull-cap or electric-chair metal cap *zzt zzt* and "BLESS YOU" he yells. I wrote more about this encounter in my memoir *All the Visions* (Ocean View Books, 1991), which I typed on a ninety-foot scroll of paper, emulating Jack K.

NOTE ON "JUNK DNA"

Written December 29, 2001, with Bruce Sterling.
Appeared in *Isaac Asimov's SF Magazine*, January 2003.

This is the third story I've written with Bruce Sterling; the earlier two being "Storming the Cosmos" and "Big Jelly," both in my anthology *Gnarl!* (Four

Walls Eight Windows, 2000.) The "Junk DNA" collaboration was tumultuous; I began finally to understand why a synergistic pair like, say, Lennon and McCartney might stop working together—no matter how good were the fruits of their joint efforts.

Although pleasant and soft spoken in person, both Bruce and I are bossy collaborators, capable of being very cutting in our e-mails. When he and I go after each other, it's like two old guys playing tennis and trying to kill the ball and blast it down the other guy's throat. *Whack!* Some of this abrasive energy shows up in the interactions between the pairs of characters in this story: Janna vs. Veruschka and Tug vs. Revel.

But the story is fun, and it rated a cover illustration when it appeared in *Asimov's*. The story also appears in Bruce's most recent collection, *Visionary in Residence* (Thunder's Mouth Press, 2006); although note that while putting together *Mad Professor*, I slightly re-edited all my stories one more time.

Bruce is such an interesting guy that he actually gets *paid* to blog, see his *Wired*-sponsored site http://blog.wired.com/sterling/.

NOTE ON "POCKETS"

Written July 18, 2000, with John Shirley.
Appeared in Al Sarrantonio, ed., *Redshift* (Roc, 2001).

I first met John at Bruce Sterling's house in Austin, Texas, 1985. We were there for the first-ever convention panel on cyberpunk. While we were walking around town, John kept sidling up to me and handing me enormous heavy rocks that I'd unthinkingly start carrying. An ant-to-ant exchange. I liked him right away, he has a charmingly skewed view of reality, and an ability to cobble nearly any situation into a story premise.

In the summer of 2000, John approached me with the first few paragraphs for this story and the invitation to join him in the *Red Shift* anthology. John figured he needed some mad professor input on how to make his higher-dimensional pockets work. Also, he and I shared an interest in using the pockets as an objective correlative for addiction and recovery. The writing of the story went very smoothly, and I get a kick out of the accent John gave Threakman. Punk forever.

In March 2003, I convinced John to go backpacking in Big Sur with me and to cap off our trip with a night in an inexpensive bunk-room at the Esalen Institute. This was not a good idea. John got blisters on the hike, and he hated the people at Esalen—as John put it, "You can't expect me to fit in at Esalen. When I had my band, I used to break beer bottles over my head till the blood ran, and dive off the stage into the audience." I quarreled with him for making our visit so hard and—let me quote from my journal:

"Then I mistakenly drank three cups of blackberry sage tea (caffeinated), thinking it was herbal, and that night couldn't sleep for a really long time. We were in a room with six bunk beds, my bed under John's, and it bothered me to be physically coupled to his creakings, also to have the plywood bottom of his bed so close to my face. In the wee a.m. hours I moved to the one other vacant bed, an upper bunk. The other guys sharing the room drifted in. Visions of a spaceship crew's quarters. Image of Shirley crawling towards me across the ceiling of the room, his fingers sticking to the dry-wall like a gecko's. Outside raged the lethal, silent energy winds of deep space, visible as in my mind's eye as Riemannian vortex meshes. At this point I actually felt some joy at being there and being embroiled in something so different from quotidien life."

We got over the argument—eventually it began seeming funny—and we still see each other every couple of months, most recently when Terry Bisson organized a joint reading for us in San Francisco as "The Dread Lords of Cyberpunk," where John read from what sounded to be one of his greatest novels yet, *The Other End* (Cemetery Dance, 2006). The book is about John's vision of what the Apocalypse might be like if the avenging angels happened to be John's kind of folks—as opposed to the angels that appear in the Christian "Left Behind" series of novels about the Rapture and the end of the world. Thus John's title—he's describing an *other* kind of end, an Apocalypse envisioned from the other end of the political spectrum.

John's latest doings can be tracked on his Web site, www.darkecho.com/johnshirley.

NOTE ON "COBB WAKES UP"

Written January 1997.
Appeared in *Other* magazine, March 2006.

"Cobb Wakes Up" is set in the world of my *Ware* novels: *Software, Wetware, Freeware,* and *Realware.* I originally intended to use this piece as the opening chapter of *Realware*, but then decided to open that book in a different way. I only happened to unearth this fragment recently, in the process of posting my writing notes for my most recent nine novels at www.rudyrucker.com/writing. Now that I'm retired, I'm industriously assembling a lifebox simulacrum of my mind online.

This tale is a self-contained vignette, a little thought experiment concerning what might happen if you could store someone's mind as software, and if you then gave that mind two separate bodies.

Rereading the story makes me miss the *Ware* worlds, and my father Embry Cobb Rucker, who was the model for Cobb Anderson. My father was a very human, sociable man: a businessman and then an Episcopal priest. I used to feel myself to be very different from him, but as the years go by, I realize we were always the same.

NOTE ON "VISIONS OF THE METANOVEL"

Written May 22, 2006.
Previously unpublished.

In the summer of 2005, I read *Accelerando*, a collection of linked short stories by Charles Stross (Ace Books, 2005). These stories had a tremendous effect on me; Stross showed that it's possible to go ahead and write about what happens after the co-called Singularity.

As many readers will know, the Singularity is a notion invented by the novelist and computer scientist Vernon Vinge in a 1993 talk—to read the original talk, just search the web for "Vinge Singularity." Vinge pointed out that if we can make robots as intelligent as we are, then there seems to be no reason that the robots couldn't plug in faster processors and bigger memories to then be *more* intelligent than people. And then—the real kicker—these superhuman robots can set to work designing still better robots, setting off an upward cascade of ever-more-powerful machines.

Some timid souls have suggested that writers and futurologists must stand mute before the Singularity, that there's no way for us to imagine the years beyond such a cataclysmic change. But, hey, imagining the unimaginable is what thought experiments are for! And Stross shows us how; he blows right past the Singularity and deep into some very bizarre and fun-to-read-about futures.

In his *Accelerando* the solar system has become concentric Dyson spheres of computing devices with only our Earth remaining like "a picturesque historic building stranded in an industrial park." And some minds in the shells want to smash Earth, simply to enhance their RAM and their flop by a few percent.

This struck me as being no different, really, from people wanting to fill a wetland to make a mall, to clear-cut a rainforest to make a destination golf resort, or even to kill a whale to whittle its teeth into religious icons of a whale god. I was outraged. But also very intrigued by the idea.

And so I began writing my novel *Postsingular* (Tor Books, projected for 2007). The novel opens with an attack of world-eating nanomachines called nants. The nants are rolled back, at least temporarily, and then one of the characters introduces a more benevolent kind of nanomachines called orphids, as described in "Visions of the Metanovel."

I'm very intrigued by the question of what kind of art we might make given vastly improved abilities. By way of researching the question, I studied Jorge Luis Borges's visionary writings, particularly his tale, "A Survey of the Works of Herbert Quain," which indeed describes an imaginary novel called *April March*. (The Quain piece appears in, for instance, Jorge Luis Borges, *Collected Fictions*, Viking Penguin, 1998.) Also of use to me in this context was Stanislaw Lem's book, *A Perfect Vacuum* (Harcourt Brace Jovanovich, 1979), in which he reviews a series of nonexistent books.

Although *Postsingular* features a kiqqie metanovelist named Thuy Nguyen, I didn't include the full text of "Visions of the Metanovel" in my novel. My sense is that people reading a novel don't want to negotiate a bulky sequence of intellectual games. But I felt that the games might seem amusing if presented as a single short piece. So here, to close this anthology, are my descriptions of imaginary metanovels, a final offering from the mad professor.